BY STARLIGHT

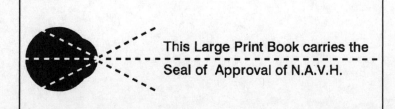

By Starlight

Dorothy Garlock

THORNDIKE PRESS

A part of Gale, Cengage Learning

Detroit • New York • San Francisco • New Haven, Conn • Waterville, Maine • London

GALE
CENGAGE Learning·

LIBRARY OF CONGRESS CATALOGING-IN-PUBLICATION DATA

Garlock, Dorothy.
  By starlight / by Dorothy Garlock.
    pages ; cm. — (Thorndike Press large print basic)
  ISBN 978-1-4104-5087-6 (hardcover) — ISBN 1-4104-5087-2 (hardcover)
  1. Depressions—1929—Montana—Fiction. 2. Prohibition—Fiction. 3. Large type books. I. Title.
PS3557.A71645B92 2012b
813'.54—dc23   2012024184

Published in 2012 by arrangement with Grand Central Publishing, a division of Hachette Book Group, Inc.

Printed in the United States of America
1 2 3 4 5 6 7 16 15 14 13 12

For Zach, Laramie, Travis, and Jake
May all of your futures be
"mint in the bag"

Why?

It's seven long years since we parted.
And I'm alone, brokenhearted.
Wanting,
Wishing,
Wondering.
Why?

And now you're near enough to touch,
Ready to help when I need you so much.
And I'm still
Wanting,
Wishing,
Wondering.
Why?

F.S.I.

PROLOGUE

Colton, Montana
July 1924

Maddy Aldridge froze as the floorboard beneath her bare foot creaked loudly. In the still dark of the night, it sounded like a gunshot. A warm summer breeze swirled through the open window of her bedroom, but it did nothing to lessen the panic that held her tight. Staring at her reflection in the small mirror over her dresser, her long red hair falling in curls across her shoulders, her green eyes looking black in the darkness, Maddy willed herself to stay still.

The last thing she wanted was for her father to wake up. Silas Aldridge wasn't the sort of man who would react well to his fifteen-year-old daughter trying to sneak out in the middle of the night. If he were to catch her now, there'd be hell to pay; even if he didn't take a belt to her, she had no doubt that he'd lock her in her room for weeks.

And that would be far too late . . .

On the other side of the bedroom, Maddy's younger sister, Helen, slept peacefully. Most nights, she was asleep as soon as her head hit her pillow, but this evening she'd prattled for over an hour about some nonsense at school. Maddy had been forced to wait impatiently, gritting her teeth.

Maddy had considered confiding her plans to Helen, had wondered if she could be trusted, but in the end had decided it was far too great a risk to take. So instead Maddy had held her tongue, waiting until she was certain Helen was sleeping before getting out of bed.

But then Maddy had stepped on a loose floorboard and made so much noise she was sure she'd awakened the dead.

Seconds ticked slowly past. Beads of sweat trickled off Maddy's brow and down the sides of her face; she was so fearful that wiping them away would make more noise that she let them crawl down her skin. Each breath she drew was agonizing.

Finally, after several long, nervous minutes, she was certain that no one had heard her. Cautiously, Maddy crossed the room, swung her leg over the windowsill, ducked under the sash, and headed into the night.

High above, the moon looked down on her, full and bright, illuminating outhouses and wood shelters and throwing shadows onto the ground. Maddy moved carefully yet quickly. Running through the dewy grass with bare feet, she wished that she'd remembered to put on shoes, but in the chaotic moments after the floor creaked she hadn't been thinking clearly. She'd also forgotten her shawl; the night air was cooler than she'd expected, especially for summer, raising goose bumps on the bare skin of her arms and shoulders. But it was too late to turn back.

Maddy didn't know what time it was, only that it was late, probably sometime just after midnight. Colton wasn't a bustling town even in the middle of the day; as she slipped between houses, dashed across a dirt road, and then hurried across the church grounds, she saw no one, set no dogs to barking, and noticed only one lamp burning behind a drawn curtain.

On and on she ran, as fast as she could, fearful she would be late.

Colton had been built into the crook between two narrow rivers that flowed out of the foothills of the Rocky Mountains. The Lewis River ran to the north, while the Clark River meandered to the south. The

11

town was small, surrounded by thick stands of evergreens, and was located only a few miles south of the Canadian border. It was the only home Maddy had ever known and, in only a few short hours, the part of it she loved most was leaving.

Maddy hurried to the bank of the Lewis River, carefully stepping through the carpet of dry pine needles that covered the ground. She gave a silent curse; her bare feet caused her to move more slowly than she liked. Beside her, the river ran low, its water gurgling over rocks worn smooth as eggs. The air was filled with the fresh, sharp scent of pine.

She hadn't gone far when a bridge loomed up out of the night before her; in the glare of the moon's bright light, its bare steel frame resembled a skeleton. Breaking into a run, Maddy padded out onto its wooden planks, looking in every direction and growing alarmed.

I'm alone.

Dread began to fill Maddy's stomach. She knew it was later than she'd promised, but there hadn't been anything she could do to get out of the house. *It's not fair!* If only her father wasn't so pigheaded stubborn, if only her sister had gone to sleep as usual, and if only —

"I was starting to wonder if you were coming."

Maddy turned at the sound of his voice, gasping in both surprise and happiness. He was sitting on the bridge's railing in shadows so deep she could've been looking right at him and wouldn't have known he was there. As she watched, he leaped down, his boots thudding on the planks.

Without saying a word, Maddy rushed to him, threw her arms around his chest, and squeezed him tight. Even though she'd been with him only a few hours earlier, it felt as if days had passed. She wanted to hold on to him, to cling jealously to the warmth of his touch, the smell of his skin, the sound of his voice, and never let him go.

"I've been waiting for almost an hour," he said softly.

"I came as quickly as I could."

"I was starting to get awfully worried," he said, gently stroking her hair. "I'd decided that if you didn't show up in the next five minutes I was going to march over to your house and bang on the door until you came out."

"My father would have answered with his gun."

"You know I'm not scared of him. Still," he chuckled, "it's probably for the best that

13

you showed up when you did."

Maddy knew that he meant it; though he was only three years older than she was, he'd always seemed sure of himself, confident, almost fearless, as if there was nothing he couldn't do as long as he set his mind to it. He wouldn't let anything get in the way of his dreams, not even Silas Aldridge's worries about his daughter's well-being. It was one of the reasons Maddy had fallen in love with him, and one of the things she'd miss most.

"I still can't believe you're leaving," she said.

"Me either," he answered.

"It's for too long!" Maddy whined, knowing that she sounded like a child.

Placing his fingers under her chin, he raised her face up until their eyes met. "I'm not going away forever," he explained. "I'll only be in Boston for a couple of years. Once I get the schooling my father's so insistent on, I'll be back. Then we can start our life together."

"We can get married —"

"And build a house, have some children, and grow so old our faces are nothing but wrinkles." He laughed, trying to cheer her up. "Everything we've dreamed about will come true. All we have to do is be patient."

14

"It's just that . . . that I'm so . . . so scared," Maddy said as tears filled her eyes. She'd promised herself that she wouldn't cry in front of him, not tonight, but knowing how long it would be before she saw him again was more than her heart could bear. "What if you decide you'd rather live there?" she began, spilling all her worries. "What if your father says that he wants you to go somewhere else after you've finished with school?"

"Maddy, stop," he tried to interrupt her.

"What if you meet someone prettier than me?" she kept on, tears streaming down her cheeks. "She could be smart and funny! You could fall in love with her and never think of me ever again! I don't know —"

Before she could say another word, Maddy felt his lips press against hers and, in that instant, all of the emotions she'd struggled against fell away. Desperately, she clung to him, squeezing his arm as she returned his passion. More than ever, she wanted their embrace to go on forever. Unfortunately, it couldn't last. He broke their kiss and wiped away her tears tenderly.

"I'm coming back for you," he said softly but firmly.

"Do . . . do you promise?" Maddy asked.

"Of course I do." His eyes searched hers,

intently. "I love you."

"And I love you, Jack."

Maddy folded herself into his embrace, her head upon his chest, secure in the promise they'd made to each other. She allowed herself to believe him, to believe that nothing, not time or distance, would keep them apart for long.

CHAPTER ONE

Morningside, Washington
June 1931

Jack Rucker was leaning against the bar when the front door of the speakeasy was knocked off its hinges and sent crashing inward, followed by a dozen policemen all brandishing billy clubs and a couple of men in suits wielding axes. In an instant, everything around him became chaotic. All of the men and women who'd been enjoying a taste of illegal alcohol jumped to their feet in panic, desperate to escape their approaching arrest. The air was filled with cigar smoke, shouts, and, soon after, the sounds of violence.

"Get your damn hands offa me 'fore I . . . !"

". . . all under arrest!"

"Would you just quit hittin' me with that thing and I'll . . ."

But Jack didn't so much as move, his eyes

never leaving the bartender.

The speakeasy originally had been a coal cellar down a darkened alleyway from a decrepit vaudeville theater. There were no windows and the inside, even with its high ceiling, made him feel cramped, almost claustrophobic. An assortment of chairs and tables had been set out and empty apple crates stacked to act as a makeshift bar. Jack had seen every nook, cranny, and dingy corner in the week he'd been coming in the door. Now it was in even *worse* shape.

The scruffy-bearded bartender had been pouring a drink when the police forced their way inside; the man had been so startled by the sound that he'd dropped the glass onto the floor, where it shattered. But his surprise didn't last long; one second later, he looked right at Jack. Maybe it was because Jack was a newcomer to the speakeasy, or that he didn't appear shocked by the appearance of so many cops: either of those things might've given him away. It was obvious that the bartender knew the truth. Jack could only hope that he would run for it or, even better, just throw up his hands in surrender.

Instead, the bartender chose to fight.

"You no-good, rotten son of a bitch!" the man bellowed as he hurried to get around

18

the pile of crates.

Jack cursed silently. All night, he'd been wondering who he'd have to fight. Whenever the law arrived, there was sure to be a brawl. Unfortunately for him, his job was to find out who was in charge, stay close, and learn everything he could. In the time he'd been coming to the speakeasy, that person was the bartender.

Now Jack was going to pay a price for his curiosity.

The bartender looked to be no stranger to fighting. Thick muscles knotted his bare forearms and his clenched fists seemed carved out of stone. His chest resembled an oak barrel and he was the tallest man in the room. Even his face showed signs of past brawls; an angry white scar zigzagged from cheek to chin. A couple of his front teeth were missing. Jack knew he was in for a tussle.

Though he wasn't as large as his foe, Jack was hardly a pushover. Turning to face the bartender, Jack caught a glimpse of himself in the mirror that had been hung crookedly on the wall behind the bar; tufts of dark hair poked out from beneath his longshoreman's cap and his eyes were narrowed, determined. He planted his feet, squared his broad shoulders, and raised his hands, ready to give as good as he got.

But then something strange happened.

Just before the bartender reached Jack, a fist cocked and ready to be thrown, his eyes wide with fury, the man's feet suddenly flew out from under him, slipping in a puddle of booze that had been spilled when the police arrived. For a moment, it was as if he were frozen in mid-air, high off the ground, before crashing painfully to the ground, the back of his head cracking against the floor. The man's eyes were wide with both shock and pain before fluttering and then closing, his head lolled to the side as he fell unconscious.

I reckon they don't call me Lucky Jack for nothing.

Suddenly, a half-filled glass of whiskey whistled past Jack's face, mere inches from hitting him. It shattered against the wall behind the bar, barely missing the crooked mirror; pieces of glass rained onto the floor as dark alcohol stained the bricks. His heart thundered in his chest.

It didn't take long for Jack to learn who'd thrown the glass. Ten feet away stood the bartender's right-hand man, a lackey who usually guarded the door. He resembled a badger, short and stocky, with a long nose and a lip curled up to reveal filthy teeth.

20

Even as a policeman brought his club down on a drunk next to where he stood, the man's narrow eyes never left Jack, burning with unrestrained hatred. The man showed no interest in trying to get away; his focus was solely on getting revenge.

I don't think I'm going to be lucky enough to avoid this one.

Without wasting any more time, the thug stepped menacingly toward Jack, a low growl rising from his throat. His first punch was thrown with anger, a wild, looping right; Jack saw it coming a mile away and easily ducked under his opponent's out-stretched arm, staying down low to throw a short left into the man's ribs. The tough grunted as the air whooshed from his lungs, but Jack held no illusions that the blow would be enough to stop such an obviously dangerous man.

"You'll . . . you'll have to do more than that," the man snarled.

"I aim to." Jack nodded.

This time, when the thug raised his fists, he feinted first with his right to draw Jack out of position before firing a left. Jack had seen it coming, but the man was as fast as a snake and the punch clipped the tip of his chin before finishing against his shoulder. Though it was a glancing blow, it still stung

21

like hell. If one of those were to land flush . . .

But Jack was no slouch when it came to fighting, either. With his hands held defensively in front of him, he shot off a couple of punches that snapped the man's head straight back, then landed a hook to the jaw that wobbled his opponent's knees. The thug managed to throw a weak punch that Jack batted harmlessly away, before immediately attacking again. The heavy's nose crunched beneath Jack's fist and the man toppled over, falling onto his back with a loud thud. His eyes rolled back slightly, looking glassy.

"Stay down," Jack ordered him.

But there was still enough fight left in the man for him to disagree; desperately, he tried to claw his way to a sitting position. With his shoe, Jack drove the man back to the floor hard, without mercy.

"I told you to stay down!" he repeated.

This time, the man understood that he was defeated, the tension dropped from his shoulders, and he stared up at the ceiling.

A thin smile curled at the corners of Jack's mouth. "You're under arrest by the authority of the Bureau of Prohibition."

■ ■ ■ ■

"So the Jack Rucker luck came through again."

Jack stood in front of Elmer Pluggett's desk, trying his best not to appear *too* pleased with the praise he was receiving. Rare afternoon sunlight streamed down out of the Seattle sky, shining through the office's tall windows and falling across the Bureau lieutenant's desk. Outside the closed door, the sound of typewriters and bits of conversation could be heard.

For the last half hour, Jack had told his superior officer about his activities in Morningside that had ended three days earlier. In great detail, he described how he'd traveled to the border town as directed and within hours had overheard a man talking about a speakeasy with a direct connection to illegal booze runners operating out of Canada. Over the course of the next week, Jack had frequented the bar and gathered as much information as possible: how big an operation it was, who was in charge, and, most important, where they got their liquor. No opportunity was missed to emphasize the lengths to which he'd gone to do his job. Finally, once he'd obtained what was needed, the bust had been set up. In the end, more than two dozen people had been arrested and the smuggling operation destroyed.

"In all my years on the job," Pluggett went on, "I can't say I've ever known someone so darn lucky. What do you reckon the odds are that the fellow you heard talking about the tavern would spill the password for getting past the doorman?" He shook his head. "Hard to believe."

"I was fortunate, sir," Jack admitted.

"If all the men working out of this office were as lucky as you are, Rucker, there wouldn't be a drop of alcohol to be had west of the Rockies and I'd be sitting in a nice, comfortable office back east." The Lieutenant grinned ironically, his eyes narrowing. "Or maybe we'd all just be out of a job."

Jack frowned inwardly. The conversation wasn't taking the direction he'd wanted. What he'd been hoping for was talk of a commendation, a medal, or, if he allowed himself to dream a little, maybe a promotion. There wasn't nearly enough praise coming his way.

What's the old man thinking?

Elmer Pluggett was like most of the senior officers Jack had met since he started working for the Bureau of Prohibition. Tough

24

and smart, Pluggett ruthlessly guarded his own place on the map while stepping on anyone who got in the way of his own advancement, all traits that Jack held in some admiration. In his mid-fifties, Pluggett was as demanding of himself as he was of the men who served under him; his face bore signs of the weariness of long hours spent tracking down those bent on breaking the law. For officers who failed to produce the results Pluggett sought, his wrath could be a terrible thing, but he also wasn't stingy with praise for those who got the job done.

So where's mine?

"How long have you been with the Bureau now, Rucker?" Pluggett asked, leaning forward in his chair. "Four years, isn't it?"

"Almost five," Jack replied.

"And in that time, how many run-down, two-bit, dingy dives have you wriggled your way into? How many con men, ship captains, hired goons, murderers, and ladies of the night have you manipulated into giving you what you want?"

"I haven't been keeping count, sir," he said, although he knew the number was greater than fifty, probably closer to a hundred.

"Quite a lot by my reckoning," Pluggett said before adding, "and all in the good name of Prohibition."

For the last eleven years, beginning in 1920 with the passage of the Eighteenth Amendment to the Constitution, the sale, production, and distribution of alcohol were illegal in the United States. In response, hundreds of thousands of speakeasies had opened across the country, pouring glasses of homemade liquor brewed in bathtubs, fermented fruit steeped in basements and outhouses, and, in the worst cases, alcohol illegally smuggled from Canada, Mexico, and other foreign ports. The law was being broken.

The Bureau of Prohibition had been created to enforce it. For the hundreds of Prohibition agents, the goal wasn't the closing of *every* speakeasy or the confiscation of *every* drop of booze but rather the dismantling of the larger criminal networks intent on making a profit from the void Prohibition created. Organized-crime syndicates had begun bootlegging alcohol, controlling the trade from brewery to speakeasy and every step in-between. For agents like Jack, it meant finding the liquor at its largest point of distribution and catching as many rats as possible in one trap.

From the moment Jack joined the Bureau, he'd taken to the work like a duck to water.

He took pride in what he did; he believed in it. While he certainly wasn't a teetotaler, wasn't above taking a nip of confiscated alcohol from time to time, he followed the letter of the law and expected others to do the same. His overbearing father had instilled in Jack a strong sense of right and wrong in among the lectures and Scripture readings; his moral compass was straight and true. Bringing down a den of criminals, smashing open their casks of whiskey, and confiscating their money was exciting work. He was very good at it.

"We've sent you to San Francisco, Buffalo, little shacks on the fishing coast of Maine, that Indian reservation in Idaho, and everywhere in-between," Lieutenant Pluggett continued, "and every time you manage to make it look as easy as taking a Sunday stroll after church."

Now this is more like it . . .

"I've done my best," he answered with a practiced air of modesty.

"That you have, my boy," the older man agreed.

What neither of them spoke of was the danger Jack faced every time he went undercover. He'd been shot at, stabbed, spat upon; a woman had tried to slip poison into his drink. He'd been tossed down a flight of stairs, thrown through a couple of windows, and in dozens of bare-knuckle brawls much like the one in Morningside. Jack had a knack for finding just what the Bureau wanted; unfortunately, that usually meant that he found trouble, too. Thankfully, his "luck" had managed to get him through it all relatively unhurt.

He *was* lucky, but he'd acquired a few mementos on the job. A nick of a scar ran along his left cheekbone just beneath his dark green eye, a reminder of a knife fight in Milwaukee. A gunshot wound pocked his right biceps and there were burn scars on both of his legs courtesy of a particularly messy night in Duluth. To Jack, they were simply the price he had to pay to uphold the law.

And to get ahead.

"It says in here that you're from Montana," Lieutenant Pluggett said, tapping his finger in a folder that he'd spread open on his desk; Jack noticed that his name was typed across the top.

"I was born and raised there, sir."

"When was the last time you were home?"

"I've been undercover in Montana twice," Jack replied.

"But what about . . . ," Pluggett began, peering down at what was written, ". . .

28

Colton?" he asked. "How long since you've been there?"

"It's . . . it's been years . . . ," Jack said, unable to keep the confusion out of his voice. "Might I . . . inquire as to why you ask, sir?"

"Because that's where you're heading next."

Instantly the confidence Jack always took great pains to project fell from his face. His eyes grew wide as his mouth dropped slightly open. With no small amount of hope, he entertained the possibility he'd misheard or that, as unlikely as it was, Lieutenant Pluggett was playing some kind of prank on him; if so, the Lieutenant was holding his cards awfully close to his vest, peering through the folder and not even bothering to look up at Jack.

"Excuse me, sir," Jack began, chuckling, "but I thought you said that you were sending me to Colton —"

"That's right," Pluggett said, still looking at his papers. "We've received a report that someone's smuggling in a lot of liquor in the area. The Canadians have their hands full and haven't been much help, but the scuttlebutt they've heard indicates the rumors have merit. We don't know if it's one of the usual suspects or somebody new,

29

but the decision has been made to check it out, and that's where you come in."

"But . . . but I thought I might be headed to Chicago," Jack said. With the success he'd been having lately, he'd hoped to be one of the first the Bureau sent after Al Capone; if he had a hand in breaking up the biggest bootlegging empire in the country, who knew how far up the ladder he could climb?

"You're going to Montana," Pluggett explained, finally peering up at Jack. The look in Pluggett's eyes made it clear that he wasn't about to brook any disagreement.

Jack's mind began working furiously, desperate to come up with something, *anything* that might change his assignment; based on Pluggett's expression, he knew he'd have to tread carefully.

"Excuse my saying so, sir," he began, "but all of the success I've had for the Bureau has come from working undercover. Most everyone in Colton will know who I am. I don't know how I could get the results you want."

"Oh, but you will," Pluggett said with a grin.

"How?"

"Because you're going to be hiding in plain sight."

"Sir?"

30

"Just because everyone in that little speck of a town can fondly recall you running around in short pants doesn't mean they have the foggiest idea what you do for a living," he explained. "You hardly strike me as the sort who writes weekly letters to his family telling them what you've been up to. Am I right?"

Jack nodded. The truth was exactly that; within months of leaving Colton, he'd acted as if it had dropped off the map. There had been no letters, no phone calls, no telegrams, nothing. The only family he'd had in Colton when he left was his demanding father, his mother having died when he was only a boy, and Jeremiah Rucker was someone Jack had no desire ever to see again. There was only one person he missed . . . one person he now worried about . . .

"No one has any idea what you are," Pluggett continued. "For all they know, you're a shoe salesman or a schoolteacher. If you're as good an actor as I think you are, they'll believe anything you tell them, especially when they have something to gain from it."

"Which is?"

"Money," the Lieutenant answered. "I want you to go to Colton under the guise of a representative of a developer from Chicago looking to buy up land to build hotels on it

31

or some such. You'll work out the details on the way there. The way I figure it, folks will be telling you every last thing you'd ever want to hear in order to get a piece of that pie."

"You want me to lie to them," Jack said.

"Isn't that what you do best?" Pluggett answered. "Besides, with your luck, it won't take more than a day or two to learn where the liquor's coming from and who's behind it all. After that who knows, maybe you'll get a crack at Capone."

Jack brightened considerably at that. Maybe it would be as easy as the Lieutenant made it out to be. Maybe he'd be out of there within a week or so. Maybe a quick visit home wouldn't be so bad. Maybe . . .

"Oh, there's one more thing," Pluggett said.

"Yes, sir."

"You won't be going alone. Agent Hooper will be accompanying you as a partner in the venture. Two heads are always better than one."

Except in this case.

For the second time in minutes, Jack knew that his face betrayed his emotions. Ross Hooper was one of the most disliked agents working for the Bureau. Loud, overbearing, sloppy in dress and work; in short, a poor lawman. Jack had never been able to figure out how Hooper had managed to keep his job for as long as he had; the best guess anyone could come up with was that he had a relative much higher up the ladder.

"You'll leave the day after tomorrow," Pluggett said, effectively ending the meeting.

As he scooped up his hat and headed for the door, Jack wondered if his vaunted luck hadn't turned into some kind of curse.

CHAPTER TWO

Maddy stood behind the long counter of her father's store, Aldridge Mercantile, and ground her teeth. In these tough times, with men unable to find work, banks suddenly closing, and families being pushed off land they'd owned for generations, she'd had to confront all kinds of emotional customers. There were those who were already crying before they opened the front door, pushing hollow-eyed children in front of them. Some talked a mile a minute, while others mumbled, never able to make eye contact. Occasionally, someone would take his anger and frustration out on her, shouting so loudly that Maddy was certain it could be heard out in the street.

But there was nothing she hated more than when someone begged.

"Please, Maddy . . . I'll pay you back. I promise . . ."

Pete Seybold stood on the other side of

the counter, his hat clutched so tightly in his hands that his knuckles were bone white. Maddy had known him for years. A joke teller, he lived with his family just outside of town, a short distance from the lumber mill he worked at, a business now closed. The effect of that closure on Pete was obvious. His face was gaunt, his cheekbones prominent, his cheeks peppered with a growth of silvery whiskers. His eyes were pleading, wet, brimming with tears.

"Times are a bit tough is all," he kept on, afraid that if he left too long a break in their conversation Maddy might fill it with something he didn't want to hear. "I've been hearin' 'bout some work down in Smulders. Talk is they're lookin' for experienced lumber men. Soon as I'm hired, I'll pay you what I owe."

Maddy pursed her lips. If rumors like this one about jobs looking to be filled were food, there wouldn't be a hungry family a hundred miles in every direction. Even if what he said was true, the competition would be tremendous. The odds of Pete getting work were one in a hundred, at best.

"I know times are hard," Maddy began, holding Pete's gaze, determined to show him that she meant every word, "but they're hard for everyone, me included. The mercantile has bills of its own that need to be paid. If I don't have the money for them, I'll eventually have to shut that door for good. I just can't afford to extend credit."

"I'm not asking for much," he pleaded, growing more desperate. "Just a bag of flour. Enough to feed my family, is all."

"I'm sorry, but the answer is no."

Outside, a peal of distant thunder rumbled over the low hills before washing against Colton. The glass in the tall windows of the mercantile shook slightly. It wouldn't be long before the summer squall broke, swelling the rivers and muddying the earth.

Pete's features were creased by an angry frown. "Your father wouldn't have turned me away in my time of need."

"My father isn't here!" Maddy snapped, her voice faltering a bit more than she liked. "But if he were, he'd make the same decision I am!"

Maddy was thankful there were no other customers in the store to hear her outburst; she thought that it was inappropriate, even unbecoming, especially for a woman. Regardless, she also knew she was in the right.

However, it appeared that her sister disagreed. Helen had been placing an order of buttons into the chest of drawers from which they were sold, her head turned slightly to help make certain she heard every word; a long time had passed since she'd put a button away. Maddy could see that Helen was frowning; for a moment, she wondered if her sister might get involved, but she held her tongue.

Maddy took a deep breath to help regain her composure. "I wish there was something I could do for you, Pete, but I can't give you anything on credit. When you get working again, come back and I'd be happy to sell it to you."

"That's . . . that's the way it's gonna be then?"

"I'm afraid so."

Pete nodded slowly. A lone tear streaked down his cheek before he angrily wiped it away, looking ashamed that it had fallen. Maddy wondered if she'd have to listen to him scream at her, ranting and raving at how unfair everything was, how she should be ashamed of herself, and worse. Instead, Pete quietly made his way to the door like a beaten man. Just as he opened it, the dark clouds above began to let loose, a teasing rain blowing against the glass.

"I suppose it was too much to hope for," he said without turning. "But what else is a man to do when he's at the end of his damn rope?"

Without waiting for an answer, he stepped out into the growing storm.

For the last two years, nearly every one of Maddy's days had been spent in the Aldridge Mercantile, struggling not to make too big a mistake as she tried to eke out a living for herself, Helen, and their father.

Built on a corner lot of Colton's Main Street just opposite the bank, the mercantile carried many of the things needed for small-town Montana life: pairs of shoes; big jars full of sweets; nails and the hammers to pound them; women's dresses; and bags of flour, oats, and beans. Maddy had heard about stores in faraway places like Denver, St. Louis, and even New York City that sold only expensive dresses, fancy plates and silverware, or pounds of chocolate, but such a place was unimaginable in Colton.

Silas Aldridge had built his business out of simpler ideas: a good item for sale for a fair price, each one sold with a smile. By ordering the hard-to-find product, allowing only the occasional perishable to go to waste, and investing some of himself into each and every person who walked through the door, he ensured that the mercantile thrived. Though his wife had died young, Silas brought up both of his daughters to understand that rewards came from hard work. But then, out of the blue, everything had changed.

When Silas had first fallen ill, there didn't appear to be any reason to worry. Over the years, he'd begun to feel a dull pain in the joints of his hands and his feet if he stood on them for too long, but suddenly the pain had become nearly unbearable. Dr. Quayle had assured Maddy that it would all soon pass, that her father just needed some rest, and that he'd be right as rain.

Instead, things had only grown worse.

The pain became so intense that Silas could get out of bed only for short periods, then only with assistance, and finally not at all. No matter what the doctor prescribed, nothing seemed to help. Often, Maddy would wake in the night to hear her father moaning, his sleep as unsettled as his days. He began to slowly wither away before her eyes, losing weight along with his vigor, no longer the larger-than-life man he'd been when she was a child.

In order to keep food on the table and a roof over the family's head, Maddy understood that she needed to step in at the mercantile. In her father's place, she had to run things until his health improved. In the beginning, she'd been terrified, nervous that she'd fail, and struggled to never let it show. Her father wrote to vendors and farmers, any supplier the store used, explaining that he was temporarily off his feet and that they should deal with Maddy when they called. She worried that many of these men, as well as customers, would find it odd to deal with a woman, but her fears had proven to be pleasantly unfounded.

Even in the midst of the Great Depression, with more and more families struggling to make ends meet, Maddy kept the business profitable. Surprising even herself, she found that she had an eye for business. She bought and sold goods shrewdly, purchasing items her father would have passed on, turning down others she felt would languish on the shelves. Maddy made the hard decisions without emotion, knowing where her ledgers stood to the penny. Most days were rewarding, even a little bit fun.

And then there were days like this one . . .

Maddy watched as Pete Seybold sat in his truck in front of the store, his head in his hands, the rain pounding down, drumming incessantly on the roof. Rainwater cascaded down the mercantile's windows, distorting her view, but she thought she saw his shoulders shaking and that he was crying.

Even as thunder roared and lightning flashed, he gave no sign of leaving, instead choosing to wallow in his misery. The streets were deserted; no one would step into such weather. She thought about running out and tapping on his window, asking him to come in from the storm, but she was probably the last person in all of Montana he'd listen to.

Maybe if Helen asked . . .

In many ways, Helen couldn't have been more different from her older sister. Four years younger at eighteen, Helen bore little physical resemblance to Maddy; her midnight black hair was cut short, her skin pale and soft, and the features of her face sharper but no less attractive. Helen always seemed to have her head in the clouds, dreaming of a life far different from the one she lived. She'd never been interested in school, had to be cajoled into doing her chores, and was always reciting bits from stories she read out of an old issue of *Glamour Confidential,* a gossip magazine she'd sent away for.

Still, Helen had done her part in helping to care for their father; she might grumble about taking him his meals, wiping his brow when he was having a bad spell, or sitting by his bedside and listening to a radio show when she'd rather be in her room pining for a more glamorous life, but she did as she was asked. Silas often remarked that Helen was the spitting image of her mother, praise the young woman cherished.

Helen had also been a great help at the store. She put away stock, swept the floors, and occasionally waited on customers, though she wasn't particularly patient; when someone hemmed and hawed about their purchase, Helen had a bad habit of drumming her fingernails on the counter. Some of Colton's young men liked to come in and try to sweet-talk her, but she disdainfully ignored them; she'd set her sights much higher.

Maddy walked the length of the counter toward the small storeroom in the back. She'd sent Helen to take an inventory of their pens and pencils so that she could place an order, but what she found when she entered was far different from what she'd expected.

Helen stood beneath the stockroom's lone bulb, working determinedly. She'd cut open a twenty-five-pound bag of flour and was scooping some of it into a smaller sack. She glanced up when Maddy entered, but didn't stop.

"What are you doing?" Maddy demanded, already dreading the answer.

"I'm helping Pete and his family," Helen replied.

Maddy quickly crossed the small room and grabbed her sister by the arm; the small sack tipped over, spilling a bit of flour and sending the scoop clattering to the floor. Helen immediately yanked herself free and turned, frowning, ready to argue.

"Don't you start going against me," Maddy began, her voice strained. "I told Pete that I wasn't extending him credit for flour and I meant it. The last person I expected to defy me was you."

"I'm not just going to stand by while that man and his family starve!" Helen shouted, her dark eyes dancing. "You'd have to be blind not to see that he's suffering! All he wants is a little something for his family to eat!"

"That doesn't mean we should give it away."

"He said he'd pay us back for it. Once he gets that job down in Smulders he'll be able to give us the money he owes." When Helen saw the way Maddy frowned, she angrily asked, "Are you calling him a liar?"

"I'm not saying he's doing it on purpose," she answered, "but you know as well as I do that even if there are jobs to be had, there'll be a line of fifty men trying to get one.

43

Times are tough for everyone. Who knows how long it'll be before he gets hired? Besides, if we start giving Pete credit, what happens when Charlie Kierscht asks, or Al Spratt, or George Erskine? Are you going to let them all have some flour, farming equipment, or clothes? When would it ever end if there's a line of desperate men standing outside the door before we open?"

"And what would be wrong with that?" Helen shot back. "If it meant that their children could sleep at night, it's a price worth paying!"

"Not if it means that we suffer in their place."

"Pa would've given Pete what he needed!" her sister shouted.

"Only if he could have afforded it."

The truth was, things at the mercantile were more precarious than ever; when Maddy balanced the books each night, she saw how much things had changed. Times in Colton were tough. Families threatened by the loss of a job or foreclosure were spending less, buying only the essentials. Maddy did her best, cutting corners wherever she could, but it didn't stop her from worrying.

But there *had* been a recent turn in their fortunes . . .

"We're not that bad off," Helen said, thinking the same thing. "Not anymore," she added, pointing a finger toward the floor.

"Stop it! Don't say another word about that!" Maddy shouted, raising her voice for the first time. "We agreed never to talk about that here!"

"Why not? It's not as if half the people in town haven't been there once or twice. Didn't you say Reverend Fitzpatrick was there two days ago? If *he* doesn't mind, there's no reason we should have to be so quiet about it!"

"Because it's wrong, that's why!" Maddy argued, fearful that someone might hear. "If Jim Utley caught wind of it . . ."

Helen folded her arms across her chest. "If you honestly believe that the sheriff doesn't know what you and Jeffers are up to, then you're an even bigger fool than I thought."

Maddy didn't know how to answer. "We can't give that flour to Pete," she finally said, no longer wanting to argue.

"We could," Helen disagreed, "but you choose not to." Angrily, she barged past Maddy, stopping when she reached the door. "I don't know how you can be so heartless," she spat. "If I thought the way you do, I don't think I'd be able to sleep at night!"

Without another word, Helen left the mercantile, hurrying into the rain as she slammed the door behind her, leaving Maddy to close up for the night.

When Maddy locked the door to the mercantile at four o'clock, the storm had blown off to the east. The bright afternoon sun drifted in and out of the trailing clouds, reflecting off of the puddles of water covering the town. A fitful breeze teased at the trees and scurried along the ground, filling the summer air with the fresh smell of rain.

Pete Seybold still sat in his truck.

Maddy had watched him all afternoon. Once Helen had stormed off, there'd only been a couple more customers, even once the weather cleared; occasionally, someone passing by would see Pete and say hello. When spoken to, he'd nod, unsmiling, but said nothing. Even after the storm passed, he hadn't driven away, hadn't so much as moved. A slight touch of worry began to worm its way into Maddy's thoughts.

If he has something he wants to say, I wish he'd just come in and say it.

When Maddy understood Pete had no intention of leaving before she closed the store, she knew that she'd have to face him.

She'd known Pete ever since she was a little girl, sitting on a chair behind the counter while her father helped customers. Pete had never been anything but kind. If there was something he wanted to say to her, she'd give him the chance to say it. She'd expected him to say something as soon as she stepped outside, but he stayed behind the wheel of the truck. But just as soon as the lock clicked, she heard him open his door, the hinges squealing, and he spoke, his voice soft.

"I'm sorry for becomin' angry with you," he said.

"You don't have to apologize," Maddy replied.

"Course I do," Pete disagreed. "Even though times ain't been easy, it don't excuse what I said 'bout Silas. I shouldn't have brung him into it."

"He'd understand why you did."

"Still don't make it right. What I should've done is ask how he's feelin'."

"He's getting stronger every day," Maddy lied easily. "He'll be back behind that counter before you know it."

Pete nodded. "Your father's a good man," he said, "and even though I been doin' business with him for more years than I can count, that don't mean he owes me nothin'.

47

'Sides, you been more than fair with me since you started runnin' things. I only asked 'cause . . . ," but his voice trailed as his eyes broke away from her, looking up the street.

Maddy knew Pete Seybold had his pride; coming to ask for a bag of flour on credit must've been hard. Pride was also what kept him sitting in his truck during a thunderstorm, waiting for the right time to say his piece. Maddy's thoughts whirled. She thought about the way Helen had looked at her, full of disdain, unaware or unable to understand the hard choices she was confronted with. She even wondered if her father would've been as conflicted as she was just then. Maddy had believed in the strength of her convictions before, but now she wasn't so sure. Maybe Helen was right; because of what Maddy had agreed to do, there was more money than before. Maybe there was enough . . .

"When will you know about that job in Smulders?" she asked.

"I'll . . . I'll know come Th-th-thursday," Pete managed to stammer, turning back to look at her with a glimmer of hope in his eye. "And I'm gonna get it, Maddy, and immediately after I get some money, I'd pay you back and —"

"That'd be fine," she cut him off, not wanting him to start making promises he couldn't keep, for both their sakes.

I hope I don't regret this . . .

"Come on in," she said, getting out her keys. "Let's see about getting you some flour."

CHAPTER THREE

"I hear Pete Seybold came asking for some credit."

Silas Aldridge sat in the chair beside his bed, a blanket tucked across his legs, his hands folded in his lap. When Maddy had entered the room, he'd turned down the volume of the radio, a luxury they'd purchased when his condition worsened; a man's voice could still be faintly heard reading news headlines. The window was open a crack, a soft breeze blowing against the hems of the curtains, filling the room with fresh air.

Even after caring for him for nearly two years, Maddy was still occasionally reminded of how much her father had changed. Gone was the larger-than-life man who had towered over her. The broad shoulders and thick biceps that had allowed him to effortlessly lift boxes in the mercantile had withered with lack of use, leaving him trapped in a wreckage of loose skin and bones. The green eyes that had kept a close watch over her were now sunken and weary, peeking out over dark bags. His thick black hair had thinned and his temples were as white as snow. His deep, booming voice sounded frail to her ears. Even his movements had changed, growing slow and careful, worried about the next excruciating flare of pain.

Arthritis had made him old before his time.

When Silas had first gone to Dr. Quayle to complain about swelling in his hands and feet, about aches and pains that didn't get better, he wasn't particularly worried. But when it got so that just getting out of bed was unbearably painful, it was time for concern. He couldn't sleep, couldn't climb the stairs, could no longer stand for hours at the mercantile. The only available relief came from the aspirins he ate like candy. Still, his condition continued to worsen. Dr. Quayle worried that Silas would eventually become completely bedridden as his joints gradually degenerated. Sometimes, when she looked in on him at night, Maddy couldn't keep the tears from her eyes.

"I suppose Helen told you what happened," Maddy said.

Silas nodded. "She came in here with a full head of steam, carrying on about how it just wasn't fair to turn down folks in need."

"She said the same thing to me in the storeroom."

A thin smile curled the corners of Silas's mouth. "That sister of yours has always had a way of letting her emotions get the better of her. Once she has her dander up, all sense of reason goes right out the window," he said, laughing. "She was even more put out when I told her I agreed with what you'd done."

"You do?" Maddy asked, surprised.

"Of course. Every good store owner knows that the decisions made in hard times are the most difficult," Silas explained, "but none more so than those where your head has to overrule your heart."

"That's what I was trying to do —"

"Then you learned something all those years you spent sitting behind the counter."

"Pete was . . . he was pretty unhappy about it . . . ," Maddy said, struggling with her emotions.

"I'm sure he was, but once he gets a chance to think things through, I'm sure he'll understand. I've known the man for more years than I can count. Heck, I bet he's sitting home right now, thinking about how to apologize the next time he sees you."

"Maybe —"

"Now don't you worry," her father said as enthusiastically as he could manage these days. "You did the right thing."

Maddy couldn't say a word, nodding quietly instead. While she walked home, she'd decided to tell her father everything, including how she'd finally decided to give Pete a bag of flour on credit. But now, seeing how proud Silas was of her, it was easier to agree. The last thing she wanted was to disappoint him; there'd already been too much of that.

Besides, it wasn't as if this was the first time she'd lied to him.

The first time Jeffers Grimm approached Maddy and proposed turning the mercantile's basement into a speakeasy, she turned him down. She did so as firmly as she dared; Jeffers was the sort of man used to getting his way.

She'd been unnerved the moment Jeffers walked in the door. Everything about him was intimidating. Extremely tall, with a chest so thick it resembled a tree trunk, he looked down on everyone he met with dark, beady eyes chiseled into a craggy face swaddled in a thick, bushy beard. His voice bellowed and his laugh frightened. Many men in Montana wore a knife strapped to their side, but when Jeffers did it, his hand often resting on the enormous steel handle, it was terrifying; to doubt he knew how to use it was to risk your life.

Jeffers's grandfather, a trapper who'd originally come down from Canada, was infamous for walking around Colton with a huge bear paw hanging from his neck. His oldest son, Jeffers's father, had gunned a man down in cold blood for looking his way and then spitting on the ground. Jeffers was cut from the same cloth. He was no stranger to violence; on the contrary, he appeared to thrive on it. Everyone in town knew he was guilty of public drunkenness, assault, stealing, and adultery; even the accusation of arson had been leveled against him.

Somehow, even with all of that, Maddy held her ground.

He hadn't seemed pleased with her rejection, but he gave a curt nod of his head, grunted, and left the store. Maddy had been more than a bit relieved to see him go.

But then he'd come back.

The second time Jeffers walked through the mercantile's door had been a couple of weeks later. He'd shown up just before closing. No one else had been in the store.

Maddy stood behind the counter, watching him cross the street to the door, too frightened even to look away. Once he'd reached the counter, Jeffers reached into his pocket and pulled out one of the thickest stacks of bills Maddy had ever seen. He slapped it down on the counter and looked at her expectantly.

"How would you like to have some of that?" he asked with a sly grin.

"What . . . w-w-hat are you talking about?" she stammered.

"I come in here a while back and give you a proposition," Jeffers answered. "I come back to tell you the offer still stands. You let me run a drinkin' establishment in the basement, open only durin' the evenings, and I'll cut you in on some of what's taken in." He paused, tapping his finger just beside the pile of cash. "I just thought I should give you an idea of how much that is. Go ahead and count it if you want."

Maddy couldn't take her eyes off the money; it was mesmerizing. Her first impulse was to agree, to let Jeffers have his tavern and make some of her troubles go away. Business at the mercantile hadn't been what it once was. She knew most people in Colton were struggling. She'd been making difficult choices, doing whatever she could to keep her family afloat, but it was hard work. What did her pride matter if it meant helping her father and sister? Still, she wondered what Silas and Helen would think if they knew what she was considering.

Maddy shook her head. "My answer's the same as the last time you were here," she explained. "What you're asking me to do is illegal."

"Don't tell me you think Prohibition's a good idea," he grunted.

Truthfully, Maddy thought it was misguided. While Colton had its share of heavy drinkers, it wasn't the epidemic that she'd heard commentators crusade against on the radio and in the newspaper. Most folks she knew had a drink from time to time, men and women. Even now, her father still had a bottle of whiskey tucked just behind the table beside his bed. Maddy wasn't a teetotaler.

"It's still the law," she said.

Jeffers snorted. "One that's been foisted on folks like us by uppity types back east who ain't worked an honest day their whole damn lives." He sneered contemptuously. "The way I see things, preachers should stay in their pulpits. There ain't nothin' I hate more than bein' told what to do by someone who ain't never walked a step in my boots."

"I imagine there isn't," Maddy agreed.

"That's why, now that I got the chance to make some money on account of a law ain't got no business in bein', I want to take it!"

"And you want me to help you?"

"Exactly!"

"Aren't you afraid of getting caught?"

"By who?" Jeffers chuckled derisively, his voice booming in the mercantile. "You think Sheriff Utley gives a damn if folks in town are sellin' a little booze? Hell, no! He'd probably be one of our best customers! And even if he weren't, even if he decided to stick his nose into what we were doin', all it'd take would be for a couple of bills to fall off this stack and land in his pocket to encourage him to forget the whole thing."

"But Jim Utley isn't the only lawman to worry about," Maddy said. "There's been a federal police force made to fight Prohibition now. The radio says they have agents everywhere."

"Bullshit. They ain't nothin' none of our concern. They're worried 'bout places like New York City. From what I heard, there's more places to get a drink, Prohibition or otherwise, in that town than there's lawmen workin' to shut 'em down! So with all that goin' on, what federal is ever gonna come snoopin' round a town like Colton?"

Maddy hated to admit it, but Jeffers had a point. Unlike the first time he'd propositioned her, he seemed to have an answer for every argument she made. Still, there was one question she'd yet to ask.

"If this is all so easy to do, with no chance of getting caught," she said, "then why do you need me?"

Jeffers smiled, his eyes narrowing; to Maddy, he looked like the cat about to eat the canary. "I've got lots of reasons," he said, "not the least of which is that folks trust you. If you were part of a place where they could have a drink, I reckon they'd think that it can't be that wrong."

Maddy wasn't buying his line. Frowning, she said, "There are lots of other people in town you could say the same thing about."

Jeffers laughed. "You might be right, but ain't none of them got a cellar as big as I'm bettin' this place does."

He was right; the mercantile had plenty of room in the cellar. But she remained suspicious. "Why do you need so much space?"

" 'Cause I'm hopin' lots of folks will be thirsty enough to buy what I have to sell," he explained. "Besides, I'm gonna need someplace safe to put the liquor."

"Now wait," Maddy said. "Even if I agreed

58

to this crazy idea, I couldn't allow much alcohol to be stored down there. It's too dangerous! We'd just be asking to get caught!"

"I told you not to worry 'bout that!" Jeffers shot back, his infamous temper momentarily showing through. Taking a deep breath, he swallowed it back down, his unconvincing smile returning. "It ain't like I'm gonna be fillin' the whole cellar. My source ain't gonna be regular, like the fella bringin' you shoes and hammers. It'll be a couple a bottles here, a case there, maybe two or three at a time — just enough so's that we can make some decent money, nothin' more. But we'll need to keep it in the cellar to keep from havin' to haul it 'round any more than we have to."

"You're asking an awful lot of me."

"Don't you fret none," he said. "You'll get paid for it."

Maddy knew she was running out of arguments. Even now, her eyes kept darting back to the stack of bills on the counter. She had to admit, it looked like an awful lot of money. Each night when she balanced the store's ledgers, she was reminded of how dangerously close she was coming to losing the business. It wouldn't take much, a missed payment here or there, and everything her father had worked all his life building would be lost.

How would I ever be able to face my father and sister? How could I live knowing I might've had a chance to prevent it?

But even though she was desperate, she still struggled against her principles; the only question now was which one would win out.

"There's one more thing you might want to consider," Jeffers said, interrupting her thoughts.

"What's that?" Maddy asked.

"You should think 'bout Silas," he answered, surprising her. "I ain't seen him in a long time, so I reckon he ain't too well off. Takin' care of him must be hard, even somethin' of a burden, though I expect you wouldn't ever put it that way." Tapping his finger next to the pile of money, he added, "A bit of this would sure go a long way toward makin' sure he got the care he needed . . . it might ease whatever worries you got floatin' round that pretty head of yours."

Ever since her father's condition had worsened to where he could no longer work at the mercantile, Maddy had told almost no one how bad his arthritis had gotten. Colton was a small town where word traveled quickly. Just the fact that Maddy was operating the mercantile in her father's stead was worthy of gossip. Still, Maddy, Helen, Dr. Quayle, and Reverend Fitzpatrick had abided by Silas's wishes and remained silent about his problem. But Jeffers was no fool; it hadn't been hard for him to piece it all together and imagine the difficult predicament Maddy was in.

Maddy could have become angry at Jeffers for trying to manipulate her into doing what he wanted. But instead, his comments made her look at things exactly as he'd intended. The truth was that she would've done *anything* for her family, even if it meant going against the law. But if she was going to stick her neck out, she decided that she'd do so on her own terms.

"All right," she said, "I'll do it, but I have one condition that isn't open to negotiation."

"Name it," Jeffers answered.

"If you want to have a speakeasy in my place of business, I'm going to be a part of it. From now on, I'm your partner."

Maddy closed the door to her father's room behind her and leaned her head against the frame. At the end of the hallway, a lamp shone beneath a darkened window; the light flickered through the wetness she wiped from her eyes. This was the moment of every night she hated the most, the time that nearly made her sick to her stomach.

Once again, I've lied to my father.

After Maddy had agreed to Jeffers Grimm's plan to use the mercantile's basement as a speakeasy, she'd needed to come up with a reason to explain her nightly absence. She hated having to lie about it, but she couldn't imagine her father would approve of what she was doing. Even if he knew how badly the store was struggling, he would never have agreed with her decision; he was a man of such high principles that he would rather lose everything than choose to do something illegal.

The only other choice she had was to let Jeffers have his run of the mercantile basement, and that was something she *would not* do. And so, she'd needed to come up with a believable story.

In order to explain why she was spending most evenings away from home, Maddy had chosen to tell her father she was going to church. She'd said that Reverend Fitzpatrick was putting together a new choir and that he'd asked her to join. She'd always loved to sing, so Silas had believed her. He hadn't shown the least bit of suspicion. In fact, he'd been quite encouraging; she wondered if he didn't hope it would lead to her finding a man to marry.

But for years now, ever since *he* left, Maddy had been determined to put all thoughts of love out of her heart. She'd had suitors, men from town who came by the mercantile and showered her with compliments, but by her actions, a lopsided smile or timely frown, they soon realized she was a hopeless cause. But that did nothing to stem her father's hopes, and so he took hope from her story of the church's choir. Thankfully, he was always asleep when she came home from the speakeasy, and never asked prying questions over breakfast.

"Are you getting ready to go?" a voice whispered.

Maddy looked up to see Helen looking out through a crack in her door.

She nodded.

"You better get going or you'll be late."

Since Maddy had come home from the mercantile, Helen had only left her room to come to dinner. She'd mumbled her way through the meal, obviously still angry about what had been said in the storeroom, looking at her sister with hooded eyes. After Maddy had taken their father his tray, she'd considered knocking on Helen's door and admitting to giving Pete the flour but decided against it; if Helen was going to act so childishly, she might as well stew about it a bit longer.

Though she and Helen had their disagreements, Maddy depended on her sister for help. While Maddy was gone, it would be up to Helen to care for their father, to comfort him if his arthritis flared. While the sisters had fought over helping Pete and his family, they had no such argument over whether their father should know about the speakeasy; they had no choice but to lie together.

"He's listening to the radio," Maddy said.

"I'll check on him in a bit," Helen said, and then added, "Be careful," the same advice she gave every night her sister left for the speakeasy.

"I will." Maddy smiled faintly before heading down the stairs and off toward another night she could never have imagined.

CHAPTER FOUR

When Maddy arrived at the mercantile, a handful of people were already milling around outside. It was nothing obvious, no one was standing in a line, but they were there nonetheless. An affectionate couple stood across the street arm in arm; a man glanced absently in the storefront window at a display of paint cans and brushes; another struck a match, bringing its flaming tip to his cigarette and puffing hard.

Maddy knew they were all waiting for her. Helen had been right to worry; she *was* running late.

"Evenin', Maddy," a voice called from the darkness.

"Good evening," she said politely in answer, hurrying around to the rear of the building.

Beside the mercantile's back door, visible in the light of a flickering bulb, was a pair of cellar doors. Maddy opened them and made her way down the steps into a gloomy darkness. Digging in her pocket, she retrieved her keys; Jeffers had installed a pair of heavy-duty locks, insisting that the only people who should have access to the speakeasy be the two of them. Maddy had agreed, although she figured he was just being paranoid.

Inside the cellar, Maddy flipped a light switch; a couple of years earlier, her father had wired the room with a couple of bulbs. The light was faint, so Maddy had added a few oil lamps. The basement was twice as long as it was wide, with two rows of support beams running its length. At the far end, the storeroom had been fitted with another set of padlocks. The ceiling was low; Arthur Pendergast, one of the tallest men in Colton, had to walk hunched over to keep from hitting his head. The ceiling and walls had been covered in an intricate white tin; Silas had purchased a large amount, but none of it had sold, so instead of throwing it out, or selling it at a loss, he'd decided to put it to good use. Maddy could only imagine how disappointed he'd be to discover what it was decorating now.

The little stock that remained in the cellar, mostly items too large to fit in the upstairs storeroom, had been placed in a far corner. In the newly opened space, chairs and tables had been set up; in the beginning, there'd only been three, but the unanticipated success of the speakeasy had soon made more necessary. Along one wall, empty crates had been stacked three high to create a makeshift bar; just looking at it unnerved Maddy; because of its length and the dark color of the crates, it reminded her of a coffin. Behind the bar, bottles of whiskey, rum, gin, and absinthe stood beside glasses waiting to be filled. An empty cigar box served as a cash register. At the opposite end of the bar, a record player had been hauled down the stairs to offer some extra entertainment; it was missing one of its legs, but Jeffers had propped it up with a couple of books.

Maddy sighed.

I still can't believe I agreed to this . . .

Shaking her head, she grabbed an apron from behind the bar, pulled her red hair back into a knot, and started getting ready for business.

". . . and no sooner were the words out of my mouth, pert' near the whole damn room burst into laughter, judge and jury included! Hell, my memory ain't what it used to be, but I think even the poor guy on trial

67

snickered a bit!"

Seth Pettigrew leaned back in his chair so far that Maddy was convinced he was about to tip over. She held her breath as his hands windmilled the air, his droopy eyes wet with tears, as he kept cackling at his own joke. But then, just as she expected him to topple backward onto his head, he somehow managed to right himself. Lurching forward, he brought his nearly empty drink down onto an empty nail crate with a loud crack. If he realized he'd been in any danger, it certainly didn't show.

"Funniest damn thing you ever saw!" he declared.

"Did you win the case?" Maddy asked.

Seth paused, his eyes narrowing, a laugh frozen on his face. "You know . . . I can't say I remember . . . ," he said before hooting even louder.

For nearly three decades, Seth Pettigrew had been Colton's only lawyer. He'd traveled back and forth to the county seat in Dewey, trying cases of trespassing, arson, divorce, drunken fights, theft, the time Felix Balizet got so bent out of shape at his neighbor that he tried poisoning his dog, and, on a couple of infamous occasions, even murder. Seth had kept accused men from prison and sent others to the gallows.

Like most law practitioners, he'd won memorable cases and lost others. He was well regarded by the people of Colton, who, in general, overlooked his greatest flaw.

He was a bit of a drunk.

Whether it was in a tavern, as he was sitting in his office generously pouring from a bottle he kept in the bottom desk drawer, or when he was imbibing an impromptu dose of liquid courage from his flask before entering the courtroom, almost everyone in the county had seen Seth drink at one time or other. Those remaining few who hadn't surely couldn't mistake the mess of burst blood vessels that colored his nose and cheeks a bright red. But Seth was a happy sort of drunkard, a backslapper always ready with a story and smile, who managed to do his job even when inebriated. After he'd retired from practicing law, handing over his practice to his oldest son, Seth had been able to drink more in earnest, no longer needing to pretend to sobriety. When Prohibition was passed, a few good-natured wagers had been made around town as to how long it would take for him to lose his wits. He'd done his best not to show it, but going without a drink began to take a toll. Maddy had no way of knowing it, but by agreeing to help Jeffers she had been the answer to Seth's prayers.

Swallowing what was left of his whiskey in one gulp, Seth ran a wrinkled hand over his stubbly chin and then up through his thinning, grey hair. A low, loud belch rumbled from his ample belly.

"By God, would I like to get the stupid bastard who thought up this Prohibition nonsense into a courtroom," he declared. "By the time I was done with him, the damn fool would be run out of town on a rail, tarred and feathered, and whatever other punishment I could come up with! Only problem is, with the number of folks here tonight, it might take some work to find an impartial jury."

Maddy looked out from behind the bar. More than a dozen people filled the speakeasy; their conversations, bits of laughter, the clinking of their glasses, and the smoke that billowed from their cigars and cigarettes mixed with the fast-stepping music playing on the record player.

Jeffers watched over the cellar from his place by the door, casting a cautious eye on everyone who came down the cellar steps. Sumner Colt, an enthusiastic crony with a gaunt, pinched-up face and an unpleasant habit of licking his lips, sat in a chair beside Jeffers. Karla Teller cleaned empty glasses from the tabletops and took them to a wash-basin at the far end of the bar to clean them. Maddy didn't know the girl well, but Jeffers had told her not to worry; Karla was a bit dim-witted, too slow in the head to go blabbing around about what they were up to.

"Now how about another drink," Seth said, holding out his glass.

"Don't you think you've had enough for one night?"

"Why, I'm as right as rain!" he argued, thrusting one pointed finger into the air as if he were addressing a jury; unfortunately for him, the swiftness of the gesture unsettled him, making him wobble so precariously in his chair that he had to grab hold of the makeshift bar to stay upright, clinging to it as if he were adrift in turbulent seas.

"Still care to disagree with me?" Maddy smiled.

"I'd hate to have to take this matter up with Jeffers." Seth frowned.

"Even *if* you managed to make it all the way to the door without falling down," she explained slowly, staring into his bloodshot eyes, "you should know by now that Jeffers doesn't tell me what to do, especially not in *my* cellar."

When Maddy agreed to Jeffers's plan,

71

she'd had one condition; the speakeasy couldn't be open without her present and behind the bar. Simply put, she didn't trust him. She wanted to be the one handling the money, serving the drinks, and making sure that no one got out of hand. To her surprise, Jeffers had readily agreed. So far, there hadn't been a single problem.

On the rare occasions when someone like Seth had a bit too much, Maddy immediately cut him off. Jeffers had applauded her good sense; the last thing he wanted was for there to be drunks out roaming the streets of Colton, causing problems and raising unwanted attention. No matter how much Seth protested, she knew he'd get nowhere with Jeffers; he'd never contradicted her decision. The former lawyer would have to go without.

But that didn't mean he'd stop arguing his case.

"One more drink isn't going to kill anyone." Seth said, smiling easily. "Besides, that way you'll still have the joy of my company."

"You can't sweet-talk your way into another drink." Maddy shook her head.

"I've got it!" he suddenly declared, snapping his fingers as if he'd just had a brilliant idea. "How about you pour me half a glass of whiskey and I'll pay you as if you filled it? That way, we both get what we want. What do you say?"

Maddy sighed. She knew that Seth would keep badgering her until she gave in; he'd be relentless. It'd be easier to give him what he wanted. Besides, if he became too rowdy, Jeffers wouldn't let him leave until he sobered up.

"And that's all you'll ask for? You won't be pestering me in fifteen minutes to give you the other half?"

"I solemnly swear," Seth lied, placing his hand on an imaginary Bible.

"Don't give me a reason to call you a liar."

"My dear, I believe I'd be offended if I wasn't so thirsty!"

When Maddy placed the drink in front of him, Seth was so happy that he patted her on the hand and said, "Compromise is the solution to all of life's problems, the doorway through which all good relationships are built. Someday, you'll make some lucky fellow the happiest husband in Montana!"

Maddy flinched; Seth hadn't meant anything by them, but his words cut her deeper than a knife.

Maddy had loved Jack Rucker with all of her heart, but now, whenever she thought of him, of what they had shared, of what all she'd lost, she couldn't help remembering each of their firsts.

The first time she'd ever laid on eyes on Jack had been the day he and his family arrived in Colton. Maddy was eleven years old. It had been a rainy, unmemorable October day, the air clutching and crisp, pushed by an insistent wind. She'd come to the mercantile to be with her father, but because of the weather there'd been no customers. With growing boredom, she'd taken to looking out the window.

Out of the sheets of rain came a lone automobile. Peering intently, she hadn't recognized it as it drove slowly closer, its windshield wipers struggling to push away the rain. In the backseat, the window down in spite of the storm, sat a boy, watching wide-eyed, his dark hair plastered to his forehead. Just as she noticed him, he looked at her. Maddy was shocked to find she couldn't look away, could hardly blink. She had the strange sensation they were talking, sharing unspoken words. When he smiled, she couldn't resist smiling back, watching until the car was again swallowed by the storm.

Six months later, under a clear spring sky, Maddy experienced her first kiss. She'd followed Jack up into the hills west of town, nervously holding his hand as they threaded their way through outcroppings of rock and across creeks swollen with melted snow. The air was full of fresh pinesap. When they finally stopped, the view was breathtaking; from far above, Colton was almost lost among the trees enveloping it, spreading as far as she could see.

Just as she turned to him, Jack leaned down and placed his lips against hers. Looking back, Maddy knew it hadn't been much, a chaste kiss between two kids who had never done it before, lasting only a few beats of her nervous heart, but she remembered it as so much more. She was a girl, but that moment was the first time she was able to imagine what it would be like to be a woman.

Two years later, on the fateful morning when her mother died of influenza, Maddy ran to the rickety bridge that spanned the Lewis River. She'd never understood how Jack had been there waiting for her; in the end, she'd simply accepted that he'd somehow *known.*

Walking toward him, Maddy was unable to hold back her tears. She'd always hidden her true feelings from others, presenting herself as a tough girl with a quick temper. But as she collapsed into Jack's arms, her body shaking from uncontrollable sobs, for the first time in her life she allowed someone to see her vulnerabilities, to see the *real* her. Stroking her hair, he hadn't said a word, waiting for her to talk. From that day forward, the bridge became their special place.

That next fall, walking home together from school, Maddy told Jack that she loved him for the first time. She hadn't intended to; the words had practically jumped out of her mouth, as if they had a life of their own. She'd been reluctant to say them, even though the feelings had teased at the edges of her thoughts for months. She was afraid that it might change things between them, that it might frighten him away; they were still so young. Instead, Jack stopped, turned to her, and smiled. When he told her he loved her in return, the kiss they shared was much more passionate than the one in the high hills.

Everything had been so perfect.

When Jack had first told her that his father was insisting he attend a college back east, Maddy had been heartsick. The thought of him being hundreds of miles away gnawed at her day and night. From that first time she'd seen him, staring back at her through the pouring rain, they hadn't spent more than a few days apart. Now he'd be gone for years. She wondered if he would ever come back, if he'd forget about her.

But Jack insisted she had no reason to worry.

Over and over, he promised he'd return to Colton just as soon as his studies were finished. He swore that he loved her, that once he'd fulfilled his obligation to his father he'd make her his wife. He vowed that they'd spend their future together.

For the first time in her young life, Maddy gave her trust to another, completely. It frightened her, but she believed Jack. And so, standing on their bridge the night before he left, she'd held him, failed to hold back her tears, tenderly kissed his lips, and said good-bye, if only for a while. The next morning, she watched as he drove away toward the depot in Dewey. A sickening feeling filled her stomach. Still, she managed to convince herself to stay strong, that even though Jack would be almost another world away, the only thing that truly separated them was time.

But the days became weeks. The weeks became months. The months became years and everything Maddy feared had come true. All of those "firsts" became worthless; memories that she should have cherished became painful reminders of a time she wished she could forget. Slowly, something else happened to her for the first time.

Maddy had learned what it was like to hate someone.

Maddy watched how Anne Rider hung on every word Mike Gilson said, how enthusiastically she laughed at every one of his jokes, and how genuinely she smiled at him with her eyes. Affectionately, she laid her hand on his, giving it a playful squeeze. Only blindness would've kept someone from noticing how deeply the young seamstress was in love, that she and the cook at the local diner would be married soon, that everyone else in the speakeasy might as well have been invisible, for they had eyes only for each other.

No matter how hard she tried, no matter how many drinks she poured, how much money she took in, or how much small talk she made with everyone who approached the bar, Maddy couldn't look away from them for long. She saw their future, their happiness, their love, all things she'd never have.

And she hated them for it . . .

Maddy was ashamed of her feelings. It wasn't fair; both Anne and Mike were two of the nicest people in Colton. But because of what had happened, of how horribly Maddy had been hurt, the idea of love had been soured for her. Her heart had been poisoned to the core. In her darkest times, she wondered if she could ever love again, could ever give a man her trust. She doubted it.

It was a pointless wish, but just for one moment Maddy wanted to have Jack Rucker standing before her. She didn't know what she'd say to him, what she might do, but she was certain of one thing.

He would *never* forget it.

CHAPTER FIVE

"Purty good crowd tonight, ain't it?"

Jeffers Grimm looked down at Sumner Colt and frowned. He hated the way the boy wanted to be all chummy. "Not bad," he grunted.

"It's a heck of a lot better'n that! If'n it gets any busier, we're gonna have to bring in more tables and chairs!"

"Just keep your eyes on the damn door!" Jeffers hissed angrily.

Sumner fell silent, just the way his boss wanted it.

The two of them stood beside the speakeasy door, at the bottom of the cellar stairs, watching the two dozen or so men and women customers have a good time. Smoke, bits of conversation, and laughter floated around the cellar. Shadows danced on the walls in the low light. A couple swayed to the music beside the record player. Maddy smiled as Seth Pettigrew cackled at another of his stale jokes.

And through it all, liquor was drunk.

Because the selling of that alcohol was illegal, Jeffers made sure someone was guarding the door at all times. He'd been careful about whom he'd told about the speakeasy, keeping it among people he knew or considered trustworthy, but he wasn't a fool, either. Word had gotten out; every night there was a new face, someone he hadn't expected. Sometime soon, there'd be a visitor who hadn't come in search of a good time.

That was why Sumner was there. He wasn't much more than a boy, barely eighteen, but thought himself far older. With his short-cropped blond hair, blemished skin, cold blue eyes, and nervous tongue, he wasn't fooling anyone. Skinny as a stray cat, he still had his uses. Though small, he was tougher than he looked. He followed Jeffers around like a dog, doing whatever he was told and only occasionally needing a beating to remind him of his place. If the kid didn't do so much damn talking, Jeffers might even have considered liking him.

"I'm gonna go take a look around," Jeffers said.

"Let's go," Sumner answered, leaping up from his chair as if to follow.

Jeffers grabbed him by the arm and squeezed hard enough to make sure he had the kid's undivided attention. "You ain't leavin' this door till you're told," he snarled. "I don't care if the damn roof is cavin' in, you stay put 'less I tell you otherwise, understand?"

"Sure, sure, sure," Sumner whimpered, rapidly nodding his head in agreement. "Whatever you say!" When Jeffers finally let him go, he practically leaped back into his chair, turning to stare at the door as if it were the most important thing in the world.

"Don't leave till I come back," Jeffers repeated.

"Got it, boss," Sumner answered quickly, his eyes never leaving the door.

Shaking his head, Jeffers made his way farther into the speakeasy.

Jeffers had never been comfortable around lots of people, but thankfully most folks were even more uneasy around him and gave him a wide berth. Even in the speakeasy, he noticed how they got out of his way; it was done subtly, a shifting of a chair here, a repositioning of the feet there, but he saw how they glanced in his direction, aware of where he was in the room. It didn't bother him; on the contrary, it pleased him greatly.

He wanted the people of Colton to be afraid of him.

Making his way through the tables, Jeffers nodded at the few patrons who were brave enough to look him in the eye. Because of his imposing size, threatening people came easy to him, almost effortlessly. He was no stranger to violence; he'd been in more fights than he could count and had never come out on the losing end. He'd shot men who'd stuck their nose into his business, had stabbed others, and even had trampled one poor bastard with his horse. Everyone knew he wasn't to be trifled with.

Everyone except Maddy Aldridge.

From the opposite side of the cellar, Jeffers watched as Maddy poured Seth Pettigrew another drink. When she took his money, she smiled so brightly that her whole face lit up. Absently, she flipped a few loose strands of hair over her shoulder. Jeffers was so caught up in what she was doing that he nearly ran into one of the cellar's support beams.

Damn, if she didn't get his heart racing.

Jeffers was surprised he hadn't noticed her much in the last couple of years. He'd see her at her father's store from time to time, but he'd never paid much attention; it was as if she were part of the fixtures.

Maybe it was because they were so completely different; she was smart and witty, always ready with a warm smile for everyone she met, and a bit easier on the eyes. She was popular and respected. On the other hand, no one would ever mistake Jeffers Grimm for Colton's finest son.

But then, gripped with one hell of an idea, he'd stepped inside Silas Aldridge's store and seen her true, maybe for the first time.

Ever since, he'd become obsessed.

Jeffers knew she was too good for the likes of him, but he didn't give a damn. It wasn't as if he wanted her hand in marriage. Maddy was pure, an example of all that was admirable and good in the world. He'd watched her talk to folks come down out of the hills, filthy degenerates without a pot to piss in, and do so with respect. As remarkable as she was, all Jeffers wanted to do was grind that goodness out of her, to make her as disreputable as he was.

He wanted her to belong to him.

Jack Rucker had been a fool to give her up. Most folks, Jeffers included, could see that Maddy was still pining for him. Though almost seven years had passed since Rucker left Colton, there was still a part of her waiting, maybe even expecting him to return, but Jeffers knew there was a better chance of hell freezing over. Better than most, he understood Rucker's leaving; Jeffers wanted the same thing, to get away to something better, somewhere *more,* to leave Colton behind forever.

Until that day came, he'd set his sights on having Maddy Aldridge. Looking at her now, how beautiful and untouchable she was, all at the same time, only made his desire greater. The whores who shared his bed couldn't hold a candle to her; whenever he rolled off one, he was usually too disgusted to look at her for long. He doubted he'd feel that way with Maddy beneath him.

We're gonna find out soon . . . whether she wants to have me or not . . .

Jeffers felt the stirrings of a smile tug at the corners of his mouth as Jared Wilkinson hurried to get out of his way, the legs of his chair scraping loudly against the floor as he shot to his feet. Without a look back, the old man practically ran toward the bar. Years before, Jeffers had lent Wilkinson some money; unbeknownst to him at the time, it had come with a high rate of interest. When the former lumberjack protested, it had taken a late night visit to help keep him paying. Even though the money had been fully paid a few months back, the man's fear remained.

Amused, Jeffers was reminded of one of the reasons he'd become attracted to Maddy; unlike Jared Wilkinson, she had a backbone.

When Jeffers had first approached her about using the mercantile's basement as a speakeasy, he'd come away impressed that she'd turned down his offer so determinedly. Though he'd seen the fear in her eyes as plain as day, she'd stood her ground. Very few people would have dared to defy him. It was at that moment Jeffers began to see her differently. He'd become attracted to her. The irony was not lost on him; the last thing he would've ever tolerated from someone like Sumner was backtalk.

The second time Jeffers had come to her, he'd been far more determined, not just because he'd needed the space but also because by then *he wanted her.* Rather than threatening her, he'd tried to make her see reason, going so far as to drag her sick father into it, anything to make her relent. Slowly, Jeffers saw her resolve weakening. When she insisted on being involved in running the tavern, it was obvious she'd expected him to argue; when he hadn't, confusion flashed across her face.

If only she knew the truth.

Jeffers walked into the thick, dark shadows at the rear of the cellar. Crates, sacks, and barrels of unsold merchandise had been stacked in piles in order to make room for the speakeasy. Weaving his way through the mess, Jeffers came to a locked door set into the rear wall. Pulling a key from his pocket, he unlocked the padlock he'd installed, stepped inside, and flipped the light switch.

The storeroom wasn't half the size of the rest of the cellar, but its ceiling was higher. In the far corner was a pulley lift that rose to the alleyway between the mercantile and the bakery next door. Thankfully for Jeffers, the tough times that had struck Silas Aldridge's business meant that the room had been nearly empty at the time his daughter agreed to open the speakeasy. That left plenty of room for Jeffers to begin filling it.

Crates full of liquor bottles were stacked three high across the room. Heavy oak barrels lined the wall opposite the lift; the contents of each had been painted on the side. A few loose bottles of whiskey were stacked on top of one of the barrels, the amber liquid dark in the faint light. Sitting beside the door was an open crate packed with straw, which held the bottles he'd set aside for the speakeasy's bar, the bottles he sold by the drink to help along his lie.

A lie that's makin' me rich . . .

When Prohibition had been enacted, most of the drinkers in Colton had bitched about the loss of drink, whining about how unfairly the new law punished them. Jeffers hadn't seen it that way; all he saw was opportunity. Wherever there was a demand for something in low supply, money was just waiting to be made. Now that selling alcohol was illegal, thirsty folks would spend plenty to get it. That was where he would step in. It hadn't taken long for him to make contact with others who thought the same way.

The border between the United States and Canada was thousands of miles long, far too great of a distance for all of it to be watched. This was especially true of the wilderness of Montana. Hundreds of pack trails, dirt roads, animal crossings, rivers, and creeks wormed their way through the thick forests that stretched between the two countries. For someone like Jeffers, a man who knew every nook and cranny of the area, it seemed impossible that someone could find him if he didn't want them to; he was a needle in a hundred-mile-wide haystack.

When Jeffers was first introduced to Jimmy Luciano, he had no idea the man worked for Al Capone. Listening to what the gangster wanted, Jeffers had a bit of trouble concentrating; with his fine clothes, cigar, and jeweled rings that dazzled from almost every finger, Jimmy was everything Jeffers aspired to be. It wouldn't have mattered *what* was being asked of him; he would've done most anything to be involved.

The plan was simple. Connections of Capone's in Canada would meet Jeffers near a little-used horse trail right on the border under the cover of darkness. Casks and crates of liquor would be transferred to a truck that Jeffers would procure. He would then drive it back to Colton and store the liquor, holding load after load until Jimmy came to retrieve it all in one fell swoop. For his work, Jeffers would be paid a lot of money.

The problem had been finding a place in Colton big enough to store the booze. He'd considered keeping it in a barn outside of town, leaving it in the truck covered with a tarp, and even stashing it beneath a bridge. In the end, none of them seemed safe enough. But getting caught wasn't an option, either; if the cops didn't lock him up forever, he could only imagine what the Mob would do to him. It was then, while walking down the street at a loss as to what he should do, that he passed in front of

Aldridge Mercantile. Through the front window he'd seen Maddy standing behind the counter, and an idea had struck him like a lightning bolt from a stormy sky.

He'd hide the liquor right in the heart of town.

Jeffers was certain that the mercantile's cellar would have plenty of room. Not only could he hide the booze there until Jimmy came to get it, but it even allowed him the opportunity to make some money on the side. Operating a speakeasy would be nothing but profit; after all, there were plenty of thirsty people in Colton. All it took was cutting a side deal with the Canadians for a couple of crates of his own and he was in business.

He just needed Maddy.

When she'd finally given in, Jeffers had set to work. He and Sumner had gotten a truck, picked up the first load of liquor, and driven back to Colton under a black, moonless sky. Careful to avoid attention, they'd parked in the alley and unloaded their cargo as quickly as they could. Jeffers had installed new locks on the doors to the cellar storeroom and pulley lift to keep any curious visitors away. A few days later, the speakeasy was open for business.

Everything had gone off without a hitch.

Jeffers had no doubt Maddy would be furious to know he'd deceived her. Because he had involved her, she was in as much danger as he was, from both the law and the Mob should anything go wrong. She was making a bit of extra money, enough to help care for her sad excuse of a father, but Jeffers stood to make hundreds of times more. Maybe after he'd succeeded in breaking and bedding her, he'd be willing to give her a bigger cut of the money. Unlike Jack Rucker, maybe he'd even take her along when he left this piece-of-shit town forever.

He was going to be rich and powerful, and there was nothing that could stand in his way.

No sooner had Jeffers locked up the storeroom and turned back toward the speakeasy when he saw something that made his blood run cold. Everyone else had noticed it, too; the whole tavern had fallen dead silent, save for Seth Pettigrew, cackling away on his stool. There, calmly walking toward the makeshift bar, a wry smile on his face, was Jim Utley, Colton's sheriff.

Furious, Jeffers's eyes snapped toward the entrance. Sumner stood in the open door, his eyes wide and his jaw slack. He looked up the cellar steps, then at the sheriff, and then over at Jeffers. Jeffers knew the boy couldn't have kept Utley from entering, but he should've done *something,* shouted out or caused a ruckus; if he had, maybe things could've been settled at the door, out of sight of the customers.

But now it was too late.

Jeffers had lied to Maddy about a lot of things, and one of them had been his lack of concern over Jim Utley. He'd told Maddy the sheriff was a pushover, nothing for them to be worried about, but the truth was he really didn't know. It could go either way . . .

Slowly, Jeffers ran his fingers over the knife in his belt.

Seth Pettigrew laughed on as if the party hadn't been interrupted. He was drunk enough not to know or care about what was happening. It wasn't until the sheriff slapped him warmly on the back that he stopped, startling so badly that his voice screeched like a phonograph needle being yanked off a record. When his bleary eyes told him who stood beside him, he looked as if he might vomit, the color falling from his face.

"Evenin', Maddy," the sheriff said, leaning his ample belly against the bar and taking off his hat. Patiently, he dug a handkerchief out of his pocket and wiped the sweat from his brow.

"Good evening, Jim," Maddy answered calmly.

"You know, darlin'," he began with a small, knowing grin, "a man doesn't spend goin' on twenty years as sheriff in a town small as Colton without hearin' 'bout every scheme goin' on, day or night." He paused, folding the handkerchief and putting it away before continuing. "So when I caught a whisper 'bout someone openin' up a speakeasy in town, well, I figured it best I go nosin' round, see if I couldn't find out where it was. You all might as well have had a sign hangin' out front, it was so easy."

Jeffers inched closer to the bar. He was the only person in the cellar moving; everyone else was frozen in place, watching.

"When word first came down 'bout this Prohibition business," the sheriff said, "I figured it was only a matter of time 'fore someone got it in their head to start sellin' illegally, but there's one thing 'bout this that surprises me."

"What's that?" Maddy asked.

"That you're a part of it," he said, nodding at her.

For an instant, Maddy's calm exterior wavered, a look of unease suddenly flashing in her eyes, and she glanced away.

Jeffers chose that moment to step out of

93

the shadows and approach the bar. The sheriff nodded when he saw him.

"I should've known *you'd* be involved in this."

Jim Utley was no stranger to Jeffers's family; the sheriff had a long history dealing with the Grimm men. He'd put Jeffers's father in jail more times than he'd likely remember and had been around so long that he'd even had a few runins with Jeffers's grandfather. Every time he had something going, it seemed the sheriff lurked close by, waiting for him to slip up.

But this time was different. Jeffers *wasn't* getting caught; no matter what it took, even if he had to gut the son of a bitch right here in front of the whole speakeasy, he wasn't going to lose what he'd gained. He and Sumner could load the truck as best they could, call Jimmy and tell him what happened and he'd leave this godforsaken town forever. But he wouldn't go to jail.

I'll kill this bastard first . . .

"Maddy and I are runnin' this together," Jeffers explained.

For the first time, the sheriff looked taken aback. "Is that true?" he asked Maddy.

She nodded.

"What do you suppose Silas would say 'bout this?"

"I don't believe he'd think too highly of it," she answered truthfully, "so that should tell you I didn't come to this decision easily. But times being what they are, I think we all need a little something to brighten our day, whether it's a few extra coins in our pocket or a drink once the sun goes down."

"Only problem is that sellin' liquor's now illegal."

"Then I reckon you need to do your job."

Jeffers stiffened. This was the moment everything hinged on. Though he desperately wanted to bed Maddy Aldridge, he didn't give a damn if she ended up in jail as long as he went free. Slowly, he began to unsheathe his knife.

"My job is more than just enforcin' the law," Sheriff Utley explained. "It's also makin' sure that the folks in this town are taken care of. Now, just 'cause some politician in Washington thinks it's a good idea to make sellin' liquor illegal, I don't know if what's happenin' here is the same thing they had in mind. Wettin' your whistle in the company of friends doesn't strike me as much of a crime."

"You . . . you mean this . . . is acceptable . . . ?" Seth asked.

"Long as no one gets drunk," the sheriff said, looking straight at the former lawyer, "and it don't go any further than this, no makin' it or distributin' it, then I'll allow it to go on. We got a deal?"

"Yes," Maddy happily agreed as Jeffers nodded.

"Now don't go thinkin' I won't be watchin'," Sheriff Utley added, "or that I won't throw you all in jail if you break our agreement."

"We won't," Maddy promised.

Fishing a shiny coin out of his pocket, the sheriff slapped it down on the bar. "Then how 'bout we seal it with a drink, huh?"

As Maddy went about pouring a whiskey, Jeffers stared silently. When the sheriff had given his warning, he'd looked in Jeffers's direction. *Does he know about what's hidden in the storeroom? He'd seemed surprised that Maddy was involved, but was it genuine? Does he know about my deal with Capone?* The only other person who knew the truth was Sumner; he'd already let the sheriff into the speak-easy . . . was he the one who told Utley about the place?

Jeffers suddenly had a lot of questions. Maybe he was going to have to use that knife after all.

CHAPTER SIX

"How in the hell is a fella supposed to get any sleep bouncin' around in this goddamn seat? It's torture! They better have a decent hotel in that town of yours or I swear —"

Jack struggled to control his temper as he steered the black Plymouth through the forested hills of Montana. The sun had just begun to peek above the eastern horizon, painting the clouds that hung in the morning sky in brilliant brushstrokes of red and orange. The car bounced and swayed as it drove the dirt road, making a symphony of creaks and groans. For the last couple of hours, things had been peacefully quiet for Jack, driving under the moon and stars. However, with his nagging companion awake, things had already begun to change.

If there was one thing Ross Hooper was good at, it was complaining.

"Ain't it just like the Bureau to be too cheap to put us in a train? A sleeper car wouldn't ruin my back! Chaps my hide, I tell ya!"

Jack considered explaining, for the third time since they'd set out from Seattle, that the reason they were driving to Colton was so that they'd have a means of escaping should things become too dangerous, but he knew his words would be wasted. Ross heard only what he wanted to hear.

As if he were trying to further annoy Jack, the man belched loudly. "Like it ain't bad enough already, now my belly's givin' me grief!"

From the moment Lieutenant Pluggett had told him who would be accompanying him on his next assignment, Jack had dreaded the thought of being in the other man's company. As soon as they'd set out, it had been one grumble after another, a seemingly endless litany; he'd fussed about the food, the weather, the time Jack had told him to be ready to travel, the task the Bureau had given them, the car they were to drive, and especially the partner he'd been saddled with, everything under the sun.

In his mid-fifties, Ross looked like a man well on his way to sitting on a porch, enjoying his retirement. With narrow, watery eyes that peered out from a particularly dull, jowly face, he was plump enough to rest his hands on the paunch of his stomach. His clothing was a mess; food and sweat stains dotted both his trousers and shirt, while his suit had been wrinkled well before he'd slept in it.

"Wonder if it was somethin' I ate," he said as he rested his head against the car window. "Just had to have been . . ."

Ross Hooper had been employed by one form of law enforcement or another since well before Jack had been born. Most of Ross's years had been spent with the Pinkerton agency, but he'd left under unknown circumstances; everyone just assumed he'd been fired. He wasn't very good at his job; Jack wasn't the only agent who didn't want to work with him. He was the type of cop who dealt with trouble by using his fists instead of his head, the sort who would rather knock a guy unconscious than let him make a confession.

Jack had to wonder if Ross was capable of pulling off their ruse. Pluggett had instructed them to pose as advance men looking to buy up land for a speculator with deep pockets back in Seattle. The thinking had been that if the townspeople of Colton figured they stood to make a windfall of money, it might loosen their tongues to talk about all the goings-on, including any rumors about someone running illegal Canadian booze. While Jack could be as silver-tongued as the devil himself when he wanted to be, Ross Hooper was the type of man who'd have trouble coaxing a starving horse to a bag of feed. If Ross wasn't good enough, if they failed at their task, Jack could forget any chance of a promotion.

And now, as if things hadn't been bad enough, he had to listen to his fellow agent prattle on about his indigestion.

Jack couldn't shake the feeling that this was *exactly* what he deserved.

The faded red windmill at Roland Gambill's farm was the first thing Jack saw that told him how close he was to his old home. Ever since the dawn broke, he'd watched out the window for something to slide by, some sign of the life left years ago, the life he'd never planned on returning to. Now there it was, whipping past, almost close enough to touch.

He was heading back to Maddy Aldridge.

In the seven years since he'd left Colton, Jack had done his best to forget all about his old life. Since joining the Bureau, he'd buried himself in his work, spending countless hours pursuing criminals, eating, breathing, and sleeping the job. From the outside, he imagined it looked as if he never gave Maddy a thought. But the truth was something quite different. She was still there, not lurking in the shadows of the past, a musty memory that occasionally floated to the surface, but one he kept returning to again and again. It didn't take much: a whiff of a woman's perfume, a voice shouted across a busy street, a song drifting over the radio; even while he slept, she visited his dreams.

Memories of Maddy filled his days and nights.

Ever since he found out he was being sent to Colton, Jack had been wondering what she was doing. Had she met another man, married, raised a couple of children, and taken over her father's business? Or was she alone and bitterly angry, unable or unwilling to so much as speak to a potential suitor? Was it somewhere between the two? He even wondered if she'd followed his example, leaving town for somewhere different and now living in Denver, San Francisco, or some other faraway city. Maybe she was long gone and his growing apprehension about seeing her again was for nothing.

But there was another possibility Jack

truly feared, one thing Maddy could have done that would pierce his heart.

Maybe she'd forgotten all about him.

Jack knew he deserved no less for what he'd done to her, but it bothered him anyway. If he were to see her now, would she just walk on past without recognizing him, or worse, would she chat for a moment, a word for an old acquaintance returned from a life she'd long since outgrown? They'd been so young, little more than children, but that didn't mean it was meaningless or any less real. Jack knew he was being selfish, but he wanted their past to still mean something to Maddy, for her to still have a bit of him in her heart. He wanted her to be happy, but he didn't want to be a discarded memory, either. That would've been too painful. He would have preferred being slugged in the face to being ignored, hated instead of forgotten.

But even so, I know I've earned the worst.

There'd been a reason for what he'd done to Maddy, for never writing back to any of her increasingly frantic letters, for never calling her on the telephone, for refusing to return to Colton. He'd clung to that reason tenaciously in the years since, as if it explained the way he'd treated her, as if it were perfectly understandable. Somehow, he'd managed to convince himself that it was all for the best, that he was doing it for her sake, but now that he was finally coming home, doubts began nagging at him.

Most of the memories of Jack's youth were hazy, out-of-focus bits and pieces of childhood, but the night he and his family had driven into Colton, traveling through a relentless storm, he'd seen a redheaded girl standing in a store window, *watching him,* and his heart had been snatched from his chest just as surely as if she'd walked out into the rain and pulled it out with her own hand.

The courtship that followed had been brief but had opened the door to an unexpected love. There'd been long walks and kisses, but there had also been a few long nights and tears, too. On the night when they'd said their goodbyes, he'd meant his promise to her, but . . .

And now, there was a good chance he was about to see her again.

During his time with the Bureau of Prohibition, Jack had willingly entered into some of the most dangerous situations imaginable: shady dives where, if his true identity were discovered, it could have cost him his life. But somehow, this assignment seemed even worse. The possibility of meeting

Maddy played havoc with his nerves and caused his stomach to toss and turn. Because he had no alias to hide behind, he felt even more vulnerable; everyone in Colton knew him. For as much as he worried about Ross Hooper not being able to do his job, Jack wondered if his problems would interfere with his own.

Jack knew he had to stay focused. Pluggett said that if he succeeded with this operation, it might mean he'd get a chance at Capone. Jack wanted to get ahead, to get a promotion, to be someone in a city so large that all of Colton would fit in one skyscraper with plenty of room left over. He didn't want to get sentimental about a life he'd left behind.

Outside the Plymouth's window, he started seeing more and more sights that spoke of the Montana he knew: Samuel Chapman's weather vane that was adorned with an iron pig instead of a rooster, the tall church spire in Faribault, and the enormous, misshapen elm tree that sat alone on an island in the middle of Mulligan's Pond. They'd be in Colton in minutes.

Over and over, Jack thought about the job, about chasing Capone, about how distasteful it was to be stuck in a car with Ross Hooper, about how he was going to look with a medal pinned to his chest. But even then, he couldn't prevent a familiar thought from intruding.

Maddy . . .

Crossing the bridge that spanned the Clark River, Jack drove the Plymouth into Colton. To Jack's eye, at first glance, nothing seemed to have changed. Majestic houses sat on both sides of the wide, elm-lined street that reached toward the center of town. In the early morning sun, dew glistened off the well-kept lawns and shrub rows and birds shook their wings in ornate baths. But when Jack looked a bit closer, he began to notice small things that were different from before: more automobiles were parked in driveways and along the street, with only an occasional horse buggy mixed in, a sign that Colton was slowly but surely becoming more modern; a couple of new houses had been built on the outskirts of town; and trees that had been little more than saplings when he'd left seven years earlier had reached a good deal higher toward the sky.

"So this is where you were raised?" Ross asked with a frown.

Jack nodded, still looking out the window.

"Huh," the man grunted, rubbing his belly and wincing.

Closer to downtown, things became even more familiar. Through the barbershop window, Jack saw Thaddeus White sweeping up a pile of clippings while Carl Hough waited for his turn in the chair. Just before they reached the Wilmington Brothers Bakery, Winifred Holland, Jack's old schoolteacher, crossed the street with a fresh loaf of bread; she was a bit more frail looking than he remembered her being, her hair a snowy white, but he would've recognized her anywhere; it took a good deal of self-control not to call out to her.

Turning the Plymouth off Main Street, Jack was thankful he wouldn't have to drive past Maddy's father's store; the last thing he wanted was to run into her the moment he arrived in town. Jack and Ross's first order of business was to check into the hotel and get settled before starting their ruse and getting information. Jack needed a shower, a bit of sleep, and maybe even a drink to calm his nerves.

"This place ain't much more than a hole in the ground," Ross sneered as he looked out the window. "If someone's sellin' booze here, I hope to hell they make a mistake and accidentally poison half the town. Ask me, they'd be doin' these sad sons-a-bitches a favor . . ."

Angrily, Jack slammed down on the car's brakes hard enough to make the tires screech; the back end fishtailed a bit before coming to a sudden, jerking halt in the middle of the street. Through the windshield, he noticed that a few heads had turned in their direction, but just then he didn't much care.

"Watch your damn mouth," he hissed at his partner.

"What's the matter, 'Lucky Jack'?" Ross smirked mischievously. "Did I hit a little too close to home?"

From the glint in the man's eye, Jack saw that Ross had been baiting him, challenging his sentimentality. All the older agent had wanted was to get under his skin, to goad him until he got the reaction he desired, and Jack, like a fool, had willingly given it to him.

Keep it together, Jack . . . Don't give him the satisfaction . . .

"Truthfully, I don't much care what you think of me," Jack began, measuring his words, "but disrespecting them," his arm waving across the inside of the windshield, "isn't going to do either of us any good. We have to be both believable and liked if they're going to buy the story we're selling. You approach someone with contempt written on your face and in your words and you aren't going to learn a thing."

"Don't you tell me how to do my job, boy." Ross chuckled, though his eyes narrowed threateningly. "I've been doing this since before you were born in this nowhere town, spending your days sucking on your mother's tit."

Jack struggled to keep his rapidly growing anger from boiling over. "Then I suggest you start acting like it. If you screw this up before we even have a chance to find out where the speakeasy is, there's going to be hell to pay. Pluggett wants results and won't stand for failure."

"Quit worryin'," Ross said dismissively. "Gettin' answers outta rubes like these will be easier than stealin' candy from a baby. Leave it to me and Pluggett and the Bureau will be kissin' both our asses. If you ask me, it'd probably be best if you just left me at the hotel and went vistin' your fine family and friends." He smiled, his voice dripping with sarcasm. "I bet there's even some old flame of yours been pinin' away the years, hopin' you'd come back to town so you could take her to bed and ravish her just like the good ole days."

Faster than a rattlesnake, Jack grabbed Ross by the neck of his shirt and practically yanked him out of his seat. Both of Jack's fists were balled tight and the desire to pound the older man in the face was hard to resist. Jack's heart thundered and he could hear his blood pounding in his ear. Fear flickered in Ross's wide eyes for only an instant before he regained his composure, a thin, sly smile slowly spreading across his face.

"Another word like what you just said and a gut ache will be the least of your concerns," Jack said menacingly.

"I'd think about that if I were you," Ross answered. "I reckon it wouldn't look too good for a fella's chances of promotion if he were to rough up a fellow agent. The Bureau frowns on that sort of thing."

Jack hated to admit that Ross was right, but he still hoped he'd made his point. Stewing in his remaining anger, he gave the man a slight shove backward as he let go of his shirt. Almost instantly, Ross's face twisted up in a grimace of excruciating pain, his teeth bared and his eyes clenched shut, his hands grasping his stomach. Jack noticed beads of sweat dotting his forehead and upper lip.

"Are you all right?" he asked, putting a hand on Ross's arm.

The older man immediately shrugged it

off. "Get your damn hands off me!" he snapped. "It's just my stomach flarin' up."

"Do you need a doctor? Steven Quayle's been here since —"

"Just take us to the hotel!" Ross shouted, cutting him off mid-sentence. "Between whatever it was I ate, your whinin' and belly-achin' 'bout pleasin' the Bureau, and the pitiful state of this town, it's a wonder I ain't keeled over dead yet!"

Jack sighed; that's what he got for showing some concern. Without another word, he did as Ross said and drove toward the hotel.

The Belvedere Hotel sat across the street from Colton's train depot on the north side of Main Street near the banks of the Lewis River. It'd been built in the exciting times just after the railway had first come to town, days filled with wishful predictions of frequent tourists and rare goods shipped from all over the country. Unfortunately, what had followed was nothing like what had been hoped for, and far from profitable. Colton had remained what it always was: far off the beaten path. Consequently, the hotel had seen better days.

Standing two stories tall, with a long porch lined with thick columns befitting a wealthy businessman's home, how majestic it had once looked. With ornate carvings framing the beveled glass of the upper windows and crisp grey and maroon paint on the building that made the unmarred white of the columns stand out, the Belvedere had been the talk of the town, a jewel to be marveled at. But now, its paint chipped bald in places, with rotted wood on the steps and a few windowsills, and even a cracked piece of glass just below where the sign hung, that former glory had long since faded.

Jack parked the car and stepped out into the early morning sun, wiping sweat from his brow with the back of his forearm. A burr of shame nagged at him that he felt relieved no one was watching his arrival.

Get over it; "Lucky Jack" . . . you're going to have to talk to someone if you expect to get to the bottom of this booze-running business.

When Jack pulled the two suitcases from the Plymouth's trunk, he found Ross leaning back against the closed passenger's door, his hands pressed against his belly and his face contorted in agony. Sweat soaked the open collar of his shirt and his skin had gone as pale as the moon.

"Listen, Ross," Jack said. "This is more

than a bellyache. It'd be best if we went to
—"

"Don't you know by now I don't give a
damn what you think!" the older man
snapped, snatching his suitcase from Jack's
hand and wobbling toward the hotel's steps.
"All I need is to lie down for a bit! You're
carryin' on like you was my mother!"

Watching Ross make his way unsteadily
up the Belvedere's steps, Jack considered
saying more but knew that anything he suggested would be turned down. Shaking his
head, he followed along behind.

The inside of the hotel had the same run-
down opulence as the outside; the crystal
chandelier was coated in a thick layer of
dust, the carved wooden ball that was supposed to be on top of the newel post at the
bottom of the long staircase banister had
been broken off, and the ornate carpet that
led to the hotel desk was spotted with stains
and laced with runs in the stitching. Once
again, Jack's memories were of something
far grander.

But there was one thing about the Belvedere that hadn't changed in the years he'd
been away; Virginia Benoit still stood behind
the front desk. She and her husband, a
former fur trapper in Canada, had opened
the Belvedere, but an unfortunate heart at-

tack made Virginia a widow before the first guest had checked in. Though her features were a bit grayer, her face lined with a few more wrinkles, she looked up at them with a smile he found warmly familiar.

"Good morning, gentlemen," she said. "Will you be checking . . . ," but her voice faltered as she looked at Jack.

"Hello, Mrs. Benoit."

"Jack . . . ? Jack Rucker . . . ? Land sakes alive . . . is that you . . . ?" she stammered, eyes wide with surprise.

"It's been a long time," he answered.

"I . . . but . . . I never expected to see you in Colton again."

Mustering up a warm, friendly smile, Jack took a deep breath as he prepared himself for the first telling of his Bureau-supplied story. It was important for him to get it right, to start laying the groundwork that explained his return to Colton and would eventually lead to whoever was circumventing Prohibition.

But before Jack could say a word, a blood-curdling scream filled the Belvedere as Ross Hooper fell onto the stained floor, his hands desperately clutching his belly, his teeth bared in a grimace of pain.

CHAPTER SEVEN

Jack stood frozen in place, unable to believe what he was seeing. He'd been in dangerous, difficult situations more times than he cared to remember, moments that required quick thinking and a cool, collected head, but this was too much. Sure, Ross had complained during the long drive about his stomach bothering him, but whatever *this* was, it was much more than whining. Tentatively, unsure of what, if anything, he could do, Jack knelt beside Ross as the man writhed in pain.

"Oh, my land sakes!" Virginia shrieked from behind the Belvedere's front desk. "What's the matter with him?"

Given Ross's current state, there was no point in asking him. Sweat dotted his pale white skin and ran in streaks down his cheeks, pooling in the recesses of his neck. The Bureau agent's hands were pressed against his stomach so tightly that the tendons stood out, his nails dug in deeply as if he were clinging to a crumbling cliff side. Sounds hissed through his clenched teeth; there were no words, only guttural noises that spoke of hurt. Frighteningly, his eyes had rolled back so far in their sockets that Jack could no longer see the pupils. Ross looked to be in such agony that Jack began to fear he was about to die right before his eyes.

It was that thought, that his partner might die if he didn't do something, that finally spurred Jack into action.

"Call Dr. Quayle and tell him it's an emergency!" he shouted at Mrs. Benoit. "Tell him he needs to get here right now!"

Without hesitation, the Belvedere's owner hurried into the small room beside the front desk. A moment later, Jack could hear her frantically dialing the operator. Thankfully, he remembered that Dr. Quayle's office was nearby, only a couple of blocks away; if he was in, he'd arrive at the hotel in minutes.

But if he isn't there . . .

Even in the short time since Ross had fallen to the floor, his condition appeared to have worsened; in addition to groaning louder, he'd begun to shake, his limbs twitching with every tremor. Unable to do more than watch, Jack felt completely helpless. He might not have liked Ross Hooper, *not a lick,* but the last thing Jack wanted was for the man to suffer.

"Doc Quayle'll be here just as quick as he can," Virginia explained, setting a pitcher of water and some old rags on the floor. "In the meantime, I reckon he needs to be cooled down a bit."

Dipping a rag into the water, Jack began wiping the sweat from Ross's brow; at the first touch, Ross reacted as if he'd been struck by lightning, his body spasming before he moaned deeply. Jack didn't know if he was helping or making things worse.

"What do you reckon's the matter with him?" Virginia asked.

"I don't know," Jack answered truthfully.

"Doc Quayle'll know what to do."

"I sure hope so."

No sooner had Jack spoken than Steven Quayle raced through the Belvedere's front door. The doctor was a wisp of a man, short and so thin he'd blow away in the first stiff breeze. Getting on in years, with severe glasses that made him look even older, he had thin white hair that barely covered a forehead well known around Colton for wrinkling whenever he considered a diagnosis. He mended children's broken bones, tended pregnant women's broken waters, and even, on rare occasions, offered advice to those suffering from a broken heart. He was a good physician as well as an honest man, sometimes brutally so, but everyone in town would put their lives in his hands.

Hurrying over to the fallen man, Dr. Quayle hesitated for an instant, surprise fading from his face as he recognized who was kneeling down beside his new patient. "What happened to him, Jack?" he asked calmly, opening his medical bag.

Jack answered by telling him about Ross's many complaints during their drive, about how he'd thought it must've been something he ate, all the way up until he'd screamed, collapsing on the floor in agony. Dr. Quayle listened, occasionally nodding, his brow furrowed.

"He only complained about his stomach?" the doctor asked.

Jack nodded.

Dr. Quayle leaned over and placed his hand against Ross's lower stomach, just above his belt. He only gave a light push, but Ross practically leaped off the floor, a howl of agony bursting from his mouth as if a knife had been slid into his belly. Jack couldn't help but recoil from the sound.

"It's his appendix," Dr. Quayle said matter-of-factly.

"Is that bad?" Virginia asked, hovering behind the two of them, one hand on her chin, poised as if she were about to stifle a gasp.

"If I don't operate," the doctor answered, "he'll die."

"You're going to cut him open?" Jack asked, stunned by how quickly events seemed to be spiraling out of control.

"It's the only way."

"Have you ever done this before?"

"Twice," Dr. Quayle answered. "Both a long time ago."

"Did they make it?"

"One did, but the other didn't, but this man will definitely *not* survive if we spend much longer talking about it."

Jack took a deep breath. "All right," he said. "Let's get him over to your office."

"There isn't time," the doctor said, shaking his head. "We're going to have to do it here if he's to have any sort of chance."

"Here?" Virginia echoed. "In the hotel?"

"I need a room that's close and unoccupied," the doctor answered, paying no mind to Mrs. Benoit's obvious displeasure at learning her home and place of business was about to be used as an operating theater.

"The first one on the right," Virginia said,

pointing toward the short hallway leading away from the bottom of the staircase. "I was about to give it to them anyways; least I was 'fore all the commotion."

"Grab his feet," Dr. Quayle ordered.

Jack did as he was told and was just about to lift Ross from the floor when the doctor stopped him.

"You're going to have to hold on to him just as tight as you can," Dr. Quayle explained. "He's in a lot of pain and moving him is only going to make matters worse. He'll be fighting us every step of the way, but the last thing we want to do is drop him."

"I won't let him fall," Jack replied.

"Then let's move him," Dr. Quayle said, positioning himself behind Ross's head and sliding his hands beneath the man, hooking them in his armpits; even with that slight touch, the man reacted as if he'd been pinched, squirming in discomfort as he issued a painful moan.

"Now."

No sooner had Jack lifted Ross from the floor than the doctor's words of warning proved to have been well-founded; another anguished scream exploded out of Ross's mouth as his body shuddered and shook, desperately trying to pull free from their grasp. Jack struggled to hold on to the man's legs as they wildly kicked and thrashed.

Virginia hurried ahead of them, holding the doctor's medical bag, and pushed open the door to the room before getting out of their way. As gently as they could, they laid Ross onto the bed. Settled, his protests subsided to a low whimper and fitful shivering. Tears leaked from the corners of his eyes. His hands never left his aching belly.

Turning to Mrs. Benoit, Dr. Quayle said, "Bring me plenty of boiled water and as many clean sheets as you can carry."

Though clearly distressed by the thought of what was about to happen to her linens, she went about her tasks.

Dr. Quayle immediately set about placing the instruments from his medical bag onto the night table beside the bed: a scalpel, a thin, long-nosed pair of scissors, as well as several other medical tools, bandages of all shapes and sizes, and a stoppered brown bottle. He placed each item meticulously, arranging them exactly as he wanted, even as Ross continued to thrash around beside him.

"What can I do?" Jack asked.

"Close the curtains," the doctor answered.

Jack pulled the drapes and turned back to the room. Two beds sat against one wall amidst sparse furnishings: a pair of tables, a dresser, and a rickety shelf only partially filled with dusty books. What decorations there were appeared to have been unchanged for decades. To combat the gloom, the doctor turned on every light and lamp in the room, throwing odd shadows against the faded wallpaper. The thought struck Jack that it would be a poor place to die.

"What now?"

"He needs to be given anesthesia if I'm going to operate," Dr. Quayle said. He took the stopper out of the bottle and, while holding a cloth against the top, turned it over. Almost immediately the room was filled with a strong, noxious smell. "Hold this against his nose and mouth and let him breathe it in," Dr. Quayle explained, handing the cloth across the bed to Jack. "It won't take long before he's under. Then I can get started."

Taking the cloth, Jack was just about to do as he'd been instructed when Ross suddenly, shockingly, grabbed him by the wrist, his grip as tight as a vise, momentarily rising out of the churning pain in which he was drowning. His eyes were wild and wide, his mouth pulled into a grimace.

"Damn . . . damn you . . . Rucker . . . ," he spat. "Damn . . . you and that . . . blasted luck of . . . yours if you don't . . . find . . . the booze . . ."

Ross's last word had trailed off into little more than a whisper, but Jack quickly looked at Dr. Quayle nevertheless. Jack had no way of knowing if the doctor had heard what had been said or, even if he had, if he understood its meaning. Fearful that Ross might say more and accidentally give away the real reason the two of them were in Colton, Jack placed the cloth against his fellow agent's mouth and nose and watched as the anesthetic slowly but surely took hold; Ross's eyes fluttered a couple of times, then his shoulders slumped, and he finally quit twitching. When Jack removed the cloth, Ross was unconscious.

Mrs. Benoit came back carrying a large pile of sheets and cloths, her distaste at their impending fate still clear on her face.

"There's water boiling on the stove," she said.

"Good." Dr. Quayle nodded as he began unbuttoning Ross's shirt; there, just above his belt, was a strange, bloated mass.

"What else do you need me to do?" Jack asked.

"Have you ever assisted with a surgery?"

"No, I haven't . . . ," he answered.

"Then there's nothing more you can do

to help," the doctor said, wiping down Ross's stomach with alcohol. "You'll need to wait outside."

"I can help," Jack determinedly insisted.

Truthfully, Jack had no idea why he was being so adamant. As a lawman, he relished being involved, being undercover with the mission's success resting in his hands. He wanted to be *there,* in the middle of things. He wasn't used to sitting helplessly by while someone else did all the work.

"You might not be the squeamish type," Dr. Quayle said sternly, staring at Jack with a look that said he wasn't in the mood for any argument, "but what's about to happen in this room is unlike anything you've ever seen. Far stronger men than you have found themselves on the floor. The last thing I need is for you to become incapable of doing what I ask. It isn't worth the risk."

"Come on, Jack," Mrs. Benoit said, tugging lightly at his sleeve. "You can help me with the water."

For a moment Jack thought about arguing further, but any delay could cost Ross his life, and that was a price that wasn't worth paying. Jack would do as he was asked. But just as he reached the door, he turned back.

"Is he going to be all right?" Jack asked.

The severe look on Dr. Quayle's face

softened a bit, though his eyes remained grim. "I'll do the best I can," he said, "but even in the best of circumstances, his condition is serious. It's likely that he's going to die."

Jack's heart thudded hard in his chest, but he managed to nod. Taking a long look at Ross, maybe for the last time, he left the doctor to his task.

Jack walked up one side of the hotel hallway, turned on his heel, and made his way back down the other. Over and over, he paced the same path, his head down, watching his feet. All the while, his hands roamed: clenched in a fist at his side, then stuffed into one of his pockets, rubbing at the back of his neck, finally heading somewhere else, always moving. Ever since Ross collapsed, Jack couldn't stay still.

Four hours had passed since Dr. Quayle had shut Jack and Virginia Benoit out of the room so that he could operate on Ross. The only time the door had opened since was so that Virginia could bring in fresh water and clean towels. She'd offered to let Jack bring a batch, to check on his companion, but he'd declined. It wasn't that he couldn't stand the sight of blood but rather because he knew himself too well; once inside the room, he'd insist on helping, on doing *some-thing* other than walking the hallway, even though he knew the doctor was right, that he'd only be in the way. That sort of dickering could cost Ross his life.

So instead, Jack paced.

Outside the Belvedere, the day had slowly descended toward night. The summer sun steadily dropped toward the western horizon, deepening the shadows across Colton. But to Jack, time felt as if it were standing still, that only minutes had passed since he'd driven the Plymouth into town, before everything had changed.

Jack hated to think what would happen if Ross were to die. There'd be a telephone call to Lieutenant Pluggett, a formal inquiry by the Bureau, to say nothing about the end of Jack's investigation. Without learning who was responsible for the illegal liquor ring, he wouldn't be any closer to a promotion, to getting a chance to chase Capone.

Suddenly, Jack was struck by the realization that, if Dr. Quayle was unable to save Ross, not everything would end badly; if he had to leave Colton quickly, there wasn't any chance of his running into Maddy. As soon as the thought occurred to him, he flushed with shame. His problems were nothing compared to what his fellow agent was going through. To think otherwise was horrible.

How can I be so damn selfish?

Even though Ross had driven Jack half-mad with all his complaining during their long drive, he knew next to nothing about the man. Did he have a wife who loved him, children who depended on him, any family that he would've wanted to be contacted? The man was a mystery. In a way, he and Ross had that in common; if they were to trade places, if Jack was the one lying unconscious on the hotel room bed, knocking on death's door, everyone in town would claim to know him, but, just like Ross, no one truly would, not anymore.

"Did you hear me, Jack?"

Lost so deeply in his troubled thoughts, Jack was startled by the sudden sound of a voice. He looked up to see Virginia standing before the makeshift operating room with another pail of steaming water.

"I'm s-s-orry . . . ," he stumbled. "I —"

"Now don't you worry none." She smiled. "Doc Quayle'll see him through, just you mark my words."

"I hope you're right," he answered weakly.

"You need to have more faith than that," she admonished him. "Besides, I have the feelin' that Lady Luck is smilin' down on that man."

Jack managed to stifle his wince; the last thing he wanted to hear about was luck.

As soon as Virginia shut the door behind her, Jack resumed his pacing, absently tugging at one of his shirt cuffs.

The moon had already started to rise, the last oranges and purples of the day desperately clinging to the western horizon, when Dr. Quayle finally came out of the hotel room. His face was drawn and haggard, his eyes filled with a deep fatigue. Taking off his round, wire-rimmed glasses, he wiped each lens with a handkerchief before placing them in his shirt pocket. When he finally looked up at Jack and Virginia, both of them staring at him expectantly, he gave the slightest wisp of a smile.

"Is he going to make it?" Jack asked, allowing himself a bit of hope.

"Honestly, it's a miracle he hasn't died yet," the doctor answered. "Nineteen men out of twenty, maybe even worse odds than that, he'd already be at the undertaker's getting fitted for a casket and a plot in the cemetery. But somehow, someway, he's still among the living."

"I told you to have some faith!" Virginia elated.

"If you're saying Ross should be dead," Jack said, unable to share in her enthusiasm, "then what happened?"

"Most every time an appendix ruptures, it spews the poisonous bile swimming around in each of us into the rest of the body," Dr. Quayle explained. With a soft sigh, he lowered himself into a chair beside the staircase. "When that happens, death is almost always sure and painful.

"But every once in a great while, the body does something miraculous. Sometimes it walls off the rupture," he said, demonstrating with his hands, "keeping an infection from spreading like a dike holding back floodwaters."

"And that's what happened?" Jack asked.

The doctor nodded. "I had to be especially careful to keep from accidentally damaging the wall, but once I'd cleaned away the bile, removed what I could, and then stitched him up, it held."

"Then he's out of danger." Mrs. Benoit smiled.

"Far from it," Dr. Quayle disagreed.

"But you just said that everything went well!"

"With the initial surgery," the doctor explained, "but that doesn't mean he's out of the woods just yet."

"What else could go wrong?" Jack asked.

"Because his body has walled off the infection from his appendix, I've had to place a couple of drains around the wound. This gives whatever bile and excess bleeding that remained inside a way out, but it also increases the chance of infection. The drains will have to be checked for blockages and his stitches will need to be cleaned regularly. He's going to need constant care."

"Who's gonna be givin' it to him?" Virginia asked.

"We'll all have to do our part."

"I ain't got time to be traipsin' over to your office, Doc." She shook her head. "I've got me a hotel to run right here."

"Good," he replied, "because he's staying here."

"I was afraid of that," Mrs. Benoit groaned.

"Now, Virginia . . ."

Even as the two of them began arguing about the hotel being turned into a makeshift hospital, Jack thought about how much Ross's condition would change what he'd been sent to Colton to do. If he was forced to spend a lot of time caring for his stricken partner, how could he possibly accomplish what the Bureau sent him to do? But what other choice did he have?

"If he recovers," Jack said, cutting off one of Virginia's complaints in mid-sentence, "how long will it take?"

"It's hard to say," Dr. Quayle answered, "but I'd expect him to be in bed for at least a couple of weeks, if not longer."

"A couple of weeks!" Mrs. Benoit shouted. "How can I run a hotel if I'm nursin' him for that long!"

"Now, Virginia . . . ," the doctor repeated.

Jack never would have said it out loud, but he was every bit as shocked as Mrs. Benoit. When Lieutenant Pluggett had first given them the assignment, the expectation was that they'd be in Montana for a couple of days, a week at most, just long enough for the famous "Rucker luck" to find out who was behind the illegal liquor. Now it appeared he was trapped in Colton.

Even if he called the Bureau and explained what had happened, he couldn't expect any help. As long as Ross's condition didn't deteriorate further, if it appeared he would recover, no one would come to assist Jack; if a doctor was sent, it would blow their carefully constructed cover, any chance of making an arrest, to say nothing of Jack's hope of advancing his career.

He was on his own.

CHAPTER EIGHT

"Why, Holmes! However did you know that Count Macalister was responsible for poisoning Baroness Piper's champagne? His alibi was unquestionable! Gallivanting around with the King's second cousin as he was!"

"It was elementary, my dear Watson —"

"Indeed!"

"And thus, our dear listeners, ends another spine-tingling adventure of the intrepid Sherlock Holmes! We here at the National Broadcasting Company, joined by our good friends at George Washington Coffee, hope that you'll tune in next week, when our legendary sleuth matches wits with —"

Silas Aldridge leaned over and turned down the volume of the radio, wincing from the effort. When he leaned back in his chair, he began to rub gingerly at the ache that had risen in his wrist. Regardless, a smile widened on his face as he looked at his older daughter.

"That sure was one heck of a radio show," he said enthusiastically. "Didn't you think so?"

Maddy nodded. "One of the best ones yet," she answered.

The truth was, sitting in the other chair in her father's bedroom, she hadn't been paying much attention. Her mind had been elsewhere, mostly on the mercantile's ledgers that she'd balanced that afternoon. Her worst fears had been realized; if it weren't for the extra money coming in from the speakeasy, the business would be in debt. Jeffers had been right, she'd needed the money he offered to continue taking care of her father and sister, but the shame she now felt at her own failings was nearly more than she could bear.

"Is something bothering you, Maddy?" her father asked, more observant than she gave him credit for.

"No, no, I'm fine," she lied, offering a faint smile.

Silas regarded her closely; try as she might, she couldn't hold his eyes for long, choosing instead to look down at her hands, restless in her lap. For a moment, an awkward silence hung in the room between them.

When her father finally spoke, his voice was soft and his words genuine. "I'm sorry I've brought you so much trouble."

"It's not like that," Maddy began to argue. "I've never —"

"Don't interrupt me," Silas cut her off, his voice suddenly full of the authority she remembered from when she was a child. "I'm an old man now and have earned the right to have my say. Hell, my voice is one of the few parts of me that hasn't completely broken down, so by God, I'm going to use it."

Maddy nodded.

Silas took a deep breath. "I know I've been a burden to you and your sister," he began. "The damn arthritis has taken a lot of things from me, but it hasn't taken my eyes. You shouldn't have to be running the mercantile and spending your nights caring for me, listening to radio shows. You should've been married by now, maybe had a couple of kids. I know this isn't what you were hoping your life would be."

Maddy felt tears start to well in her eyes, but she did everything she could to stop them from falling. She wanted to tell him he was wrong, to contradict him, but doing so would have made her a liar.

This wasn't what I was hoping for at all.

But that didn't mean she wasn't proud of what she'd done. If she'd abandoned her father to his illness, if she'd put the burden of his care on Helen, she couldn't have looked at herself in the mirror. What she'd done she'd chosen willingly; it was how she'd been raised.

Unfortunately, that decision had come with its share of consequences.

"Still," her father continued, "as bad as things might've turned out, I'm glad you're not married to that worthless fool Jack Rucker!"

Maddy winced as if she'd been pinched at the mention of Jack's name. Undoubtedly, her reaction was made worse because she'd just been thinking about him only the night before, watching Mike and Anne show their affection in the speakeasy. Still, she really shouldn't have been surprised.

Her father had *always* hated Jack.

While Maddy had been interested in Jack from the first time she'd seen him, her father's reaction had been just as immediate; he despised the boy from the first time they met. For years, Maddy had struggled to understand why. She wondered if it was because Jack's family came from old money while Silas had to struggle for every cent, if the boy's self-confidence came off as cockiness, or if Silas simply hated the idea of someone replacing him in his daughter's heart.

Once, she'd managed to work up the courage to ask.

"There're just things a father knows that his daughter can't," Silas had explained. "And this is one of them!"

Things had worsened after the death of Maddy's mother. In the days after Jack had held Maddy on the bridge, after they'd finally declared their love for each other, Silas suddenly became enraged at every mention of Jack's name. Silas had even gone so far as to tell Maddy she was no longer to spend time in Jack's company. Once, Silas had threatened to get his gun. But instead of abiding by her father's wishes, Maddy took to sneaking out in the middle of the night.

But then Jack had left and she'd never heard from him again.

Maddy had been surprised that her father hadn't gloated when Jack abandoned her, at least not *too* much. She supposed it was because it had been clear, even to Silas, that she was devastated. Before he fell ill, there was an occasional snide comment here and there, but he seemed more concerned about her sadness than proving his point.

"I can only imagine what that heartless son of a bitch is doing right now," her father continued. "As horrible as he was to you, I imagine he's being paid back in full even as we speak! He probably never amounted to a hill of beans and is living in a cesspool! I know you don't want to hear it, Maddy, but you're better off without him, I can tell you that!"

Earlier Maddy had wanted to interrupt her father, but now she found herself speechless. There was much of her that agreed she was better off now, but there was still a part of her heart that belonged to Jack, that would *always* be his, and right then, as she listened to her father's hard words, it ached.

"Come on, Maddy! Let me go tonight! Please . . ."

Maddy finished the last of her water, set her glass beside the sink, and took a deep breath before looking at her sister.

Helen was dressed for a night out on the town. She wore a slightly outdated flapper dress, cream colored and sleeveless, with a deep, revealing neckline, stockings, and high heels. Her short black hair had been pulled back to one side, pinned up with a jeweled brooch that sparkled in the light of the kitchen. Maddy recognized the look; her sister had shown it to her again and again in the yellowing pages of her romance magazine. She stood next to the stove, her arms nervously crossing and uncrossing over her chest, her face hopeful, waiting for an answer. Helen looked just exactly like what she was: a young woman, scarcely more than a girl, trying desperately to be older.

Ever since Maddy agreed to let Jeffers start a speakeasy in the mercantile's basement, Helen had been pestering her to go. She imagined that it was glamorous, filled with drinking, smoking, and flirting with men, a night doing all the things she'd spent her whole life being told not to do. To Helen, every evening Maddy went to the illegal tavern was straight out of Hollywood or the ridiculous love stories she loved so much.

But Maddy had always said no.

"I'm good with customers in the store, so there's no reason to think I couldn't help out behind the bar," Helen kept on, pleading her case. "Or if not that, I could always clear tables, wash glasses, take drinks to people, whatever you needed me to do. I'd even sweep the floor when we closed."

"You don't look like you're dressed to do

much work," Maddy said.

Looking down at her clothes, Helen gave a dismissive laugh. "Well, you can't expect me to work the *whole* time I'm there, can you?"

Maddy knew it would be easy to give in. She was tired from all the troubles at the mercantile, her days followed by too many long evenings spent behind the speakeasy's bar, and that was before she'd listened to her father's despising words about Jack, which made her heart a topsy-turvy mess. Because of all of that, the last thing she wanted was to have to watch Mike and Anne, or any other couple, make eyes at each other all night. What she *really* wanted to do was put her head on her pillow and go to sleep.

Even Jeffers had suggested she take a break, pointing out that she didn't have to be there every night. He'd even mentioned that Helen could take her place if she wasn't comfortable leaving it in his hands. This made Maddy even more nervous; the last thing she wanted was for her younger sister to be alone with men like Jeffers Grimm and Sumner Colt. Heaven only knew what they might do if given the chance. Even if she were there with them all, she knew she'd spend the whole evening worrying.

It was better not to take the chance.

"I'm sorry, Helen," Maddy said, "but I can't let you go."

"But it's not fair!" her sister fumed.

Maddy sighed. "I know," she admitted. "Maybe some other night you can come to see what all the fuss is about, but right now, I need you to stay here. Dad wasn't feeling very well earlier and —"

"I got it, I got it!" Helen shouted, crossing her arms and sticking out her lower lip in the best pout she could muster. "I'll do it, but I want you to know I'm getting sick of you telling me what to do all the time! If this is how you act at the speakeasy, no man is ever going to be interested in you! You'll die a spinster!"

Helen's words cut deep. Whether her sister knew it or not, her ruthless remarks were nearly enough to make Maddy throw up her hands and march up to her room, anything rather than having to listen to more. In that moment, the burden of providing and caring for her family had never felt heavier. Her chest tightened with emotion and she struggled to hold back tears. Ever since her father had become bedridden, she'd taken pride in not showing weakness, but it wasn't easy.

Instead of surrendering, she gave a weak

laugh that nearly became a sob. "I don't know what you think you're missing," she said, "but it isn't as if I'm going to meet the love of my life tonight."

Grabbing her hat, Maddy left without another word.

Jack lay in his bed in the Belvedere, staring at the ceiling. A near-darkness filled the room; even with the drapes open, little light filtered in from outside. The rhythmic, steady sounds of crickets drifted through the open window, mixing with the ticking of the clock on top of his dresser. He had no idea what time it was, the gloom too thick for him to see clearly, only that a couple of hours had passed since he'd decided to retire for the night. While his body was still, his fingers laced together on his stomach, his mind was crazed with activity as he tried to sort through everything that had happened.

Things can't get much worse.

Ross slept in the room across the hall. Dr. Quayle had taken Jack and Mrs. Benoit in to see him and demonstrate how to care for him in the coming days. Shocked by how drawn and haggard Ross looked, Jack had trouble believing the man was still alive. He'd watched closely to be certain Ross's chest was still rising and falling; relief filled him when he saw the blanket covering him move, though it did so shallowly.

"He doesn't look so good," Virginia had said.

"He's been through an awful lot," Dr. Quayle replied. "The next couple of days will tell whether he'll live or die."

Jack hadn't said a word.

Even as the doctor began explaining the steps needed to be taken to ensure that the drains protruding from Ross's lower abdomen remained unclogged, Jack struggled to pay attention. His mind kept wandering back to the predicament he was in. He was trapped in Colton, trapped in his disguise as a land speculator, trapped until Ross recovered, if he did at all.

He was trapped with no chance of escape.

Again and again, Jack turned things over in his head. The list felt endless: he thought about what would happen if Ross survived or if he died; he remembered everything he'd done to advance his career at the Bureau and wondered if it was in jeopardy of being flushed away; he wondered if Mrs. Benoit hadn't already spread the news that he was back in town; and he considered what he could do to uncover the illegal liquor operation.

But over and over, his thoughts kept returning to Maddy.

Though he had no way of knowing for certain, Jack was convinced she was still in Colton. In a matter of minutes he could be standing in front of her house or looking in the windows of her father's store, walking the streets they had strolled down hand in hand, or even crossing their bridge. He wasn't even safe in the Belvedere; he couldn't remember if they'd ever been in the hotel together, but they had walked past it dozens of times. She was everywhere around him, close enough to touch.

With everything racing through his head, there was no way he'd be able to fall asleep, even though he was exhausted; he'd been up half the night before driving over mountains and through forests in order to get to Montana. It should've been easy to nod off, but his nerves were frayed and his heart and mind raced. No matter how long he lay there, no matter how many sheep he counted, there was no way he'd get any rest.

"Damn it all," he muttered.

Frustrated, Jack got up and went to the window, raising it all the way open and enjoying the feel of the cool night breeze on his skin. In the faint starlight, he checked his pocket watch and was surprised to find that it wasn't yet midnight.

Jack felt foolish for even considering it, but he began to think about heading out into the night to see if he couldn't learn something about the illegal liquor operation the Bureau had sent him to investigate. Right now, there was nothing he could do for Ross; Dr. Quayle would be checking on him throughout the night in case he took a turn for the worse. It was worth a try; after all: Jack knew that it was highly unlikely anybody would get a good look at him under the cover of darkness. He'd have a chance to walk around town and see what, if anything, had changed in his absence. Maybe it would even get his mind off of Maddy.

Who knows . . . maybe I might get lucky.

Outside the Belvedere, Jack ran a hand through his dark hair and stared up at the thin moon; it was little more than a sliver surrounded by tens of thousands of stars. While he watched, a comet streaked across the sky, a brief trail of light that was there one instant and gone the next, making him smile; he'd spent so many years in cities that he'd forgotten how beautiful the night heavens could be.

A surprising chill in the air, especially for

June, caused Jack to rub his arms for warmth. He'd left his jacket back in the hotel, along with his Bureau-issued pistol; even in his wildest of hopes, he couldn't imagine that he'd have reason to use it his first night back in town. Besides, now that he was outside, he wasn't going back; he'd manage without either.

Leaving the hotel, Jack walked to Main Street and turned north. He passed the barbershop where he used to get his hair cut, the bakery where he used to purchase sweet cakes by the bagful, and the church where his father made him sing in the choir. Other than a new coat of paint here or a tree grown taller there, Colton remained just as he'd left it.

Because of the late hour, Jack had expected to have the sidewalks to himself and was therefore surprised when he heard bits of conversation and laughter grow steadily stronger from the other side of the street. Quickly he ducked into the dark shadows of the alleyway between the library and Wallace Narveson's shoe shop and watched. Soon a couple appeared at the intersection farther up the street. Seconds later a pair of men followed, one smoking a cigar as the other smacked him playfully on the back, their laughter carrying up into the night sky. All of them were headed in the same direction; they crossed the street before disappearing somewhere ahead of Jack.

What in the hell's going on here . . . ?

Jack had worked undercover for the Bureau of Prohibition long enough to know when something looked strange.

Why are four people out walking in the middle of the night? Where could they possibly be going? One couple might have been believable, but two . . .

What he was seeing just didn't add up. It was this sort of hunch that had led to his success working undercover, to the arrest of dozens of criminals, and had never steered him wrong. Jack would've bet his badge they were headed for a speakeasy.

If his memory served him right, they would have turned at the corner opposite of where the bank stood. If he hurried, he'd be able to catch up and stay in the shadows until they showed him where they —

Suddenly Jack stopped dead in his tracks. Farther ahead of him, moving quickly in his direction on the same side of the sidewalk, was a woman. She was far enough away that he couldn't make out any of her features, especially considering that she was walking with her head down, but he knew, he just *knew,* that it was Maddy. It might've been the way she moved, something about the sway of her hair, he couldn't have known for certain, but he was convinced he was looking at the woman he'd loved and who had once loved him.

The woman came closer and closer, but Jack remained frozen in place, unsure of what he should do. His instincts told him to hide, to watch her as he'd watched the others, but there was also a part of him that wanted to walk toward her, that wished to see her face and hear her voice again. It was this indecision that made it impossible to move.

But then the woman made the decision for him; just like the others, she turned ahead of him and was lost to sight.

This time, Jack began running, his feet pounding the sidewalk.

CHAPTER NINE

Maddy glanced up at the clock on top of the bank and cursed herself for being late. A trickle of a breeze blew down Main Street, rustling store signs and pushing a discarded newspaper. Though it was early summer and the days were warm enough to make men pull out their handkerchiefs and wipe their brows, the nights remained cool; Maddy was so chilled that she shivered, pulling her wrap tighter around her shoulders.

Even as she quickened her step, Maddy frowned; she knew there would be customers milling about outside the mercantile, waiting for her to open the door. She'd noticed people out and about, something that was no longer a strange occurrence after midnight in Colton; no doubt they were on the way to her illegal tavern. But even though Sheriff Utley had given her and Jeffers his word that he'd look the other way as long as things at the speakeasy didn't get out of hand, she hadn't been able to erase her worry that they were about to be found out, that it was all about to come crashing down around their heads. She half-expected her comeuppance to leap out of the dark shadows all around her, like a pack of wild dogs or a monster; even now, she felt as if she was being watched.

The worst part of all the sordid business she'd gotten herself involved with was that Maddy had come to rely on the money the bar provided. With business at the store growing steadily worse, being able to care for her family was becoming harder and harder. Jeffers had been right when he'd shown her the huge stack of bills; it had made some of her problems go away.

Too bad the money can't make me happy.

Maddy was exhausted, filled with a weariness she felt in her bones. She spent so much time trying to make everyone else happy that there wasn't any time left over for her. This night had been particularly trying. All she wanted was to sleep, to close the door to her room and somehow forget her burdens, just for one night. But that was a dream, a fantasy that could never become real. So here she was, trudging on, knowing she could never turn back; too much was depending on her.

There was no use complaining. She'd made a deal with the devil; it wasn't as if she'd never expected to get burned.

Jack raced around the corner at a run, stopping to stare into the darkness of the street before him. He'd expected to see the woman he still believed to be Maddy walking away from him, but there was nothing except the deep, impenetrable shadows that blanketed the town. Glancing quickly toward the opposite side of the street, he only found more gloom.

Where in the heck did she go?

Slowly, Jack's eyes began to make out details in the dark: the weather-beaten sign that hung above the door to Hagen's Diner; a Ford Tudor parked along the street, a couple of dented milk canisters strapped to its luggage rack; and an old mutt that stopped to look at him while crossing the street. From somewhere ahead of him came the faint sound of laughter, but because of the way the road intersected up ahead he couldn't tell if it was coming from his left or his right. There was no sign of the woman.

There was only one thing he could do; he had to make a choice. There wasn't time to waver. If he was going to reach her, discover whether it really was Maddy, he had to —

"Jack?" a man's voice asked from the darkness just beside him. "Jack Rucker? That you?"

Jack froze; hearing his name, as well as the closeness of the sound, unsettled him. For an instant, it felt he'd been found out, that his identity as an agent for the Bureau of Prohibition had been discovered and he was in grave danger. He knew the reason for his fear was that he was using his name, his *real* name, for the first time; usually, he was Eli Carter, Lawrence Scott, "Foggy" Murdock, or some other alias he slipped into as easily as a raincoat. Now, he felt vulnerable. Desperately, he tried to put on his mask, to become the land purchaser's man, but he knew he looked startled.

From the thick shadows beneath the barbershop's awning a figure emerged into the scant starlight and slowly began to walk toward him. It was a man, so shockingly thin that he resembled a scarecrow, with wild, scruffy hair and an equally unkempt beard. As he came closer, he was slightly hunched over, his head moving from side to side as if he were a bird peering at a crumb.

"By God," the man said. "That *is* you, ain't it . . . ?"

The stranger stopped short just a few feet away, his face split by a broad grin. A glimmer of recognition flared in Jack's memory; though the man's face was rough around the edges, lined and worn, they had to have been about the same age. Jack struggled to remember the man's name, came tantalizingly close, but the right one stayed just out of reach.

"Yeah," Jack answered, giving a wide smile, "it's me."

"I'm startin' to wonder if I ain't dreamin'." The stranger chuckled. "You've been gone for years."

"I just got back this morning."

Though he still couldn't remember the man's name, Jack began to recall memories of when they'd been younger; back then, the stranger had been somewhat chubby, an awkward boy who hadn't made friends easily. Jack had a faint recollection of watching him sit on the shore of the Clark River, eating mud pies and grinning like —

Got it!

"Heck," the stranger said, smirking. "It's been so long since you've been in these parts I bet you don't even remember my name —"

"Clayton Newmar," Jack said quickly, as if it were the easiest thing in the world. "How could I ever forget?"

Clayton smiled brightly; in that instant, Jack saw him as he'd been years before, a child beside the river, mud smeared all over his face. "I was just funnin' ya." He chuckled. "I knew you wouldn'ta put me out of your mind! Not after bein' friends all them years!"

"You got that right," Jack replied, going along with it.

"But what in the hell're you doin' here?" Clayton asked. "I figured you weren't ever comin' back this way."

"Business," Jack answered simply, instinctively knowing that if he offered any more, it would be lost on Clayton; maybe later, once word got around about the money that could be made, he might throw his line out to see if the man bit.

"I was so excited to be home that I couldn't sleep," Jack continued. "I thought I might walk around a bit, see what had changed."

"Ain't nothin' in this town's changed much." Clayton shrugged. "A few folks've died and a few others are busy havin' babies, but it's still the same ole dull place it ever was."

"It wasn't that bad," Jack said quickly, somewhat surprised that he'd actually meant it, "but having been gone for so long, I suppose you'd know better than me. So tell me, what passes for fun in Colton these days?"

Clayton looked him over, his brow knitted and his lips pursed, as if he was weighing a decision. "I'm wonderin' if you're the same fella you were when you was a kid," he said, his voice low, a conspiratorial whisper. "You still the trustworthy type . . . the sort who can keep a secret?"

"Of course," Jack answered.

Clayton nodded. "Thing is," he began, taking a look over his shoulder at the dark and deserted street, "somethin's new in town and it's more'n a bit fun; it's just that —"

Instantly, with Clayton's words hanging in the air between them, Jack knew exactly what the man was going to say. *I know it!* It had happened to him too many times before for him not to understand. But he still had to play along; raising an eyebrow, he tried to look curious, as well as a bit clueless, with a touch of excited thrown in for good measure.

"Do you do any drinkin'?" Clayton finally asked.

"You mean alcohol?"

"That's the only kind far as I'm concerned," he answered, his face lighting up a bit in the faint starlight. "So do you?"

"I used to," Jack replied, growing comfortable in the role he'd played many times before. "But isn't it illegal now on account of Prohibition?"

"Don't tell me you agree with all that claptrap," Clayton hissed, his voice tempered in volume but not disgust.

"No, no, of course not," Jack said quickly. "It's just that the new law makes it harder to get, is all."

For Jack, the most difficult, delicate part of working undercover was gaining the trust of the very people he meant to arrest or, as in this case, someone who could lead him to them. Most were rightfully paranoid, unwilling to give that trust to anyone, yet Jack had to somehow make them believe that he should be brought into their confidence. Therefore, he had to be authentic. On the one hand, he couldn't seem ignorant of the law; he had to voice his concerns and fears of being caught and his awareness of the consequences. On the other hand, he had to look interested, to be able to commiserate about the unfairness of the law or his own love of drink. Too far one way or the other could spoil everything.

"Truth is, I've always fancied a glass of

whiskey," he added.

"Now that's what I'm talkin' 'bout!" Clayton exclaimed, slapping Jack's shoulder so hard he was sure it would bruise. "Now what if I told you that glass of whiskey was just a short walk away?"

"But how . . . ?" Jack asked.

"You've heard 'bout them taverns been openin' in all the big cities . . . speakeasies, they call 'em," Clayton explained. "Well, now we got one right here in Colton."

"You don't say . . . ," Jack said; he'd hit the jackpot.

"It's supposed to be kept quiet, kind of a secret I suppose, but seein' as you're back in town, no one's gonna be upset I told ya."

"Where is it?"

"Come with me and I'll show ya!"

For a moment, Jack thought about the woman he'd been pursuing. Until Clayton had surprised him, he'd been convinced it was Maddy, but now, the more he thought about it, he was certain it had been wishful thinking. Why would Maddy have been out so late at night? It wasn't as if she was going to the speakeasy. Whoever it had been, she was long gone; besides, *this* was what he'd been sent to Colton to do.

"How far away is it?" Jack asked.

"Quit askin' so many questions and follow me." Clayton laughed. "You're gonna feel like you never left home! And since you'll be so happy 'bout it, only seems fair that you're the one buyin' the first round!"

"Deal," Jack said, chuckling.

As they headed off into the gloomy streets, Jack thought about how, once again, his luck hadn't steered him wrong.

Clayton led the way down Colton's darkened sidewalks and then suddenly darted into an alley. The gloom was even deeper there, with only a sliver of stars visible in the sky high above. Jack had to stay close to his companion as he took one turn, then another, and then yet another, for fear he'd be left behind. It didn't take long before he had no idea where they were; it was like being in a twisting maze.

Suddenly Clayton stopped. Before them, a faint light shone above stone steps that led down to a cellar. Jack felt lost; as he looked around, he had a nagging feeling that it was familiar, but try as he might, he still couldn't place it.

"Here we are," Clayton announced.

"Down there?" Jack asked, still playing along.

Clayton smiled. "Just a few short steps and you can have that drink that's bein' unfairly denied to you. Come on."

At the bottom of the cellar stairs, a thick door blocked their way. Clayton rapped on it a couple of times, which was followed by the sound of a lock being slid back, and then the door opened a crack. From inside, a young man's scraggly, frowning face regarded them warily. Voices, laughter, and the faint strains of music drifted from over his shoulder.

"Who in the hell'd you bring with you, Clayton?" the man asked.

"Oh, come on now, Sumner." Clayton chuckled. "You ain't so young you really don't know who this is, are ya?"

Sumner looked closer at Jack, his eyes narrowing further, his frown growing deeper. Jack tried a soft smile, but it only seemed to make matters worse. "I ain't never seen him before in my life."

"It's Jack!" Clayton exclaimed. "Jack Rucker!"

"Nice to meet you," Jack offered, but there was no reply.

"You ain't supposed to be flappin' your gums 'bout what goes on here," Sumner chided Jack's newly rediscovered companion. "When Jeffers finds out, there's gonna be hell to pay."

Jack knew exactly who Sumner was talking about. Jeffers Grimm had been a nasty piece of work back when Jack lived in Colton; he imagined that the passing years had done nothing to improve the man. He was violent, seedy, and far from above doing something illegal to make some money. If there really was someone running booze over the border, Jeffers would have to be involved. Anyone who got involved with him would be just as guilty, as well as a fool.

"He ain't gonna like that you was talkin'," Sumner continued.

Clayton looked into the illegal tavern. "Where is Jeffers anyway? He's usually right here beside you —"

"He's got business to take care of, so he left me in charge," Sumner said with no small measure of pride. "When he gets back and I tell him what's been happenin', he ain't gonna like it one bit."

But Clayton didn't appear much concerned about the warning. "What Jeffers ain't gonna like is that you've got two fellas wantin' to wet their whistles, who got money burnin' a hole in their pockets, and you're too paranoid to open the damn door! Come on, now! We're thirsty!"

There must have been a grain of truth to Clayton's words; though he was clearly unhappy about it, Sumner pulled the door open wide enough for Jack and Clayton to slip through before slamming it loudly shut behind them. Up close, he looked far younger to Jack's eyes, little more than a kid. When they left him, Sumner was grumbling to himself.

"Now this is more like it!" Clayton crowed.

The speakeasy was much like a dozen others Jack had been sent to investigate, ramshackle furniture hastily arranged to provide some measure of comfort to those who sought to enjoy what the law said they could no longer consume, all done in the dead of night, under dim lighting, and through a haze of tobacco smoke. Jack could only see the far end of the bar where the record player stood, but it, too, looked to have been cobbled together.

"I still don't know where we are," Jack said.

"This is the basement of the mercantile," Clayton explained. "You remember, don't ya? Silas Aldridge's place."

Jack's eyes widened as the bottom fell out of his stomach. He'd been in the mercantile's basement before and, now that he looked closely, he saw that Clayton was telling the truth. Confusion tore through him like a storm. How could Silas Aldridge be

159

involved in something like this? Though he
remembered how much the man hated him,
it was simply impossible for Jack to imagine
that a man as honest as Maddy's father was
would willingly break the law.

But before Jack could try to comprehend
what he was seeing, he began to realize that
his arrival was attracting attention. It started
as a ripple, one or two faces noticing him,
their gaze lingering long enough to recognize him, before it seemed as if everyone at
the tables nearest the front door was staring, their mouths open. Slowly, he began to
hear them whispering.

". . . thought he'd never come back . . ."

"I'm tellin' you it's him . . . it's Jack
Rucker . . ."

". . . doesn't look a bit different . . ."

While more and more of the speakeasy's
patrons began to turn in his direction,
someone jumped up out of his seat, shook
Jack's hand, clapped him on the shoulder,
and offered to buy him a drink. Within
seconds, it seemed as if the whole room
stood beside him, a sea of voices washing
over him in waves. He hadn't known what
sort of a reception he'd get, but all the
friendly smiles and faces genuinely touched
him.

It was standing there, surrounded by

people he'd once known as well as himself, that Jack was reminded of how wonderful it felt to be surrounded by friends and loved ones. For a moment, he forgot all about doing whatever it took to get ahead, the pressure of chasing a promotion, and the cold calculating involved with reaching for the next rung on the ladder. He was honestly surprised by how nice it felt.

More and more people rose to greet him; it felt like the whole bar. He saw a few women glance nervously toward the bar, but before he could wonder what they could be looking at the whole mob headed in that direction, a few of the men nearly coming to blows over who would buy the first round of drinks.

But then, just in front of the bar, voices began to fall silent; in seconds, there wasn't a sound to be heard except for the scratch of the record player's needle as it played Al Jolson. Before him, the crowd began to part. What he saw when the last person moved out of his way made his heart stop, then thunderously pound in his chest; it was as if he'd been slugged in the stomach, all of the air driven from his lungs, leaving him gasping and helpless.

There, standing behind the bar with a bottle of whiskey in her hand, was Maddy.

CHAPTER TEN

Maddy had just finished pouring Seth Pettigrew a glass of whiskey when she noticed a commotion at the front of the speakeasy. There were too many people crowding around for her to see what was happening, but she could still see Sumner, and from the look on his face, he was anything but happy. Still, everyone else was smiling and pointing, rising from their chairs to join in on the fun, far different from the reception Sheriff Utley had received when he'd unexpectedly shown up a few nights earlier.

"Tastes as good as if it were the nectar of heaven itself," Seth declared as he wiped his mouth with the back of his hand, setting the empty glass down on the makeshift counter. Whispering to Maddy, he added, "But don't tell Reverend Fitzpatrick I said that. I wouldn't want him to think I'm a blasphemer."

"Your secret's safe with me." She smiled.

Ever since she'd arrived at the speakeasy, Maddy had regretted coming. Everything she did took effort; smiling at the customers, listening to Seth ramble on about cases he'd tried years earlier, and even the music on the record player unnerved her. When Karla had dropped a tray of glasses she'd cleared off of a table, Maddy had nearly jumped out of her skin.

Even Jeffers's absence wasn't enough to brighten her mood. She'd been surprised to discover that he wouldn't be at the speakeasy tonight; he always insisted on being there from the moment the first customer arrived until the last one left. Sumner would only say that he'd been called away on business and that he'd be back the next night. Normally, she would've been thrilled that he wasn't skulking in the shadows, looking like he was about to tear some poor customer limb from limb.

But it wasn't enough to put a smile on her face or still the whirlwind of thoughts whipping around her head. She kept thinking about what her father had said about Jack, the money problems of the store, Jack, the dangers of being caught running a speakeasy, Jack, and then Jack some more.

Maybe I should've let Helen come instead . . . Maybe I shouldn't be here.

163

"Maddy?" Seth asked, coughing into his fist to get her attention.

"Oh!" she exclaimed, startled. "I'm sorry. My head was somewhere else."

"That's quite all right, my dear." He smiled. "I was just saying that now that we've agreed to keep a secret from the good reverend, I thought I might celebrate with another drink."

Maddy laughed. "What better way?"

"Indeed!"

Reaching for the whiskey bottle, Maddy noticed that the mob of people was making its way toward the bar. But no matter how closely she looked, she still couldn't understand what all of the fuss was about. A strange sensation began to worm its way down her spine, similar to what she'd felt earlier that night, walking the streets in darkness. It was like someone was watching her, but *different.* It made her feel uncomfortable, as if something bad was about to happen.

"Better make it a double," Seth said, "on account of the occasion."

Maddy was about to pour when she realized that the speakeasy had fallen silent. Looking up, she was surprised to see dozens of faces were turned toward her. Half of the room seemed to be standing just in front of her, on the other side of the bar. Slowly, a couple of men stepped to the side, showing her exactly why there'd been such a commotion.

It was Jack.

Maddy stood dumbstruck, her heart thundering, her breath trapped in her chest, and her thoughts empty and aflame all at the same time; she was vaguely aware that Jack looked every bit as shocked as she did. No one said a word. Through a haze, Maddy set down the whiskey bottle, walked out from behind the bar, and stood in front of Jack. She felt as if she were dreaming, walking on air and not herself; she wondered if she wouldn't wake up and discover that she hadn't gone to the speakeasy at all, that she was in her bed at home, because what she was seeing was impossible.

"Maddy . . . ," Jack said weakly.

She couldn't answer. Instead, she looked into his green eyes, searching out all of the things that had changed about him with the passage of years. There were a few more lines and creases around his eyes. His hair was longer than she remembered and a bit darker. He looked stronger, thicker across his chest and shoulders. Still, she couldn't help but notice how much there remained of the young man who'd left Colton seven

165

years before, whom she'd thought she would never see again.

Convinced that she *was* dreaming, Maddy reached out her hand, the ends of her fingertips shaking slightly, and placed it against Jack's chest; she couldn't stifle a gasp when they touched. Unbidden tears rose in her eyes as she looked up at him. Slowly, he began to smile.

And that was when she slapped him.

The sound of the blow was surprisingly loud, filling the cellar. There were a few gasps that quickly faded, leaving only the record on the phonograph to fill the silence, playing a slow ballad about lost love. Jack recoiled from the slap, reacting more out of surprise than pain.

Maddy was as shocked as anyone by what she'd done. She'd reacted without thinking, hitting him so hard her hand ached. Staring into his eyes, seeing his sorrow as he looked back, she couldn't keep herself from trembling. For a long moment, time stood still. She knew everyone was looking at them, the whole speakeasy wondering what was going to happen next, but as far as Maddy was concerned, she and Jack were the only two people in the room.

"I'm sorry," Jack said, his voice a low whisper.

Those two simple words were enough to shatter the dam she'd placed around her churning thoughts. Tears filled her eyes as the first sob clenched her chest. And so, there in the basement of her father's mercantile, in front of everyone, *in front of Jack,* she did the only thing that made any sense.

She turned and ran.

For an instant Jack wondered if he shouldn't just let Maddy go. The truth was, he never imagined she'd be there, not in the illegal speakeasy in the cellar of her father's store! He knew now that it had been she he'd seen walking the darkened streets, and that she'd been heading here. His head was spinning from what all of that meant.

I'm a lawman and she's behind the bar of a speakeasy.

Seeing him again had upset her more than he'd anticipated. The slap she'd given him was unexpected yet not undeserved. In his head, he knew she needed time to digest his return, time to yet again soothe the wounds he'd given her years before. But the urge to talk to her was too great to ignore; it banished all of his earlier worries and compelled him to race after her.

"Maddy, wait!" he shouted, but she was

halfway across the room and didn't look back.

Hurrying after her, Jack saw the faces of those around him change; the smiles that had blossomed at seeing him after so many years slid into frowns, another reminder of what he'd done to Maddy.

Sumner, the thin, scraggly man who'd been so difficult when Jack and Clayton arrived, looked completely taken aback by what was happening. He halfheartedly tried to stop Maddy, but she brushed past him, threw open the door, and ran up the stairs. When Sumner saw Jack approaching behind her, he seemed more determined to assert his authority, bracing his feet and looking willing to fight.

"Now, just you hold on a second," he ordered.

"Get the hell out of my way," Jack snarled, shouldering into the smaller man and knocking him to the side. Taking the steps two at a time, Jack was up the cellar stairs, staring out into the night, trying to figure out where Maddy had gone.

There was no sign of her in the inky darkness. He strained to hear a sound, anything that would tell him where she'd gone. Faintly, he heard footsteps off to his right, so without hesitation he again raced after her.

Desperation gripped him. He'd spent the days after Lieutenant Pluggett told him he'd be returning to Colton dreading what would happen if he ran into Maddy, but now that he had, all he wanted was to have her before him again, to be able to talk to her, to say something that might ease the pain he was now all too aware of having caused.

But he had to catch her to get the chance.

Jack raced down an alleyway, dodged an old crate but accidentally caught the edge of a barrel in the hip, momentarily slowing him. Over the pounding of his heart and the panting of his breath, he listened for Maddy's footfalls. He ran from one intersection of alleys to another, across the street beside the Lutheran church, and then back into another gloomy space between two buildings. He'd have thought he would've caught up to her already, but fear must've been pushing her forward. Finally, he came to Main Street. From the mouth of an alley, the light from the stars and the sliver of moon made the town appear strangely bright. He saw Maddy right away; she was across the street, only a hundred yards away. He'd catch her in an instant, and then he could tell her that —

Suddenly a hand clamped down hard on Jack's shoulder. Without a second's thought, he spun, throwing a cocked fist, and saw a pair of wide, surprised eyes looking back at him. He felt his punch crash into his mysterious assailant's face, the sound of cartilage breaking filling the alley. With a groan, a man crashed onto his back in the dirt, his arms limp at his sides, his mouth open, unconscious. It was all over before Jack had any idea what'd happened. Peering down into the gloom, he discovered that he'd floored Sumner.

"Damn it all," Jack hissed.

Turning back to the street, he no longer saw Maddy. He took a couple of hesitant steps but then stopped. Though she was out of sight, he knew she couldn't have gotten far. Finding her would be little trouble; either she'd be home or she'd go to the bridge they'd once shared, but he was slowly coming to realize that confronting her now would only make things worse. He had to let her go.

"Hell . . . and holy water . . . ," someone swore behind him before giving a low whistle. "What in tarnation . . . happened here . . . ?"

Jack looked back and found Clayton leaning down over Sumner, his hands on his knees, breathing heavily.

"He startled me. Came up from behind and put a hand on my shoulder. I hit him before I even knew what was happening." Jack took a deep, frustrated breath. "Why was he following me, anyway?"

"I don't think . . . he took too kindly to the way you . . . pushed him aside . . . ," Clayton said. "Either that . . . or he went a runnin' for the same reason I did . . . He just had to know . . . what happened . . ."

"He shouldn't have grabbed me like that."

"I reckon he'd do it different if'n he had the chance," Clayton said with a grin. "Remind me never to surprise you in a dark alley."

"It was an accident," Jack insisted.

"Oh, I believe you, but I doubt Jeffers is gonna be as understandin' when he learns you knocked out his right-hand man. He ain't the forgivin' type. When he finds out, there's gonna be hell to pay."

"Is Jeffers as bad as he used to be?"

"Worse," Clayton answered. "Rotten to the core and then some. Most folks steer clear of him day or night. Shows you how bad we all want a drink if'n we're willin' to set foot in Jeffers' speakeasy to get it."

Suddenly things fell into place in Jack's mind, sending a sickening feeling racing across his gut. "That's Jeffers' place?" he asked, shocked. "What the hell is he doing in Silas Aldridge's cellar?"

"I don't know for certain if Silas is in on it, on account of he ain't round much anymore. Word round town is he's sick," Clayton replied, looking away from Jack as he added, "but there ain't no doubt that Maddy's a part of it, is there . . ."

Jack held his tongue. What could he say? Clayton was right. Jack had seen it with his own eyes; Maddy had been *behind the bar,* she'd had a bottle of whiskey in her hand when he'd first seen her, and it was her father's cellar. What other explanation could there be? She was involved in Jeffers's illegal liquor operation.

And I was sent here by the Bureau to do a job . . . and if I do it, Maddy will be put behind bars . . .

"I reckon part of this is my fault," Clayton said.

"How do you figure?"

" 'Cause I knew Maddy was there," he replied. "Hell, she's poured me a few drinks since the place opened, but I was so happy to see you I plumb forgot 'bout the history 'tween you, which is pretty stupid of me 'cause there ain't no one in town don't 'member how the two of you was together, or how hard it was on her when you left. I shouldn't have took you there."

"It wasn't your fault," Jack replied honestly.

"I feel bad 'bout it all the same," Clayton admitted. "Tell you what, how 'bout we go back and *I'll* buy the first drink."

"I appreciate it, but I think I've had enough excitement for one night."

"You sure? After all you done been through, I reckon you've earned a drink or two."

"Maybe some other time."

"Fair enough." Clayton nodded. "But what're we gonna do 'bout him?" he asked, nodding down at Sumner. "Maybe we oughta get him back to the speakeasy."

"Leave him," Jack said. "When he comes around, he'll be madder than a bee with a bear's paw stuck in its hive. It'll be better if we're as far away from him as possible when that happens."

"Sounds like good advice to me," Clayton agreed.

They said their good-byes and Jack headed back into the night, thinking about how some folks would look at what had happened to him as a stroke of good luck, but to him it seemed nothing but the worst.

■ ■ ■ ■

Maddy finally stopped running only when she made it home. Even then, she expected Jack to be right behind her. Ever since she'd left the speakeasy, she'd heard him running to catch her; whenever she looked over her shoulder, he'd been there, relentless, getting ever closer, but she'd lost sight of him when crossing Main Street and hadn't seen him since.

But that didn't mean she was safe.

Resting against the gate in the picket fence her father had built with his own hands before the arthritis had robbed him of their use, Maddy stared up the walk at the darkened house. Everything was still and silent. She realized that no one inside, not Helen or her father, knew what had happened to her.

Maddy looked up at the second floor window and her bedroom beyond. Years earlier, she'd sneaked out of that very window to be with Jack; now, all she wanted was to get back inside. For a moment she had the hope that it was all an unwelcome dream, that at any moment she'd wake, the sun on her face, and look out the window at where she now stood and find no one there.

Jack . . . how can he be back . . . ? It has to be a dream.

But Maddy knew she was lying to herself. She'd touched him! He'd stood right in front of her! She'd slapped his face! It was useless to deny what had happened. Running away had been another mistake, a childish act of desperation, but she couldn't face him; *she just couldn't!*

By morning, if it took *that* long, everyone in town would know what had happened, that Jack Rucker was back and that their reunion had been anything but straight out of a pulp romance. What people actually saw would mix with rumor, with hearsay and gossip, until it was unrecognizable. Wherever she went, there would be unwelcome stares, whispered words, probably even titters of laughter. Her reputation would be in tatters . . . again . . .

And then there was Jeffers . . .

She could only imagine how upset he'd be that she'd left the speakeasy. As dangerous as he seemed while calm, she could only imagine how fearsome he'd be when irate. Maddy had no idea what Sumner would tell him, though she had little doubt Jeffers would think her weak. She couldn't really blame him; her emotions had put them all in danger, regardless of what Sheriff Utley had said.

But right then, Maddy didn't care. All she wanted was to go inside, check on her father and Helen, and get in bed. Somehow, she'd slip off to sleep, wrap herself in a pleasant dream, and, if only for a little while, escape her troubles.

CHAPTER ELEVEN

Jeffers Grimm groaned, then cursed at the thin sliver of sunlight that managed to slip through the curtains, falling unwelcome across his face as he lay in bed. Squinting, he blinked a couple of times, struggling to wake. For a moment he was unsure of where he was, the lingering effects of a bottle of rum clouding his head and making the room twist and turn.

Shading his eyes, he sat still, listening with growing confusion to the sound of light snoring, rising and then falling. Turning his head, he found a woman lying on her face beside him, her mousy blond hair falling over her bare shoulders and obscuring her face. Slowly, memories of the previous night floated back.

It was then that he started getting angry.

Whipping off the worn blanket, Jeffers got out of bed, stumbled across the room, and threw open the door to his cabin. He stood naked in the sunlight, it was undoubtedly more afternoon than morning, and emptied his bladder onto the ground. Absently, he scratched at his whiskers.

"All the goddamn things I gotta deal with . . . ," he mumbled.

The cabin Jeffers lived in was at the base of the foothills east of Colton. It wasn't much to look at and had begun listing to one side. His grandfather had built the place when he'd first come to Montana decades before and since then it had been passed down to successive generations, each of them getting a more run-down, dilapidated property than the last. It was less than half the size of the mercantile's cellar, with busted windowpanes, furniture that was missing legs, and a stove with a partially blocked pipe that filled the place with smoke when it was lit.

While meticulous and ordered in his criminal dealings, Jeffers was anything but that at home. Stubbed-out cigar butts littered dirty dishes, mingling with clothes tossed onto the floor, marked here and there by an empty liquor bottle, dropped where it had been finished. He'd noticed a few visitors wrinkling their noses at the lingering smell of rot, but it had been that way for so long that he no longer noticed. Outside, weeds grew everywhere, even as high as the bumpers of his truck.

Still unsteady on his feet, Jeffers wobbled over to the stove, shoved some wood inside, struck a match, and put it to the kindling. Reaching for the old coffeepot, he knocked over a stack of empty bean cans, his usual choice for dinner, sending them falling to the floor in a clatter.

"Quit makin' so much noise," the woman said from the bed, her voice a mumble since her face was still pressed into the dirty mattress.

Annoyed, Jeffers purposefully made even more noise, dropping the lid of the coffeepot, rapping a spoon against the stove, even though the clanging did nothing but aggravate his own hangover.

"Aw, Jesus," she swore, smothering herself with her pillow to quiet the unwanted sounds.

Deb Wehmeyer wasn't a whore in the usual sense; while she didn't charge anyone for a roll in the sheets, she was willing to spread her legs for almost any man in the county providing she got something out of it: a drink, a blouse; some nights, even attention would do. She was getting a bit long in the tooth, a bit plumper than usual, but whenever Jeffers came calling she did what he asked. Last night, after he'd discovered what had happened at the speakeasy in his absence, he'd taken a couple of bottles of booze, picked her up, and made her screams fill the cabin and spill out into the night. He'd done all of the things he wanted to do to Maddy, though he knew she'd never be as accommodating as Deb. His hope had been that it would soothe his anger, and for a while it had.

But now it was back with a vengeance.

Once the coffee was finished, Jeffers poured the steaming liquid into a mostly clean tin cup, took a bitter drink, and thought about all the ways in which his life had gone to hell.

Jeffers's night had begun much differently than it had ended. Just as he was about to leave for the speakeasy, he'd gotten a call from Jimmy Luciano telling him to come to an important meeting and not to be late. Without any other options, he'd entrusted the speakeasy to Sumner, believing that the boy had proven himself. Besides, with Maddy there, Jeffers felt he had no reason for concern.

Pulling up to Luciano's place, Jeffers had been nervous; he'd read a few dime novels and seen enough serials where the Mob called a meeting to rub out a stool pigeon to cause his imagination to run wild. Instead, Jimmy met him with a big grin and a stiff drink, telling him how pleased he was with their partnership. He explained to Jeffers that it wouldn't be long before they'd come for what was being stored, but that there was going to be another load crossing the border, a big one. Jimmy even mentioned that Capone himself had heard what Jeffers had done for the organization and that it looked as if he'd have a hell of a future. There had been more drinks, good cigars, food, and laughter. Leaving, Jeffers had felt as if he were finally somebody, as if he'd soon be more than the only fish in a pond as small as Colton.

And then he'd come back to the speakeasy and found that his big plans had hit one hell of a snag.

Jeffers first realized that something was wrong the second he set foot inside the speakeasy; Sumner was nowhere to be seen. Instantly Jeffers was furious. *If there was one thing I'd told that stupid son of a bitch time and time again . . .* Every head in the place turned to look at him; Jeffers heard plenty of whispering, as well as the titter of a woman's laughter. He understood that he was the only one who didn't know what had happened, which only made him angrier.

Stomping through the speakeasy, Jeffers found Sumner at the bar. The boy was slumped forward on a stool, resting his head on his arm, his mouth open and a wet towel pressed against his nose. It looked like he was sleeping, drunk, or both.

But that wasn't the only surprise.

Seth Pettigrew stood behind the bar, pouring glasses of liquor, taking money, and placing it in the cash box. His cheeks were the rosy red that only people well oiled with alcohol had, his head lolling sleepily on his shoulders as if it took effort to keep it upright. Jeffers's blood boiled. It was only later that he realized he shouldn't have been so angry with the old lawyer; though it undoubtedly cost Jeffers a full bottle of booze poured down the man's throat, at least *someone* was still taking money, and in that regard Seth was probably the most trustworthy man in the room.

"Want sumthin' to wet yer whishle?" Seth asked Jeffers, the words a slurry leaving his mouth. "There's shtill plenty to go round . . ."

Jeffers had to bite his tongue to keep from shouting. "Where's Maddy?" he asked through clenched teeth.

Seth looked around as if it was the first

time he'd even considered her absence. "I guess she left," he said matter-of-factly.

"Goddamn it," Jeffers muttered.

Snatching Sumner by the arm, Jeffers roughly yanked the boy from his stool and dragged him toward the back of the cellar, determined to get answers. Sumner stumbled along, unable to get his feet under him, moaning and groaning as if he was in pain. In the dark recesses of the room, Jeffers grabbed Sumner by the throat and slammed him into the locked storeroom door, behind which his entire future lay; as the back of his head struck hard Sumner yelped and then began whimpering, sounding more like a child instead of the man he wished to be.

"What in the hell went on here tonight?" Jeffers growled, inches from Sumner's trembling face.

"It . . . it weren't my fault, Jeffers," Sumner pleaded. "I swear it weren't!" As he spoke, the towel slid from his face, giving Jeffers a look at the devastation that had been wrought; even in the murky gloom of the cellar, he could see the swelling, the new crookedness of the boy's nose, and even the beginnings of the black eyes that would last for weeks.

"Who did this to you?"

"I didn't want to let him in; honest I

didn't!" Sumner cried. "Clayton Newmar brung him, acted all surprised I didn't know who he was, tryin' to make me look stupid! I told him I ain't never seen him before, but —"

"Just tell me who he was!" Jeffers snapped; from the terrified look in Sumner's eyes, it wouldn't take much more and he'd be in tears.

"Rucker," the young man answered, his teeth chattering. "He said his name was Jack Rucker."

Jeffers froze. Of all the names he'd expected to hear, Jack Rucker's was definitely *not* one of them. How could it be? He'd been gone for years, long enough that everyone in Colton, himself included, figured he was never coming back. But if what Sumner was saying was true, and judging by the damage on his face he wasn't lying, then things had suddenly become much more complicated.

"Why'd he beat you like that?"

Sumner recounted the whole story; he explained how everyone had been so happy to see Rucker back in town, how the room had been silent when Maddy came out from behind the bar, how she'd slapped his face before running away, how Jack had barreled into him when he followed, and finally how he'd given pursuit, determined to make the man pay for knocking him over that way, only to get punched in the face.

"You should've stayed here," Jeffers snarled. "Leavin' meant there weren't no one to watch the place."

"I know," Sumner whined. "But I was just so damn mad! That bastard got lucky, s'all! If he hadn't surprised me, I woulda showed him a thing or two! He'd a been damn sorry for what he done!"

Jeffers didn't correct his bravado; truth was, Sumner was dangerous in his own right, but there was a lot more bark than bite. If Jeffers remembered the kind of fella Jack Rucker had been, he would've been able to handle Sumner even if the boy had brought a brass band to announce his coming.

But Sumner's tale did explain one thing . . .

"Maddy ran off when she saw him?" Jeffers asked.

"After she slapped him," Sumner replied. "What in the hell's up with that, anyway? The two of them have a history?"

Jeffers was surprised that Sumner didn't already know the story; everyone else in town did. Maybe it was because he'd been too young when Jack left, or maybe it was because he wasn't the sharpest knife in the drawer.

"Somethin' like that," Jeffers answered.

What happened had been an inconvenience, one that could've been worse, but Jeffers felt uneasy. Something nagged at him. If nothing else, Jack Rucker would be another obstacle in his pursuit of Maddy, but one that he could take care of; unlike Sumner, he wouldn't go down so easily. Nothing was going to stand in the way of Jeffers's becoming rich and important like Jimmy Luciano, or even Al Capone. If there was another problem, he'd solve it, with either his fists or a bullet, but it *would be taken care of.*

"You ever do somethin' like that 'gain," Jeffers threatened Sumner, "and a broken nose is gonna be the least of your worries."

"I'm sorry, I'm sorry, I'm sorry . . . ," the young man repeated, finally dissolving into tears, the fear finally overwhelming him.

Jeffers left Sumner determined to take back control of his speakeasy and to find something, or someone, on whom he could take out his mounting frustrations.

Jeffers swirled the last bit of coffee around in the bottom of the cup, watching the dregs float this way and then that. He'd been thinking about what had happened for so long that the brew had grown cold in his hand. Absently, he flung the last bit into the sink before letting the cup fall with a loud clatter.

Deb groaned again before rolling over, leaving her saggy, bare breasts exposed in the same sliver of sunlight that had woken him.

Seeing her like that made him think of Maddy.

Ever since he'd first approached her with the idea of using the mercantile's basement as a speakeasy, he'd wanted her. The more he watched her work behind the bar, the more he stared at her curves, his feelings of desire grew to infatuation. He saw her as something beautiful he could defile, someone he could bring down and make roll around in the muck of his life.

But now Jack Rucker's return complicated things. Jeffers wasn't a big enough fool to believe they were on equal footing for Maddy's affections; truthfully, he didn't give a damn. What worried him was that Maddy's thoughts would be a mess; she'd be moody, unpredictable, and that threatened the sweet deal he had going with the smuggled booze. If she got it in her head that she wanted out of their partnership, then Jeffers could be left twisting in the wind and lose everything he'd worked so hard for. She had to stay levelheaded long enough for Jeffers to bring in the last load from Canada and for Luciano to come for it all. After that, she could do whatever the hell she wanted; Jeffers would be off to bigger and better things. He'd have a talk with her, something similar to the one he'd given to Sumner, threaten her until she saw it his way. Maybe he'd have to have a talk with Rucker, too.

Still naked, Jeffers glanced down to see that thinking about Maddy had aroused him. He only wished that she were the one lying in his bed, but since she wasn't . . .

With a growing anger, Jeffers yanked the sheet off of Deb's naked body, then placed his hand on her breast and gave it a hard squeeze.

"Ouch!" she shouted. "What the hell do you think you're doin'?"

"Takin' what's rightfully mine," he snarled.

Just like he always did.

Slowly and as carefully as he could, Sumner put a finger to each side of his nose and gave it a little push. Stars of pain immediately flashed across his vision and he gave a yelp as his eyes started to water. Long

188

seconds passed, but still the pain didn't go away. Looking at himself in the faint light of his mother's bathroom, he felt every bit as pathetic as he looked.

"What a goddamn mess . . . ," he mumbled to himself.

His face looked as if it had been in a car wreck. The swelling on his nose was huge, like a balloon. It was too early to tell how crooked it was going to be, but there was no denying that it was off-center; that was why he was trying to push it back. Purple, brown, and black bruising underlined both of his eyes; it reminded him of the outrageous makeup of a clown in the traveling circus he'd seen as a child.

And it was all that bastard Rucker's fault . . .

A light knocking on the bathroom door startled Sumner so badly he jumped. "Are you about done in there?" his mother asked.

"Not yet," he said.

"It's just that I have to get ready so that I can —"

"Goddamn it! I said I ain't done yet!" he exploded, spit bursting from his mouth to splatter the mirror.

After a moment's silence, he finally heard his mother walk away without any further protest. Sumner breathed a sigh of relief.

From the moment his father abandoned him and his mother, leaving one winter's night when Sumner was seven, he'd lived with the sense that he was nothing but a disappointment. What had happened last night when he'd run after Jack Rucker had only made that feeling worse.

Waking up alone in the darkened alley and staggering back to the speakeasy had been painful and humiliating, but it was nothing compared to the embarrassment Sumner had suffered when Jeffers found out what'd happened. All Sumner had ever wanted was to please the man, to make him see that he could be his partner, that he could be trusted. Only hours earlier, when Jeffers had explained that he'd be gone for the evening and that Sumner was in charge, his chest had swelled with pride; unfortunately, that meant he'd have that much further to fall. Now he'd be lucky to be trusted with a pack of matches for fear he might accidentally burn the place to the ground.

Struggling to hold back tears, Sumner turned on the faucet and began splashing cold water onto his face; even that made his nose ache. His pride was also bruised. He knew that for the next couple of weeks, everywhere he went, people would snicker behind his back, would joke about what had happened; after all, it was written right there on his face.

There was only one thing that made Sumner feel better, a thought he held close in his heart, an unyielding fire he took care to stoke.

Revenge!

No matter how long it took, no matter how it ended up being done, he would make Jack Rucker pay for what he'd done. If it meant taking the man's life, spilling his blood, then that was what he'd do. He remembered what Clayton had said when they'd entered the speakeasy, that everyone in town knew who Rucker was, but that didn't deter him in the slightest; if anything, it made his fury burn even hotter. Maybe then, people around town would start to look at him the same way they did Jeffers: with fear and respect. Maybe he could be someone important, could make some serious money and finally escape from his mother's house.

He'd prove himself by taking care of Jack Rucker. He'd show Jeffers, his mother, the whole town, even himself, that he wasn't weak, he wasn't a child. Before he was finished, that bastard would beg for forgiveness.

"You're gonna pay for what you done, you son of a bitch . . ."

CHAPTER TWELVE

Maddy leaned back against the mercantile's long counter, absently watching the summer rain as it fell in torrents outside the windows. The air was still, humid, and heavy; she'd propped the door open to provide some relief from the heat, listening to the steady patter of raindrops hitting the sidewalk, the awning of the barbershop across the street, and the few cars that drove past. It had been a particularly slow morning and early afternoon of business; weather like this meant there'd be few customers, leaving her plenty of time to get lost in her own troubled thoughts.

"I still can't believe it . . . ," she mumbled to herself.

Lying in her bed, Maddy had stared up at the ceiling, replaying what had happened over and over in her mind; sleep had been a long time coming, and fitful when it finally had. She'd awakened with a start just as the sun broke the horizon, panic gripping her chest, unable to think about anything other than Jack.

Questions to which she had no answers kept asking themselves in her head . . .

Why had Jack come back?

Where had he been for the last seven years?

How did he know about the speakeasy? Had he come because he'd known I would be there?

Maddy shook her head and sighed; there was a part of her that was thankful for the rain. While the downpour meant that there wouldn't be much money coming into the cash register, making the task of keeping the business afloat that much harder, it also meant that she would be undisturbed. She was certain that word of what had happened at the speakeasy had spread through town like wildfire. Wagging tongues would spread news of Jack's return far and wide. She'd expected to be visited by gawkers, women who came with sympathy and compassion but hoped to leave with some nugget with which to telephone their friends, some news they could brandish about as if it were a jewel on a finger. To avoid such a circus, Maddy had considered staying home, lying in bed with her head under the covers, but she knew that her problems would only get worse. Thankfully, the downpour had lent her a hand.

But the rain wouldn't last forever.

The sudden sound of pounding footsteps out on the sidewalk startled her. Instantly her mind leaped to all sorts of wild conclusions; Jack was coming to confront her, or Jeffers would barge in to curse her for abandoning the speakeasy. Even as a figure raced past the windows with a newspaper spread over her head in a futile attempt to keep from getting wet, Maddy still wasn't certain who it was. It wasn't until her new visitor was inside the store, the soaked paper tossed to the floor and an angry face turned to glare at her, that she knew.

"Why didn't you tell me what happened?" Helen demanded.

That morning, once she'd finally convinced herself to get out of bed, Maddy had said little, mumbling her way through breakfast and her duties in caring for her father before hurrying off to the mercantile. Her head had been a mess. The thought of telling anyone about Jack's return had seemed impossible, especially her father, who knew nothing about her business with Jeffers Grimm and who'd made his distaste for Jack abundantly clear. But now, her sister standing before her with her hands on her hips, Maddy couldn't help but feel a little guilty.

"Why didn't you say something?"

"I just couldn't," Maddy answered.

"Not even to me? Your own sister?!"

"I . . . I was just so surprised to see him that . . . well . . . I didn't want anyone else to know until I'd figured it out . . . ," Maddy struggled to explain.

"Well, it's too late for that!"

"What do you mean?"

"It's already all over town!" Helen shouted, throwing up her hands, gesturing out into the rain-soaked afternoon. "Every-where I've been today, it's the only thing anyone's talking about!"

"Oh, no," Maddy groaned.

"I can't believe you didn't tell me first!"

"What are they saying?" Maddy said, knowing that her worst fears had started to come true.

"That Jack showed up at the speakeasy with Clayton Newmar, which is kind of strange," her sister explained, "and that no one could believe what they were seeing. I heard Bill Tottlebunner say that no one in the whole room made a sound when Jack approached the bar and you saw each other for the first time in years."

"They didn't," Maddy agreed.

"Marjorie Kessler said that she nearly fainted when you came out from behind the bar, walked up to Jack, and kissed him on the lips!"

"What?!" Maddy exploded, unable to believe what Helen had said. "I didn't do that! I didn't kiss him! I swear I didn't!"

"That's not what Marjorie was telling all the women standing in line at the bakery," Helen said, shrugging. "The way she told it, it was like something out of a Hollywood picture, although I doubt a frumpy old thing like her could be considered much of an expert," she added, insinuating that because of the magazine she'd read cover-to-cover countless times she was.

Maddy felt physically ill. It was even worse than she'd feared. One exaggerated story mixed with the next and then the one after until it had been changed beyond recognition. In this way, lies became the truth. By nightfall, she expected half of the town to swear that they saw Jack get down on one knee and ask for her hand in marriage.

"I didn't kiss him," she insisted.

"So I suppose the part where you slapped him didn't happen, either . . ."

Maddy looked away quickly, shame reddening her cheeks. She shouldn't have been surprised to discover that that part of the story was being spread around town.

Helen saw her reaction and immediately understood. "You actually did it, didn't you?" she pounced, a grin of disbelief slowly spreading across her face. "You slapped him!"

"I didn't mean to!" Maddy said. "Or maybe I did . . . I don't know . . ."

"I can't believe it!" Helen gushed. "But why? What did he do?"

Instead of answering, Maddy sighed deeply, ran a hand through her red hair, and went to the window, not knowing how she could possibly explain. As if to further darken the clouds hanging over her life, the afternoon sky was split by a bolt of lightning, followed by a deep rumble of thunder that shook the windows.

"He said my name," she answered simply.

To her surprise, Helen didn't immediately press her for more details.

"I've spent the last seven years hating Jack for what he did," Maddy continued, admitting something she'd kept locked in her heart. "I've tried as hard as I could to go on with my life, but seeing him again, hearing his voice, it brought all of the anger and hurt back and I lashed out. It happened so fast I'm sure I looked as shocked by what I'd done as Jack did."

"What did he say after you hit him?"

"I didn't stay to listen," Maddy answered. "After it happened, I ran away as fast as I could. I was angry, embarrassed, frightened, all at the same time. I just couldn't face him.

"But he followed. I could hear him running somewhere behind me. He shouted my name a couple of times, but I didn't respond. I just kept going. Eventually, he must've given up."

For a time, neither of them spoke. Telling Helen what had happened made Maddy feel a bit better, but she still had no idea what she should do next.

"Don't you want to know why?" her sister finally asked.

"Why what?"

"Why he came back? Why he was at the speakeasy? Why he chased after you?" Helen said. "If I was you, after all you shared, no matter how many years had passed or how angry I was at him for how he left, I wouldn't be able to sleep until I'd looked him in the eyes and asked every question I could think of. I'd demand to know the truth!"

Maddy looked at Helen with no small measure of surprise. Usually, her favorite way of communicating was by arguing mixed with long periods of silence, by complaining about how unfairly she was being treated, whining about how she never got to do anything fun, or wishing that she was all grown-up so she could move far away and live her life the way she wanted. Suddenly, right before Maddy's eyes, Helen seemed more mature than her years; she wondered if it might not be a glimpse of the woman she'd someday become.

"I do want to know some of those things," Maddy admitted.

"Then ask him."

"I . . . I don't know if I could . . ."

"Yes, you can!" Helen insisted.

"I'd be too ashamed. Besides, I don't know where he is. He's probably at his father's place, but —"

"He's staying at the Belvedere," her sister said matter-of-factly.

Maddy could only stare in answer.

"What?" Helen asked incredulously. "Did you really think that everyone's only talking about *one* of you? From what I heard, Virginia Benoit's keeping the switchboard operator plenty busy."

Just like that, Maddy knew that if she protested any more, she'd only be making excuses for herself. Helen was right; she should confront Jack and get all of the answers she'd long deserved. All she had to do was walk over to the hotel, find out what room he was in, and knock on the door . . .

Still, she wavered.

"I don't know . . . if I can . . . ," she said, tears welling in her eyes.

Helen walked over and gently took her hand. "Even if he doesn't give you the answers you want, heck, even if he refuses to answer, at least you'll have tried. That has to be better than spending years wondering why. Who knows? Maybe he has a reason for what he did, although I can't think of what it could be." She smiled. "Either way, no matter what happens, you can finally get on with your life."

With her heart nearly bursting at the seams with nervousness and excitement, Maddy made her decision; she'd go to Jack. She wouldn't wallow in her own misery, or act like nothing had happened, or even wait for him to come to her. She'd take control of her own life and learn the truth.

It was the only way.

"Go," Helen said. "I can handle the store."

Maddy undid her apron, gave her sister a kiss on the cheek, and hurried off into the rain.

"If he gets out of line," Helen shouted after her, "just give him another slap!"

■ ■ ■ ■

Jack leaned against the railing of the Belvedere's porch and watched the rain slowly diminish, listening to the steady pitter-patter of drops striking the Packard and puddle on the empty street. The air was full of the fresh scent of the storm, billowing and blowing from the west; looking in that direction, he saw the storm begin to break and the clouds lighten, showing patches of blue.

But his mind was still a raging tempest, full of thoughts that threatened to blow down all he'd painstakingly built.

Unlike every other time he had gone undercover for the Bureau of Prohibition, lying through his teeth and putting his life in danger, all for the greater good, *this time* he had absolutely no idea what to do next. His vaunted luck had proven to be a double-edged sword. On the one hand, it had brought him right to what he'd been sent to Colton to find: the illegal liquor. On the other hand, he'd discovered that the woman he'd once loved was somehow involved. Ever since he'd left Clayton in the dark alley, Jack had been filled with indecision. He'd spent long years striving for a promotion, to advance in the Bureau so that he could go after infamous criminals like Capone. He'd be one step closer if he'd just contact Lieutenant Pluggett and tell him what he'd found.

And that was just one of his problems . . .

Ross Hooper had yet to wake. Dr. Quayle had come at sunrise to examine him and had declared that his condition had improved, but only just a little. So far, the incision and drains showed no signs of infection, though it could be several weeks before he'd be up and around. Jack hated to admit it, but he was thankful Ross couldn't ask him any questions. Before now, Jack never would have been able to lie to a fellow agent, but how could he tell Ross about Maddy's involvement? Still, he wouldn't be able to avoid the problem forever.

Jack heard footsteps behind him and turned to find Virginia Benoit wiping her hands on a towel.

"I just took a pot of soup off the stove," she said, "and was wonderin' if you'd like some."

"Thank you, but I'm not very hungry."

"Take my word for it," Virginia said with a smile, "what with takin' care of your friend, you're gonna need to keep your strength up. 'Sides, like my dear Jean-Pierre used to say, I make the best darn chicken vegetable soup this side a the border."

Jack gave a friendly laugh. "I'll have some later. I promise."

Virginia nodded and looked like she was about to leave, but she lingered longer. "I'm sorry 'bout how things went last night with Maddy," she finally said. "What with bein' away so long, I reckon that wasn't the welcome you was hopin' for."

"You heard?" Jack asked, surprised, though deep down he knew he shouldn't be; it felt like half of Colton had watched Maddy hit him.

"Everyone in town has, but don't be angry 'bout that," Virginia explained. "What with how hard things have been round here, gossipin' 'bout the two a you is darn near the most excitin' thing to happen in months."

"I'm glad my misfortune can entertain everyone," he replied, a touch of bitterness in his voice.

"It ain't like that, I said. It's just that folks round here 'member what you was like together 'fore you left. 'Cause a that, we all just assumed, myself included, that you'd be married and havin' babies by now. There weren't a woman in town who didn't sympathize with Maddy when you left. So to see you come back to town outta the blue, well, it was a surprise that no one woulda expected."

Jack frowned; he knew Virginia was right and that he had no one to blame but himself. Still, that didn't mean he liked it.

"It's too late to change things now," he said.

"Well . . . ," Mrs. Benoit said.

He looked at her, puzzled. "What could I possibly do to make things right?"

"I've been thinkin' 'bout this for pert' near the whole day," she explained, kneading her hands together. "See, while everyone in town's busy talkin', flappin' their gums 'bout what happened, seems to me that the two people who should be hashin' it out, bein' you and Maddy, you ain't sayin' a word."

"She doesn't want to see me." Jack shook his head. "She hates me."

"You don't know that for certain."

"She slapped me last night!"

"Maddy's spent the last seven years wonderin' if you was ever gonna come back. Part of her was hopin' you would, while she was also worryin' what would happen if you did. Hittin' you and then runnin' away couldn't have been much of a surprise. Truth is, you deserved what happened last night."

Jack clenched his jaw and looked away.

"Hard to hear, ain't it?" Virginia asked.

"Yes," he admitted, "but you're right . . . I had it coming to me . . ."

"And now that it's happened, the best thing you could do is clean up the mess you made. Find her and talk to her. She deserves that much."

Finished, Mrs. Benoit left him to the rain.

While they'd talked, the storm had mostly blown over, leaving only a few drops still falling from the last trailing clouds. Off to the near west, brilliant shafts of sunlight streamed down, glaringly bright in the aftermath of the summer squall.

And maybe Jack's mood had brightened, too, if only a bit.

If he was able to admit it to himself, he wanted to talk to Maddy again, to try to apologize for last night, for the last seven years, for everything he'd done to her, even if he had no idea what to say. She was as beautiful as he remembered, even more so; the memory of her behind the bar made his heart beat faster. He didn't know how she'd react, if she'd hit him again, curse him, or just refuse to listen, but he had to try.

What Jack could never tell Mrs. Benoit, or anyone else for that matter, was that seeing Maddy again meant that he'd have to make a difficult choice: confront her about working at the illegal speakeasy or hold his tongue. As a Bureau agent, he was obligated to follow the law. By arresting her and everyone else involved in the operation he could use her to advance his career. Then he'd leave town and never give her another thought. Or he could —

Suddenly Jack saw someone running toward the hotel. Just like the night before, he knew exactly who it was.

Maddy.

CHAPTER THIRTEEN

Maddy suddenly stopped at the bottom of the hotel steps, blinking up in surprise at the man she saw standing there, watching her. It looked as if Jack had been waiting for her. Running through the rain had plastered strands of her long red hair to her forehead and face, making it hard for her to see clearly. She nervously wiped her eyes clear as her heart pounded and her breath came in ragged gasps.

For a long moment, neither of them said a word, things between them as awkward as they'd been the night before at the speakeasy. She'd run over to the Belvedere ready to talk, eager to confront him and get all of the answers Helen had spoken about, answers Maddy knew she deserved, but now, with Jack right in front of her, she wondered if she hadn't made a mistake.

Maybe I shouldn't be here . . .

"Maddy," Jack said, the sound of his voice

sending a shiver racing up her spine. Making his way down the steps toward her, he held out his hand and said, "Come out of the rain."

Trying to keep from trembling, she accepted his hand and joined him on the hotel porch. Their touch lingered, she was surprised by the warmth of his fingers, but she was determined to shake herself free of their older, more pleasant memories, so she pulled her hand free. He stared at her, but she found it too difficult to return his gaze, choosing instead to look at her feet, the latticework beneath the railing, back out into the dwindling storm, anywhere but into his eyes.

"I'm sorry for what happened last night," he began, his voice deeper than she remembered. "I didn't mean to startle you the way I did . . . I'd only just gotten into town yesterday and . . . well . . . ," he stumbled, trailing off.

"You couldn't have known I'd be there," she replied.

"That doesn't mean I'm not sorry for surprising you like I did."

"If anyone should apologize, it ought to be me," Maddy said, stealing a quick glance into his eyes. "I slapped you."

"It's still my fault." Jack shook his head.

"I've given you plenty of reasons over the years to hit me."

"That's why I'm here," she replied, gaining the courage to tell him the truth about why she'd come. "There are so many things I want to ask you, no matter how difficult they might be for us to talk about, but that shouldn't —"

"Wait," Jack said, stopping her just as she was getting started. "You're absolutely right. We need to talk, but I don't want to do it here," he explained, looking back over his shoulder into the depths of the Belvedere. "We've already given everyone in town plenty to gossip about. There's no point in throwing more gasoline on the fire. We need to go somewhere private."

"But where?" she asked.

"I think we should go to the bridge."

Jack's words struck Maddy like a blow, stealing the air from her lungs. The bridge over the Lewis River, one of the two main routes into Colton, had always been their special place. Since he'd left, she'd stayed far away from it, only crossing when she had no other choice. It was too painful. The idea of returning there with him was unsettling, but she couldn't fault his reasoning; what Marjorie Kessler told everyone in the bakery, *an outright lie,* was only a taste of the gossip to come. If they really wanted to talk, if they wanted to be alone, the bridge would give them some privacy.

"All right," she agreed.

"Then let's go," he said, heading down the steps.

With her heart in her throat, Maddy followed.

Jack led the way around the side of the Belvedere and away from the center of town. It would take them longer to reach the bridge going this way, but Maddy understood his reasons; nothing would cause more of a ruckus than the two of them walking down the street together. Going this way meant they could avoid being seen.

"Do you remember how to get there?" she asked.

"How could I forget?" he replied with a smile.

Maddy looked away, embarrassed.

As they walked, the rain finally stopped falling. Brilliant sunlight shone from the nearly cloudless sky that followed the storm. Though Maddy had gotten wet when she'd run to the hotel from the mercantile, the sun quickly warmed her. Water glistened on everything; it clung to the leaves in droplets, cascaded in newly made streams down muddy hillsides, and collected in puddles and pools.

They walked on in silence, as if they were saving themselves for the bridge. Maddy stole a glance at Jack as they turned down a street on the edge of town. She'd looked at him in the speakeasy, but the gloominess of the cellar, as well as the intensity of her shock, hadn't let her see him clearly. But now, in the afternoon sun, she saw that he was more handsome than ever. Even the way he moved was attractive; he held his head high, confident, sure of every step. It made her blush; she was suddenly thankful *he* wasn't watching *her.*

The Lewis River was already swollen from the runoff of the storm. Usually a clear blue, meandering along at a slow, steady pace, it now ran muddy and fast. Occasionally, pieces of debris floated past; a broken tree limb, the lid of a crate, even a boot bobbed along, all swept up by the squall.

As they crested a small rise at the edge of the Pierce property, the bridge came into view. The sun had begun its slow descent behind it; looking up at the framework, Maddy had to shield her eyes from the glare. Though it had been repainted a couple of times in the seven years since Jack

212

left, had one of the railings replaced, and its boards were worn from having weathered the changing of the seasons, to her eyes it didn't look to have changed at all.

Maddy couldn't help but think about all the times she'd come to the bridge to meet Jack. Whether it was surrounded by a kaleidoscope of changing leaves in the middle of autumn, in the dead of a humid summer night, or with the wind blowing a brutally cold winter snow off the Rockies, she'd rushed along the path she now walked, almost breathless with anticipation to be with him. Now, years later and with Jack again by her side, she was still filled with a nervous excitement.

Remember why you're here . . .

They reached the bridge and walked out onto its worn, wooden planks, the sound of their footfalls echoing off the trees on the other side. Jack beamed, his smile as bright as the sun. He reminded Maddy of a child as he ran his hand along the railing and then up onto one of the support streets, peering over the edge into the water, before looking back at her to see if she was watching.

"Do you remember when I jumped in?" he asked.

"How could I forget?"

It had been a lazy day in early spring. The

river had been higher than usual with the melting of mountain snow, but not as turbulent as today. They'd sat together on the railing, their feet dangling over the edge, when he'd wondered aloud what it would be like to jump in. Maddy had laughed; the Lewis was rarely deep, only in springtime and after a strong storm, and was littered with large rocks between the occasional pool. To dive in would be dangerous. She'd jokingly said that he should find out, never thinking for a moment he was serious, but seeing the mischievous twinkle in his eyes, she'd immediately known that she'd played right into his hands. Without another sound, he'd sprung off the railing and plummeted toward the water, leaving her to scream in shock. He had hit the water with a loud splash, come up laughing, and then swum toward the shoreline. He'd laughed walking back across the bridge, but she'd been so angry that she'd made him promise never to do it again.

"I thought you were crazy," she said.

Jack looked over the railing and down to the river. "Maybe you were right," he said. "It sure looks a lot farther down than I remember."

Both of them laughed at the memory. For Maddy, it was comfortable, easy, a happy recollection of how things had once been. But no sooner had she started than she stopped. This wasn't a time for laughter. She'd spent seven long, miserable years alone, wondering what had happened.

She thought about the last time she'd stood on the bridge with Jack, a summer night before he'd left for school. He'd promised to return as soon as he could, had sworn that they'd be together, as husband and wife. He'd held her in his arms and told her he loved her. All of it had proven to be lies. That night, she'd admitted her fears, that he wouldn't come back, that he might find someone else, but he'd told her she was being silly, that he'd never leave her. Yet more lies.

"Do you remember that other time when — ," he began.

"Just stop, Jack," she demanded. "Stop it!"

For an instant he looked disappointed, but then he nodded, understanding that things between them wouldn't be so easily mended.

"Tell me why!" she asked.

Jack didn't answer, looking away.

"I've waited seven years to be able to talk to you," Maddy said, struggling to contain the emotions she'd held back for so long.

"Seven years! Whatever your reason, I have a right to hear it! I deserve to know why you never wrote back to me, why you never called to tell me what happened, why you disappeared from my life! Why, Jack? Why did you lie to me?"

"I didn't lie to you," he insisted, his voice calm. "When I stood here and told you that I was coming back, I had every intention of keeping my word. I thought it'd be just like I said . . . I'd go to school and then I'd come back to you. But then . . ." He stopped, his voice trailing off.

Maddy remained silent, waiting for more.

"When I got to Boston," Jack continued, leaning on the railing and looking out over the swollen river, "I couldn't believe what it was like. There were cars and people everywhere, so much going on. It was the most incredible thing I'd ever seen. Whenever I turned around there was something new. Different foods. Baseball. I'd sit in a classroom and listen to a lecture from a professor that made me look at the world differently. Within a matter of weeks, I knew I couldn't come back to Colton."

"Then why didn't you tell me?" Maddy shouted. "I'd have listened. I would have understood! We could still have had our life together! All you had to do was be honest and I'd have come to be with you!"

"I know you would've," he admitted, "and that's why I didn't tell you."

"What?" she exclaimed in surprise.

"If I'd written and told you the truth, that I didn't want to leave Boston, how I couldn't return to Montana, and asked you to join me, you would've done it in a heartbeat, not knowing that it would make you miserable."

"How can you say such a thing?" Maddy asked. "You don't know that —"

"Of course, I do," Jack answered, moving away from the railing to stand before her, his eyes dancing across her face. "I lived here with you for too long not to have understood what this place means to you. It's your home. It's where your family lives. This is where you've always wanted to be," he explained, sweeping his arm out toward the forested hillsides and then back at Colton. "You wouldn't be happy living in a city. Eventually, you would've resented me for taking you there; you would've hated me for ruining your life."

"But you still ended up making me hate you!"

Jack nodded. "I did it on purpose."

Maddy was struck speechless by his admission. She simply couldn't believe what she'd heard. It seemed impossible to her that Jack would do such a hurtful thing, but his confession said otherwise.

"Wh-why . . . why would you . . . ?" she managed.

"I wanted to protect you," he answered. "I knew that the only way to keep you from making the mistake of following me was to make it so that *you didn't want to.* I had to give you a reason to stay in Colton, so that you'd have a chance to forget about me and get on with your life." Looking down at her, his eyes were full of such intensity, as if he was pleading with her to understand, that she had trouble returning it, though she refused to turn away. "I couldn't bring myself to write you a letter filled with lies, so I chose to let you think that I'd abandoned you, that I no longer cared. That way —"

For the second time in as many days, Maddy slapped Jack's face. But this time, he was the only one of them startled by it.

"How dare you!" she shouted, stepping right up to him; unlike the night before in the speakeasy, this time she wouldn't run away.

"I did what I thought was best," he said, his hand on his cheek, the skin beneath it turning a bright red.

"That wasn't your decision to make! It should've been my choice, not yours!" Maddy chastised him. "And even if I always expected to live my life here in Colton, it was because I believed it would be the two of us. After everything we talked about, after all the promises we made, what else could I have thought? The most important thing to me was that I was going to live my life with you!"

"But was I the only person that mattered to you?" Jack argued. "What about Helen? What about your father? Would you have left them behind?"

For the first time, Maddy felt there was a bit of truth to Jack's reasoning. If she'd left town before her father's condition had deteriorated, who would've cared for him or taken over running the mercantile? Helen was too young to carry the burden alone. As bad as things were now, they surely would have been worse if Maddy weren't around.

"Besides," Jack continued, "your father would never have approved of your leaving. He would've come after you no matter where you went, all because you were with me." He shook his head before adding, "Hell, if he could see us standing here now, he'd run me out of town!"

"He couldn't," Maddy said simply. "He's too sick for that."

Jack frowned. "What?"

"My father is ill," she explained, suddenly tired from all the troubles weighing down on her. "His arthritis is so bad that he can't get out of bed without help."

"Wait . . . ," Jack said. "Silas isn't working at the mercantile?"

"How can he? He can't stand up on his own."

Jack looked away, a look of confusion crossing his face. He raised a hand and ran it through his dark hair, then held it against the back of his head.

"But what about the cellar?" he asked. "Does he know it's being used as a speakeasy, because —"

"This isn't about my father!" Maddy snapped, cutting him off. "This is about us!"

Just like the first time she'd shouted at him, Jack again nodded. But now, instead of moving away from her, he came closer, gently taking her hand in his own; he surprised Maddy with his tenderness, so much so that, even though she was still upset over the confession he'd made, she couldn't bring herself to pull away.

"I never expected you to accept my reasons," he began, his thumb rubbing the back of her hand; the sound of his voice and the nearness of him set her heart to thundering.

"I don't," she agreed.

"I know I've hurt you, but I swear it wasn't my intention. I can see now that I made a terrible mistake. You deserved better than I gave you. I'm sorry for that. Can you ever forgive me?"

"I don't know if I can . . ."

"I wouldn't blame you if you didn't."

Tears began to fill Maddy's eyes as she looked at him. So much of what he'd said were the things she'd been waiting seven long years to hear. It was possible that he was being honest, that he'd made a misguided attempt to do right by her. Still, there were so many questions she'd yet to ask, things that had to be answered.

"If you decided that you were never coming back to Colton, then why are you here?" she asked. "You've been gone for so long that I don't know anything about you. What do you do for a living? Is Boston home? Is there another —"

Before Maddy could ask him whether or not there was a woman in his life, Jack leaned down and kissed her. She was so shocked, so flabbergasted he'd acted so brazenly, that she gasped into his mouth.

221

Every instinct in her body told her to pull away, to slap him yet again, but the impulse lasted only for a moment before she felt his passion rise, his arms pulling her close, his lips against hers, and she gave in. For that brief moment she was a girl again, returning to a simpler time when she and Jack were happy together, their whole lives in front of them. Then, though Maddy felt anger rise at herself for returning to the past, she wondered if maybe, just maybe, it was the only way they could go forward.

Gently, Maddy reached up and ran a finger along Jack's jaw and then down across the back of his neck before slipping her hand up into his hair. His lips devoured hers and Maddy slipped into happiness she'd long since forgotten and had long since given up hope of finding again. When their kiss finally ended, she felt dazed.

Jack leaned back and looked at her, a faint smile on his face, the sun a brilliantly bright halo behind him.

"I've missed you," he said, and she knew he meant it.

But just as a smile began tugging at the edges of her mouth, Maddy shook it away, knowing that things between them couldn't be so easily mended.

"But what about the questions I asked?"

she prodded. "I need to know so many things. I need to —"

"Shhh," Jack said as he placed a finger softly against her lips. "I promise that I'll answer them all, but not now. There's already been too much arguing between us. Besides, there's something else I'd rather do."

With that, he leaned down expectantly, wanting another kiss; Maddy noticed that he stopped partway, waiting, leaving it up to her whether his declaration of desire would be fulfilled. She paused only for a moment.

In her heart, kissing him was what she wanted, too.

CHAPTER FOURTEEN

Jack hurried down the steps of the Belvedere, pulled his hat down low over his brow, and headed off into the night. Dodging puddles, he moved with a new purpose. Unlike the night before when he'd wandered aimlessly, unsure of what, if anything, he would find, he now knew exactly where he was going.

He was headed back to the speakeasy.

Walking in the crisp night air, Jack hoped to clear his muddled thoughts, though he knew it was a fool's errand. Spending the afternoon with Maddy had been as exciting as it was troublesome, making him wonder where his loyalties lay; were they with his head or his heart? Being at the bridge had given them the privacy they needed, but it had also brought back powerful memories. Smiling and laughing with her, feeling her touch, it had begun to make him question himself.

And that was all before I kissed her.

Even now, hours later, he swore he could still feel her lips against his, could still taste her. Just thinking about it made his pulse race. He'd acted impulsively, recklessly, and had half-expected to receive yet another slap for his impetuousness.

But then he hadn't.

Jack had a couple of reasons for taking Maddy in his arms and kissing her. The first was because she was a breathtakingly beautiful woman; even when he'd seen her running toward him in the rain, strands of her luxuriant red hair sticking to her face, he'd felt the first tremor of desire course through him. Taking her hand and leading her up the hotel steps had nearly been his undoing; he'd wanted to kiss her on the spot. Eventually, being with her, listening to her voice, and looking into her eyes had proven to be too much.

But there'd been another reason; Maddy had begun asking questions he couldn't answer. Up until now, he hadn't lied to her. The answers he gave about why he'd never contacted her, while unpleasant to hear, had been the truth. But when she'd begun to delve deeper, asking him about his job and where he lived, he knew he was in a pickle. Should he give her the story the Bureau concocted? Should he lie? Was it possible for him to tell her something closer to the truth?

But how can I when she's obviously involved with the speakeasy?

No matter how hard he tried, Jack simply couldn't ignore the reason he was back in Colton. He was a lawman, sent by the Bureau of Prohibition to ferret out the source of an illegal liquor operation. And within a matter of hours he'd done just that. Unfortunately, standing there, clearly involved in it all, was the woman he'd once loved and hoped to marry.

Maddy's revelation about her father's health had also been a surprise. Jack's first instinct about Silas's involvement in the speakeasy had proven correct; there was no way he'd be a part of such a thing. But that left many other questions unanswered. Why was his daughter there? Had Maddy willingly entered into a business relationship with a known troublemaker like Jeffers Grimm? Was Jack supposed to throw her in jail for violating Prohibition?

Jack walked down the darkened steps to the mercantile's cellar and knocked on the speakeasy's door. After a moment's pause, it was cracked open just far enough for a narrowed eye to look him over suspiciously and then widened to show the deep frown of the man on the other side. Sumner Colt sneered contemptuously at him, rage written on his face. Both of his eyes were as black as lumps of coal and his nose leaned slightly to the side.

"What in the hell're you doin' here?" he snarled.

Ever since he'd knocked the man unconscious in the alley, Jack knew he was going to have to eat a heaping pile of crow in order to regain entrance to the speakeasy. Though Sumner was nothing but a lowlife, fit for little more than being a crony to a stronger man like Jeffers, he couldn't be ignored, either. Because he handled the tavern's front door, gaining entrance without his approval would be difficult. Besides, it was too early in Jack's undercover ruse to already be making enemies.

Holding up his hands, palms out, Jack said, "I'm really sorry about what happened last night."

"Save it," Sumner growled, " 'cause I ain't buyin' the crap you're sellin'."

"I'm just glad you weren't hurt too badly."

"Yeah, I sure feel great," the younger man spat sarcastically.

"I didn't do it on purpose," Jack offered

truthfully. "How was I supposed to know you were behind me? You grabbed me and I just reacted. It was an honest mistake, one I'd take back if I could. Just let me in, I'll buy you a drink, and we can let bygones be bygones."

Sumner's face soured even further. "Why don't you just go to hell and —"

Before Sumner could finish, another hand grabbed hold of the door and pulled it all the way open.

Jeffers Grimm stood there looking even more menacing than Jack remembered. Though Jack was hardly a small man in his own right, Jeffers stood a couple of inches taller and, with his thick beard and hard stare, he would've unnerved even the strongest man. But what really set the man apart, what really made him look intimidating, was his enormous bulk; he looked strong enough to pick up a car by its bumper without breaking a sweat. Jack knew that Jeffers was the most dangerous man in the room.

His eyes lingered on Jack for a moment, sizing him up, then turned toward Sumner.

"Go check on the bar," Jeffers growled.

"But I was just —"

"Do what I said," Jeffers cut him off; his voice hadn't changed, but the threat in his words was as clear as if he'd pulled out a knife.

With one last look of hatred at Jack, Sumner left them alone. Neither Jack nor Jeffers watched him go; they were too intent on each other.

"I don't think he likes me very much," Jack said.

"Can't say I blame him," Jeffers answered. "Breakin' a man's nose first time you meet him ain't gonna get things off on the right foot. If I was you, I wouldn't turn my back on him."

"It was an accident."

Jeffers shrugged. "Don't make no difference to me if you two wanna kill each other," he said. "Problem I do have is that it all started in here. Way I been told, you was the one started the ruckus." Jeffers's gaze narrowed, his lip curling up in a snarl. "Give me one good reason why I should let you back inside."

"Because I give you my word nothing like that will ever happen again," Jack replied. "Besides, I just got back into town. I've got money in my pocket and drinks I'd like to buy for all the people I haven't seen for years. You're smart enough to know that's good business."

Jack waited nervously as Jeffers fell silent.

229

He'd hoped to appeal to the man's basest instinct, greed, but the longer Jack stood there, the more he wondered if he wouldn't be turned away. He was just about to try a different approach when Jeffers finally spoke.

"What the hell're you doin' back here, Rucker?" he asked. "Ain't nobody figured they'd ever see your face round these parts again. Why come back? You gonna make good by Maddy?"

Just like that, as if a switch had been flipped, Jack slipped into the role that had been prepared for him. Leaning closer, he lowered his voice. "I'm here for the same reason you are," he explained. "I want to make some money. I came on behalf of a man in Seattle, someone with money to burn. He wants land and lots of it. He sent me here to see if there was any for sale. Who knows, if things work out the way I expect, maybe you could get your hands on some of the cash he'll be spreading around . . ."

A wicked smile slowly crept across Jeffers's face; Jack could see the gears begin to turn in his head. "I'd like that." Stepping out of the doorway, he added, "Go buy them drinks."

Jack was filled with relief. Stepping past the much larger man, he'd only taken one step inside the speakeasy's door when Jeffers grabbed him by the arm, *hard*. "Hold on," he growled into Jack's ear. "You'd best remember that I'll always be watchin' you. Step outta line and I'm gonna hurt you bad. You start botherin' that pretty redhead behind the bar, the one you used to be so damn keen on, it's gonna be even worse. I'll make you wish you never even *thought* 'bout comin' back. Don't make either one a us regret me bein' generous, you understand?"

Slowly, Jack turned to look at him and nodded. With one last squeeze of Jack's arm, Jeffers let him go.

No matter what it takes, I'm going to put you behind bars.

Jeffers watched Jack Rucker walk away into the speakeasy. Immediately people began getting up out of their seats to greet him, laughing and smiling, a loud clamor rising throughout the cellar. Everyone seemed truly happy to see him, excluding Sumner, who stood beside the bar, scowling.

In this way, Jack was good for business; the place was the fullest it'd been since they opened. With word having spread around town about all that had happened the night before, folks had come hoping to get a repeat performance. The same curiosity had held true for Maddy; people had been streaming to the bar since they'd opened, offering their sympathies while buying drink after drink. The cash box had to be near full to overflowing.

"It's like a goddamn zoo," Jeffers mumbled under his breath.

Though he couldn't have said why, Jeffers felt there was something odd about Jack's story, that it didn't ring true. Maybe it was that he'd so willingly offered up a chance at his rich boss's money. Maybe it was that Jeffers never trusted anyone at first glance. Maybe it was because he didn't like the thought of Jack coming back to town and once again sweeping Maddy off her feet. No matter the reason, something didn't feel right.

Still, Jeffers had plenty of things to worry about other than whether Jack's story held water or not, particularly the last shipment of booze he'd be hiding for Al Capone. Jeffers hadn't been contacted by Jimmy Luciano yet, but he knew it could come at any time. He couldn't afford to make a mistake. He had to be ready.

But that don't mean I ain't payin' attention to what's happenin' here.

He'd meant what he'd said to Jack; he'd be watching.

■ ■ ■ ■

When Jack stepped inside the speakeasy, Maddy was behind the bar, doing her best to follow Seth Pettigrew's instructions for a drink she'd never heard of before; he called it a Dubonnet and swore that it was the drink of choice among high society. It was made by combining gin with equal parts of a specific type of wine, one that Seth just happened to have hidden away and had secreted across town for the occasion. His eyes were practically glowing as she poured the results of their work into a glass.

"I hope you like it," she said, handing it to him.

"Coming from your able hands," he replied, raising the glass in a toast, "I cannot fathom it would be anything but heavenly." Taking a small sip, he theatrically closed his eyes, savoring the taste with a smile. "Stupendously delicious!" he declared.

"Whatever it is, with praise like that, I'll have to have one."

Maddy looked up to see Jack standing before the bar, smiling at her. Butterflies immediately began dancing around in her stomach. Thankfully, Jack had been allowed to approach the bar alone; everyone seemed to want to give them some privacy, though she was sure they were all straining to hear every word she and Jack said. Memories of their afternoon filled her thoughts; she felt certain that everyone in the place knew exactly what she was thinking. She worried that the color she felt rising in her cheeks could be seen on the other side of the room.

"You'll have to ask Seth," Maddy replied. "It's his wine."

"I'll gladly pay you for it, Mr. Pettigrew," Jack offered.

"Nonsense, my boy," the former lawyer answered jovially. "Another connoisseur of fine drink is always welcome by my side, although if you ever address me so formally again, I'll make you pay double!"

"Fair enough," Jack said, laughing.

"Get this man some libation!" Seth shouted.

While Maddy began preparing Jack's drink, her thoughts drifted back to their time together on the bridge. It felt as if it'd been a dream. There'd been laughter, tears, and even some of the answers she'd spent years seeking. Jack's explanation for why he'd abandoned her had been painful to hear, but that didn't mean he wasn't telling the truth. She knew it would take a long time for her to be able to completely forgive him, if she ever really could, but she still hoped they had a chance for a new beginning.

And then there'd been the kiss.

Over and over, she'd replayed it in her mind: the surprise she'd felt when he put his lips against hers; the way her own passion had risen as she hungrily returned his advances; and even how easily her worries had been quieted. When she and Jack parted, she'd walked back into town feeling as if she were floating on a cloud. Her head had been such a mess that she'd nearly burned dinner. Helen had looked at her questioningly all night, but Maddy hadn't said a word. How could she? She could scarcely believe it herself.

But she and Jack had a long way yet to go before Maddy would truly be able to start trusting him again. He was mysterious, a riddle without an obvious solution; she still didn't know why he'd returned. She felt as if she had countless questions yet to ask, and she *was* going to ask every last one. If Jack were to answer them all . . .

For the first time in seven years, Maddy felt a flicker of hope.

". . . and when I pointed out that Carl Tanner couldn't possibly have stolen that truck on account of the fact that he was, at the very moment it was taken, having relations with his neighbor's wife in the horse barn, good ole Jim Utley snorted so loud it sounded like a gunshot!" Seth exclaimed, dissolving into cackles of laughter as he finished his story.

Jack joined in, chuckling. "Speaking of the sheriff," he said, looking around the speakeasy, "doesn't he know about this place? Heck, I was in town for only a couple of hours before I found out. This town's way too small to keep a secret for long. If he doesn't, what'll happen when he finds out?"

"He already knows." Seth shrugged. "Just the other night he sat right where you are and had a drink with me."

"You're joking," Jack blurted.

"I am not!"

"He isn't," Maddy agreed, setting Jack's drink down in front of him; he took a sip and nodded appreciably. "Jim said that as long as things don't get out of control, as long as he doesn't have to deal with any public drunkenness or the like, we could stay open."

"Even though it's against the law?"

"My dear boy," Seth tutted, "take it from me, an old lawyer who's been around long enough to know, when I say that there're many different ways to look at every rule on the books. When one of them is broken, it's done in degrees. Some folks just tip over the line while others take a flying leap. Some acts are committed on purpose while others are accidents.

"Take this Prohibition nonsense. If those dimwits enforcing the laws believe that everyone who goes to a place like this one to have a drink is a criminal who deserves to be locked behind bars, well, it isn't going to take long before half the country's in jail! When people are struggling to make ends meet and put food on the table, all this worrying about liquor should be the least of our concerns! It's poppycock! Let a man have a drink, by God!"

"I can see both arguments," Maddy interjected. "While I understand alcoholic drink can be a problem, the majority of people who drink are harmless. Someone can become addicted to anything. In here, people can forget their troubles for a little while, just like if they bought a ticket to the movies," she explained. "What do you think, Jack?"

"I believe in following the law," he said simply.

"I hate to tell you," Seth chuckled, "but I think you're involved in the breaking of one right now."

"I didn't say *which* one I was going to follow, did I?"

They all laughed at Jack's joke, but Maddy could see that he wasn't entirely kidding. There was a hint of seriousness in his eyes, as if he was weighing a difficult decision. She'd seen that look before, years earlier, back when he was wondering whether he should listen to his father and leave Colton for school out east. Whenever she would ask Jack what he was thinking, he'd lie and say that everything was fine. He'd wanted to spare her any suffering, but that had been a mistake; maybe if they'd talked about it then, things would have been different. If she asked him now, she wondered if he would tell her.

Right then and there, Maddy made a decision.

If she wanted to believe that they had a future together, that what they shared that afternoon on the bridge was the first step toward rekindling their love, then she couldn't keep waiting for answers; she'd have to demand them. It was the only way she'd know the truth, the only way they could go forward.

She just had to ask.

CHAPTER FIFTEEN

It was well after midnight when the last customer left the speakeasy. Sumner had closed the door behind him, leaving Maddy alone in the basement. She stood over the washbasin beside the bar, cleaning the last of the glasses Karla had cleared from the tables. After all the commotion of a cellar full of drinking men and women, the room seemed unusually quiet; the only sounds came from the wiping of Maddy's cloth across the glasses and the faint strains of Ruth Etting singing "Ten Cents a Dance" on the record player.

"Ten cents a dance . . . that's what they pay me . . . ," Maddy sang along softly.

Jack had left almost an hour earlier, offering to make sure Seth made it home safely, even if the former lawyer protested that he *wasn't* drunk and *didn't* need any help. Maddy had been slightly disappointed; she'd hoped that the two of them might've had some time together. There were still so many things they needed to talk about, especially —

From somewhere nearby Maddy heard the sound of a door being locked. Looking into the dark depths of the cellar, she saw Jeffers walking purposefully toward her. The sight of him startled her; every night since the speakeasy had opened, she'd closed by herself, cleaning up and counting the money that had been made. She'd thought she was alone.

And now she felt certain she was about to get yelled at.

Jeffers had yet to say anything to her about what had happened when she'd run off and left the speakeasy. Thankfully, nothing too bad occurred in her absence; Seth had gone on and on about how much fun he'd had behind the bar, though she wondered how much liquor he'd poured into his stomach instead of customers' glasses. But she also knew Jeffers would find no humor in it; instead, he'd think she was ridiculous and irresponsible, *a woman,* weak in every way, and would want to teach her a lesson. Jack's knocking Sumner unconscious only made things worse. Ever since Jeffers had arrived at the speakeasy, she'd been waiting for him to give her an earful. But it hadn't come, at least not yet.

"Here," Jeffers said, hefting a crate of liquor bottles up onto the bar. "This oughta replace what you poured tonight."

While Maddy restocked the alcohol, Jeffers opened up the money box and began thumbing through the bills and coins.

"Looks like we done pretty damn good tonight," he said.

"More than that," she replied. "Once it's all counted up, I'd be surprised if tonight wasn't our best night yet."

"You reckon it was 'cause people wanted to see if Jack was gonna chase you round the room again?"

Maddy winced. For the briefest of moments she'd wondered if Jeffers was going to ignore the problem and let the matter pass without comment. Now she knew she wouldn't be so lucky.

"I'm sorry about what happened," Maddy said, straightening up and looking directly at him, just like she'd done the day he came to the mercantile and proposed opening a speakeasy. "I know I was wrong to leave, but I never would've expected that Jack was going to show up here. When he did, I panicked. It was a mistake."

"You're damn right it was!" Jeffers snapped, tossing the cash box down so hard its contents spilled out, sending a couple of coins clattering to the floor. "If a fool like Sumner does somethin' stupid and runs off half-cocked, I ain't a bit surprised, but you know better! What woulda happened if Utley had come sniffin' round again, huh? What if that drunk, worthless lawyer'd started pourin' free drinks or passed out and the place got robbed blind? What then?"

"I said I was sorry," she answered truthfully.

"Words ain't good enough," Jeffers spat. "You wanted to be partners in all this, but it looks to me like you don't know what that means. This here is dangerous! Both our asses is sittin' on the line. One of us gets caught, one of us goes down, the other's gonna be sharin' the cell next door."

Maddy knew he was right; even though Sheriff Utley had given them some leeway, that didn't mean they weren't still breaking the law. She'd understood what Seth's argument had been earlier, that there were degrees of lawbreaking, but she wondered what an honest-to-goodness lawman would've thought if he'd been sitting there listening. He probably would have arrested her on the spot. No matter how she tried to look at it, in order to provide for her family she'd taken an incredible risk in going into business with a man the likes of Jeffers Grimm.

"It won't happen again," Maddy said firmly.

Jeffers didn't answer, choosing instead to stare at her; no matter how badly she wanted to do so, Maddy didn't look away. Neither of them spoke, their silence growing deeper when the record suddenly finished, the player's needle skipping near the label.

Suddenly Jeffers began to grin, then folded his arms and rested them on the bar; the crates groaned loudly from holding his considerable weight. Maddy imagined he thought this was all some kind of game. "Seemed like you weren't none too concerned 'bout seein' Jack tonight," he said. "What happened? The two of you spend the day kissin' and makin' up for lost time?"

Maddy blanched, her eyes widening with shock. Immediately she knew she'd made a mistake; from the way Jeffers's eyes narrowed, he'd understood the truth just as surely as if she'd come out and said it.

"I was . . . I was just . . . surprised to see him y-y-esterday . . . ," she stammered, looking away in a clumsy attempt to cover up for her error. "It took me off-guard is all . . . Tonight, I knew he was coming . . ."

"You gonna see him when you leave here?"

"No," Maddy answered quickly before again wishing she'd lied.

Jeffers chuckled, a sound that only served to unnerve her further. "What the hell's wrong with you?" he snorted. "Even after all them years you spent wonderin' why he left you like he did, he just waltzes back into town and it's just like it used to be. He must have a hell of a way with words. Your heart didn't get stomped on good enough you want more? You ain't nothin' but a fool."

Maddy was so flabbergasted by what she'd heard that she could only stare. Never in her life had she been spoken to in such a way. There was a part of her that was glad Jeffers was on the other side of the bar; if he'd been just before her, she might've reacted just as she'd done with Jack and slapped him; the consequences of that were too terrible to imagine.

"It's not like that," she said, her voice raw.

"Sure it is."

"I'd never let myself get hurt like that again."

"If you meant that, you wouldn't be givin' that scoundrel the time a day, let alone swappin' spit," Jeffers chided her.

"Don't talk about him like that," Maddy replied, so upset she worried she'd start shaking. "You don't know him."

"Don't lie to yourself that you do," Jeffers replied. "If you know so much, then why'd he come back here?"

Maddy's heart began to race faster and faster. She hated to admit it, but Jeffers was right; she *didn't* know why Jack had returned to Colton. She'd tried to ask him, but he hadn't given her any real answers. Still, she just couldn't give Jeffers the satisfaction of being right.

"He came to see his father," she lied.

"Bullshit," Jeffers sneered.

"It's the truth . . . ," she insisted, doubting that she was very convincing.

Jeffers laughed. "When he come in tonight, he told me he's workin' for some fella back in Seattle wantin' to buy up land round here for somesuch," he explained, showing that he already had the answer. "He ain't here 'cause he's feelin' sentimental. He's here 'cause a money."

"He told you?" Maddy asked, too shocked to try to disguise it.

"Maybe he's more forthcomin' with me 'cause he knows I'd have an interest in what he's sellin'," Jeffers suggested. "He remembers I got a way with business. That I got the stomach for takin' a chance." He paused, looking at her so intently that she began to feel uncomfortable. "So why ain't he tellin' you his reasons?"

Maddy's head was spinning like a top. Was Jeffers telling the truth? Was Jack here because he'd been sent on an errand by his rich boss? Had Jack made Jeffers an offer? It sounded unbelievable. She didn't know what to think.

"Kinda puts a cloud over that fancy future you musta been plannin'." Jeffers chuckled, obviously enjoying himself.

"I'm not doing anything of the sort," she answered.

"Don't give me that crap," he snapped, an edge to his voice, as if he were giving an order. "I ain't like them rubes standin' on the other side of the bar, willin' to believe anythin' so long as you're pourin' me a drink."

"I'm not lying. After what happened between me and Jack," Maddy explained, "I'd be a fool if I wasn't being cautious."

"That's good to hear." Jeffers said with a nod. "Otherwise, I'd be worried you was headin' for another heap a trouble."

Maddy paused. "What do you mean? What trouble?"

"You get your hopes up," he explained, "Jack's just gonna knock 'em all down. He ain't the type to go givin' your trust to."

As he spoke, Jeffers moved around the corner of the makeshift bar and began to approach her. Maddy felt more and more uncomfortable, but there wasn't much she could do about it; because of the empty liquor crates and boxes full of glasses crowding the tiny space, there wasn't anywhere for her to move. She found herself pressed back against the cellar's brick wall, watching the space between them slowly shrink.

"Why would you say that about him?" she asked.

"Use your head," Jeffers replied. "He's been livin' in the big city all these years, spendin' time at fancy restaurants and clubs, listenin' to music with every kind a broad you can think of lookin' him over, seein' a picture whenever he feels like it. He's been citified. After all that, whatever'd make you think he could come back to a place like this and be happy? A little nothing town like this one, he'd be bored outta his skull in no time. Hell, odds are he's already countin' the days till he can leave. He don't belong in Colton no more'n Hoover or Howard Hughes do. He ain't for here no more . . . he ain't for you . . ."

No matter how hard she tried, Maddy couldn't keep her lower lip from trembling.

Jeffers was right. Jack himself had told her so; once he'd gone to Boston, once he'd seen what a big city had to offer, he'd known he couldn't come back. It was the reason he'd refused to contact her. So why now, after all the years he'd spent away on the East Coast, in Seattle and who knew how many places in-between, far away from her, could she have ever expected him to suddenly change his mind?

So what does that make our kiss this afternoon . . . ?

Maddy hated the first answer that leaped to her mind; he'd needed to come back to Colton for business, just like he'd told Jeffers, and since she was still here, he'd decided to have himself a little fun for old times' sake. What could it hurt? And when it was over, he'd leave just like before, no matter what it did to her . . .

"You don't need him."

The sudden sound of Jeffers's voice startled her. She'd been so lost in her own thoughts that she hadn't realized how close he'd come; he towered in front of her so completely that she could see little else. Placing one hand against the brick above her head, he leaned in, leering down at her. Try as she might, Maddy couldn't retreat any farther.

"What you need is someone who'll make you feel like a woman," he continued, his voice a low growl. "You need a real man." Lowering his hand, he took some of her hair between his fingers.

"Jeffers, please . . . ," she said uncomfortably, turning her head to the side, as far away from his touch as she could get.

"Someone who'll please you," he kept on as if she hadn't said a word of protest. "Make you cry out in pleasure late in the night, make you want him inside you again and again and again." His breath began to come fast, insistent. "I could make you feel that way . . ."

"Please, don't . . ."

"I'd make you feel like you ain't never felt before . . ." As his last word trailed into the heavy silence of the speakeasy, Jeffers ran his finger down the side of Maddy's cheek; to her, it felt as if he were dragging a razor blade against her skin.

In that instant Maddy knew that if she did nothing, he was going to force himself on her whether she wanted him to or not. He was going to rape her in the basement of her father's mercantile. Jeffers Grimm wasn't the sort of man who gave a damn that a woman said no.

But it wasn't until he grabbed Maddy's

breast that she acted.

Unlike the almost delicate way he'd touched her face, Jeffers gave her breast a hard squeeze, making her yelp with pain. Just like when she'd slapped Jack, Maddy reacted without thinking, driving her elbow into Jeffers's stomach while stomping on his foot with the heel of her shoe. It felt as if she were hitting a mountain. She harbored no illusion that she'd hurt him but was hoping to surprise him instead; it was unlikely that he was used to a woman fighting back. To her amazement, he backed up enough for her to squeeze by and hurry to the other side of the bar.

When he turned to face her, a thin smile creased his hard face; he reminded Maddy of a wolf toying with wounded prey. "I like it when a gal gets a little playful," he growled.

Maddy didn't answer, watching him carefully, ready to make a run for the door if he came after her. Instead, Jeffers popped the cork out of a bottle of whiskey and took a slug, wiping his beard with the back of his hand.

"You know what I like 'bout you?" he asked.

Maddy remained silent.

"You got a spine," he answered anyway.

"Stay away from me," she warned.

Jeffers laughed; listening to him, Maddy realized how futile her warning was; if he wanted to take her, her only hope was to run. She was so unnerved that she started walking backward toward the door. He didn't follow. It wasn't until she was unlocking the door that he spoke again, his voice clear all the way across the basement, and just as menacing as if he were right beside her.

"When you realize Jack ain't the man you think he is," he said, slamming the now empty liquor bottle down on the bar, "I'll be waitin'."

"Are you sure you'll be all right?"

Jack watched as Seth turned back to him, the man's eyes looking off somewhere over his shoulder, bloodshot and wild, before slowly drifting back and narrowing as he tried to focus. His mouth hung slack, his lips wet with spit. Standing in the foyer of the old lawyer's home, a dim lamp lit inside the door, Jack could see how flushed Seth's cheeks were, how unsteadily he tottered and slumped into an old chair.

"Never been better!" Seth declared, punctuating his statement by raising a finger into the air so quickly that he nearly tipped onto the floor.

"Do you need help getting to bed?"

"Nonsense, my boy," Seth pooh-poohed. "I'll just sit here a minute, catch my second wind, and then retire for the night. Go on. I'll be fine."

Jack shook his head. He knew there wasn't any point in arguing further. It'd already been like pulling teeth to help Seth home safely. He had complained every step of the way. Even if he fell asleep right where he was, at least he was home.

Back outside, Jack considered heading back to the speakeasy to see if Maddy was still there. They'd agreed to meet the next day at the mercantile, but right then he was filled with a desire to be with her again, to revisit what had happened on the bridge. Still, it was precisely because of that desire that he finally decided to make his way back to the Belvedere.

Maddy Aldridge is driving me crazy . . .

Jack knew he was in a tough spot with the Bureau. He was supposed to be focused on his job, to be immune to every surprise or distraction, but this was unlike any other assignment he'd ever been given. His head was as big a mess as Seth's, but it wasn't because of alcohol. Still, Jack couldn't deny that his famed luck had produced results.

In a matter of days, he'd discovered that there was an illegal liquor operation in Colton, successfully infiltrated the speakeasy without raising suspicion, learned that Jeffers Grimm was the man in charge, and now only needed to learn where in Canada the booze came from to tie the whole thing up with a bow and hand it over to Lieutenant Pluggett. Once the arrests were made, Jack could return to the promising professional life he'd taken such pains in constructing. But there was a problem.

Maddy was mixed up in it all.

There was no use denying it; there were plenty of hard questions he'd have to ask.

He hated to think what she might ask of him in return.

Completely lost in thought, Jack looked up to find that he'd already made it back to the hotel. Inside, the front desk was empty; it was late, well past the midnight hour, but he wondered if Mrs. Benoit might be tending to Ross, so he walked down the hall to the recovering man's room, put his head against the closed door, and listened. He didn't hear a sound. Carefully, he opened the door.

Only a sliver of the faint light from the hallway fell into Ross's room, illuminating only the bottom half of the bed. Jack saw one of the man's hands lying limp, palm up toward the ceiling. Though it wasn't much, Jack got the strong impression that Ross was weak, possibly clinging to life.

Before he got too pessimistic, Jack reminded himself of what Dr. Quayle had explained: that it would take quite some time before they'd know for certain whether Ross would pull through. He needed plenty of rest. But just as Jack was about to give it to his fellow agent, to close the door and try to get some fitful sleep of his own, a gravelly voice croaked at him in the darkness.

"I guess . . . you ain't so . . . lucky after all . . . ," it said, ". . . 'cause if you was . . . I reckon . . . I'd be dead . . . by now . . ."

CHAPTER SIXTEEN

Jack stood frozen in place as Ross's hand rose, trembling from the effort, the hotel room bedsprings groaning as he tried to move. Hearing the older man speak had been startling. Jack had thought Ross was sleeping, that it would be days before he'd come around, peacefully stuck in a drug-induced haze so that his body could heal. But now he was awake, for both better and worse.

"I didn't mean to wake you . . . ," Jack managed.

"I bet . . . you was hopin' . . . I wasn't ever gonna . . . be a bother . . . to you . . . again . . . weren't ya . . . ?" Ross answered, and then dissolved into a fit of coughs.

"You should lie still," Jack cautioned. "Dr. Quayle said that you needed to have plenty of —"

"I don't . . . give a . . . good goddamn . . . what some . . . two-bit . . . small-town . . .

quaok . . . thinks," Ross interrupted with a growl. "Quit whinin' . . . and turn on the . . . light so I can . . . look at ya . . ."

Jack did as the man asked and switched on the lamp beside the bed. After the darkness, the sudden light was almost blinding.

Ross looked haggard and worn-out, as if he'd been forced through a knothole. With everything he'd suffered, it wasn't surprising that it looked as if he'd aged ten years. His hair was a sweaty, disheveled mess. Dark bags hung beneath his wet, narrowed eyes. His skin was a sickly, pale color. Stubble peppered his cheeks and his lips were as dry as paper. Looking at him, Jack was reminded of an old drunk he used to see around Boston, a disaster of a man who sat at the mouth of an alley, spilling whiskey down his chin while getting drenched by the pouring rain. He looked weak, tired, as if he'd been forced to stay awake for days. He looked terrible.

"I bet . . . I look . . . like hell . . . ," Ross said.

"With everything that's happened, you shouldn't be complaining," Jack answered, seeing no point in lying to the man. "From what Dr. Quayle said, you're lucky to be alive."

"Lucky . . . I'm . . . lucky . . . ," Ross

snorted. "I ain't . . . so sure . . . Right now . . . things feel so bad . . . maybe death . . . would be better . . ." Once again, he had an attack of coughs. "Get me . . . somethin' to . . . drink . . ."

Jack poured a glass of water from the pitcher on the dresser and brought it to the suffering man. Carefully, he placed his hand behind Ross's head and lifted him up high enough to put the glass to his lips, tipping it so that he could drink. After a couple of gulps, Ross suddenly gagged, sputtered, and then angrily slapped the glass away, sending it skittering across the floor.

"What'n the hell're you tryin' to do?" he complained. "Drown me?"

It was a struggle, but Jack managed to hold his tongue. Though he'd had hopes, it appeared that Ross's ordeal had done nothing to improve his mood; he remained as surly and unlikable as ever. Jack knew he needed to be understanding, that he shouldn't hold it against the man.

But that didn't mean it was going to be easy . . .

"How long've I been out?" Ross asked, rubbing a hand across his chin, wincing as he shifted on the bed.

"A couple of days," Jack answered. "From what I was told, you weren't supposed to have awakened yet, if at all."

"Look at this mess," Ross said, pulling up the bedsheet and revealing the tubes and stitching that marred his abdomen. Blood and pus stained his skin and Mrs. Benoit's bedding. "I'm like some damn cadaver who doesn't have the sense to know he's dead."

"It's going to take a long time for you to get back on your feet," Jack replied. "Like I said, you're lucky to still be alive."

Ross gave no reaction, his head lolling to the side, away from his visitor. For a moment Jack wondered if he hadn't fallen asleep, still worn-out, slipping to unconsciousness without a fight. But suddenly Ross turned back to face him, his eyes sharp and intense.

"So where was it?" he asked.

Jack stumbled, unsure of what his fellow agent could possibly be talking about. "Where's . . . where's what?"

"The booze," Ross answered. "If I've been sleepin' for a couple a days, that goddamn luck a yours shoulda led you right to it. So let's have it . . . what did you find . . . ?"

Jack felt as if he'd been punched in the stomach. This was the moment he'd been dreading but thought he'd have more time to prepare for. Eventually, he knew Ross would ask him about their investigation, whether he'd found a speakeasy or any clue that would lead to the arrest of the crooks behind the illegal booze operation. He'd dreaded the moment it might happen. But just as he had felt in his dilemma with Maddy, Jack didn't want to lie. Until he crossed that line, he could convince himself there was still some ambiguity to his actions, to the strange situation he'd entered into, and where he wasn't being derelict to his duty. But now he was going to have to make a decision.

In for a penny, in for a pound.

Jack slowly shook his head. "I haven't found anything."

"Nothing?" Ross asked, surprised.

"Nope." Jack shrugged. "Not yet."

"Huh," the other man answered; Jack wondered if, despite his earlier claims to the contrary, Ross hadn't been as firm of a believer in Jack's vaunted luck as the rest of the Bureau.

"You been askin' round?" Ross pressed further. "You been tellin' people the story like we was supposed to, wavin' the money in their faces?"

"Some," Jack answered evasively, fearful of digging the hole for his lie that much deeper.

"Then what'n the hell've you been doin'?"

Ross snapped.

"What I could," he shot back defensively. "I've spent most of the time worrying about what was going to happen to you."

"What'n the hell for?"

Jack could only stare silently in answer.

"You shouldn't give a damn 'bout me," Ross continued angrily. " 'Cause I tell you one thing, if our places was reversed, if it was you lyin' here, poundin' loud on death's door, I wouldn't give a rat's ass whether you lived or died." At this thought, a thin smile curled at the corners of his mouth. "I'd be out there doin' what I'd been sent to this shithole town to do, movin' on up the ladder no matter who I had to step on to do it, you can bet on that!"

Jack struggled to hold back his surprise. He was so used to thinking of Ross as a poor, lazy excuse for a lawman that it was shocking to see him show some devotion to the job, even if it was selfish and mean-spirited.

"What'd Pluggett say when you told him what happened?" Ross asked.

"He doesn't know," Jack answered truthfully.

Ross looked as if he were going to complain some more, but he stopped just short, a look of contemplation crossing his tired features. "You know, that's probably a good idea," he finally said. "If you'd said anythin', the Bureau woulda shut the whole thing down. With my damn guts burstin', it wouldn'ta made a difference if they'd brought the best doctor west of the Rockies with 'em. This way, don't matter if I keep breathin' or start pushin' daisies, you can go right on investigatin'." Ross's eyes narrowed as he looked up at Jack. "Probably work out pretty good for your career that way, won't it?"

Jack didn't blink or turn away, though he was ashamed that when Ross had first collapsed he'd thought the same thing. But now things had changed. He needed to be able to operate without calling the Bureau for an entirely different reason.

He had to figure out what to do with Maddy.

"How long am I gonna be like this?" Ross asked.

"Dr. Quayle said it could take weeks, maybe longer."

"When I hit the floor, when I was outta my head from my guts bein' torn 'part, did I let it slip what we was here for?"

"Almost," Jack answered, "but no one heard."

Ross nodded. "You tell anyone the truth

why we're here?"

"No one."

"Then we can still do what we was sent to do," he explained. "We stick to the ruse, you start askin' round, we find out where the booze is at and where it's comin' from, and then we call Pluggett and get the hell outta here."

"You shouldn't be doing anything but getting plenty of rest."

"I told you not to worry 'bout me!" Ross snapped. "We do our jobs right and there'll be medals, I tell ya! Medals!"

Jack nodded in agreement, his head racing to come up with a way where this wasn't going to end in a catastrophe, where he wouldn't have to lie and mislead at every turn, where he wouldn't be fired from the Bureau, where the woman he'd once loved and couldn't deny he was once again developing feelings for wouldn't find herself behind bars.

What in the hell am I going to do?

As soon as Maddy entered her father's bedroom, carrying his breakfast on a tray, she knew something was wrong. Silas slammed shut the book he'd been reading, abruptly turned off the radio program mid-sentence, and stared at her as she rounded the end of his bed and placed his food on the mattress beside him, exactly as she'd done ever since his arthritis had started getting the better of him. However, unlike most mornings, when her father would greet her with a joke, a comment about the weather just outside his window, or explaining something he'd just discovered in his reading, today he was silent.

"I thought you might like some bacon and eggs this morning," she said cheerfully. "You've had oatmeal so much lately that I half-expect it to start coming out of your ears."

Maddy looked down at him with a smile, but what she saw on his face was anything but pleasant. As a matter of fact, it was a look she found very familiar, though it had been years since she'd last seen it.

He was disappointed, with a dash of anger thrown in for good measure.

"We need to talk," he finally said.

Immediately Maddy knew there was trouble. Clearly, her father had learned something about her, something she'd wanted to keep hidden, something he didn't like, not one bit. It had to be the speakeasy. She wasn't sure how it had happened, but he'd learned about what she'd been doing in the cellar of the family business. Her father would be furious, dead set against what she'd done, horrified that she'd do something that flew in the face of his principles. Ever since she'd agreed to Jeffers's plan, this was the moment she'd been dreading, all the while hoping it never came. Now, it was too late.

"Why didn't you tell me?" he demanded.

"Let me explain," she started, panicked. "It's just that —"

But her father cut her off, his voice laced with disgust. "Why didn't you tell me Jack Rucker had come back to town?"

Maddy was so stunned that she couldn't speak, just like she'd been when she first saw Jack standing in front of the speakeasy's bar. She could only stare at her father, his face creased in an angry scowl, trying to think of something to say, feeling as if she were floundering in a raging river.

"I . . . I thought it would upset you," she finally managed.

"You're damn right it does!" Silas shouted. "And to think, I'd been talking about that worthless cur just a couple of days ago! He must've been lurking underfoot even as I spoke! Have you seen him?"

Maddy could only nod.

"When?" he pressed, growing more and more agitated. "Where was it?"

"At the store," she answered, the strange mixture of lie and truth coming easily to her tongue. "He came by just after he got back to town."

"And?" Silas pressed. "Don't make me pull every little detail out of you. There must be plenty you're not saying."

Maddy knew her father couldn't have been more correct. But what could she possibly tell him? The truth? That she'd been so shocked by Jack's appearance at the illegal tavern she ran in the cellar of the family store that she slapped him and ran away into the night? That she'd met him at the Belvedere and together they'd gone to the bridge that had once meant so much to them, where Jack then took her into his arms and they'd kissed passionately, rekindling memories and feelings she'd spent years trying to keep buried?

She had no choice but to lie.

"We didn't talk for long," Maddy offered evasively.

"He didn't tell you why he left?" Silas asked angrily. "He didn't explain why he ran off the way he did, abandoning you here?"

"No," she said simply. "I didn't ask."

"What?" her father exclaimed, his eyes wide with disbelief. "Why on earth not?

With all that bastard put you through, the least you could've done was make him tell you why!"

"Maybe it's like you've always told me," Maddy offered, hoping that a small lie might be enough to convince him to let it go. "Maybe I realized it's better left to the past."

Silas nodded. She hoped that her answer would be the end of it, but her father's interest couldn't be quieted for long. "What does he look like?"

"About the same as when he left, just a bit older," Maddy explained, seeing no point in telling Silas that she found Jack more handsome than ever.

"Did he tell you why he's in Colton?"

Maddy took a deep breath and looked away. She knew that her father would keep on pressing her, question after question, relentless in his attempt to wring every last bit of information out of her that he could. But the truth was that she didn't have many of the answers he sought, most of them things she would've liked to have known herself.

"Who told you about him?" she asked, changing the topic.

"Steven Quayle," Silas told her. "The two of us had quite the conversation last night after you left for choir practice. He told me that Jack's over at Virginia Benoit's place and that it's all anyone in town's talking about." He frowned a bit before adding, "Not that either of my daughters so much as mentioned it to me."

"We didn't want to upset you," Maddy explained.

"Fat lot of good it did you." Her father shook his head, the look of disappointment returning to his face. "I reckon I looked like a proper fool in front of the doctor once I learned you've been keeping secrets from me. Makes me wonder what else I don't know."

Maddy could only imagine how her father would feel if he knew how right he was to be suspicious. Everything she'd kept from him, from the speakeasy to Jack's sudden reappearance, had been done to protect Silas; what he didn't know couldn't possibly hurt him, could it? She just hadn't counted on the doctor appearing in the middle of the night and the two of them —

Wait a minute!

"Why was Dr. Quayle here last night?" she exclaimed, suddenly worried that something terrible had happened while she'd been out breaking the law by pouring illegal drinks, as well as trying to fend off Jeffers's unwanted advances. The thought that she'd been negligent made her stomach turn. "Did something happen? Are you all right? Did you have another bad spell?"

Silas shook his head. "It was nothing like that," he answered.

"Then why was he here?"

"Because he's been so busy the last couple of days that he hasn't had time to check up on me, that's all. He called and asked if I'd mind if he came by after he saw a new patient of his," Silas said, his jaw tightening a bit before he continued. "I guess it's something pretty bad, something that has to do with Jack . . ."

"What are you talking about?" Maddy asked. "What does Jack have to do with it?"

"Turns out that Jack didn't come to Colton alone," her father said, letting it sit there long enough for Maddy's imagination to grab hold of it and run wild; she wondered if Jack had brought another woman with him, maybe his future bride, for a trip to see where he'd grown up.

But just as soon as Maddy had those troubling thoughts, she shooed them away. No matter what had happened between her and Jack seven years before, he wasn't a big enough louse to have taken her to their bridge and kissed her if there was someone

268

else in his life. He was better than that.

Still, it did nothing to satisfy her curiosity. "Who is it?" Maddy asked.

"Some fella," Silas answered. "Doc Quayle figures they must work together. I guess they'd no sooner set foot inside the Belvedere when the other fella's stomach burst. Steven says he's lucky to have survived the surgery, though he isn't out of danger yet. What did Jack say about it?"

"Nothing." Maddy shook her head; it was just another in a long line of things the two of them needed to talk about, and soon. "Did Dr. Quayle mention the man's name?" she asked.

Silas thought about it for a moment. "Hoover or Hooper . . . ," he said. "Something like that."

Maddy's imagination once again started to race. There was plenty that Jack hadn't told her, secrets folded over into riddles; she wondered if it wasn't all mixed together with a heaping helping of lies.

Who is this other man?

Is he the reason Jack was so secretive about why he'd come back to Colton after so many years away?

Why are the two of them here?

"What else did the doctor say?" Maddy asked.

Before her father could answer, his face was suddenly twisted into a painful grimace; grabbing his left hand with his right, he began squeezing the spasming fingers hard, stretching them out as they fought against him, involuntarily curling, as if they were trying to make a fist. "Damn these things," he growled. "If I didn't think it'd hurt like the dickens, I'd ask you to cut them off with a hatchet!"

Maddy hurried over and sat beside her father on the edge of the bed. She took his stricken hand and began working just as he had, kneading his fingers and pulling them straight. Silas occasionally grunted and groaned, but she continued until the arthritis relaxed its grip, the spasms subsiding, and eventually his hand returned to what now passed for normal.

"Thank you, sweetheart," he said.

"No thanks needed," she answered.

For a long moment, they sat in silence. Finally, Silas spoke, his voice soft yet firm. "I'm sorry to give you so much grief about Jack coming back," he said. "It's just that you're my daughter and I love you. The last thing I want is for him to hurt you again."

Maddy smiled tenderly, fighting to keep tears from her eyes. "Then we both want the same thing," she said.

"Just be careful."

"I will," she said, leaning close to embrace him, laying her head on his shoulder as she began to wonder, given all of the problems she now had in her life, from money to Jeffers to Jack, what she was going to do next.

CHAPTER SEVENTEEN

Jack walked Colton's streets as if his feet had a mind of their own. Leaving the Belvedere, they marched to the intersection where his old school still stood, all of the windows thrown open to give the place a good airing out, trod right on past the barbershop where a patron, all lathered up in the chair, pointed excitedly at him as he crossed the large window, and strolled past Morgan's Blacksmithing, looking in through the open doors at the shower of sparks flying off the piece of metal being pounded. Unlike the first night after he'd returned to Colton, hurrying through darkened alleyways behind Clayton on the way to the speakeasy, with no idea where he was, he now had no trouble finding his way. His feet knew the route well; with where he was going, they'd never forget.

He was headed to Aldridge Mercantile.

Jack thought about all of the times he'd

waited for Maddy outside her father's store, standing under the awning and watching the spring rain, staring at the autumn leaves as they lazily fell from the trees, kicking about in the freshly fallen snow, or sweating under the blazing summer sun, much like today. Because of the way Silas felt about him, it was better for all of them that he wait outside. No matter where he was in Colton, he'd would've been able to find his way to her. Even after seven years away, he imagined he could do it with his eyes shut.

But this is the first time I've ever been so nervous.

When Jack said good night to Maddy at the speakeasy the night before, they'd agreed to meet the next morning at the mercantile. Jack had no doubt as to what she wanted to do; even as he'd kissed her at the bridge, he'd known he was only postponing the inevitable, delaying her desire to ask countless questions that he had no idea how to answer.

I don't want to lie, but how can I tell her the truth?

Things had become even more complicated after his conversation with Ross. If he expected Jack to bring him results, to tell him every little detail of his investigation into the illegal liquor ring in Colton, if he

273

wanted a spectacular arrest as a means of advancing both their careers in the Bureau, then Jack was faced with a tough decision; either he had to throw Maddy behind bars with Jeffers Grimm, Sumner Colt, and anyone else involved with the speakeasy or he had to find some way to protect her. There was no middle ground. The problem was that, looking at things from the outside, Maddy appeared just as guilty as the others; after all, it all took place in the basement of her family's store, with her behind the bar. Jack had no doubt how Ross would look upon her involvement. After a sleepless night spent tossing and turning, Jack was no closer to finding a way out of the mess he had lied himself into.

Rounding the corner at the bakery, his mouth watering at all the delicious smells, Jack came to a stop and looked across the street at Aldridge Mercantile. Like much of the rest of Colton, it appeared unchanged to his eyes; there was the same crisp lettering painted on the front windows, which displayed new goods, the familiar knobby, worn front door, now opened in the summer heat. Jack couldn't help but smile; it was as if he were sixteen again, waiting for Maddy to burst outside so that they could be together.

But today was different. Now, he'd have to be careful, have to hope that she didn't become too angry, that he didn't paint himself into a corner from which he couldn't escape. He hated that he'd have to be on guard but knew there was no other choice. Suddenly, another hope fluttered in his chest: that he might kiss her again, knowing that he shouldn't but then feeling certain that, if he got the chance, he'd take it.

Swallowing hard, Jack tried to calm his nerves, told himself that he'd been in far more difficult situations dozens of times where things came out fine. Finally, he crossed the street.

With that darned luck of mine, what's the worst that could happen?

Jack stepped inside the mercantile. Everything appeared just as he remembered, all the way up to the ceiling fans turning lazily in the summer heat. What felt the most familiar was the smell: a strange, almost intoxicating mixture of candies, leather, wood, and mothballs. He was the only person there; no customers and no Maddy.

"Hello?" he called.

In answer, there was a rustling in the storeroom at the far end of the counter. Jack expected to see Maddy come through the door and greet him, so he was surprised when a woman he didn't know stepped through. She was younger than Maddy, with short, dark hair and sharp features, wearing a dress far more cosmopolitan than he would have ever expected to see in Colton, even if it was a bit out of style. He had the impression that she was trying to look older than she actually was, more sophisticated. When she saw him, she gave him a thin smirk.

"I'm sorry, I w-w-as . . . ," he stammered. "Is . . . is Maddy here?"

"She's down in the cellar fetching a few things," the young woman answered. "She should be up in a minute."

"Oh . . . thank you . . . ," Jack replied, stuffing his hands in his pockets, unsure as to why she was staring at him so intently. He imagined that she was like most everyone else in town, gawking at him, unable to believe he'd returned.

"You don't recognize me, do you?" she asked with a chuckle.

Jack looked at her closely and, for a long while, still had no idea who she was, though she clearly had no such problem with him. Then slowly, steadily, the realization dawned on him; it was something in her eyes and

276

the curve of her chin. The truth had been right in front of him all along; frankly, he felt stupid for not having figured it out sooner.

"Helen," he said, unable to keep from smiling.

When Jack left Colton, Helen had still been a child, just eleven years old. She'd always been underfoot, a sharp-witted, rambunctious girl who often fought tooth and nail with her older sister. Even back then, Helen and Maddy had been different, yet still close in the way that only siblings could be, despite it all. Helen had found him funny and had always wanted to tag along, occasionally to Maddy's displeasure. She'd been gangly, even awkward, nothing like the young woman who stood before him now.

"If you hadn't said something, I don't know if I would've recognized you." He grinned. "I can't believe how much you've changed."

"Not you," she answered. "You're exactly the same. No wonder you're the only thing anyone in town is talking about."

"I didn't mean to cause such a fuss."

"Well, you did," Helen said with a laugh. "Virginia Benoit's become the most popular woman in town because you're staying at her hotel. Half of Colton's rung her telephone to find out where you've been all these years and why you've suddenly come back."

"Why don't they just ask me instead?"

Helen shrugged. "Maybe all the wondering is more fun than the truth."

"Seems kind of silly to me."

"Me too," she agreed. "So where *have* you been for seven years?"

Jack was momentarily taken aback by her bluntness; not even Maddy had been so abrupt. Still, the answer he'd give Helen could lack many of the details her older sister would insist on. "Just about everywhere," he answered. "Boston, Chicago, Seattle, San Francisco, Los Angeles —"

"You've been to Los Angeles?!" Helen shouted, her face suddenly brightening like a movie marquee when the switch was thrown. She raced over to where he stood and grabbed hold of his hand, clenching it tightly. "What was it like? I bet it's just like it looks in the magazines! Did you go to Hollywood? Have you ever met any movie stars? Tell me everything!"

"I . . . I was only there for business," Jack tried to explain, purposefully leaving out the names of the movie stars he'd seen coming and going from the speakeasy he frequented, "but it seemed nice."

"I can't wait to go there!" Helen enthused. "As soon as I can, I'm going to do just what you did and leave this worthless town! I want to go where there's excitement and glamour, somewhere fun!"

Although Jack's reasons for leaving Colton had been different from Helen's, there was a part of him that could relate to her desires; small-town life could be as different from the big city as night was from day. Still, coming home had given him a new perspective, had softened the resolve he'd held firm to during his years working for the Bureau.

"Take it from somebody who's spent plenty of time in cities," he said. "There's plenty to like about a place like Colton, too."

"Aw, nuts." Helen frowned. "It's too boring for me."

"Once you spend a couple of months listening to honking car horns when you're trying to get some sleep, never getting a minute's peace and quiet, living in a place no bigger than a closet, fighting your way through a crowd just to make it to the grocer, only to find out they've sold out of what you wanted, you might think about it differently."

"I doubt it," she huffed, looking at him like he must be crazy for bad-mouthing life in the big city.

Jack couldn't help but laugh. "All right, all right," he gave in. "Go and find out for yourself, then. Who knows, maybe I'll be able to show you around someday."

"You've already got enough problems with one Aldridge girl," a voice spoke from behind him. "Do you really think it's a good idea to get involved with another?"

Jack turned to see Maddy standing at the top of the cellar steps, a crate in her hands. From the look on her face Jack couldn't tell if she was really annoyed or if she was pulling his leg.

"Maddy, I didn't mean it like that," he began defensively.

"Don't worry about it," Helen cut in. "He's not old enough for me anyway. I want someone who's been around long enough to make tons of money, like a movie producer or an oil baron. Jack couldn't afford me."

At that, both Jack and Maddy dissolved into laughter, while Helen seemed unable to understand what could possibly be so funny.

Maddy led the way out the mercantile's back door and into the alleyway with Jack right behind her. The noon sun stood high

280

in the sky, leaving few shadows to darken the ground around them. Maddy noticed Jack glance toward the steps leading down to the speakeasy before quickly turning back, giving her a faint smile. They were completely alone.

Though Maddy was thankful that Helen had agreed to watch the store while the two of them talked, she was still filled with feelings of unease. After her emotional run-ins with Jeffers and her father, she'd been up for most of the night wondering what she was going to say to Jack; though each of them did so in different ways, both men had put the idea in her head that he was keeping something from her. No matter what, she knew the time had come for answers.

"I can't believe how much your sister's changed," he said, chuckling. "What happened to that little girl I used to know?"

"She grew up," Maddy answered. "You've been gone for a long time."

"It doesn't seem like it's been *that* long."

"That depends on who you ask."

"She sure seemed excited about going to Los Angeles."

"It's because of those ridiculous magazines she likes to read."

"If she ever gets there, it won't take long for her to see that Hollywood's not a whole lot like they make it out to be."

"The problem is that she'll have to leave here to find out," Maddy said, growing a bit angry at the thought of another person she loved going away. "I hope she'll have enough concern to write once in a while."

"Maddy, I didn't —"

"I wasn't looking for another apology," she cut him off.

Maddy immediately regretted her choice of words. She hadn't intended on being so brusque with him. Still, she wasn't going to apologize, either. Instead, neither of them spoke, standing under the blazing sun.

Eventually, she felt his eyes fall on her.

"Why didn't you find someone else?" he asked.

"Why would you say such a thing?"

"It's just like you said," Jack explained. "No one knows better how long I've been gone than you. So why didn't you meet another man, get married, have children? There had to have been suitors."

Maddy thought about all the men who'd tried to gain her affections, most of them much earlier than she would've expected chivalrous, only to discover her scowling, unpleasant face far less attractive than they'd imagined. Eventually, everyone got the hint she wanted to be left alone.

"I never gave anyone a chance," she answered truthfully.

"Why not?"

"Because I never stopped loving you," Maddy explained, finally turning to look at him; Jack's gaze never wavered from her, though his jaw tightened. "Because I never allowed myself to stop hoping that you might change your mind, and that you might come back to me."

"You would've have had every right to forget all about me," he said.

"I couldn't."

"The whole way back to Colton, I imagined you had a new life, a husband, everything we'd always talked about."

Maddy shook her head, unable to listen to more. "What about you?" she asked, turning the conversation back on him just as she'd done with her father the night before, finally giving voice to the question that had been nagging at her relentlessly, the one she'd been both unable and unwilling to ask, even as Jack had kissed her on the bridge. Bracing herself for an answer she didn't want to hear, she tentatively added, "Did you find someone else?"

Jack paused, looking straight into her eyes, making her heart rise into her throat, before shaking his head. "No," he said. "I didn't."

"Why not?" she pressed breathlessly.

"Looking back on the years since I left, all I remember is being in a hurry to get somewhere else," he explained, looking up into the sun. "I was always busy moving from one place to the next, from one job to another. I never had a chance to settle down, to make friends."

Maddy struggled to hide her disappointment. Jack's reasons for remaining alone, for not finding someone else to love, were different from hers. While she'd resisted any and all advances, he'd simply been too busy to receive any. If he'd lived a different life, if he'd been able to see a head turned his way, had noticed one particular girl's smile, he wouldn't be here with her.

"But that's not the real reason," he said suddenly, turning back to look at her, the sun dancing on his skin.

This time, Maddy struggled to contain her hope.

"I suppose I was just like you," said Jack, smiling. "No matter where I went, no matter what I was doing, heck, even in my dreams, you were still in my thoughts. The truth is I never stopped loving you, either."

Maddy gasped, her hand rising to her mouth as tears began to fill her eyes. She'd spent the last seven years wondering whether Jack ever thought about her or he'd simply walked away from her without a look back. Now, the hopes she clung to, the ones that occasionally made her feel foolish, had proven to be anything but.

"I told you why I made the choices I did," he continued, "but now, being here again, spending time with you, I feel like I made a mistake. But my life is so complicated now that I don't know how to fix things, I don't know . . . ," he finished, his voice trailing off.

"What is so complicated?" Maddy asked.

Jack sighed deeply. "It's because of my job."

"What job? What do you do?"

As he looked at her his eyes softened and a wisp of a smile creased his face; Maddy thought that he looked tortured, as if the truth was agony.

"I can't tell you," he said.

"Why not?"

Jack took a couple of paces in the alley before kicking a rock and sending it skittering into an old barrel. Absently, he ran a hand through his dark hair before turning back to face her.

"The man who I work for is very demanding," he began. "He asks me to do dangerous things all over the country. Once I finish a job, it's only a matter of days before I'm sent to do another. I'm often put in a position where I have to betray people's trust, lie to their faces, do whatever it takes to get the results that are expected. There've been a couple of times where I was lucky to have come out alive."

"Who is it? Who do you work for?" Maddy pressed.

"I said I can't tell you."

"Jack . . ."

"Trust me when I say that this is better . . . for both of us . . ."

It was clear that Jack didn't want to tell her any more, regardless of how desperate she was to hear it. Learning the truth was going to be difficult. Still, she had to try.

Though it disgusted Maddy to think about what had happened between her and Jeffers in the speakeasy the night before, especially the feeling of his hand on her breast, painfully squeezing it, she remembered what he'd told her about Jack, things that were meant to put doubts in her head.

"Jeffers told me that you offered him money," she said bluntly. "He said you were working for a man in Seattle and that you were back in Colton because he'd sent you to buy land for him."

Jack laughed out loud. "He sure didn't

waste much time. I reckon he had plenty to say about me, but I doubt any of it did me any favors."

Maddy paused. She thought of all the things Jeffers *had* said, about how Jack couldn't be trusted, about how he'd only come back to town long enough to do some business before he'd leave as he'd done seven years before, about how he was only using her for cheap thrills for old times' sake. But then she recalled Jeffers's own declarations toward her, his unwelcome advances, the way he'd touched her, and the fear she'd felt at being alone with him.

Her revulsion must've been plain on her face, for Jack suddenly asked, "What happened, Maddy? Did Jeffers do something to you?"

"Nothing," she answered with a slight hitch in her voice. "It's nothing."

"If he did anything . . ."

"I told you it's nothing," she said angrily, though much of it was toward herself for how she'd behaved in the cellar. Maddy knew it would be easier to tell Jack what had happened. From the way he'd reacted there was little doubt that he'd confront Jeffers. But that wasn't what she wanted. What had happened in the speakeasy was for her to deal with. She'd fight her own battlon. "Nothing that I can't handle. I'm not the frightened girl you knew."

Jack didn't argue further, but Maddy could see he wasn't happy.

"Is what Jeffers said true?" she asked again, refusing to let the matter go.

Jack slowly shook his head. "No," he said. "I was lying to him. I've been lying about it to everyone in town."

"But why?"

"I already told you," he repeated slowly, "I can't tell you why. Just understand that if the man I work for found out that I'd told anyone my real reason for being here . . . I don't want to imagine what he'd do to me."

"What about the man Dr. Quayle's caring for at the Belvedere? Does he work for the same man you do?"

Jack looked shocked. Then, just as she thought he was about to ask her how she came to know such a thing, he gave a short chuckle. "Is there anything about my coming back to Colton that Virginia Benoit hasn't spread all over town?"

"I doubt it," Maddy answered truthfully.

"Ross works with me," he admitted. "We were sent here together, but we'd only been in town for an hour when his appendix burst. If it wasn't for the doctor, he'd probably be dead."

"And no one knows why the two of you are here?"

"You know more than anyone," Jack replied, his green eyes holding her in place with intensity.

Maddy felt the truth about Jack's return as a tickle in the back of her head, as something tantalizingly close but just out of reach. It was there in what he'd told her, mixed in with the lie he'd given Jeffers, in things he'd said on their bridge. Remembering the questions he'd asked about her, her father, about goings-on around town, suddenly brought it all into a clearer focus until she felt something slip into place.

"This all has to do with the speakeasy, doesn't it?" she asked.

Jack looked away quickly but not fast enough to keep Maddy from seeing that her guess had struck true.

Slowly, Maddy began to put the pieces of Jack's puzzle together. She thought about everything he'd told her, about how the man he worked for was demanding, how Jack had to do difficult, dangerous things, how he seemed afraid to imagine what would happen if he failed to complete the task he'd been given, and how he claimed she'd be better off not knowing the truth. Now she knew that it was all connected to the speak-

many. When she added all of these things together, there was only one possible conclusion she could reach.

Jack is working for the Mob!

Maddy couldn't believe it, yet there it was, right in front of her! She couldn't imagine the man Jack had been, the person *she loved,* being caught up in such a dangerous way of life, but what else could it be?

"Are you all right?" Jack asked; once again, her face must have given her away.

"I'm . . . I'm fine . . . ," she answered, unable to meet his eyes.

"Maddy . . . ," Jack said, hurrying her; eventually, she looked up at him, his face shielding her from the sun, and she felt her heart skip. "I know it's hard to —"

"Shhh," she said, placing a finger against his lips. Right then, with everything she'd begun to understand about him, she realized that none of it really mattered, not so long as she knew how he felt about her. "Do you love me?" she asked him. "Right now, right here, just tell me."

Jack's eyes warmed as they searched her face. She knew this time was different, that he wouldn't be evasive like he'd been on the bridge, that he wouldn't tell her to trust him and that they'd talk about it later. This time, whether she agreed with the answer or

290

not, she'd know.

"I do," he said, melting her heart. "I've never stopped."

Maddy couldn't have said which one of them initiated their kiss; as she listened to him tell her the words she'd longed to hear, her own desire was so great, her passion to feel his lips pressed against hers so overwhelming, that she may have acted first, grabbed hold of his arm, pressed herself against him, leaned up as she closed her eyes, and begun to hungrily kiss him. Or it could have been Jack. Either way, she let herself go, feeling the heat of his skin, listening to the sound of her heart in her ears, smelling the familiar scent of his skin, and tasting his tongue as it pressed against hers. There, by the back door to her family's store, she finally felt as if the barrier between them had been broken through, that somehow, someway, they would find their way back to each other. Even if Jack was involved in something as dangerous as the Mob, she'd find a way to set him free.

No matter what, she'd make sure that they were together, just as they'd always meant to be.

CHAPTER EIGHTEEN

Jack walked back to the hotel with his hands in his pockets and his head somewhere up beside the wispy clouds that had begun to blemish the otherwise clear sky. Replaying his conversation with Maddy over and over in his head, he wrestled with conflicting emotions; on the one hand, he was angry with himself for telling her as much as he had, but on the other, he knew he couldn't lie to her.

I'd have told her everything if she wasn't involved with the speakeasy.

But no matter how much he wished otherwise, she *was* involved and there was nothing he could do to change that. His career as a lawman had been spent investigating and arresting criminals who'd done exactly what Maddy was doing now. She was guilty, and he knew it. Still, he'd done nothing to report her to Pluggett, had told Ross nothing about what he'd discovered, but instead, all he *had* done was tell her that he was still in love with her.

Jack knew that kissing her again only made things more complicated, but there was no point in denying that holding her in his arms, feeling the passion explode between them, was exactly what he wanted.

"If I'm so blasted lucky, how come I'm making such a mess of things?" he mumbled to himself.

Nearing the Belvedere, Jack stopped on a street corner and wiped the sweat from his brow. As he was putting his handkerchief back in his pocket, he heard the low grumble of an engine and the complaint of shifting gears. Looking up the road, he saw a truck coming toward him, a large one with wooden-slat railing up both sides of the trailer bed. Two men sat in the cabin, but they were too far away for him to see clearly.

Jack couldn't have said why, but there was something about the truck that made the hairs on the back of his neck stand up. Rather than cross the street and go on his way, he waited, watching as it approached. As luck would have it, the driver turned directly in front of him, giving a clear view of the cab.

Sumner Colt sneered out the passenger's side window at him, staring daggers with a throat that didn't need to be spoken. Across the cab, Jack saw Jeffers Grimm behind the wheel, his eyes never leaving the road, his face a mask of determination and menace. Even as they drove away, Sumner leaned out the open window to look back at Jack, as if he were a growling dog.

Where are the two of them going in that truck?

"Did you see that stupid son of a bitch just standin' there?" Sumner almost shrieked, pulling his head back inside the truck's cab. "You shoulda just run us up on the corner and squashed him like a bug!"

"Quit your bellyachin'," Jeffers growled, his eyes never leaving the road or the task at hand. "Just 'cause he knocked you flat on your ass ain't 'nough of a reason for us to try and kill him in broad daylight. Hell, he probably didn't have no idea who we was."

"He was lookin' right at me!"

"That's 'cause you was stupid enough to be hangin' out the window!"

"I still owe him a lickin'," the boy threatened. "He best not think I'm gonna forget it, 'cause I ain't!"

"You'll get your chance."

Jeffers drove the empty truck over the Lewis Bridge and then off the main road and up into the hills outside Colton. The way immediately worsened, full of deep holes and grooves washed out by rainwater that pulled the truck first one way and then another, bouncing the two of them around in the cab. It'd be like this the whole way. Thankfully, they'd be at their destination within an hour.

"You reckon he knew what we're up to?" Sumner asked.

"How would he?"

"He saw the truck."

"What in the hell would that tell him?" Jeffers snapped. "Jack Rucker's too busy chasin' after Maddy Aldridge and tellin' everyone in town what a big shot he is to pay us any notice. He ain't got no more idea what we're doin' than a damn dog sunnin' his balls by the side a the road would!"

The truth of it was, Jeffers had far more important things to worry about than someone watching them drive by; the phone call he'd gotten from Jimmy Luciano that morning telling him it was time to come pick up the last load of booze from Canada was enough. He would rather have waited until near nightfall before setting out, when it was dark enough for them not to draw any unwanted attention, but Capone's lieutenant had been adamant; they had to go now because of the Canadian side's timetable. Once all the hooch was stored in the mercantile's basement, Jeffers was to call Luciano and they'd set up a time for it all to be handed over. Once that happened, Jeffers would get paid a hefty sum, he'd have proven his worth to Al Capone, and he'd be out of Colton and off to better, more lucrative things somewhere like Chicago or Kansas City.

This is my big chance, and I ain't gonna mess it up.

"I can't stop thinkin' 'bout what I'm gonna do with all that money!"

Jeffers glanced over at Sumner; the boy was bouncing around in his seat and it wasn't all on account of the rough road. He was bubbling over with so much impatient excitement that he looked like a kid waiting for Christmas morning.

"What're you gonna do with your share?" Sumner asked.

"Ain't no use thinkin' 'bout it till we have it."

"Aw, where's the fun in that?"

"What we're doin' is business," Jeffers snarled. "It ain't fun, boy."

"I know, I know . . ."

"You better."

What Jeffers *didn't know* was what he was

going to do with Sumner once the job was completed. To Jeffers, Sumner Colt was a useful fool but a fool nonetheless. Though the boy was a loyal flunky who did everything he was told passably well, Jeffers still couldn't imagine bringing him along when he moved on to bigger and better things; it was embarrassing enough to deal with the Canadians with Sumner loitering around; most of the time, Jeffers made him stay in the truck until business was finished. Then there was the matter of Sumner leaving the speakeasy unattended. How could he be trusted completely? What if the next time the mistake was even worse? Jeffers's only flunky was a failure.

Jeffers knew exactly what *he* himself was: strong, ruthless, *and* smart. He had the brains to plan big crimes and the toughness to carry them out. Once he got somewhere better, he'd have no trouble finding others to work for him as he rose up to Capone's heights, maybe even higher.

As for Sumner, he'd have to be dealt with. There was no point in leaving any loose threads to dangle.

Before he left Colton for good, there was one other thing Jeffers swore he was going to take care of; he was going to tear every last shred of Maddy Aldridge's dignity from her. After last night, when she'd rejected his advances, going so far as to look offended, even disgusted, by them, he knew he'd have to take what he wanted by force. It would be violent, full of screams, blood, and tears.

It'll be fun.

Maybe he could kill two birds with one stone. Maybe he'd give Sumner what he so desperately wanted and let him loose on Jack Rucker. Maybe he'd let the boy carve that bastard up while he had his way with Maddy in the other room. The thought caused a hardness to grow in his pants.

Jeffers gripped the steering wheel tighter as he began to smile.

Determined to find out where Jeffers was going, Jack decided to find someone who might know. He headed for the Lewis Bridge, cut through a tangle of evergreens, almost lost his footing hurrying down a sharp, rocky incline, and then leaped over a rotten wooden fence beside which stood a pile of cordwood and an axe buried several inches into an old tree stump. His legs and lungs burned, but he knew there wasn't any time to waste; who knew how far Jeffers and Sumner could get before he set off after them? The thought made him run even faster, regardless of the pain.

Ahead of him was a cabin that had seen far better days: shingles that had fallen off the roof lay here and there on the ground; a burlap flour sack had been placed over a broken window; and a pile of old food tins leaned precariously against a front door that looked to be off its hinges, resting against the frame. He could only hope that his memory was correct and that the person he needed still lived there or was even home.

Skidding to a stop, he pounded on the door, grabbing it quickly before it fell inside the cabin.

Long seconds passed with no answer, but just before he was about to knock again, a pair of hands grabbed the door from the inside and pulled it away.

"Why, I'll be! Jack Rucker! What the heck're you doin' here?"

Clayton Newmar stood in the doorway looking like hell; Jack wondered if either he hadn't gone to sleep yet or he'd just waked up. Heavy dark bags underlined narrow, bloodshot eyes. His shirt was buttoned up only halfway, the buttons done up out of order. One thin hand scratched intensely at his scraggly beard, as if he had an itch that wouldn't quit. Jack couldn't help but wonder if Clayton was in any condition to give him what he needed.

"I need your help," Jack said, knowing he had no choice but to ask.

"Well, you done come to the right place, buddy." Clayton beamed, suddenly showing more life. "What do you need?"

"Your family used to trap up in the hills around town, didn't they?" Jack asked. Besides sitting with him at the side of the river eating mud pies, his strongest memory of Clayton was of the boy working beside his father as they skinned the animals they'd caught: red-tailed foxes, rabbits, squirrels, beavers, and every once in a while an enormous bear or fearsome wolf. Once they'd scraped the pelts clean, they'd put them out to dry and all the children around town would come to look. If Jack's recollection was right, that meant that Clayton would know all of the many ways in and out of the woods, all of the secret trails and roads that were off the beaten path. If Jeffers was doing what Jack thought he was, going to pick up another load of illegal liquor, Clayton would have the best idea as to where he was headed.

"Sure did," Clayton answered, looking at Jack curiously. "You wanna go huntin' somethin' up?"

"In a way," Jack replied. "Can you think of anywhere someone would go, up in the

300

hills, if they didn't want anyone to see what they were doing?"

Clayton kept scratching at his beard. "There's lots a places," he said. "There's that trail that winds round Cooper's Outcrop, the valley where the Shannonburr River's dried up most a the summer, you could hike up the trail south a the Barston Ridge, but the goin's so rough you'd be better off hitchin' a ride on the back of a mountain goat, then there's —"

"Not like that," Jack said, cutting him off. "What I'm looking for is somewhere you could drive a truck, a big one, somewhere wide enough for it to fit."

"A big truck?" Clayton repeated. "Huh . . . well, I reckon there's a couple of spots up north could do it." He finally stopped his scratching, his eyes narrowing before he asked, "Why're you askin'? You wantin' to drive somethin' up there?"

Jack knew that in order to gain Clayton's cooperation he'd have to be more forthcoming than he would've liked. The more he revealed, the more questions the other man was sure to have. But Jack had no choice but to plunge ahead.

"I need to follow someone," he said.

"Who?"

"Jeffers Grimm."

Clayton sneered as if he'd suddenly smelled something gone rotten. "Messin' with Jeffers ain't the best way for a fella to make sure he stays upright," he explained. " 'Member I was sayin' to you the other night that he ain't the sort you should go gettin' tangled up with."

"All I want to know is where he's going," Jack answered. "Believe me, I don't want trouble with Jeffers any more than you do. I may've been gone for a while, but I haven't forgotten how dangerous he can be. But I need someone who knows his way around the woods. If I go after him on my own, I'll get lost faster than you can snap your fingers."

Clayton looked as if he was mulling it over. Jack braced himself for the barrage of questions that was sure to follow. What did he think Jeffers was doing out in the woods? Why did he want to go after him? Even if they did find him, what were they going to do next?

Instead, Clayton nodded his head slowly up and down, a big grin showing through his beard. "You know," he said, "I ain't never liked Jeffers nohow."

"You'll do it?" Jack asked hopefully.

Instantly the other man brightened, the sleep falling away from his face as he clapped his hands together, excitement coursing through his scrawny body. "Sure as rain, I'll go! Buckle up, old buddy! We're goin' on an adventure!"

Half an hour from Clayton's home, Jack wondered if he hadn't made a mistake.

"Are you sure this thing will get us there?" he asked.

"Don't you worry none," Clayton answered. "It's been up and down all these hills 'nough times to know the way on its own!"

Jack held on to the beat-up, worn-down truck's rickety door frame for dear life as they sputtered and clanked their way down the road. When Clayton had first led him to it, he'd had to stifle a laugh. To say that it had seen better days would be an understatement: rust had eaten through so much of the truck's body that there was a hole in the floor of the cab; the seat upholstery was so badly ripped that springs had worked through, digging into Jack's back; and there was a dent in the hood so deep that rainwater had pooled in it. The steering wheel looked as if it was about to come off in Clayton's hands. Even the windshield wiper was in a state of disrepair, occasionally swinging back and forth as if it had a mind of its own, making a screeching grate against the glass.

"It just likes wavin' to folks now and 'gain," Clayton explained.

The only thing worse than the truck's condition was the way it handled on the road. Going around even the gentlest of curves made the vehicle's frame shudder so violently that Jack worried it was about to slide off the undercarriage, leaving the wheels to go on without them. Every tree on the side of the road suddenly became a threat, something they were about to smash into, the truck racing out of control.

"I rode on a donkey once that was a smoother ride than this," Jack said.

"Now don't you go makin' fun of ole Roger here," Clayton replied, his voice a bit wounded as he patted the seat beside him as if the truck were a horse, a companion, even a friend. "You'll hurt his feelin's."

"Roger?" Jack asked. "Your truck has a name?"

"Course he does! That way it don't seem so awkward when I'm talkin' to him while we're drivin'. Ain't you ever named somethin' ain't 'live?"

"No, I haven't."

"I hate to tell you," Clayton chuckled, "but y'er missin' out! Makes things a hell of a lot easier when you need to cuss it out!"

Clayton drove the truck down into a recess of the valley perpendicular to the river before turning it up toward the hills. Stands of elms and oaks, interspersed with evergreens and cinquefoil bushes, lined both sides of the road so deeply that they choked out most of the sunlight. Jack had a faint memory of traveling this road as a boy, but he couldn't even have said what direction they were heading. After a series of winding bends, Clayton slowed before picking his way through some overgrown brush onto a road so faint Jack hadn't even noticed it until they were on it.

"I had no idea this was here," he marveled.

"Ain't many folks do," Clayton replied. "My pa was the one who cut it through the brush as a shortcut to the better trappin' spots. Every other year or so I gotta bring the axe up here to keep the woods from takin' it back."

Jack imagined that that was a heck of a chore; even now, branches and leaves scraped against the truck's door and reached through the open window to claw against his arm. For several minutes they crawled along the wilderness path before Clayton slowed, a patch of huge thistles blocking the way.

"Looks like I ain't been as good 'bout my weedin' as I thought." He chuckled. "We gotta get past, so Roger'll have to push 'em flat."

Revving the engine, Clayton eased the battered truck forward and slowly forced their way through. Once on the other side, Jack was amazed to find a wide road snaking through the woods.

Clayton took the still-rumbling truck out of gear.

"Gonna have to take a closer look," he said before jumping out of the cab as Jack followed. Clayton ambled over to the road they'd met and knelt down, inspecting the ground at his feet.

"Just like I figured," he crowed, pointing at the unmistakable sign of tire tracks that had cut through the dirt and dust, crushed leaves and grass flat, and smashed a couple of fallen sticks. "A truck's just been through here," he explained. "Big one, too. The way I reckon it, it's gotta be the one Jeffers is drivin'."

"What's up ahead?" Jack asked, pointing up the secluded road.

"A lake that collects snow runoff, a couple a clearin's, and if you keep goin' far 'nough, you'd wind up in Canada."

With that, Jack knew that his hunch had

led him to the right place. Undoubtedly, he'd been lucky to be standing on the street corner when Jeffers and Sumner drove past. He'd also done the right thing by going to get Clayton. Somewhere up ahead, Jeffers was picking up illegal liquor from Canada, just as the Bureau had suspected. To go ahead now would be dangerous, but Jack had to be certain. He had to see it for himself.

"Let's go find that truck."

CHAPTER NINETEEN

Clayton drove the truck up the rough road Jeffers and Sumner had taken for another ten minutes before pulling off to the side and into a narrow gully notched between two trees. It was a tight fit; Jack could barely squeeze out of the passenger's side door. Clayton rustled up broken tree branches and uprooted small bushes, placing them around the rear of the truck and the side that faced the road.

"If they was comin' up the same way we just did, then only a blind man could miss seein' it sittin' there," he explained. "But since they'll be drivin' the opposite way, odds are they ain't gonna notice it when they go past."

"How much farther is it to where you think they stopped?"

"It's a bit of a walk, but the border's just over that ridge," Clayton said, pointing farther up the road. "Since this is the only place big 'nough to hide Roger, it's as far as he goes. The rest is on us."

As they made their way up toward the crest of the hill, Jack gazed up through the thick canopy of trees, the leaves shifting in the slight breeze. The sun had begun its descent, but there were still hours of daylight left. If Jeffers was doing what Jack suspected he was, it was odd that he'd be brazen enough to act in the middle of the day; most booze runners did their business under the cover of darkness. Still, it was hard to imagine that Jack had misunderstood what he'd seen. Why else would they be driving such a large truck up into the hills? There had to be a reason.

At the top of the hill, the road went down a bit before turning sharply to the left and out of sight.

"We best pick our way through the trees from here on out," Clayton suggested. "It ain't but a ways farther."

Pushing into the trees and bushes, nearing the end of their search, Jack began to feel the familiar pangs in his gut, the unmistakable feeling of danger lurking somewhere ahead. Not for the first time since he'd set off after the truck, Jack wished that he had his Bureau-issued pistol, but it was still in his dresser drawer in the Belvedere; there'd been no reason to take it with him to meet Maddy and he hadn't yet gone back to his room before seeing Jeffers and Sumner drive past. But now, faced with the possibility that he might need to use it, Jack felt vulnerable. If they could just stay out of sight . . .

"What is it you suspect Jeffers is doin' up here?" Clayton asked, pushing through an overgrown bush and holding it until both of them had passed.

Jack took a deep breath before deciding on the truth. "I think he's picking up a load of liquor from Canada."

"For the speakeasy?"

Jack nodded.

Clayton looked to be mulling the matter over, chewing on the inside of his lip. "So what's that matter to you?"

This was the question Jack had been waiting for Clayton to ask. There were a couple of lies Jack could try to pass off, he could always try to stall, to put it off like he'd done with Maddy, or he could tell the man the truth. After everything Clayton was risking in leading them to Jeffers, the least he deserved was an honest answer, but giving him one would destroy the cover Jack had been instructed to use.

Sometimes, the only thing to do is take a

"There's a reason I needed you to get me here," he began. "It's why I came back to Colton. I need to know what Jeffers is doing because I work for —"

But before Jack could say another word the unmistakable sound of men laughing loudly sounded ahead. Instinctively, he and Clayton crouched low to the ground and began to work their way through the underbrush, toward the sound. Jack followed as Clayton dropped beneath the boughs of an evergreen, crawling among fallen pinecones and across a carpet of dried needles. Clayton signaled to slow, easing toward a rocky outcropping; it wasn't until Jack was beside him that he realized the tree clung precariously close to the edge of a short but sheer hillside. Slowly, he leaned up and peeked over the edge.

Jack looked down into a valley that had been carved between two rocky outcroppings, their sides worn smooth over countless years of rain, wind, and ice. The ground between them was littered with fallen stones. The road he and Clayton had been following snaked down out of the trees and into the depression. There, at the widest spot of the valley floor, stood two large trucks, their engines rumbling as they idled.

As Jack watched, Summer slammed the back hatch of one of the trucks shut, closing the door on dozens of oak barrels and crates. Several other men dawdled between the two vehicles, smoking and talking. There, in the thick of it all, was Jeffers.

"Looks like yer hunch was right," Clayton whispered.

"It was *your* good thinking that led us here."

"You reckon that's booze in the back end a that truck?"

"As sure as we're lying here."

"Makes me thirsty just lookin' at it," Clayton observed with a wink. "So what do we do now?"

Truthfully, Jack didn't have an answer. He had what he needed: visual proof that Jeffers was bringing liquor illegally across the border. All it would take was a message to Lieutenant Pluggett and the Bureau of Prohibition would come raining down on the whole operation.

But that included Maddy . . .

There was another burst of laughter and it looked like things were breaking up. The Canadians walked back toward their own truck; as they went, Jack caught a glimpse of machine guns slung over shoulders. Moments later, the truck began moving with a grinding of gears. There was just enough room in the valley for the driver to turn it around. The man in the passenger's seat gave a wave before driving out of sight, leaving Jeffers and Sumner alone in the woods.

Almost alone.

Jack couldn't help but watch Sumner. The young man stood at the rear of the truck, looking like a petulant child who'd just been told off by his father. Angrily he kicked at rocks at his feet, his hands sunk in his pockets, his face creased by a deep scowl that looked an awful lot like the one he'd directed at Jack when they'd first driven past. Something had happened, but Jack had no idea what.

"Get your ass in the truck," Jeffers growled. "We gotta get back so we can stash this away."

"Okay, okay," Sumner mumbled in answer.

But then, just as he was about to do as he was told, rounding the end of the truck, he looked up and came to a sudden stop. It took Jack a moment too long to realize that the thug was staring *right at him.* Sumner's eyes grew wide with surprise, then narrowed in fury. What he did next was even more shocking.

Instead of shouting out a warning to

Jeffers or cursing Jack's name, Sumner pulled out a pistol and started firing.

Jeffers was just pulling open the door to the truck's cab, his mind turning over how he'd have to hide the alcohol somewhere, maybe even out at his place, until they could unload it at the mercantile after nightfall, when the sudden, shocking sound of gunfire began to echo off the rock walls around him. His first thought was that someone was trying to take what was rightfully his, to put a bullet in him and steal the liquor he'd just loaded, cutting in on the business arrangement he'd built with one of Al Capone's top lieutenants. Jeffers's hand flew to his waistline and yanked his gun free, and he quickly pointed it in one direction, then another, and then yet another in the hope that he'd see someone to shoot before he was cut down. But then, even as the sound of the last gun blast ricocheted all around him, he heard Sumner shouting.

"I seen ya, you son of a bitch! I seen ya!"

Goddamn it! What in the hell's he doin' now?

As if Jeffers hadn't already had his fill of problems with the boy, Sumner had not taken kindly to being told to stay in the truck while Jeffers dealt with the Canadians. Instead of just doing as he'd been told, he'd

314

whined and moaned until Jeffers finally relented, snapping at him to help load the booze into the truck. Even then, the few times Jeffers had glanced Sumner's way, it was clear the boy was out of sorts. And now, to make matters even worse, he was firing the gun Jeffers had reluctantly given him, shooting into the woods.

Jeffers raced around the rear of the truck just as Sumner fired yet again, the gun bucking in his hand, the sound deafeningly loud. Furious, Jeffers yanked the weapon from the boy's hand, the barrel hot against his skin, and then grabbed a fistful of Sumner's shirt and spun him around.

"What in the hell're you doin'?" Jeffers shouted.

Sumner looked crazed: his eyes were wide and wild; spittle wet his lips, his fury barely restrained. He tugged relentlessly against Jeffers's grip, trying to get loose, as if he were a dog on a leash, tired of being tied up on a hot summer day.

"I seen him!" Sumner shouted. "I seen him up that hill!" he pleaded, pointing up at the tree line to the south. Jeffers's gaze followed, but he couldn't see anything but evergreens and rocks.

"There ain't nothin' up there," he growled.

315

"He was there, Jeffers!" the boy insisted. "He was!"

"Who was it?"

"That bastard Rucker! He was pokin' his head over the edge and watchin' us! He musta followed us from town and now he —"

Jeffers slapped Sumner in the mouth with the back of his hand as hard as he could; it sent another crack echoing around the small valley. The boy's head snapped to the side and blood immediately began to trickle down his chin from a cut on his lip. Jeffers had hit Sumner because he wanted to knock some sense into his thick head, to make him see how crazily he was behaving, but when he looked back at Jeffers he seemed as unhinged as before, maybe worse.

"It was him!" Sumner refused to back down. "I swear it!"

When Jeffers raised his hand to hit him again, the boy shied away in fear, still trying to get free from the larger man's grasp, but he didn't stop pleading.

"I saw him!"

"You're imaginin' things," Jeffers snarled.

"I'm not!"

"Think 'bout how crazy you're talkin'! How in the hell would he a known what we were doin'? How could he follow us? You think he *ran* all the way out here?"

Sumner's head kept looking back over his shoulder, back up to the hilltop he'd been pointing at. "I don't know how he done it," he said. "All I know is what I saw! He was there, Jeffers, honest!"

Jeffers couldn't have said exactly what it was that made him wonder if there wasn't some truth to Sumner's claims. Maybe it was the fact that the boy had stuck to his story even after getting popped in the mouth and threatened with another. Maybe it was because there was something about Jack Rucker that still didn't sit quite right with Jeffers. Or maybe it was because he was cautious by nature and especially now, so close to the reward he'd worked so hard for, he wasn't in the mood to take any chances. Besides, it would hurt nothing to check things out . . .

"You saw him up there?" Jeffers nodded toward the hilltop.

"I did!" Sumner persisted.

"Then let's go take us a look."

Jack pressed himself flat on the ground beneath the evergreen tree as the first bullets whizzed overhead, ripping through the branches and careening off the rocky hillside. It wasn't the first time he'd been shot

317

at, but it was something he'd never gotten used to. Even though he knew he was out of Sumner's line of sight, he still held his breath, fearful that the next shot would tear through him. Somewhere over the ringing echo of the gun blasts, he could hear shouting.

"We gotta get outta here!" Clayton hissed beside him.

"Let's go," he agreed.

Without another word, Jack burst out from under the tree and began running as quickly as he could. Dodging boulders, ducking low-hanging branches, and pushing through bushes in his path, he ran through the woods as fast as he could, straining to get away from Jeffers and Sumner as if his life depended on it, which it did. Without his revolver, there was no chance that he and Clayton could overcome the two criminals. If they caught up to them, they wouldn't survive; they'd be shot down like dogs, without mercy.

On and on, Jack ran, his heart thundering in his chest. He expected to hear Jeffers shouting his name behind him or the crack of another gunshot just before the bullet slammed into his back, but there was another part of him thinking about Maddy, about how much he wanted to see her again, to hold her in his arms, to kiss her lips and tell her the honest truth about his life. It was that desperation that fueled him forward, that made him run faster, until his legs and lungs burned from the effort.

I've got to get away! I've got to!

But just as Jack jumped a fallen tree, its branches cracked and rotten, he had to struggle to stop himself, his skidding foot kicking a few loose rocks over the edge of a precipitous drop, sending them tumbling toward the churning river far below. For a moment Jack could do nothing but stare dumbfounded, completely unsure of where he was. Looking down, he understood that the cliff face was too sheer to descend and the water too far below and too fast to even consider jumping.

He was trapped.

Seconds later, Clayton pulled up beside him, his hands on his knees, breathless. But instead of being as surprised as Jack was, he looked angry. "What'n the hell're you doin' runnin' *this* way?" he asked.

"What are you talking about? I was trying to get away!"

"You run out from under that tree sideways." Clayton frowned. "You been goin' 'longside the valley 'stead of away from it. To the west, it curves backward till it runs smack into the Lewis," he explained, pointing to the river down below. "I was tryin' to get your 'tention, snappin' my fingers and such, but I couldn't make too much noise for fear them fellas'd know we was there. All I could do was follow till you stopped."

Angry at himself, Jack spat, "Damn it!"

"Ain't no point in gettin' worked up 'bout it now," Clayton answered. "What's done is done. What we gotta be concerned 'bout is gettin' back the way we come, then to Roger, without bein' seen."

"Can't we just skirt along the river?" Jack suggested, pointing along the cliff face and against the water's flow.

Clayton shook his head. "Brush is too thick round these parts," he explained. "With where we'd have to go, tryin' to work through that'd take all night and into tomorrow. Only choice we got is headin' back the way we come."

Jack frowned. That way was back toward Jeffers and Sumner, back toward bullets being fired at them, back toward danger. Still, the thought of spending the night hacking through the underbrush wasn't appealing, either. Besides, it would take too much time. They had to make it back to the truck so that he could get back to Colton, decide what to do with his discovery, and make sure that Maddy was protected from the two criminals who'd somehow ensnared her in their plans.

There was no other way.

But just as Jack made his decision, something occurred to him.

"You could've gone on without me, you know," he said to Clayton. "If you'd kept running the right way, you'd have made it back to the truck and be safely headed back toward Colton by now. Coming back for me only put you at risk."

"Can I ask you somethin'?" Clayton answered.

Jack nodded.

"If this was your neck of the woods, if you was the one knew your way round, if I'd been the one run outta there without a clue where I was goin', would you a come after me or would you a saved your own hide?"

"I would've run after you," he answered truthfully.

A huge grin spread across Clayton's face. "That's 'cause a real friend don't leave the other in a tight spot no matter how stupid a thing he mighta done." He chuckled. "Now let's get the hell outta here!"

"I know he was up here! I seen him!"

Jeffers watched with growing annoyance

as Sumner thrashed around beneath an evergreen tree. This was the spot where he swore he'd seen Jack Rucker watch them load smuggled booze into their truck. They'd hurried up the narrow road and then plunged into the woods, but so far they'd found nothing and no one. Jeffers was beginning to feel foolish for having bought into the boy's claim.

"Look at this!" Sumner suddenly shouted, pointed excitedly around the base of the tree. "Somethin's been rootin' round in here!"

"It coulda been a rabbit or squirrel, maybe a fox." Jeffers shrugged.

"Naw, it's too much for that," Sumner insisted.

Jeffers walked over and looked down at the ground; it *did* look like more than an animal could make, but for all he knew, Sumner had stirred it up and was trying to convince himself it was something more.

Jeffers sighed. Looking around, he saw only the forest staring back, nothing but trees and rocks and bushes as far as he could see, which wasn't very far. Undoubtedly, it stretched on for miles without end.

"He ran on this way," Sumner exulted, walking with his head down, following something as it led away to the west.

"You a tracker now?"

"Just come on," he insisted, scurrying off.

Jeffers walked along behind halfheartedly for a couple of minutes as Sumner led them down a gentle depression and through a tight grove of trees; as he hurried along, the boy seemed to be mumbling to himself. Suddenly Jeffers was struck by the absurdity of what they were doing and stopped walking.

"We ain't goin' no farther," he declared.

"Come on, Jeffers," Sumner pleaded, looking back at him. "We just gotta find him! We gotta! He was watchin' us!"

"Right now, I don't give a damn if Rucker was up here or not," Jeffers snapped. "The only thing that matters is gettin' that truck back to town. We're fools for wanderin' off into the woods and leavin' it unguarded. We gotta get back to town."

"Then I'll go on by myself," Sumner argued.

"I said *we* gotta get back," Jeffers growled, wondering how far the boy was willing to push the matter. "I ain't unloadin' it by myself."

Sumner looked desperate. "But he could be just up ahead," he argued. Pointing at a couple of large rock outcroppings twenty feet away, he said, "He could be hidin' right behind them for all we know!"

"Now why in the hell would he stay round here with the way you was shootin' at him?" Jeffers asked. "If I was him, I'd be long gone from here by now."

"But the tracks —"

"Come on," Jeffers snarled. "We're leavin'."

This time, Sumner did as he was told, though he looked as enthused as he'd been about every other thing Jeffers had ordered him to do all day. As he trudged past, his feet dragging in protest, Jeffers knew that the time was coming fast when he'd have to figure out what to do with the boy once and for all.

Jack and Clayton waited quietly behind the rock outcropping they'd hurried to at the first sounds of Jeffers and Sumner approaching. For several long and anxious moments, they'd stayed frozen in place, listening to the two criminals argue about whether they should go farther; Jack found himself rooting for Jeffers to win out. As the argument dragged on, Jack had been too frightened to breathe for fear he'd give him and Clayton away. Sumner had no idea how right he'd been; they *were* behind the rocks, just as he'd suggested. Fortunately, he and

Jeffers hadn't come any closer. Still, it wasn't until well after the two men had walked away and the sounds of the heavily liquor-laden truck had long since quieted that Jack and Clayton dared to venture into the open.

"That was closer than I woulda liked," Clayton sighed with relief, "but long as they didn't see us, everythin' worked out."

"Except for the fact that Sumner's still convinced he saw me."

"I wouldn't worry 'bout that none. After all, he hated you plenty 'fore he suspected you of followin' him into the woods."

Jack knew that Clayton was right. Still, he knew that the next time he set foot in the speakeasy he and Sumner were going to have fighting words; if the man started firing bullets into the woods at the sight of his face, what would happen when Jack was standing right in front of him?

"We best be gettin' back to Roger 'fore there ain't no light left to the day," Clayton said.

In some ways, Jack was thankful he'd have the whole ride back to Colton to figure out what he was going to do next.

CHAPTER TWENTY

"So what was it like kissing Jack again after so many years?"

Maddy spun around from the kitchen counter where she'd been cutting carrots and looked at Helen. She sat at the small table nearest the window, absently thumbing through her favorite Hollywood gossip magazine. Though she was looking down, acting as if her question was nothing out of the ordinary, Maddy could still see the faintest wisp of a smile.

"How . . . how did you . . . ?" she stumbled, so taken aback that she was nearly speechless.

"Because I was watching you through the window in the back corner of the storeroom," Helen replied as if it were the most obvious thing in the world. "You really didn't expect me to stay at the front counter, did you?"

"You shouldn't be spying on people,"

Maddy said, annoyed.

"Oh, come on, now." Her sister laughed, closing her magazine and finally looking up, her eyes full of mischievousness. "The two of you are the most exciting thing to happen in this town in I don't know how long! Everyone is talking about you, so when I have the chance to watch something happen firsthand, I *have* to take it! I almost broke my neck climbing up on a stack of crates to get a better view, although it was worth it. What I saw was sure better than what's written in here," she explained, rifling the pages of her gossip magazine. "Besides," she added with a frown, "I figured you would've told me all about it by now. I didn't expect you'd keep it to yourself . . ."

The truth was, Maddy had had a hard enough time understanding what had happened between her and Jack that it would have been impossible to tell someone else. She just couldn't believe that Jack was a *gangster!* Over and over, she tried to come up with another explanation for what he did for a living, something that would explain the things he'd said, the way he described the man he worked for, or his reluctance to give her many details about the life he'd led for the last seven years. But she hadn't been able to come up with anything. Instead, she'd kept their conversation, and their kiss, to herself. The problem was that she hadn't counted on someone spying on them. Still, she understood why Helen was disappointed.

"I would've told you eventually," Maddy offered.

"When?" her sister asked. "After he'd asked you to marry him?"

"Helen!"

"I'm kidding." The girl laughed, raising her hands as if she were surrendering. "You're not really mad at me for watching, are you?"

"No," Maddy admitted.

"Good! Then you won't mind telling me what it was like," Helen prodded again, her voice practically dripping with excitement. "Tell me everything!"

"I don't know . . ."

"Please!" Helen pleaded.

Maddy sighed; her sister wouldn't let up unless she told her *something*. "Well . . . it *was* nice . . . ," she began, remembering how it felt to be in Jack's arms and to have her lips against his. "Whenever I'm with him now, sometimes it feels like nothing's changed between us, but at others, it's completely different. I still get upset about how he left, but there's no use denying how I feel about him."

"How *do* you feel?"

"I love him," she answered, a flutter racing across her heart.

"Did you tell him?" her sister asked.

Maddy nodded.

"Well, what did he say? Did he tell you he felt the same?" Helen pestered her. "I swear it's like pulling teeth to get anything out of you!"

"It's not that bad," Maddy said, laughing. "I just don't believe in spreading my business around like the women you read about in your magazine."

"Aw, you're no fun! Give me something!"

"I told you," she said. "It was nice."

"I suppose I can understand why you can't come up with anything more to say. Jack's more handsome than ever!" Helen observed. "I think his good looks have you tongue-tied."

"Really? Do you think so?"

"Absolutely! With his dark hair, *those eyes* that go on forever, and his broad shoulders, he looks like he could be an actor up on a movie screen. I could see Jack playing a soldier or a cowboy or a policeman —"

"Or a gangster," Maddy blurted out before she could stop herself; immediately she flushed bright red with embarrassment, looking at her sister to see if she'd given her fears away, but Helen didn't seem to have noticed.

"No," she answered, crinkling up her nose as she gave the idea thought, "he's not rough enough to play a part like that. It just wouldn't be believable." Suddenly Helen's eyes brightened. "But I could sure see him in a romantic feature after watching the two of you kiss! Wouldn't he look great up on the screen beside Jean Harlow?"

"I'd rather he was next to me." Maddy frowned.

"You know what I mean!"

As the two of them laughed, Maddy thought about how it felt to be loved by Jack Rucker after all the years they'd spent apart. Helen was right; he was still incredibly handsome, as well as smart, funny, and everything else Maddy had ever wanted in a man. No one else compared. She thought about the vow she'd made to herself as they'd kissed behind the mercantile; no matter what, she'd help him break free from the mobster life he'd somehow gotten himself involved with. Their love would prevail. They'd make up for the years they'd spent apart and start anew together.

"So what are you going to do when Jack

leaves you again?" Helen asked, her voice soft and cautious, breaking into Maddy's pleasant thoughts.

"What do you mean?"

"Well, I hope you don't think that he's going to stay here forever," her sister explained. "Virginia Benoit told Eunice Manfreddson that Jack came back to Colton for business. That means he's going to eventually go away."

"Not necessarily," Maddy argued.

"Maddy, he told me that he's been to places like Chicago and San Francisco, even Los Angeles. If he's been to cities as big as those, as exciting as those, what possible reason would he have for wanting to stay here?"

Though it pained Maddy to hear Helen making some of the same arguments that Jeffers had buffeted her with in the speakeasy, she wasn't particularly surprised. Everyone in town was enjoying gossiping about her and Jack's unexpected reunion, but no one expected their love to last. But then, no one had seen them on their bridge or on the back steps of the mercantile; what everyone remembered was when she slapped Jack in the mercantile. What Maddy wanted was to prove everyone wrong, to love and be loved in return.

In the end, Maddy had to believe that she knew the answer to Helen's question. She hoped that there *was* a reason Jack would want to stay.

Me . . .

". . . estimate that the amount of money being lost to organized-crime operations totals well into the millions of dollars nationwide. This scourge is rampant! Whether it's prostitution, the shakedown of honest businesses for protection kickbacks, drugs, murder, or especially the proliferation of alcohol, an act that the government has deemed illegal through the enactment of Prohibition, it is the undeniable duty of every honest American to stand up against this foe and fight for the sake of self and country! Only then can we be safe! Only then —"

Silas leaned over with a groan and shut off the radio, breaking the hold that the on-air preacher's sermon had held on Maddy. She'd stood at the end of her father's bed with his dinner tray in her hand for a long minute, mesmerized, hanging on the firebrand's every word, but in the silence that followed she shook herself free of his grasp and offered her father a weak smile.

"He seems passionate," she offered.

"Pastor Mead's a bit of a blowhard if you ask me," Silas shrugged, "but that doesn't mean I disagree with the message. If you want to hear the rest, I could always turn it back on."

"No, I'm fine," Maddy answered a bit too quickly. "I just got caught up in it for a minute, that's all."

Even as she placed her father's meal on the bed beside him, Maddy thought about what she'd heard on the radio. Living in Montana, far removed from the hustle and bustle of city life, it was hard for her to imagine the impact organized crime could have. All she knew was what she'd read in the newspaper and heard on the radio. With all the problems at the mercantile and her family's struggles dealing with Silas's deteriorating health, she already had plenty to worry about. Still, what she knew seemed frightening and dangerous.

And somehow, Jack has gotten himself tangled up in it.

Maddy had taken some solace in Helen's declaration that Jack didn't look the part of a gangster, but now, minutes later, she was already wavering. It was true that Jack didn't resemble the men Hollywood cast as thugs, mobsters, and cutthroats, driving dark cars and firing machine guns, but that was the movies. What sort of people were they in real life? Was it really possible that Jack Rucker, the man she'd loved so passionately, had believed would be her husband, had wanted to spend the rest of her life with, had become involved in something so corrupt? Thinking about how he'd held and kissed her, Maddy couldn't bring herself to believe it.

Maddy began tidying up her father's bedside table, but just as she was about to leave and start getting ready to go to the speakeasy she noticed that he was staring at her, his hand absently turning his spoon in his stew.

"Is there something wrong with your meal?" she asked.

"I'm sure it's fine," he replied, still watching her.

Maddy hesitated. It was as clear as the moon rising outside her father's window that there was something he wanted to talk to her about; from the grim look creasing his face, she doubted that it was anything she wanted to hear.

"Are you going to choir practice tonight?" he asked.

"As soon as I finish cleaning up in the kitchen."

"How's it going?"

"Pretty well," Maddy answered, a sliver of unease flaring in her stomach. "I don't think my singing is ever going to turn heads, but I'm getting better."

Her father nodded, his jaw clenched so tightly that it looked to her as if he was gnashing his teeth. For a long while, he didn't say a word in answer, letting the silence between them drag on so long that Maddy's discomfort steadily grew.

"Did I tell you I had a visitor earlier this afternoon?" he finally asked. "Someone who came by while you were at the store?"

"No, you didn't," Maddy replied.

"Reverend Fitzpatrick was nice enough to stop by," Silas explained. "He stayed for about an hour. We talked about all sorts of things."

Maddy could only stare as her knees grew weak; she felt as if the floor beneath her were dropping away. Her heart pounded and her mind raced. This was the moment she'd worried about ever since she'd agreed to Jeffers's scheme. This was when all of the many lies she'd spoken would come home to roost.

"Dad, I —"

"The reverend came to see me because he said the Good Lord had given him some perspective on how I've been feeling," Silas said, talking right over her. "Apparently, he's been so sick for the last week that he's been unable to get out of bed and had to cancel church on Sunday."

"Let me explain —"

"When I asked him if that included the choir practices, he said it had," her father continued with a hint of a smile, as if there was something funny in his daughter having consistently lied to him. "He said he was so sick that if he'd tried to stand there and conduct, he was liable to either pass out or throw up, and neither one was very appealing to him."

"Just listen for a —"

"And then I started thinking about all of the times last week you brought me my dinner, just like tonight," he said, the anger in his voice growing more pronounced with every word. "I remembered you saying that you were going to practice a couple of times, but after what Reverend Fitzpatrick told me, I imagine it must've been pretty hard to practice if you were the only one there."

With that, Maddy's father fell silent, but now, without him interrupting her every attempt to explain herself, she suddenly found herself unable to muster any words in her own defense. Instead, she stared and worried. The reverend hadn't known what guarded secrets he'd been revealing, but Maddy couldn't help but wonder what else he'd let out of the bag. Had he told her father about the speakeasy? After all, the reverend had been a regular customer and may have assumed that Silas knew what was happening. If her father had learned the truth, she could only imagine how disappointed he must be.

"Don't you have something to say for yourself?" he demanded.

"I think you already know," she answered.

"That you lied to me again!"

"I didn't mean to hurt you —"

"And yet you did precisely that by not telling me the truth!" Silas thundered. "Why is it that I keep getting visitors who tell me all of the things my daughter is doing? The secrets she's keeping! What else aren't you telling me?"

"Nothing . . ."

"That's what I thought the last time. And that's why I want to hear you say it! I want the truth! I want you to admit what you've done!"

At this point, Maddy wondered what the harm could be in doing what her father wanted; it was obvious that in talking to the reverend he'd learned something about the speakeasy. But just as she was about to steel herself and attempt to offer an explanation he talked over her yet again.

"I want you to admit that you weren't going to your choir practice because you were spending time with that no-good Jack Rucker!"

For the second time in a matter of days, Maddy was both relieved and surprised that her father hadn't learned the truth about the speakeasy. Both times, her relief had come at Jack's expense. But this time instead of listening demurely as Silas ranted and raved about the man to whom she'd given her heart, Maddy began to grow angry.

"The last time we talked about Jack," she explained, "you only told me to be careful. You didn't say that I shouldn't see him again."

"I don't want you to get hurt!"

"Then you have to start trusting me a bit," Maddy said. "I'm not the girl I was seven years ago."

"But if he were to leave —"

"Then I'll deal with it." In her heart, Maddy knew it was true. Maybe Helen, her father, and even Jeffers were right: As soon as Jack got the chance, he was going to bolt back to wherever he'd come from. He'd come back to Colton for business and all she was to him was a distraction from his past. He'd have his fun and then go. If that happened, she'd look like a fool around town. Everywhere she went, people would lower their voices, whispering about poor Maddy, about what a pathetic laughingstock she was, gullible enough to believe in love twice.

Or maybe something else will happen.

Maddy believed that her faith in Jack would be rewarded, that the love she again felt blossoming between them would be enough to make him abandon the dangerous life he'd become involved with and let them have the future she'd always dreamed of. She clung to it tenaciously, ready to fight whoever she had to, do whatever it took to make it so, even if she risked failure.

But whatever happened, the consequences were hers to bear.

"But why didn't you tell me the truth?" Silas continued, not willing to let his argument go. "Why did you have to lie?"

"Maybe it's because I'm tired of having to listen to all of your complaints about Jack," she snapped back, finally allowing her anger and irritation to show. "Ever since the day his family came to town, you've never given him a chance. No matter how hard he tried, no matter what he said or did, you turned your back on him and made certain you told me he wasn't worth my time!"

"You're my daughter," Silas offered. "I only wanted to protect you."

"Until Jack left the way he did, he'd never done anything to deserve the way you treated him! You should've been happy for me! You should have wanted him to be the son you never had, for us to get married and have a family of our own! But you couldn't do that. Instead, you did everything you could to keep us apart, making him wait outside the store out of sight, making it so unbearable that I had to sneak out my bedroom window in the middle of the night just so we could be together!"

"You did what?" her father asked incredulously at the secret she'd just revealed to him after keeping it hidden for years.

"But I'm not the girl I was then," Maddy vented, ignoring his question. "I'm a woman now, and I'm going to make my own decisions, right or wrong, regardless of what anyone else thinks! If that means I want to spend time with Jack, if I want to tell him I love him, that I want to be with him, then that's exactly what I'm going to do!"

With that, Maddy stalked from her father's room, slamming the door shut behind her,

her heart pounding and her head spinning.

From behind her, she heard Silas shout out to her, "Maddy! Maddy, wait! Let's talk about this! Maddy!"

But she kept right on walking, down the hall and then the steps. Tonight she'd tell Jack everything. She'd insist that he tell her about how he'd gotten tangled up with organized crime, and together they'd find a way out. She'd offer him her heart and trust that he wouldn't break it again.

And to hell with whoever disagreed.

CHAPTER TWENTY-ONE

"Stop here."

Clayton did as Jack asked and pulled the battered truck to the sidewalk in front of the bakery. Outside the dirty windshield and open windows, night had descended on Colton, wrapping it in a blanket of stars. Even at such a late hour, just like the first night after his return, there were people out and about, many more than before, most of them headed in the same direction.

Maddy's speakeasy.

The trip back to town had taken far longer than Jack hoped. He and Clayton had waited a long time to be certain Jeffers and Sumner had really gone and weren't lying in wait, watching to see who might eventually walk out from the trees. When they'd finally made it back to the truck, Clayton had driven them on a different, winding road that had initially led them even farther from Colton, before eventually curving back. While it had only taken a couple of hours to get to the site of the illegal liquor transaction, the return had lasted nearly three times as long; even with the long days of June, enough time had passed for night to descend. Finally, they'd entered town from the opposite direction from which they'd left. Still, it had been the right decision; there was no point in taking the chance of being seen, even if it was well past sunset.

"You sure you don't wanna go back to the Belvedere?" Clayton asked. "After all we just been through, can't say I'd blame you fer wantin' a hot meal and a bed. Ain't no shame in callin' it a night."

Jack didn't answer, watching the people head toward the tavern, his mind spinning, a plan forming.

"I don't much like that look you got in yer eye," Clayton said, correctly reading Jack's intention. "I ain't much of a gamblin' man, but I'd put some coins down that yer thinkin' 'bout goin' to the speakeasy."

"I am," Jack admitted, nodding slowly.

"You sure that's what you wanna be doin'? After all, Sumner just shot bullets at you. You come walkin' through the front door, he's gonna have an easier time of it than firin' blind into the trees."

"All the more reason to go."

Clayton scratched his beard. "Talkin' in riddles like that ain't doin' nothin' but confusin' me."

"Just listen," Jack said, warming up to the idea that was taking form in his head. "If Sumner believes he saw me in the woods, would he expect me to come to the speakeasy tonight? No," he answered his own question. "He'd figure I'd stay far away. This way, he has to wonder about what he saw. It'll confuse him. Hopefully, it'll give me a chance to learn what they did with a truck full of alcohol."

"I think yer givin' Sumner too much credit for thinkin'," Clayton disagreed. "That boy ain't one for usin' his head."

"There's a first time for everything."

"Rollin' the dice like that seems risky to me."

No matter how much Clayton tried to dissuade him, Jack had made up his mind; he was going to the speakeasy. But there was more to his reasoning than he was willing to admit to. Though he'd seen what Jeffers and Sumner were up to with his own two eyes, there were still unanswered questions, first among them being where they had taken the liquor. Still, as much as he remained determined to do his job as an agent of the Bureau of Prohibition, to smash the illegal liquor operation and arrest those responsible, he was equally resolute in wanting to protect Maddy. If she was at the speakeasy, he was convinced she was in danger. He had to keep her safe.

Jack opened the door and stepped out onto the sidewalk. Clayton got out from behind the wheel, looking at him over the truck's roof.

"Yer gonna go through with this crazy idea?" he asked.

"I have to."

"Well then." Clayton said with a chuckle. "I reckon that means I'm goin' with ya."

"This isn't your fight," Jack replied.

"Aw, hush that talk! What kind a friend would I be if'n I let you go alone?" With a wink, Clayton added, " 'Sides, last time you treated me to one hell of a show!"

"Here you are."

Maddy placed the glass of whiskey on the makeshift bar in front of Seth Pettigrew anticipating that it would quickly disappear, so she was more than a little surprised when he didn't reach for it right away; it wasn't often that a drink set before the former lawyer remained in place for more than a few seconds. She was even more mystified when she looked up to find him staring at her intently.

"Is . . . is something wrong . . . ?" she asked.

"With me, no," he answered. "But I can't help but wonder the same of you."

"What makes you say that?"

"My dear." Seth smiled easily, his face turning up as smoothly as a well-oiled door. "You don't spend as many years as I did trying to pry the truth out of witnesses, information most of them were hell-bent on keeping to themselves, without learning how to read what's written on a face."

"And what is mine telling you?"

"That you're lost in thought, with a touch of worry and unease thrown in for good measure."

As much as Maddy would've liked to contradict him, she knew there wasn't much point; after all, Seth was right. Ever since she'd left home and walked hurriedly to the speakeasy, her thoughts hadn't drifted far from the heated argument she'd had with her father. It wasn't like her to raise her voice like that, especially toward Silas, but when it came to her relationship with Jack it often felt as if *everyone* was determined to stand against her, against *them*. Though she had let her frustration boil over, Maddy didn't regret it.

"Is it that obvious?" she asked.

"As the nose on your face." Seth chuckled before finally picking up his drink and downing it in one swallow. "Now, if I were standing in a courtroom, trying to convince the members of the jury to see things my way, the next question I'd ask was whether your current doldrums had anything to do with Jack Rucker . . ."

"You must've been a pretty good lawyer."

"One of the best, if I do say so myself."

"Then I'm sure you'd be happy to know you're right," she admitted. "Ever since Jack came back, it feels like he's the only thing on my mind."

"Understandably so."

"When I first saw him, I couldn't help myself; all of these emotions came rushing back and there wasn't anything I could do . . ."

"What I witnessed from this very stool that night was quite a testament to that," Seth agreed. "But then I think most everyone in this room would have agreed that Jack had at least one good slap coming to him."

"When I ran out of here . . ."

"You didn't want to talk just then, you were overwhelmed . . ."

"But then when I saw him again, it was easier, I listened to his explanations, and things began to change . . ."

"After all those years together, things couldn't have changed that much . . ."

Maddy wondered if this was like being a witness in one of Seth's trials, baring her thoughts, eased along with words of encouragement until she'd spilled every last secret she held. It occurred to her that it might be best to hold her tongue, but now that she'd started she didn't feel like stopping.

"Now that we've spent time together, now that we've . . . ," she explained, trailing off, unable to speak of their kiss, "there's a part of me that wonders if we might still have a chance to be together, that we can start over, but everywhere I turn, it feels like everyone's against me, like I'm a fool for even hoping . . ."

"That's because most people are either unwilling or unable to take a chance," Seth replied with a hint of pity. "They're afraid. Whatever the reward, it isn't worth the risk. But that's not how I see things."

"It isn't?"

"Absolutely not," Seth answered, giving her a smile that must have been quite successful in the courtroom. "I've always been a bit of a risk taker, and while things haven't always worked out as I would've liked, even with a couple of complete disasters mixed in, I don't have many regrets. But when it comes to love," he explained with a wink, "my advice would be to take that leap of faith. If your number comes up, it'll change your life."

"But what if it doesn't work out? What if I fall flat on my face in front of everyone?"

"Then you get back up, dust yourself off, and try again." He shrugged. "You've already done it once. Remember, you might not like how folks in this town flap their gums about you and Jack," he said, cutting her off, "but that's because they all remember the unmistakable love you had for each other. Most people live their whole lives without a single taste of what you've had. That's why, if you don't take the chance you've been given, you'll spend the rest of your life regretting that you didn't try to get it back." Seth looked at her long and hard, letting his words slowly sink in, before his face broke into a wide grin. "Now how about another one?" he asked, holding up his empty glass.

"On the house," she said, before placing her hand lightly on his and adding, "Thank you for that."

"You're quite welcome, my dear."

Maddy lifted the whiskey bottle and was just about to pour when she happened to glance across the crowded bar and see Jack coming in through the front door with Clayton Newmar. Jack was staring right at her, but their eyes met only for an instant, long enough for a flutter to race across her heart, before Sumner Colt blocked her view, his hands balled into tight fists, his body coiled like a rattlesnake, confronting Jack in such a way that Maddy knew, without a shadow of a doubt, that there was going to be trouble.

Jack betrayed no emotion as Sumner whipped open the door to the speakeasy, took a half step back, and looked at him with disbelief, as if he couldn't bring himself to accept who was standing before him, as if the dead had suddenly come back to life. In the awkward silence that followed, Jack stepped carefully inside. He had just enough time to look toward the bar and find Maddy's eyes. Relief flooded him that she was safe and sound; it was a struggle to keep his features calm. Clayton entered right behind him.

"What'n the hell're you doin' here?" Sumner asked, his voice low but full of bristling menace.

"I thought I might have a drink," Jack answered.

"Don't tell me we're gonna go through this whole song and dance again," Clayton added. "Where's Jeffers? I wanna talk to him."

Sumner's eyes never left Jack's face; he wondered if the flunky had even heard a word Clayton had said.

"I done saw you," Sumner hissed, his face contorted in fury. "I saw you watchin' us up there'n the hills. I know you was there!"

With all of his years as an undercover agent to draw on, Jack had no trouble making his face reflect bewilderment. "What are you talking about? What hills?"

Rather than giving Sumner a reason to doubt his claim, much as Jack had hoped, his denial only served to enrage the thug further; he'd taken a chance, one that appeared to have failed miserably. Angrily Sumner stepped closer, his hands balled into tight fists, looking like he wanted to tear Jack limb from limb.

"Don't lie to me none," Sumner threatened, his breath hot and sour. "I saw you with my own two eyes! I don't know where you went when me'n Jeffers was lookin' for ya, hidin' like the coward you is, but I know you was there! If you'd a shown your face a

351

second longer, I'd a put a bullet right 'tween your eyes!"

"You *did* see me today," Jack said, making Sumner straighten up at the admission, "but it was when you and Jeffers drove past me near the Belvedere." Now that he'd knocked the man off-guard, Jack decided to try to keep him that way. "What were you hauling in that big truck, anyway? Whatever it was, it couldn't have been small. Or were you picking something up?"

"And what's all this nonsense 'bout shootin' a gun?" Clayton interjected. "I reckon he musta been drinkin' too much of what's bein' sold in here. That's 'bout the only way I figure he coulda come up with such a cockamamie story like that."

"Look, I understand you're still mad about what happened in the alley," Jack added. "Let me buy you a drink and we can let bygones be —"

Before he could say another word, Sumner attacked, either unwilling or unable to hold his fury back any longer. Though he'd anticipated such a thing happening, Jack was surprised by the speed with which his foe struck, and a glancing punch landed against his jaw, dazing him with pain.

"I knew you was trouble from the moment I laid eyes on ya!" Sumner snarled, his fists raised, the sinewy muscles of his arms tight. "I told Jeffers you was no good, that you was gonna have to be dealt with, so now that's exactly what I'm gonna do!"

Jack had never understood why, at the beginning of a fight, men suddenly started talking. By ranting and raving, Sumner had given up his advantage, allowing his opponent a moment's respite to find his footing and chase the cobwebs from his head. Now it was up to Jack to make use of the gift he'd been given.

"I guess I'll just have to show you how much trouble I can be," Jack replied.

Fast as a bolt of lightning, Jack's fist shot out and hit Sumner flush against his already-broken nose, snapping his head back, causing his eyes to water, and forcing a yelp of pain to jump out of his mouth. Jack followed up with a hook to the ribs, driving the air from Sumner's lungs and sending him scrambling backward, surprise and pain written across his face.

An audible gasp rose from the crowd around them; Jack didn't dare risk a look, but he imagined every face in the speakeasy was turned in their direction. Snippets of conversation drifted across the cellar.

". . . can't believe it!"

"I ain't gettin' involved with all that!"

"Jack better be careful!"

That last comment caused a smile to curl at the corners of Jack's mouth. Everyone in the bar, heck, everyone in Colton, would've been surprised to know how many fights Jack had been in. Before he'd left town seven years earlier, he would've been far more likely to try to talk his way out of trouble than use his fists. But one of the lessons he'd quickly learned during his time with the Bureau was that, on occasion, there was no choice but to fight.

This was one of those times.

In coming to the speakeasy, his intention had been to learn more about what Jeffers had done with the illegal liquor he'd loaded, not to get into a brawl. But he'd underestimated Sumner's hatred for him. He'd knocked the bootlegger unconscious once already; he'd have to do it again.

"You're gonna pay for that, you son of a bitch," Sumner groaned.

"You're welcome to try."

Once again, Sumner came at Jack swinging, but this time there was nothing unexpected about it and it was easy to sidestep the blow. The young man's fist hit nothing but air. Now with Sumner unable to defend himself, it was easy for Jack to land another heavy blow to his midsection; immediately his face twisted into a grotesque mask of agony as he was driven off his feet. Sumner landed on the floor in a heap of arms and legs, knocking over a couple of chairs and nearly upending a table, forcing people to scatter out of the way.

"You done bit off more'n you could chew," Clayton said to Sumner, rubbing salt in the wounds of his defeat.

Sumner looked as if he wanted to get up and continue the fight or, at the least, say something to defend his wounded pride, but he remained still and silent. Jack felt no pity for the boy, after all, he'd started their fight, but he felt no sense of victory, either; that wouldn't happen until Sumner and Jeffers were behind bars where they belonged.

"Now how 'bout that drink?" Clayton asked.

"I suppose I've earned —"

Jack never saw the blow coming. He was struck on the side of the head with enough force to lift him off his feet, just as Sumner had been, and send him hurtling through the air. Pain grabbed him so hard that he wasn't really aware of landing on the cellar floor and only faintly heard the shattering of glasses and the panicked scraping of chair legs trying to get out of his way. Blackness filled the edges of his vision, threatening to overwhelm him and drag him down into its inky depths. The side of his face was hot and numb, all at the same time. He struggled to remain conscious

"What . . . what's . . . ," he mumbled.

Before Jack could do anything else, a hand grabbed a fistful of his shirt and lifted him from the floor. He hung there like a child, unable to do anything to defend himself.

"What in the hell're you doin', Rucker?" a voice bellowed.

Even if he hadn't been able to see through the haze clouding his eyes, Jack would have known who it was immediately.

Jeffers.

CHAPTER TWENTY-TWO

Maddy gasped as Jeffers stepped from the darkened shadows at the rear of the cellar and punched Jack in the face. Only seconds before, she'd marveled at the beating being given to Sumner, but now, as she watched the man she loved awkwardly crash to the floor, sending chairs and people scattering in every direction, fear clutched tightly at her heart. It was as if Jeffers had simply appeared out of nowhere; everyone in the speakeasy had been fixated on the fight. Now, as Jack's almost unconscious body was effortlessly lifted from the floor, no one moved a muscle.

Except for Maddy.

For the second time since Jack had returned to Colton, Maddy found herself running across the speakeasy. But unlike that first night when she'd been desperate to escape but unsure of where to go, this time she had no such confusion; regardless of the danger, she'd make it to Jack's side and keep him safe, no matter what. Even as Jeffers bellowed a threat, his deep voice rumbling across the smoky cellar, making everyone near him cringe with fright, Maddy wasn't afraid.

I won't let him be hurt.

"You think you're gonna come in here causin' trouble?" Jeffers ranted. "No one fights in my place! No one!"

"It's my place, too."

Jeffers's head snapped around quickly at the sound of Maddy's voice. She immediately worried he was about to attack her, too, his eyes narrow and full of rage, like a bull pawing a hoof against the ground, readying to charge. Even with her thundering heart and knees that threatened to quiver, Maddy refused to back down or show weakness; a man like Jeffers would devour her if she did. Instead, they stared at each other, the silence of the speakeasy deafening.

"This ain't your problem, Maddy," Jeffers finally warned.

"You made it mine when you attacked Jack."

"He went at Sumner."

"Who everyone in here will tell you started the whole thing."

"I ain't in the mood to be disagreed with."

"Neither am I. Put him down," Maddy demanded.

The glare Jeffers gave her was nearly as unsettling as the feeling of his hand on her breast. Maddy knew that there weren't many people who'd ever spoken to him in such a way and walked away unscathed. Everyone in town knew Jeffers wasn't a man to mess with; even Clayton looked taken aback by her boldness. But to protect Jack there was no risk she wasn't willing to take.

"I said, put him down," she repeated forcefully.

Maddy expected Jeffers to argue with her, to spit curse words and threaten her with all sorts of terrible things, but the thin smile that spread across his face was far more frightening. He did as he was told and lowered Jack gently to the floor, letting go of his shirt and stepping back; Maddy was surprised that he hadn't dropped Jack down with a thud.

Without another word, Maddy hurried over and knelt down by Jack's side. Already his face had begun to swell and bruise. Looking up at her with dazed eyes, he looked disoriented, as if he were lost in the woods. Absently, his hands tried in vain to push himself up off the floor.

"Don't try to move," she told him. "Everything's going to be all right."

"But I . . . I . . . I have to . . ."

"You don't have to do anything but let me take care of you."

Maddy didn't know if Jack understood what she was telling him, but he nodded and stopped moving. As she brushed a stray lock of hair from his forehead, her heart swelled at being able to save him from whatever punishment Jeffers had been hell-bent on dishing out. Remembering Seth's words of encouragement, Maddy was more determined than ever to stand up for the love she again felt blossoming between her and Jack. Gently, she slipped her hand in his and smiled when he gave it a light squeeze.

"Listen up!" Jeffers suddenly shouted. "It's time for everybody to get the hell out! Bar's closed for the night!"

Even after Maddy had successfully stood up to him, there were only a few grumblings to Jeffers's demand.

". . . just got here . . ."

"But I haven't finished my drink yet . . ."

". . . the fuss if the fight's over?"

Jeffers snarled as he roughly yanked Sumner back to his feet; from the bared-teeth grimace on the younger man's face and the hand that never left his ribs it was obvious he was still in a lot of pain. "Any of you here when Utley came through know I ain't gonna take no chances," Jeffers snapped, meaning that if the sheriff got wind of there being a fight there was a chance the whole operation could be shut down. "We'll be open again tomorrow."

Slowly but steadily, people began making their way toward the cellar door. As they passed, Maddy looked up into faces that showed a mix of both admiration and concern for what she'd done. She knew their worries were well-founded; the last thing she wanted was to be left behind with an irate Jeffers and Sumner.

Hoping to slowly clear the cobwebs from Jack's addled head, Maddy placed her hand on his chest and leaned down close.

"We need to get out of here," she whispered.

Jack made no answer, his head turned to the side.

Worrying that he'd finally succumbed to the pain of Jeffers's punch and slipped into unconsciousness, she shook him gently. "Jack," she said more urgently, "You have to wake up!"

"I'm . . . I'm fine, Maddy . . . ," he replied in a voice stronger than she would have expected.

It was then that she realized Jack's eyes were open and that instead of resting, he was looking at something. Following his gaze, Maddy peered through the mess of people still filing out of the speakeasy and into the dark gloom at the back of the cellar. There she could faintly make out the open door of the storeroom and glimpsed the mess of boxes and crates that filled it. Usually, Jeffers kept that door locked, telling Maddy that it was to protect the small amount of liquor he'd set aside to sell; he must've been inside when he heard the commotion of Jack and Sumner's fight and forgotten to close the door when he left. Now, she couldn't help but wonder if he'd been lying to her; even if the room held most of the mercantile's overstock prior to the opening of the speakeasy, there shouldn't have been *that* much.

"Help me get to my feet," Jack asked of her.

Grabbing him by the elbow, Maddy tried to lift him, but she wasn't strong enough, especially since he wasn't yet steady enough to help. But even as she wondered how she was going to get Jack out of the speakeasy, Clayton Newmar bent down and hooked his arm beneath one of Jack's.

"C'mon now, pardner," Clayton said.

"I'll get the other," Seth Pettigrew announced, having been reluctantly forced off of his beloved barstool.

Once Jack was upright, still as shaky on his feet as a newborn calf, the bruising on his face growing darker with every passing second, he looked at each of them in turn and gave his thanks.

"Like I done told you earlier, bein' in this here tavern with you is a guarantee of seein' some entertainment," Clayton answered with a booming laugh. "If the only price I gots to pay for it is helpin' you up a flight a stairs, well, that seems more'n fair, you ask me."

"Since you were kind enough to help me home the other evening after I'd had too much to drink, reluctant though I am to admit it," Seth explained, "I wouldn't be much of a gentleman if I didn't return the favor."

Maddy couldn't contain her smile. With help from Clayton and Seth, she'd be able to get Jack out of the cellar and home safely. Now all they had to do was make their way past Jeffers and Sumner.

"Let's go," she said, joining the last of the speakeasy's patrons as they headed toward the door.

"Where'n the hell do you think you're goin'?" Jeffers snarled as they approached. Sumner had fallen into his usual chair by the door but didn't look up; it was clear from his pained expression that he'd gotten the worst of the brawl.

"You said it yourself," Maddy answered. "We're closed."

"I wasn't talkin' 'bout you."

"She's . . . coming with us . . . ," Jack said valiantly.

"I'd a thought you'd took enough of a beatin' to keep you from mouthin' off."

"It takes a tough man . . . to strike someone . . . when he isn't looking . . ."

Jeffers sneered. "Next time, I'll let you know I'm comin'." Turning back to Maddy, he added, "There's things we gotta talk 'bout."

"We can talk about them tomorrow," she replied.

"We'll talk now," he growled.

Standing up as straight as she could, steeling herself, as well as remembering that there were three men standing behind her, Maddy moved a step closer to Jeffers. "Whether you like it or not, I'm taking Jack home, *right now,*" she explained, her voice firm, her eyes never leaving those of the much larger man. "But you're right, with everything that's happened tonight, there are plenty of things we need to talk about, but they're going to have to wait. Understand?"

Jeffers's only answer was the deepening of his scowl.

With that, Clayton and Seth led Jack over to the cellar door and began to slowly help him up the steps. Maddy followed along behind, but just as she thought she was going to get away without any problems Jeffers's hand shot out and grabbed her arm, squeezing it like a vise.

He moved up close behind her, his weight pressing lightly against her back, his breath rustling her hair as he leaned down close. "You had better start rememberin' who it is you're talkin' back to," he threatened. "The last skirt who stood up to me ain't never stood right 'gain, *understand?*" he added with an agonizingly painful squeeze of her arm before he released it.

Even though she'd been set free, Maddy stood still for a moment longer; she couldn't have said if it was out of defiance or fear. Finally, without a word or another look back, she went up the stairs and out into the dark night.

"Land sakes! What happened to him?"

365

Virginia Benoit clutched her nightdress to her chest as she rushed out from behind the front desk of the Belvedere and helped Clayton and Seth steer a still-dazed Jack across the lobby and down the hallway toward the room. Maddy hurried to keep up with them, all of their shadows dancing wildly across the faded wallpaper and closed doors. To her surprise, even at the late hour there'd been a light on in the back room when they'd opened the front door; Maddy wondered whether Mrs. Benoit had been awake in order to tend to Jack's mysterious partner, the man Dr. Quayle had told her father about.

"He run 'foul a Jeffers, is what happened," Clayton explained.

"Why on earth would he tangle with *him?*"

"I'm afraid he didn't have much choice in the matter," Seth answered. "The dear boy never saw it coming."

"Up till then, he'd handled himself perty good," Clayton added.

Looking over her shoulder, Virginia asked, "I take it he was over in the mercantile's cellar?"

Maddy nodded; there was something in the older woman's tone and the expression on her face that made her feel as if she was being held accountable for Jack's condition, which, in a way, she was.

Halfway down the hall, Mrs. Benoit threw open a door and led them all inside before hurrying over to the nightstand and turning on a lamp. When Maddy entered, she was surprised by how clean and orderly it was; if it weren't for the closed suitcase slid between the dresser and a rickety old chair beside the window, she would have wondered whether anyone was even staying there.

Clayton and Seth put Jack on the bed as gently as they could, though he still groaned when his head came to rest on the mattress.

"Should I go fetch Doc Quayle?" Virginia asked.

"It's . . . it's not that bad . . . ," Jack struggled to answer; ever since they managed to get him out of the speakeasy, he'd had moments of clarity, talking and making light of what had happened, but others when he could only moan an occasional word or two. "I . . . I just need some rest . . ."

"Sounds to me like you ain't in much shape to be offerin' an opinion."

"I've seen fellas take a hell of a lot harder knocks'n the one he got and be all fine come mornin'." Clayton shrugged. "What he needs is a good night's sleep."

"Still, it wouldn't hurt to be cautious,"

Seth offered.

"Won't Dr. Quayle be coming by tonight to check on Jack's partner?" Maddy asked; Clayton and Seth both looked at her with expressions of confusion, but Mrs. Benoit's face was full of surprise. "Mr. Hoover, is it?"

"Hooper," Virginia answered. "But no, he's already come. He ain't gonna be back till mornin'."

"Then I guess I'll just have to stay and watch over him."

No one disagreed with her; in the end, the only person to speak up against it was Jack. "You . . . you don't have . . . to do that . . . ," he attempted to argue. "I said I'll be . . . I'll be . . ."

"I'm *not* leaving," she replied firmly.

Knowing that it was a fight he wasn't going to win, as well as being in no condition to contest it, Jack nodded, laid back his head, and closed his eyes.

"If he worsens, I'll come get you," Maddy said to the older woman.

Seth and Mrs. Benoit stepped out into the hall. "Get some sleep, buddy," Clayton said before pulling the door shut behind him, leaving Maddy and Jack alone.

Moving to his bedside, Maddy looked down at Jack. The faint light of the lamp did little to chase away the shadows that filled the room; looking right at him, she couldn't tell whether his eyes were open or closed. The darkness also covered the bruising on his face, though she could still see that it was badly swollen. Regardless, she still found him handsome, as well as brave for standing up to Sumner.

"Are you comfortable?" she asked. "Is there anything I can get you?"

When the only response she heard was the sound of his measured breathing, Maddy understood that he'd already fallen asleep. Placing two fingers against her lips, she gave them a light kiss and then pressed them tenderly against his forehead.

"Sleep well, my love," she whispered.

With that, Maddy let him be and tried to figure out just how she was going to rest in that beaten-down old chair.

Maddy awoke with a start. For a panicked moment she had no idea where she was and had to struggle to calm the pounding of her heart. Blinking, she managed to crawl from the haze of sleep that enveloped her and looked around Jack's hotel room. Nothing moved. She wondered if she hadn't been woken by footsteps in the hall, maybe Mrs. Benoit was checking on them, but as Maddy continued to listen there wasn't a sound to be heard. She was just about to chalk it up to a bad dream when someone spoke.

". . . going in that truck . . ."

Maddy froze. The man's voice hadn't been loud but close, so close that it sounded as if he'd been in the same room as her. She was so frightened that she didn't dare breathe.

". . . have to know . . . he puts it . . ."

Though fear had sunk its claws into her deep, Maddy eased out of the chair in which she'd fitfully slept. She imagined that it was Jeffers and Sumner, wanting vengeance and come to take it. Slowly, she crept toward the door.

". . . only way . . ."

Halfway there, she realized that the sound was coming from behind her.

". . . only way . . . save . . . Maddy . . ."

As soon as she heard her name, Maddy understood what was happening. Moving to the side of the bed, she looked down to see Jack's arms twitching, his face all screwed up as he mumbled in his sleep. While she watched, whatever was worrying him seemed to slowly pass, his expression softening, his movements relaxing until they eventually stopped as he again drifted off into a deep sleep, leaving Maddy to wonder what it was he'd been dreaming about, as

370

well as why it had bothered him so.

It's just one more thing to add to the growing list of what I don't know about Jack Rucker . . .

Because of the way she'd woken, Maddy couldn't imagine going back to sleep. With her mind once again reviewing the secrets Jack was keeping from her, she decided to search his room for clues. In her heart, Maddy knew that it was wrong, that she shouldn't even be entertaining the idea, but the lure was too great. Looking back at Jack, seeing the swelling on his face, she began to convince herself that if she snooped through his things, if she found evidence that he was involved with the Mob like she believed, she'd be that much closer to saving him.

I'll just take a quick look.

She pulled Jack's suitcase out from beside the chair, but as soon as she picked it up she knew it was empty. When she popped the latches anyway, her suspicion was confirmed; he must have put away all of his things. Careful not to make too much noise, she began searching the dresser drawers. Each squeak made her cringe; the last thing she wanted was for Jack to wake and find her rifling through his belongings. In the third drawer, far in the back, neatly tucked away between the folds of a pair of pants, her hand touched something surprisingly solid. Working her fingers around it, she pulled it free and out into the bedroom's faint light.

It was a gun.

Looking at it, Maddy first felt disbelief, then a sickening cramp in her stomach she struggled to put down. Other than in the movies, she'd never seen one before. Her father didn't own one, and she was surprised by how big it was, by how heavy it felt in her hand. Her worst fears had been realized; what other reason could there be for Jack to have a gun than he was mixed up with organized crime? The truth repulsed her so violently that she wanted the gun out of her hand, back where she'd found it. Frantically, she jammed her hand back into the drawer's depths, tears welling in her eyes.

Why am I such a fool? How could I've ever thought Jack and I could have a future? Everyone else was right about him! My father, Helen, even Jeffers knew that he —

Then, just as she'd put the gun back between the pleated folds of Jack's pants, her hand had brushed up against something else that felt equally out of place among his clothes. Her heart hammering, Maddy grabbed hold of it and pulled it out.

It was a wallet.

Maddy desperately wanted to open it, but so far all her curiosity had brought her was more misery. Still . . .

After that gun, how much worse could things get . . . ?

Taking a deep breath, Maddy opened the wallet. There, shining brightly even in the meager light of the hotel room, was a badge, on which was written four words:

AGENT — BUREAU OF PROHIBITION

CHAPTER TWENTY-THREE

Jack woke slowly from a hazy dream, its details already fading from memory, replaced by the dull roar echoing around his skull. Even with the curtains drawn, his room in the Belvedere seemed abnormally bright, as if the sun were streaming directly into his head. Moving a hand to shade his eyes only served to make him dizzier; the room momentarily lurched one direction and then the other. Touching the side of his face set off a burst of pain like fireworks lighting up the sky on the Fourth of July; it felt tender and puffy. He could only imagine how wrecked it looked. Flashbacks of the previous night surfaced in his memory: fighting with Sumner, being completely blindsided by Jeffers, Clayton and Seth helping him back to the hotel, and Maddy insisting on spending the night in his room.

"Maddy . . ."

Though it sent a pounding sliver of pain

piercing throughout his aching head, Jack leaned up and looked around the room. It was empty. For a moment unsettling thoughts raced around his head; she'd been so insistent on getting him out of the speakeasy safely, worried about his being hurt, and brooking no argument against spending the night so she could watch over him that it seemed strange that she'd be gone now. *Did Jeffers come while I slept?* Jack knew he was being paranoid, she'd probably just gone to get something to eat, but it was worrying all the same.

The inside of Jack's mouth felt like it had been stuffed with cotton, sticky like glue, so he rolled over to the bedside table in search of the glass of water he habitually kept there. The lamp had remained on all night and its light burned bright in his eyes. Closing them, he fumbled in darkness to find the switch and turn it off. Once it had been extinguished, he groped in search of the glass but was surprised when his hand found something else instead.

"What in the . . . ?"

Cautiously, Jack opened his eyes. Squinting, he saw something that made his blood run cold and his stomach sink, as if he'd jumped off a cliff and was plummeting to the rocks below. It was his special wallet, open and folded in such a way that his badge, the one issued to him by the Bureau of Prohibition, was staring him in the face.

Even with everything that had happened to him in the last day, as hectic as it had been, even after getting punched in the face by Jeffers, Jack knew that before he'd gone to the mercantile to meet Maddy, the last time he'd been in the room before last night, he'd placed his badge, along with his pistol, back in the dresser drawer, hidden in the back inside of a pair of pants. No matter what, he wouldn't have left it lying out on his bedside table.

So what was it doing there . . . ?

Jack already guessed the answer. Maddy had found it. For whatever reason, she'd gone through the dresser's drawers and discovered his hiding place. Undoubtedly, she'd found the gun, too. She'd arranged his wallet so that, as soon as he woke up, he'd know that she'd learned his secret.

"Damn it all," he swore.

Though it was agonizing, Jack rose from the bed and lurched over to the washbasin on the dresser, where he splashed his face with water, trying to clear the cobwebs. Not for the first time since he'd returned to Colton, he cursed himself for not telling Maddy the truth about what he'd become in the long years since he left. He'd had the best of intentions, had hoped that there would be a chance to confide in her, but things between them were far more complicated than he would have ever anticipated. No matter how much he wished it weren't so, Maddy was involved in the illegal liquor operation he was duty-bound to destroy. Now his worry was that it was too late to fix their problem.

Whipping open the dresser drawer, he retrieved his pistol, stuffed it into the waistband at his back, and snatched his badge off the nightstand. Catching a hurried glimpse of himself in the mirror, he cringed; he looked like hell. But it didn't matter, not now. No matter what it took, he'd make things right. He'd find Maddy and explain himself.

Out in the hallway, Jack's head swam and his knees buckled, sending him crashing sideways into the wall. For a moment he worried he'd black out, but somehow, clawing against the plaster, he willed himself forward. He'd only managed a couple more steps when a voice shouted from behind a closed door.

"Rucker!"

Jack paused. His first instinct was to walk on and let Ross Hooper yell himself hoarse.

Though Jack had agreed to keep his fellow agent updated on what he'd found out about their investigation, this was different. Right now, he had far more important things to do than report to a man he detested, a man who'd have no idea what he was going through.

"Rucker! Get in here, damn it! Don't leave me outta things!"

He knew that talking to Ross would only complicate things further, so Jack pushed on, weaving down the hall.

"You worthless son of a bitch!" Ross shouted behind him. "I'm gonna call Pluggett and tell him everythin'!"

Even if the bedridden man went through with his threat, even if it cost Jack the career he'd painstakingly built, he was far past caring.

Out in the Belvedere's lobby, Jack stopped and stared out the windows. He'd thought it must be morning, surely no later than ten o'clock, but from the color of the sky, the western horizon streaked with purple and orange, he realized that much of the day had passed.

"What're you doin' out of bed?"

Jack turned to find Virginia Benoit coming out of the back room; from the way she looked at him, he knew she was honestly surprised to see him.

"What time is it?" he asked.

"Almost six," she replied. "You slept most of the day. I was worried 'bout you, thinkin' you was hurt worse'n we thought, but when Doc Quayle came by, he checked and said there weren't no reason to worry. You just needed your rest, is all."

If he'd slept for longer than fourteen hours, Jack knew that Jeffers must've rung his bell harder than he'd thought. But right then he wasn't the least bit concerned with his own well-being. "Where's Maddy?" he asked. "I remember her being there when I fell asleep, or did I imagine that?"

Virginia shook her head. "She stayed with you through the night," the older woman answered, "but she lit outta here so early the sun weren't barely up. Hurried right past me and out the front door without a word. Seemed more'n a touch upset."

Jack knew she had every right to be. He might not have outright lied to her face, but he hadn't been honest, either. If she was angered at discovering that he was a law officer, that he'd evaded her questions by spinning a web of half-truths, dodges, and feints, he'd earned her wrath. The only thing he could do now was give her the explanation she deserved.

He was just about to the door when Mrs. Benoit spoke.

"I may've gabbed more'n my share round town 'bout you bein' back after so many years," she said gravely, "but I give you my word I ain't gonna say nothin' 'bout what I seen in your room. Doc Quayle told me he'll do the same."

Jack immediately understood that she and the doctor had seen his badge. If he was going to be able to wrap up what was left of his investigation, it was imperative that his real identity remain a secret, at least for a little while longer.

"Thank you," he answered.

"Just promise me one thing," Virginia said.

"What's that?"

"When this whole thing's over, you'll tell me all the juicy details so's I can be the one spreadin' it round town."

"Deal," he agreed.

"Then you best get goin'. She's waitin' out there somewhere."

And that's exactly what he did.

Hurrying down Main Street, Jack tried to imagine what he might say to Maddy to make up for all he'd kept from her. Over and over again, he tried out the words, but every time he thought of something it sounded hollow, as if it wouldn't do justice to how he felt. Eventually, he stopped trying; whatever he finally said to her would have to come from his heart.

Because it was much later than he'd expected, most of the shops had closed for the day. When Jack arrived at the mercantile, its door was locked and the inside dark. Desperate, he knocked on the door, hoping to see a head poke out from the door to the storeroom, but everything remained quiet and still. Racing awkwardly around back, his head still splitting, he stumbled down the stairs to the cellar doors and found them similarly locked. Jack pounded on the door, understanding that he risked it being opened by Jeffers or Sumner, but his desperation to make amends with Maddy was great enough to take that risk. But there was still no answer.

"Now what?" he muttered out loud.

His first instinct was to walk the short distance to Maddy's home; if she wasn't still working at the mercantile, that was where she had to be. Even the prospect of confronting Silas Aldridge, a man who'd never made a secret of his contempt for his daughter's suitor, who must have spent the last seven years secretly glad that Jack had left Colton the way he had, wasn't enough to dissuade him. Even if Silas was as sick as Maddy claimed, Jack knew that the old man's protectiveness would cause the fire to rage in his belly. Jack didn't give a damn. After the years he'd spent convincing himself that he'd made the right decision in turning his back on Maddy, only to then discover how big a mistake he'd made, he understood what was at stake. For Maddy, for whatever chance they might have at a future together, he'd have walked through the gates of hell. After that, Silas didn't seem all that daunting.

But Jack had only taken a couple of steps before he stopped. Just like that, he knew he was wrong. After everything that had happened between them, after what Maddy had just learned, there was only one place she would go. It was where they'd always gone when things got rough.

Our bridge . . .

Even if she wasn't there now, she soon would be. Jack headed there as fast as he could.

Absently, Maddy kicked a stone with her foot and watched as it fell from the bridge, tumbling end over end from shadow into the fading light of the approaching dusk until it splashed into the slowly moving water of the river below. It disappeared from sight, swallowed up by surroundings that were no longer familiar, going from the bright of day to the dark depths of the water in an instant.

Maddy knew *exactly* what that felt like.

Until she had discovered Jack's gun and the badge that declared him an agent of the Bureau of Prohibition, she'd thought that he'd somehow become involved with the Mob and had been determined to save him. She couldn't possibly have been more wrong. Over and over, she'd replayed whatever she remembered of their conversations, sifting through every word, every gesture he'd made, every smile and frown, all in the hopes that she could find something that she should have recognized, something that might have given him away. But there was nothing. Once again, Jack had lied to her face.

And once again, I'm the biggest fool in Colton.

She'd left Jack's room in the Belvedere around dawn, after she'd placed his badge on the nightstand where she was sure he'd see it when he woke. Her trembling fingers had nearly dropped it on the floor. Ever since she'd found it and the gun, her head had been spinning. She'd walked past

Virginia Benoit without a word and kept right on going, up one side of town and then back the other way, trying to comprehend what she'd learned. She was glad that Helen was supposed to open the mercantile that morning and she'd had no other responsibilities needing her attention. Occasionally, she wondered how Jack was feeling, if his aches at Jeffers's hands had lessened, but it took only a second for her anger to flare. Eventually, she'd made her way to the bridge.

If he wakes up, he'll come here. Then I'll demand he tell me everything, no lies, no avoiding my questions, no —

"Maddy . . ."

Looking up from the water, she found Jack standing at the end of the bridge. Brilliant sunlight bathed him, the setting sun's orange glare painting his face, interrupted only by the gentle breeze that lazily blew through the tree branches, their leaves creating shadows that danced over his skin. Even from where she stood, Maddy could see the bruising on the side of his face; dark and swollen, it undoubtedly caused him pain, but his eyes showed no sign of it, watching her steadily. Sweat ringed the open collar of his shirt and glistened on his forearms; he must've run to her.

"Why, Jack?" she asked, her voice almost breaking.

He made no answer, still staring at her.

"Tell me why! Why did you lie to me?"

The irony wasn't lost on Maddy that she was saying the exact same things, asking the same questions of Jack, that she had when they'd last been on the bridge together.

"I didn't lie," he said, giving her the same answer as before.

Once again, Maddy found herself rushing toward Jack, tears filling her eyes while anger burned in her heart. She stomped across the bridge until she was standing before him, looking up into his eyes. Her instincts told her to slap him, just as she'd done twice before, but this time she simply couldn't. For his part, Jack looked as if he expected it to happen, but he didn't flinch or turn away.

"Why didn't you tell me the truth?" she asked, her voice pleading. "Why didn't you tell me that you were a lawman?"

"I couldn't," he answered simply.

"That's not good enough!" Maddy snapped. "There was no reason not to!"

"Yes, there was." Jack took a deep breath; it was clear that he was carefully weighing what he should tell her. "I'm an agent working undercover," he explained. "That means that no matter where I am, who I'm with, or what I'm doing, I'm always in danger. Whenever an agent forgets that and allows his secret to slip, that's when he ends up getting himself killed."

"And telling me would have put you at risk?"

"It could have."

The bluntness with which Jack answered her question made her momentarily uneasy; she could see that he believed the truth of what he'd said. Maddy couldn't imagine what that must be like, constantly worrying that his real identity might be discovered, always in danger. It frightened her.

"Why would you do that to yourself?" she asked, unable to come up with an answer on her own. "Why would you live your life that way?"

"Because it's my job," Jack answered, stepping away from her, walking over to the bridge's edge, and looking down into the river. Leaning against the railing, he ran a hand through his dark hair. "I've been working for the Bureau for four years now, and in that time I've learned that there are all kinds of bad people lurking in the shadows. By putting myself at risk, I take a chance that I can do my part to put them where they belong, behind bars."

"And that's why you're here . . . ? To put someone in jail . . . ?"

"The reason I'm here . . . is complicated . . ."

Again, Maddy rushed to Jack's side, grabbing him by the arm and turning him to face her; for his part, he didn't look away, but his eyes wore a pained expression far deeper than the bruises encircling one of them.

"Don't avoid me," she said determinedly.

Jack stared silently.

"You're here because of the speakeasy, aren't you?" Maddy asked, voicing the suspicion that'd been troubling her from the moment she'd seen his badge.

Slowly, he nodded.

"But why this one? Why here of all places?" she prodded. "I might live in some backwater town in Montana, but I know enough about Prohibition to guess that there're thousands of speakeasies around the country, tens of thousands, so why would a government agency care about the one in Colton?"

Again, Jack didn't answer, at least not directly. "I came here because my lieutenant told me to, because this was once my home."

"Then what about the man who came

here with you, Hooper, the one Dr. Quayle saved . . . ?" Maddy asked, trying to piece it all together.

"He's an agent, too."

"Is he your partner?"

Jack sighed. "I suppose so, but really he's nothing but a big pain in the ass who isn't very good at his job. I hate to say it, but having his appendix burst was a blessing, in a way."

"That's a terrible thing to say."

"It is," he admitted. "I'm glad he didn't die, but I'm just as happy that he's not running around underfoot, making my job harder."

"What job?" Maddy asked again, desperate for an answer.

Jack looked over toward the horizon; the sun had melted down into the tops of the trees, but the light still played across his face, making his eyes sparkle like jewels. "Before I left Seattle," he said, "I was given a cover story I was supposed to stick to. Ross and I were to present ourselves as buyers for a rich businessman who was looking to buy up land around town."

"The story you gave to Jeffers . . ."

"Exactly," he answered.

"So everything you told people was a lie?"

"One that I never told to you," Jack said,

staring hard into her eyes. "As a matter of fact, I went so far as to tell you that it *was* a lie."

Maddy faltered; he'd admitted as much to her behind the mercantile.

"I swore to myself that, no matter what, I *wouldn't* lie to you," he continued, gently taking her hand in his own; the warmth of his touch sent a shiver racing through her heart. "It's one thing to try to put something over on a man like Jeffers. To people like him, lying is as natural as taking a breath. When I'm undercover, I have to act like them, lie like them, *be like them,* but that couldn't be any further from the man I really am."

"And who's that?" she asked softly.

He moved a half step closer, his eyes searching her face. "I'm not that different from the boy you loved."

Maddy's heart thundered. In that moment, all she wanted was to take his answers without question, to melt into his arms and feel his tender kisses fall hungrily upon her lips. It would be so easy.

And that was why she let go of his hand and turned away.

Not until I have all of the answers . . .

"Why are you here in Colton, Jack?" she said with steel in her voice.

For a long moment, he was so silent that Maddy thought he was going to try to avoid the question yet again, but then he finally spoke. "I'm here because the Bureau of Prohibition got a report that there was an illegal liquor operation somewhere in town. Normally, you'd be right, the government doesn't have the time or manpower to chase down every speakeasy, but the information on this particular place was different. Rumor was that it was being smuggled in from across the Canadian border. Ross and I were sent here to find out if it was true." He paused for a moment before adding, "It didn't take long to discover that it was."

Maddy's voice felt faint, far away, to her own ears. "So what happens next?"

"As a federal agent acting on behalf of the United States government, I'm supposed to arrest everyone connected to the operation," Jack answered, the inevitability of the next words hanging in the air, "including you."

CHAPTER TWENTY-FOUR

Ever since the day Jeffers Grimm had darkened the doorway of the mercantile, slapping a pile of money down on the counter and proposing that they open a speakeasy in the cellar, Maddy had known she was on borrowed time. Even after it had become easier to pay the rapidly multiplying bills and care for her father's illness, she'd remained worried about the fact that they were breaking the law, that they would be caught. Initially, she'd thought it was going to happen the night Sheriff Utley had sauntered down the steps, but somehow, luck had shone on them. Still, she'd worried. Her father had always told her, if you play with matches, you're going to get burned.

I just never would have suspected that the man I love would be the one wielding the flame.

Jack may have fallen silent, but his words

echoed again and again in Maddy's thoughts. Faster than she could've snapped her fingers, whatever hopes and dreams she'd rekindled about spending the rest of her life with him were dashed, gone up in smoke. She'd be the biggest laughingstock in the state of Montana once word got out.

"I'm . . . I'm going to go . . . to jail . . . ?"

Jack slowly crossed the bridge to stand just behind her. Placing his hand on her shoulder, he gently turned her around and looked down at her, his eyes searching her face. Even with everything that had just happened, with the declaration that he was going to put her behind bars, Maddy couldn't keep herself from reaching up and tenderly placing her fingers against his bruised cheek; instead of flinching in pain, he leaned into her palm, sending conflicting shivers of fear and pleasure racing throughout her.

"You're going to arrest me, aren't you?" she asked, her voice faint.

"No, I'm not," he whispered in answer.

Maddy went weak in the knees. At first, she wondered if she hadn't misheard him, but from the way he looked at her, with a smile slowly spreading on his face, she knew she'd understood perfectly. Unbidden tears filled her eyes. For a moment her mouth opened and closed without sound. Eventually, she said, "But you just told me that —"

"I told you what, as a federally deputized lawman, I'm *supposed* to do, but that doesn't mean I'm going to do it."

"But why not?" Maddy asked in confusion. "I'm involved with the speakeasy just the same as Jeffers and Sumner. It's set up in the basement of my family's business with my permission. Worse than that, I've sold drinks to practically the whole town!"

Jack's smile faded slightly. "Where did Jeffers tell you he was getting the alcohol?" he asked.

Maddy thought back to the days before the speakeasy first opened. "He told me that he knew someone who could get us a couple of bottles of what we needed, enough so that we could make some money."

"A couple of bottles . . . ," Jack echoed. "Yesterday, Clayton and I followed Jeffers and Sumner up into the hills along the border and watched as they loaded up a truck with so many crates and boxes of liquor that the springs groaned."

"What?" Maddy blurted, stunned.

"They were met by another truck crossing over from Canada. I can't say for certain, but from the look of the men driving it,

393

they're connected to the Mob. Regardless, they were up to no good."

Maddy's head swam faster than the river's current. Her heart was in her throat. From the moment she'd agreed to Jeffers's plan she knew that she was making a deal with the devil, but she never would have imagined, wouldn't have dreamed, that *this* was what he'd do. He'd used her, plain and simple. She remembered the warning he'd given her in the cellar, that if one of them were caught it would mean both their heads, but he hadn't been particularly truthful; while both of them were taking plenty of risk, he was getting much more of the reward. Still, she understood why he'd lied; there was no way she would've agreed to such a thing.

While Jeffers's bootlegging scheme meant plenty of trouble for her, Maddy suddenly realized that it had made problems for Jack, as well.

"This is why Sumner attacked you, isn't it?"

Jack nodded grimly. "He saw me watching them," he explained. "I got careless, and even though he didn't get a good look at me, it was enough for him to pull out his pistol and start firing blind into the woods. Clayton and I ran off and hid when he and

Jeffers came looking for us, but Sumner's as paranoid as they come. He was convinced. I thought that my coming to the speakeasy would give him a reason to doubt himself, but all I managed to do was set him off."

"He had a gun?" Maddy said, her mouth going dry.

Gently, Jack put his hands on her arms, steadying her. "When Jeffers Grimm was born, he was already as dangerous as a wounded bear," he said. "If my suspicion is right, if he's working for some mobster and running booze out of Canada, then that means he has a lot to lose if he gets caught. There's nothing he won't stoop to, and no one he won't destroy to protect his stake."

"How would he get involved with all of that?"

"Trouble finds men like Jeffers as easily as flies find rotting fish. Everything he's done so far has to be at someone else's request. He just isn't smart or connected enough to have come up with it on his own. This wasn't the first shipment he's stored. More than likely, it's one of the last. Once he's gathered everything he's been told to get, someone will come for it, he'll get whatever payment he's been promised, and the law will be left in tatters."

"But if Jeffers has brought back more than

one loud of alcohol, where is he hiding — ,"
Maddy started to ask, but then stopped
without finishing; she already knew the answer.

"It's all in the mercantile's storeroom,"
Jack said. "I didn't know for certain until
after Jeffers hit me and I fell to the floor."

Maddy had seen it, too, looking past the
storeroom's open door at all the crates and
barrels.

"I'm such a fool," she chided herself.

"He took advantage of you."

"I should've known what he was doing,"
Maddy insisted.

"How could you?" Jack asked. "He used
your need to take care of your father against
you. You couldn't have known that he was
lying to your face, manipulating you for his
own gain."

All at once, Maddy realized the enormity
of what she'd done. In trying to protect
those she loved, she'd put everything she
cherished in jeopardy. No longer able to
control her emotions, she plunged tearfully
into Jack's arms and buried her face in his
chest. He ran his hand through her long red
hair, doing what he could to calm her.

"It wasn't your fault," he soothed.

"I was a fool," she disagreed. "I should go
to jail right along with him."

"No, you shouldn't."

"I'm guilty! I broke the law!"

"Not willingly."

"But it's your job to arrest me. Why wouldn't you do it?"

"Because I love you."

Slowly, Jack leaned down and placed his lips against hers. All her worries of what lay ahead immediately fell away, replaced by a fierce longing to cherish the present, together, standing beneath a rapidly darkening sky on their special bridge. The passion of their kiss increased with every second, the gentleness of the first touch becoming a fevered longing as Maddy lost herself, her mouth opening to allow him to taste her tongue, to feel her desire; in all of their years together, she wondered if they'd ever kissed so intensely.

"And I love you," she said, never meaning it more.

When Jack took her by the hand and led them from the bridge and back toward town, Maddy knew, without any doubt, what he wanted to happen between them, and she went willingly.

Maddy was still holding Jack's hand when they hurried up the stairs of the Belvedere and into the small lobby. Outside, the sky had steadily darkened toward night, the sky brilliant, with thousands of more stars growing visible each passing second. The warm summer day cooled with the setting sun. Lights burned in open windows, but it was still several hours before she was expected to open the speakeasy, which she had no intention of doing. In that moment, being by Jack's side was the only thing that mattered.

The whole walk from the bridge, Maddy had been embarrassed to pass anyone on the street, on the one hand because she and Jack were still the talk of the town, but also because she was convinced that their barely contained passion must be obvious to anyone who saw them. For that reason, she was thankful that Virginia Benoit wasn't behind the front desk; the hotel's owner was too perceptive, too prone to gossip.

Jack led the way past the desk and down the short hallway before stopping in front of his room. He paused for a moment, looking at the door across the hall, his head turned as if he was listening; Maddy heard nothing; she wondered if it wasn't the room in which his Bureau partner was staying. Finally satisfied, Jack opened the door, and she followed him inside.

The room was dark, with only a sliver of

faint light falling through the crack that split the curtains. Only hours before, Maddy had fled from this room, feeling that she'd been lied to, manipulated by Jack's withholding of his true identity. Unable to help herself, she glanced over at the dresser, remembering the feel of the gun in her hand. Where before it had unsettled her, she was surprised to realize that now that Jack no longer had any secrets from her, now that she'd been told the truth, she felt *safer* that he had a pistol, especially because of what Jeffers and Sumner were up to.

"I can put it somewhere else," Jack said, following her eyes.

Maddy shook her head.

"I don't want it to upset you."

"I'm not," she replied. "It doesn't matter anymore. The only thing that matters to me now is you."

Breathless, Maddy was enveloped by Jack's embrace as he pulled her close. His mouth found hers hungrily as one hand slid up the side of her cheek, brushing past her ear and then finally nestling in her thick hair.

"Maddy . . . ," he breathed between kisses.

His passion ignited her own. Her kisses grew steadily stronger as she caressed his muscular arm, his shoulder, and the length of his back, stopping at his waist. Excited by the strength of her desire, she tugged his shirt free of his pants, only to be surprised when he stopped their kiss and stepped back.

"Did I do something wrong?" she asked.

"No," he said with a soft smile, "but I want you to be sure this is what you want. I don't want you to have any regrets."

Maddy looked right into his eyes, her gaze never wavering. "I'm no longer the girl I was when you left, naïve about the ways of the world. When you took my hand on the bridge, I knew that this was where we were going."

"I just don't want you to —"

"Stop," she said, quieting him. "All I want is to make love to you."

Jack didn't say a word in reply, but Maddy could see a flare of desire erupt in his eyes. Telling him what she wanted, actually saying the words out loud, had removed the last barrier between them. It made her feel free to have been so honest, so forthcoming. It was what she wanted, to finally give herself to this man after so many years apart, so much time spent wondering why he'd left.

This time, when Maddy began to pull Jack's shirt free from his pants he made no move to stop her. Sliding her hands along his bare waist, she brought them up and over his rib cage before pressing against the hard muscles of his chest; the sensation of her touch caused him to moan into her open mouth.

Clumsily at first, she began to undo the buttons of his shirt, her lips never leaving his. With each one that was threaded free, she grew faster, confident, and more excited. Finally finished, she pushed the shirt over his shoulders, watching as it fell toward the floor at his feet; before it had even touched the ground Jack had begun to undo her shirt, although with his larger fingers and her smaller buttons he wasn't nearly as fast.

"Let me help you," she whispered.

"The darn things won't go quite where I want them . . ."

Maddy laughed softly. "You must not have had much practice doing this."

Jack stopped, his face serious as he looked at her. "There hasn't been anyone for me other than you," he said insistently. "No one."

"I know," she answered. "It was the same for me."

Before Jack had left for Boston seven years earlier, Maddy had considered giving herself to him. After everything they'd been through, experiencing both happiness and tragedy, her love for him had been so powerful that there was nothing she wouldn't have shared with him, including her own body. But in the end, she'd been too young, too frightened, to go through with it.

But now she was no longer scared.

And I'm a woman, one who wants to share myself right here, right now, with the man I love.

Jack led Maddy over to the bed, where she lay down, her long red hair cascading around her. He joined her, the bed's springs only complaining for an instant, and looked down at her from above, his face visible in the faint starlight that managed to find its way inside.

The next few moments were a blur of images, sensations, and memories Maddy knew she would never forget. There was a passionate kiss, her thumb running along his jaw, and the feeling of his stubble against her skin. More buttons were undone as one item of clothing after another was unceremoniously tossed to the floor. Tremors of pleasure raced across Maddy the first time Jack's hand touched her bare breast. His thumb ran lazy circles around her nipple as his lips planted gentle kisses across her pale chest, and she drew in sharp breaths through clenched teeth. When he'd at last slipped her undergarments past her bare feet, leaving her naked before him, she felt no embarrassment, only rising anticipation.

When Jack had shed the last of his clothing, they began exploring each other's bodies in delighted ways. His hand slid up Maddy's calf, dallied on her knee, then traced a path along one thigh before finally pressing against the wetness between her legs; from that first touch she felt a surge of pleasure greater than any before, more than in her wildest imagination. In return, Maddy ran her fingers along Jack's hip before veering down, following the crease that led to his sex, smiling with amazement at the hardness of him, and the heat that radiated off his skin. Just as he'd done to her nipple, she ran her thumb along the length of his penis, then over the soft tip, feeling him spasm in her hands, the rest of his body growing rigid, then relaxing, then jumping again.

"Maddy . . . ," he gasped. "Your touch is almost more . . . than I can bear . . ."

Jack's fingers passed over a spot between her legs that made stars dance before her eyes; she knew exactly what he meant.

With her breath coming short and fast, as sweat began to bead on her brow and chest, and as her longing for Jack grew to the point where she believed she could no longer contain it, Maddy spread her legs as he shifted on the bed and rose above her.

"I love you, Maddy," he said with a glimmer in his eye that reminded her of the boy she'd known years ago.

"And I love you," she answered. "I always will."

Slowly and carefully, Jack began to enter her. When a wave of pain momentarily washed over her, she forced herself to relax, and soon began to feel a sensation she'd never known before. She gasped and tossed her head back on the pillow, her chest arched. Pleasure mingled with the last remnants of discomfort as Jack eased himself all of the way inside her. With his face buried in the crook of her neck, he began to dot her skin with kisses, his breath hot in her ear.

"Are you all right?" Jack asked. "If it hurts you too much . . ."

In answer, Maddy pulled him as close as she could, her hands reaching across his broad back, her fingers digging into the tight, muscled flesh. She knew in her heart that this was the beginning of the future she'd craved for so long, had been wanting ever since Jack had boarded the train for

Boston. Now they'd never be apart again.

Jack began to move inside her, slowly at first, his hips sliding up and then back down again, rhythmically. Soon he began to go faster as his own excitement grew, his breathing ragged. Maddy's hands raced all over him, from his forearms to his shoulders, and then from his hips across his chest. Everything felt so wonderful, so fulfilling, that she didn't ever want it to stop. In time, her movements began to synchronize with his; when he moved away, she did the same, then came back to meet him, their sweat-slickened bodies meeting together.

As their lovemaking grew more frenzied, Maddy struggled to keep quiet. The pleasure boiled inside her frantic to be released, the pressure building. She turned her head, doing her best to stifle her cries.

On and on, Maddy's pleasure rose, like a tornado pulling her toward the sky. Finally, Jack's breathing grew stronger and his movements faster; she knew he wouldn't last much longer.

"Maddy . . . ," he managed.

She leaned up to kiss him, and the moment their lips met Jack's body shuddered, the convulsions rippling across his body, and Maddy felt a warmth fill her, answered by a quivering of her own.

"Jack! Oh, Jack!" she whispered fiercely.

When their ecstasy finally subsided, Jack let his weight down, gently resting on top of her, while Maddy held him tight, never wanting this night to end. Everything that she'd suffered, every night she had spent wondering what could possibly have gone wrong between them, vanished in an instant. This was what she'd desperately wanted, had waited her whole life for: she and Jack together as man and woman.

This *is what love is.*

CHAPTER TWENTY-FIVE

"You've got to be kidding!"

Maddy laughed out loud, walking beside Jack down the darkened streets toward home. They made their way under a brilliant sky, starlight pouring down all around them, the moon a winking sliver in the east. The breeze rustled branches, kissed her skin and swirled the hem of her skirt, cooled the summer night and caused the dew to shimmer on the grass.

After making love to Jack, Maddy had lain in bed beside him, talking for hours, sharing memories as well as soft kisses. She'd wanted to spend the night nestled beside him, but Jack worried about what people would think if they found out, especially her father, so even though it was almost three o'clock in the morning, he'd insisted on walking her home.

And it was then, walking hand in hand under the stars, that she'd told him a secret of her own . . .

"I mean it!" Maddy insisted. "I really thought you were a gangster!"

"What in heaven's name would've given you that crazy idea?" Jack asked incredulously, although he *was* smiling.

"It's because of what you said in the alleyway behind the store," she explained. "You were being so secretive about why you were back in Colton and wouldn't give me a straight answer. You've got no one to blame but yourself!"

"But why would you leap to such a ridiculous conclusion?"

"Because when you started talking about how you didn't want to imagine what your boss would do to you if anyone found out the truth, it was the only explanation I could come up with!"

Jack laughed again. "Wouldn't my lieutenant love to hear that . . ."

"Considering what you gave me to work with," Maddy said, joining in the fun, "I think it was a pretty good guess."

"That's because you've read too many dime novels and go to the movies too often."

"You forgot radio shows," she added, remembering the preacher's rant against organized crime.

"Those too!"

"Well, I'm sorry to say you couldn't be more wrong," Maddy explained. "As a matter of fact, the one person who came to your defense and said I was jumping to wild conclusions was Helen, and the *only* thing she likes to do is bury her nose in those horrid gossip magazines."

"Why did she stand up for me?"

Maddy blushed a little. "She said that you were too handsome."

"I'm not going to argue with her on that count!"

"I bet you wouldn't," she kidded him. "Was what you told Helen the truth? Have you really been to Hollywood?"

Jack nodded. "I was working, so I didn't get to see all the glamorous places the tourists go, but from what I saw of the place, it isn't the paradise your sister thinks it is."

Listening to Jack talk so casually about traveling to some faraway place she'd only read about, Maddy wondered what was going to happen between them now, especially after what they'd just done. From this moment on, things would be different, forever . . . They'd declared their love, had willingly given their hearts and bodies to each other, but there was still much that was unsettled. Difficult decisions still needed to be made. Could she truly ask him to stay in quiet little Colton with her after he'd seen the world? Would he have to give up his job? Was she ready to follow him? Could she live somewhere as big and bustling as Chicago or Los Angeles? What about her father and Helen? Though she desperately wanted answers for all her questions, and many more to boot, Maddy knew that now was not the right time.

But soon . . .

"Were you angry that I thought you could be a criminal?" she asked instead.

"A little," Jack said with a wink.

"That'll teach you to keep secrets from me." She laughed, slipping her arm into his, putting her head on his shoulder, and smiling contentedly.

Listening to Maddy laugh, Jack stole a glance at her beneath the star-filled sky and couldn't help but think that she was the most beautiful woman he'd ever seen. She was breathtaking. He felt just as he had when they were younger, when he felt lucky to simply be by her side, when one smile from her would keep him up half the night, when the sound of her voice was music to his ears.

But what happens tomorrow?

Jack hated himself for thinking about it,

especially since they'd just consummated their love, but he knew that they'd soon have to make a decision. Could he leave the Bureau? If he asked, would she come with him?

Suddenly Jack stopped, his thoughts interrupted by a sound that grabbed hold of his attention and refused to let go.

"What's wrong?" Maddy asked.

They stood opposite the bank, in nearly the same spot where Jack had watched customers heading for the speakeasy the first night he'd been back in Colton; but tonight they were the only people about.

"I thought I heard something," he replied.

"What was it?"

Before he could answer, Jack heard the noise again; this time it sounded closer, clearer.

It was the throb of a vehicle with a big engine, its gears grinding as they were shifted. Jack knew exactly what was happening.

Jeffers was moving the booze.

For a moment Jack thought about turning away, to walk Maddy home and deal with things in the morning. After all, he had her safety to consider, and besides, there was a chance he was mistaken. But in his heart, he knew he was lying to himself. He was

411

still an agent of the Bureau of Prohibition and it was his job to uphold the law, regardless of how inconvenient that might be.

"You're going to have to go on without me," he said to Maddy.

"Why?" she asked, confused. "What's wrong?"

Jack didn't want to tell her any more than he had to, but he knew that she'd keep asking questions until he gave her something. "It's Jeffers," he said reluctantly. "I think he's moving the liquor out of the cellar."

"Then we have to stop him!" Maddy answered immediately, and with great determination.

"This is my responsibility, not yours," Jack explained. "No matter what, I don't want you to get involved. It's too dangerous."

"I'm not a child!"

"Maddy, you're too important to me for you to take the risk."

"But this is my fault!" she pointedly argued. "Jeffers isn't just breaking the law by smuggling alcohol into the country; he's hiding it in my family's store. He's used me to get rich! And even though you've decided that I shouldn't be arrested for what I've done, that doesn't mean I'm not guilty for the part I've played in all of this. Because of that, I'm going to help you."

"Just listen for a —"

"I'm not leaving," she cut him off, the look in her eye almost daring him to say more.

Jack sighed, knowing that he couldn't win. "Stay close to me and don't make a sound," he finally said. "I need to see exactly what they're up to."

Quickly but quietly he and Maddy made their way up the darkened street, ducking into doorways shrouded in thick shadows before scurrying forward along the sidewalk, heading toward the mercantile. Even at such a late hour, Jack didn't want to take any chance of their being seen. From somewhere ahead of them he again heard the sound of a truck complaining as its gears were forced into place, followed by the growl of a large engine. With every step, he became more and more convinced that his suspicions were about to be proven correct.

Turning just past the barbershop, they slipped into an alley, following it toward the increasingly loud sounds; a door was shut and a few bits of conversation drifted on the wind. They moved cautiously, careful not to give themselves away. Finally, they crouched low behind a half-filled rain barrel, its sides mossy and damp. Jack eased around the edge and took a look.

Jeffers stood outside the mercantile with his back to the same large truck Jack had followed into the woods the day before. He was looking down into the shaft of the store's lift that was used to load and unload product into the storeroom, where he'd stashed all of the bootleg liquor. While Jack watched, a load of boxes slowly rose into view, shuddering to a halt before Jeffers threw open the gate and started to haul boxes to the truck's gate, his large, muscular arms straining from the effort.

"Get your ass up here and help!" he snarled once he'd returned to the lift.

Jack knew that he had to be shouting at Sumner; he couldn't hear the young man's response, but Jeffers clearly didn't like it.

"I don't give a damn!" he barked. "I ain't tellin' you again!"

"Why are they loading it all back into a truck?" Maddy asked from over Jack's shoulder, her voice soft in his ear.

"He's moving it somewhere," Jack answered. "I don't know if it's because he's spooked or if he's been told to get it ready for the Mob to pick up, but regardless, I've got to stop him."

"How do we do that?"

Jack thought about it for a moment. With his gun back in the dresser drawer, he'd be at a distinct disadvantage if they saw him; he needed to improve his odds, and there was only one way he could think to do it. "I need you to go get Sheriff Utley."

"I told you that I wasn't leaving you," Maddy insisted.

"That's not the reason I'm asking you to go," he explained. "One of us has to stay here and keep an eye on them in case they drive off. Once they have everything loaded, there's no telling where they could go. We've come too far to take the chance of losing them now. But I can't handle them alone. Once the sheriff is here, then we'll do everything in our power to make them pay for what they've done. It's our only chance."

Maddy thought about it for a moment, still reluctant to part from him, but she eventually agreed.

"His house is on the edge of town," she said. "I'll be back as soon as I can."

"Be careful," he told her, his eyes searching her face in the dark.

"You too."

"I love you, Maddy."

Jeffers lugged another crate full of bottles over to the truck, hefted it up into the back, then wiped the sweat from his brow. All around him, Colton slept. He couldn't be sure of the time but figured that it was still a couple of hours until dawn, long before anyone would be poking their heads out to see what he was doing, and plenty of time to finish the task he'd been given.

That afternoon, when he was sleeping off a bit of a drunk at his place, Deb Wehmeyer once again naked and snoring at his side, the phone had rung, startling him so badly that he'd fallen out of bed. He'd answered angrily but swallowed his threatening words when he'd understood that it was Jimmy Luciano on the other end, telling him that it was time to get all of the liquor together and ready it for transport to Al Capone.

Jeffers had gone to the speakeasy as usual and, on the one hand, been furious that Maddy hadn't shown up for work, but he'd also been happy that he was leaving this backwater, piece-of-shit town forever; he'd been in such a good mood that he'd given that drunken old lawyer a drink on the house.

But Maddy's absence annoyed him. After the way she'd openly defied him when he'd hit Jack Rucker, he'd wanted to completely embarrass her, to degrade and destroy her; he'd been so worked up by the idea that he'd left Deb in a puddle of her own sweat and tears the night before. Still, he refused to be too bothered by it; there'd be plenty of other women, not to mention money, when he was working for Capone.

"How many more cases are we gonna have to load?" Sumner asked, struggling with a smaller cask, his face caked with sweat.

"As many as it takes," Jeffers grunted.

"And how many is that?"

Shortly after they'd closed the speakeasy, Jeffers had gone for the truck and started filling it with the alcohol they'd amassed, taking load after load out to the abandoned house he'd chosen for the pickup location. Now, hours later, completely drenched with sweat and tired, they were almost finished. So far, they hadn't been seen by anyone.

"We should be able to get the last of it with this trip," he answered.

"Good," Sumner said. "I don't want to do no more liftin', that's for sure."

"You'll do as much as it takes."

Jeffers frowned as his lackey went off grumbling. He knew that the time had come for him to end their so-called partnership. Once they were safely at the meeting place, he'd put a bullet in the back of Sumner's head and leave his worthless body in the woods for the animals. No one would ever be any the wiser; hell, Sumner's own mother would probably be just as glad to be rid of him as Jeffers was going to be. He didn't need the boy's deadweight dragging him down when he was trying to climb Capone's ladder.

In a bit more than an hour, there was nothing that could stop him.

Maddy ran down the dark, sleeping streets as fast as she could, her breath short and her heart pounding. Fear gripped her, urging her forward. She knew Sheriff Utley's house was another five minutes away and that then she would need time to wake him, tell him what was happening, and convince him to come with her. Even if they drove his car, who knew how much more time would pass?

Suddenly Maddy stopped, her hands on her waist, panting, looking back at the center of town.

In her heart, she knew that Jack was in terrible danger; worse, she was leaving him to face it alone. Jeffers Grimm wasn't a man to take lightly. Remembering the night she'd been alone with him in the speakeasy, the sleazy feel of his hand on her breast, made her feel sick to her stomach; the only memory more unbearable was the sight of Jack lying on the floor, bruised and battered by Jeffers's hand.

What happens if they find Jack watching them? Sumner shot at him with no more than a second's glance.

Maddy knew she should listen to what Jack told her, that she should trust that he wouldn't do anything rash until she returned with the sheriff so that together they could arrest both men for what they'd done, but her heart told her it wasn't that simple. She couldn't let anything happen to him, the man whose bed she'd just shared, the man she passionately loved.

I just can't . . .

Without any more hesitation, Maddy ran back toward town.

Time flew past as Jack watched Jeffers and Sumner continue to load the truck. Silently, he cursed himself for not having his department-issued gun; this was the second time he'd had to deal with the two criminals without it. He could only assume that Sumner, at the very least, still had his gun and was possibly even more anxious to use it here than in the woods.

Every so often, Jeffers stopped and looked around them, watching to see if they had any unwanted company; Jack had to admit that while the man was stronger than an ox, he wasn't as stupid as one. Once, while Jack was taking another look, he was nearly seen by Sumner. Jack ducked just in time, a breath trapped in his chest.

I need to find a better place to watch them.

Carefully, Jack maneuvered back down the alley, raced through the streets, and approached the mercantile from a different direction. This time, he was looking right at the truck; from where he stood, it would be much more difficult to be caught watching them. He watched as Jeffers once again berated Sumner for not working fast enough, and wondered how much time remained before they'd have everything loaded.

What am I going to do if they get in the truck and drive away? What if Maddy isn't back yet with the sheriff? How can I stop them?

Before Jack could begin to consider his options, he heard a faint scuffling behind him, and then a second later, before he could even turn around, he was grabbed roughly by the arm as a hand clamped down on his mouth.

CHAPTER TWENTY-SIX

Panic gripped Jack even tighter than his unknown assailant. Even as he struggled to get free, he knew he'd been a fool to think that Jeffers and Sumner had been acting alone in their smuggling operation. Jack didn't know if it'd been someone watching just out of sight or if an overseer had been sent from the Mob to make sure nothing went wrong, but either way, he'd let his guard down. Now he just might pay for it with his life. If only he could —

"Quit fightin', dang it!" a voice hissed in his ear. "It's me! Clayton!"

Freed, Jack spun around in the darkness to find his friend grinning back at him. He was happy and relieved but more than a little angry, too.

"What in the hell do you think you're doing sneaking up on me like that?" Jack swore. "You scared me half to death!"

"What choice did I have? Weren't like I

could call out your name," Clayton explained. " 'Sides, you done come up on me all sudden like. If I'd a tapped you on the shoulder, you'd a been so surprised you'd a yelled out. Coverin' your mouth was the only way I could figure to keep you quiet."

Even though his heart was still hammering in his chest, Jack knew that Clayton had a point; if he'd been startled enough, there was a good chance he might have made enough noise to attract Jeffers's or Sumner's attention, and then everything would have been lost. Still, Jack was surprised to find that he wasn't the only person watching what was happening at the mercantile.

"What are you doing out here?" he asked.

"Same thing you are, I reckon." Clayton smiled, nodding over to the rapidly filling truck. "Watchin' them two."

"But why?"

" 'Cause I figured that after everythin' that happened yesterday, from gettin' shot at in the woods till Jeffers knocked you upside the head, someone needed to keep a close eye on what them two was up to. Since you wasn't in too good a shape, that left me to do the job."

"Messing with those two is dangerous," Jack said. "You said it yourself."

"It's also kinda fun."

"This isn't a game."

"Didn't say it was," Clayton replied. "When my father took me trappin', he'd say that even though we was huntin' critters that'd tear our throats out if'n they could, even if it was rainin' or snowin' somethin' miserable, there was somethin' 'bout the hunt that made it all worth doin'. Sounds an awful lot like dealin' with Jeffers, you ask me. Hell," he added. "I'd a thought you'd be happy I was doin' this."

"I am, but I don't want you getting hurt on account of me."

"I can take care a myself."

Jack nodded. Clayton had already put his life in danger by helping him with Jeffers and Sumner. Once Maddy returned with the sheriff, maybe they'd be enough to stop Jeffers and Sumner.

"What've they been doing?" Jack asked, nodding at the truck.

"Been at it since shortly after closin' the speakeasy," Clayton replied. "This here's the third time they loaded up. First time they drove 'way, I was panicked they was goin' for good so I followed 'em with Roger all the way out to a 'bandoned house 'bout twenty minutes east. The old Perkins place. Stayed a ways back so they didn't see me. Eventually, they come back for more. I figure this here's the last load they're haulin'. Can't see there bein' 'nough room for much else."

"Then we don't have much time."

"So what're we gonna do?"

Jack frowned. Without his gun or the sheriff, there was little chance he could survive a confrontation with the two criminals. To try would likely be suicide. Even if he followed them in Clayton's truck, watched as they handed off the liquor to whomever they were holding it for, what then? He'd have no way of contacting Lieutenant Pluggett while surrounded by men who'd kill them without hesitation.

He had to stop them here and now.

But how? I could always —

"You're a lawman, ain't ya?" Clayton suddenly asked, his words striking Jack as hard as a hammer hitting a nail.

Jack turned slowly to find Clayton staring expectantly at him through the gloom. When they'd followed Jeffers and Sumner into the woods, he'd feared being asked for his reasons, but Clayton had only skirted the issue. Now, with everything the scraggly man had done, for all that he continued to risk, he deserved to know the truth.

"I am," Jack answered. "I'm an agent of the Bureau of Prohibition."

"I knew it!" Clayton said with a low chuckle. "Ever since we drove up into them woods, I been wonderin' what reason you could have for knowin' what shenanigans they was pullin'. Took me a while, but I guessed it."

"Does it change your mind about doing this?"

"Hell, no!" he replied, looking a bit offended. "No matter what reason you'd a had for takin' Jeffers Grimm down a peg, I'd want in. That fella's been askin' for it for years. 'Sides," Clayton added with a grin, "I figure my helpin' you out might shine a different light on my own drinkin' of that liquor. Maybe I could earn me some a that, what's it called, complacency —"

"Clemency," Jack corrected him.

"That's the stuff! Can I have some a that?"

But before Jack could explain that, according to the law, he'd done nothing wrong by buying a drink, the night was split by a sound that froze his blood, terrified him, and made him sick to his stomach, all at once.

It was a woman's scream.

Maddy inched her way through the inky darkness of the same alleyway that she and Jack had originally come down to watch

Jeffers and Summer load their illegal contraband from the mercantile's cellar. She'd run so fast after deciding not to get Sheriff Utley that her breathing was labored; she covered up her mouth for fear of making too much noise. As she neared the alleyway's end, she wondered what Jack would say to her, how mad he'd be at her for having not done as he'd asked.

He'll just have to get over it . . . I'm not leaving his side . . .

But when Maddy reached the mossy rain barrel behind which they'd hid, she was shocked to find that Jack was no longer there.

"Jack?" she whispered as loud as she dared. "Where are you?"

Seconds passed with no answer.

Fear grabbed Maddy at the thought that something had happened to Jack, that he'd been found out and was even now suffering at Jeffers's hand. Rising up to take a look around, she accidentally knocked over an empty bottle she hadn't seen, sending it clattering to the ground. In the otherwise still quiet of the night, it sounded as noisy to her ears as a wailing trumpet. Terrified, she ducked down behind the rain barrel, too scared to do anything but tremble.

Oh, no! Oh, no, oh, no, oh, no!

Time trickled slowly past. Maddy desperately wanted Jack to be by her side, to keep her safe, but she knew she was alone. At any moment she expected Jeffers to roar out her name, fling the rain barrel aside, and grab her by the arm. But nothing happened.

Slowly but steadily, Maddy began to believe that she'd somehow been lucky; maybe they hadn't heard the bottle because they'd been too busy hauling crates of liquor, maybe they were too far away, or maybe it wasn't quite as loud as she'd thought. Finally, confused and curious, Maddy took a deep breath and hazarded a look.

Jeffers was headed back to the truck with another large crate of bottles, just as he'd been doing when she and Jack had arrived. Relief flooded Maddy. Her hopes had been well-founded; Jeffers and Sumner hadn't heard the bottle after all. It didn't look as if they'd discovered Jack, either. Now all she had to do was find out where he'd gone and then —

Suddenly, she was grabbed by the arm and yanked violently to her feet. Maddy was so startled that she screamed, but it only lasted an instant before a hand clamped down on her mouth.

"Lookee what we got here!" Sumner

shouted, pulling her out from behind the rain barrel and dragging her over toward the truck. No matter how hard Maddy struggled, it was pointless; he was far too strong for her to resist. "Now we got ourselves some company!"

Oh, Jack! Help me!

The sound of Maddy's scream grabbed Jack by the heart and squeezed. He jumped to his feet, but from where he and Clayton were hidden he couldn't see much of anything past the truck. He didn't know what had happened, if Maddy had brought the sheriff with her as he'd asked or if something had gone wrong, but there was no doubt that she was in great danger.

I've got to rescue her!

But just as he was taking the first step to run to her aid, Clayton grabbed him by the arm and held him back.

"Now just hold on a second there, pardner," he said.

"What in the hell are you doing?" Jack asked angrily, trying to shake himself free of the other man's grasp. "We've got to help her!"

"I ain't tryin' to tell you otherwise, but this right here's the sort of thing you can't go into half-cocked," Clayton explained.

"You go runnin' over there, intendin' to do right, it's gonna get us all killed. They'll hear us clear as if we was a couple a hound dogs howlin' at the moon. Sumner'll be shootin' 'fore he sees us. We don't get the drop on 'em now, we ain't gonna get 'nother chance."

Though it pained him, Jack knew Clayton was right. "How else are we going to get her away from them?" he asked. "Those two are animals!"

Even in the dark, he could see Clayton's thin smile. "I got me an idea."

Maddy looked all around her for some sign of Jack, some avenue of escape, for anything that might help her, but there was nothing. Sumner's grip was as painful as it was strong. Slowly but steadily, she was dragged toward the store Silas Aldridge had built with his own two hands, toward the crates of alcohol she'd unwittingly allowed to be stored in the cellar.

And toward Jeffers Grimm.

Leaning against the rear of the heavily laden truck, he had a thin smile on his rough face, making him appear even more intimidating; it was as if he was savoring what was about to happen. Maddy remembered the way he'd spoken to her the night they'd

429

been alone together in the speakeasy, the way he'd leered at her, the way he'd *touched* her, and grew even more frightened.

"Why ain't I surprised to find you here?" Jeffers growled.

"She was over by that barrel watchin' us," Sumner added; from the look that crossed Jeffers's face, he wasn't happy his flunky was talking. "I heard her rustlin' round so I took a look and found her."

"What're you doin' here, Maddy?" Jeffers pressed.

"I should ask you the same thing," she said, turning the question around, unwilling to back down, even now that she'd been caught. Her mind swirled, wondering where Jack could be, why he wasn't coming to rescue her. "What are all of these crates doing in my father's cellar?"

Jeffers patted the barrel beside him, his large hand pounding hard on the wooden frame. "This here's a lot of money."

"You're a smuggler! This is against the law!"

"So's sellin' drinks out of a speakeasy to half the damn town."

"I didn't agree to anything like this!"

Jeffers shook his head. "You got *exactly* what we agreed to. When I showed you that pile a money, your eyes lit up like a marquee. I promised you'd make enough that tough times'd be easier, and that's what you got."

"But you lied to me!"

To that, both Jeffers and Sumner laughed.

Maddy could barely contain her anger. "I never should've trusted you."

"But you did," Jeffers said, shrugging. "The mistake you made was underestimatin' how bad I want outta this piece-of-shit town. All of this," he explained, waving around at the crates, "is my ticket outta here."

"*Our* ticket," Sumner corrected him, but Jeffers kept on, ignoring him as if he hadn't said a word.

"There ain't a damn thing gonna stand in my way," Jeffers snarled threateningly. "Not you, not the sheriff, nothin' or no one! I've worked too damn hard to let it slide outta my grasp now. Hell, I woulda figured you'd be used to this by now, what with how Rucker ran out on you. Him and me ain't that different . . . we both had our fun while you was handy, then tossed you away first chance we got."

"Where is that son of a bitch, anyhow?" Sumner asked, tugging so hard on Maddy's arm that she nearly flew off her feet. "He's still got a beatin' comin' to him for what he done to me."

Maddy looked back at Sumner; ever since he'd startled her, she'd been too preoccupied with Jeffers to give him more than a quick glance. What she saw startled her. His face, already a mess of bruising from having his nose broken in the alleyway, had worsened; swelling puffed at the corner of his mouth and cheek, and there was a trickle of dried blood that had seeped from a still-leaking cut above his eye. Jack had beaten him badly.

"He's probably lurkin' round, too," Sumner said, looking around wildly, one hand fishing into his pant pocket.

"Jack's still laid up in bed," Maddy lied quickly, hoping it would give Jack more of a chance to come to her aid. "After what you did to him," she added, looking directly at Jeffers, "he needs all the rest he can get."

"He shouldn't a stuck his nose in my business."

"You must really be worried about him if you hit him when he wasn't looking," Maddy replied. "You're nothing but a coward!"

Jeffers's grin dropped. He moved a couple of steps closer, towering over Maddy as if she were a child. "You best watch that mouth a yours," he said, trying to intimidate her.

"It must be hard to hear the truth," she replied defiantly.

"I ain't got much unfinished business 'fore I leave," Jeffers smirked, leaning down, "but I been hankerin' to slap that pretty mouth a yours, tear everythin' off a you till you was stark naked, and then have my way while you screamed." With obvious pleasure, he reached out and once again grabbed one of her breasts, squeezing until she yelped in pain; Sumner laughed at her discomfort. "Up till now, the only thing holdin' me back was makin' sure this booze was delivered safe and sound. With that 'bout to be taken care of, there ain't no reason I can't make you regret the way you been talkin'."

Even as terror paralyzed Maddy, she became aware of something else, a sound . . . It was faint at first, distant, but it continued to tug at her, insistent, growing louder, closer; she knew she wasn't imagining the noise because it seemed to have drawn Jeffers's and Sumner's attention, too.

"What the hell . . . ?" Sumner wondered aloud.

As if in answer, a beat-up truck suddenly exploded out of the alleyway in which Maddy had been discovered. It was traveling fast, its engine roaring, and showed no sign of slowing. Wide-eyed with shock, Maddy watched dumbfounded as it came right toward her, smashing into a pair of crates and sending splinters of wood, shards of glass, and plenty of liquor flying through the air. In the ensuing chaos, Maddy jabbed an elbow into Sumner's ribs, freeing herself and leaping out of the way. The truck skidded to a halt as the criminals were showered in a barrage of destroyed contraband, the doors flying open.

Maddy gasped to see Jack out of the passenger's side door in a flash.

"You're under arrest," he shouted, "by order of the Bureau of Prohibition!"

CHAPTER TWENTY-SEVEN

Jack's feet hit the ground running before Clayton's beat-up old truck had come to a complete stop, the last sounds of the destruction they'd caused still echoing off the surrounding buildings. Broken glass and splintered wood were everywhere. Sumner looked at Jack as if he'd seen a ghost, his eyes wide and mouth slack, while unconsciously backing away.

"You're under arrest by order of the Bureau of Prohibition!" Jack shouted as loud as he could, still wishing he had his badge and gun but hoping that a bit of confusion and fear of arrest might make their dangerous, difficult job easier.

"Ain't no point in puttin' up a fight!" Clayton bellowed, jumping from the driver's side door. "It's all over now!"

Clayton's plan had been a bold one: to drive his truck right into the middle of the landing in order to give them the element of surprise they so desperately needed. If it worked, they'd have a chance to rescue Maddy while simultaneously putting an end to the illegal liquor operation.

Now all they had to do was take advantage . . .

Desperately Jack searched for Maddy; his biggest fear barreling down the narrow alleyway, their lights off so that they wouldn't give themselves away, had been that they'd accidentally hit her when they burst out into the open. Clayton had assured him that she'd be fine, but the worry had continued to gnaw at him. Finally, he saw her lying unharmed on the ground beside the broken remains of a crate and his heart filled with relief.

"Jack!" she shouted, her face brightening.

"Get somewhere safe!" he shouted at her before turning away; now that he knew she hadn't been hurt, he could turn his attention back to putting an end to the two criminals' schemes.

No matter what, I'm going to stop them!

Without hesitation, Jack ran right at Sumner. Though he knew Jeffers was the more imposing of the two, undoubtedly the more dangerous in a brawl, that didn't mean that the younger man wasn't the bigger threat. Jack knew Sumner had a pistol, one he'd shown no reluctance to fire. If Jack could get to him quickly, before he had a chance to draw it . . .

As he struggled to best his shock, Sumner's hand fished wildly in his pant pocket; he was doing just as Jack had expected, but so far he'd been unable to pull the pistol free. If he'd had it in his rear waistband, within easier reach, he'd already have been shooting; Jack guessed that he'd put it in his pocket in order to more easily move the alcohol.

It only took Jack a few seconds to reach the man, but they were the longest of his life. Finally, just as Sumner managed to draw the gun, Jack was on him, a fist smashing into the thug's jaw and sending him sprawling, the gun flying from his hand and, much to Jack's relief, clattering over the edge of the mercantile's lift before plummeting into the darkness below.

"Now you'll have to fight me like a man," Jack said.

"I'm gonna kill you with my bare hands!" Sumner shouted back, and came charging right at him. He threw a wild haymaker that a blind man would've had a good chance of dodging. Jack nimbly moved to the side, let the fist fly past, and took immediate advantage of Sumner's vulnerability to smash a punch into his exposed ribs. As the air whooshed out of his lungs, Jack kept at him, cracking him on his chin and sending him sprawling onto the ground in a faceful of dirt.

Maybe things were going to be easier than Jack had imagined.

Maddy could scarcely believe what she was seeing. Just as Jeffers had told her that he planned to rape her, put his hand on her breast, and squeezed until tears welled in the corners of her eyes, just as any hope of rescue had begun to fade, here was Jack coming to her rescue. Her ears still rang from the sound of the crash, but shouting his name had cleared her spinning thoughts. Even though he'd ordered her to leave, to go somewhere safe, she couldn't bring herself to look away, watching him pummel Sumner senseless yet again.

Glancing quickly at the other side of the old truck, Maddy saw Clayton slowly circling Jeffers, his hands raised like a boxer, looking for an opening.

"Don't tell me you're scared a fightin'," Clayton taunted the much larger man. "Put 'em up!"

Maddy was unnerved by Jeffers's reaction; instead of being goaded into action, cuss-ing, or making threats of his own, he smiled. She was reminded of the day he'd first come to the mercantile and proposed the speakeasy; Jeffers Grimm was at his most dangerous at a moment like this.

No matter what she'd been told, Maddy knew she couldn't run away, even if it meant she was in danger. Jack and Clayton needed her.

I've got to do something to help them . . . But what . . . ?

Suddenly she had an idea. Hurrying to the truck's passenger's side door, she threw it open and slid inside. Pieces of glass littered the seat from the window that had shattered in the collision. Careful not to cut herself, Maddy got behind the wheel. If she could blow the truck's horn, she might be able to wake the sleeping town and draw attention to what was happening. If everyone came running, the odds could tilt in their favor.

But before Maddy could make a sound she was yanked out of the door and onto the ground, landing hard on her side. From where she lay, she saw Clayton's crumpled body.

"You ain't gettin' away from me that easy, bitch," Jeffers growled.

This time when Maddy screamed, there

was no attempt made to keep her quiet.

Sumner spat the coppery tang of blood from his mouth, desperately trying to clear the cobwebs from his head. Bright stars spun at the edges of his vision, blinking and turning, and the ground seemed to tilt one way and then the other, making it hard to get back to his feet. Even that bastard Jack Rucker looked out of focus, like there was more than one of him, standing above Sumner, his fists balled, gloating.

That son of a bitch!

Somehow Sumner had been knocked on his ass for the third time. Unbelievable as it was, it was still a fact: first in the alleyway, then in the speakeasy, and now yet again. He knew it wasn't because Rucker was a better fighter but rather that he was luckier than a cat on its ninth life! He had to be! If Sumner ever managed to get his hands on him . . . All he needed was to pull himself together, get back on his feet, and get his revenge.

"Shoulda known . . . you was a . . . goddamn copper . . . ," he muttered.

But the bastard didn't respond.

"Gonna . . . gonna kill you . . ."

"Stay down," Rucker ordered him. "You'll only get hurt worse."

Suddenly a woman's scream split the night like a thunderbolt. Jack spun at the sound, looking back over the wreckage he'd caused, his face twisting in distress. To Sumner, the sound had a different effect; it was like beautiful music. Where a moment before his head had been addled and his muscles a quivering mess, he now felt clearheaded and strong.

This was his chance. This was what he'd been waiting for.

With an animal growl rising up and out of his chest, Sumner sprang to his feet and charged the other man, slamming his full weight into his back and driving him to the ground. Sumner's entire body felt charged, possessed, and he began raining down punches on the back of Rucker's head and shoulders. When Sumner's hand struck bone it flared in agony, as if it had been broken, but he ignored the pain and kept right on punching, knowing that this was his only chance. He'd win; he'd show Jeffers he was a worthy partner; he'd kill Rucker like the dog he was; he'd —

Without warning, Jack suddenly thrust up his hips and flipped Sumner off him and onto his back as easily as a dog shaking off water. He landed with a thud, his enthusiasm for the fight momentarily gone, but as he struggled to regain what he'd lost Jack was on him, driving an elbow into his midsection.

"Maddy!" Jack shouted, his concern somewhere other than on the man he was fighting. "I'm coming!"

Not if I got anythin' to say 'bout it!

Sumner and Jack rolled around on the ground, each fighting for an advantage. At one instant Sumner felt victorious, but in the next it was gone.

But then things changed.

When he was once again thrown hard on his back, Sumner's hand knocked up against the stem of a broken liquor bottle. Grabbing it tightly, he thrust quickly upward, driving the sharp glass deep into the meat of Rucker's shoulder. Instantly blood seeped from the wound as the man shouted in pain.

Exultant, Sumner pressed his gain. Roaring, he pushed Rucker off him and quickly straddled the fallen man's waist, their positions reversed. With a smile curling his bloodied lips, Sumner raised the broken bottle above his head and prepared to drive it into his opponent's exposed throat.

This was the moment Sumner had been waiting for, his glorious triumph, the death of that no-good son of a —

Before Sumner knew what was happening, his whole world turned upside down. Beneath him, Jack had grown desperate; knowing that he only had one chance, the threat to his life dangerously real, his shoulder burning from where he'd been stabbed, he grabbed Sumner just beneath the ribs and, pushing upward with every ounce of strength he had left, threw the man off him. Sumner flew forward, tumbling end-over-end, his smile frozen on his face.

But instead of landing hard on his back, the fight's momentum again swinging in the other direction, Sumner just kept on falling. Even as he plummeted down, he knew what had happened; while they'd been fighting they had rolled beside the mercantile's lift, the same lift he'd been using to bring the crates of liquor up to the truck. He was dropping down the open shaft.

Before he even had time to be frightened, Sumner smashed into the remaining casks and boxes. Agony such as he'd never known before exploded across his back, but then, like a candle being snuffed, it was suddenly gone.

". . . kill you . . . ," he muttered.

Then everything went black.

Without a glance back to see how Sumner was faring with Jack Rucker, Jeffers dragged

Maddy toward the truck. She fought him every step of the way, but she was no more trouble to him than if she were a child. Although there was no chance to get the rest of the alcohol in the mercantile's cellar, most of it had already been loaded; along with what had already been taken to the pickup location, Jeffers knew there'd still be plenty to give to Jimmy Luciano and then on to Capone. He couldn't deny that he was shocked by Jack's being a lawman, he wondered if *he* was the reason the bastard was back in Colton, but there wasn't time to waste thinking about it. All he had to do was drive the truck out to the meeting place one last time.

And then I can have my way with this meddling bitch.

Jeffers stepped over Clayton Newmar's moaning body and kept right on going. In the aftermath of the crash, even as the other man had circled him, running his mouth, Jeffers had seen the fear in his eyes; he was used to making men feel that way. When he'd struck, Clayton hadn't seen it coming.

"Let me go!" Maddy shouted, trying to pry Jeffers's hand from her arm.

"Shut your damn mouth," he hissed, squeezing until she gasped.

Whipping open the driver's side door, he

threw Maddy inside. Like a flash, he was right behind her, fast enough to grab her before she could slide across the seat and escape out the other door.

"You try'n run and I'll hurt you in ways you ain't never imagined," Jeffers warned, his eyes flat and menacing.

Maddy said nothing, but the fear in her eyes spoke plenty.

Jeffers was going to enjoy breaking this woman, giving in to every twisted desire he'd ever had, every fantasy that had caused a twinge between his legs. Whenever he finally stopped, she'd wish she was dead. By then, her own father wouldn't recognize her. Before Jeffers bellied up to the table with the big boys, he was going to have Maddy Aldridge as an appetizer.

The truck started without any fuss, its engine rumbling. Throwing it into gear, Jeffers drove away from the mercantile, from Jack Rucker, from this godforsaken town, with a grin on his face.

Ain't nothin' stoppin' me now.

Jack looked over the edge of the lift's shaft and saw Sumner's limp body lying on top of a shattered crate. He lay still and silent. Jack hadn't meant to throw the dangerous criminal over the edge, but his life had been in danger and he'd simply reacted. But he wasn't going to waste any time on regrets, either. He had more important things to do.

I've got to save Maddy!

Jumping to his feet, Jack ran after the heavily laden truck, losing distance as it slowly gained speed. Within a dozen steps, he knew he wouldn't be able to catch up; it was already moving too quickly. So instead, he raced back to where Clayton was struggling to get to his feet, one hand on his jaw.

"I feel like I been run over by a truck," he complained, wiggling one of his teeth to see if it'd been knocked loose.

"We've got one we need to catch," Jack explained. "Do you think you can catch it?"

"Are you kiddin'?" Clayton exclaimed, his eyes growing a bit brighter. "Runnin' into a bunch a boxes ain't gonna stop Roger!"

"Then let's go!"

As fast as they could, they ran over to the beaten truck and leaped inside. Clayton tried to start the engine, but it sputtered and stalled.

"Come on now, old boy," he soothed. "Don't make a liar outta me . . ."

Roger coughed to life on the next try, Clayton jammed down on the gas and the engine roared. Shattered wooden crates rattled around beneath the undercarriage, making the vehicle bounce around a bit before it finally hit the road and took off in pursuit. Wind whipped through the remains of the windshield, but Jack never took his eyes off the accelerating truck.

"Where'd Maddy get to?" Clayton shouted to be heard. "She run to safety once we gave her a distraction?"

Jack frowned. "Jeffers got her. She's in the truck with him."

"Oh, Sweet Jesus," he replied. Shaking his head, he added, "It's my fault she's in this mess. It's all 'cause I let Jeffers whup me good."

"You did the best you could. It's like you told me," Jack said. "Jeffers Grimm isn't the sort of fella you want to mess with."

"You got that right," Clayton agreed, rubbing his jaw. "What happened with you? Sumner get what he had comin' to him?"

Jack closed his eyes and once again saw Sumner lying at the bottom of the lift shaft. "He won't be giving us any more trouble," he answered grimly.

Clayton drove his truck as fast as it would go through the darkened streets. Nearer to the mercantile, a few lights had been turned on; Jack guessed that they'd heard the commotion of the crash. But the farther he and Clayton got from the center of town, the night pressed back in, the sky dark save for thousands of stars. Up and down a low hill, they raced toward the river. Taking a corner fast, Roger's tires screeched, sliding slightly. Slowly, the distance between the vehicles began to close.

"What're we gonna do when we catch up to 'em?" Clayton asked. "Jeffers ain't just gonna pull over . . ."

No matter how much Jack wished otherwise, there was no easy answer. He knew they had only one chance. "We're going to have to run them off the road."

Clayton's eyes grew wide and he whistled low. "I don't know if Sumner done knocked the sense outta your head, but if we hit that there truck, we'll go bouncin' right off like a mosquito flyin' into a brick wall!"

"Not if we do it right," Jack replied, warming to the idea. "All you need to do is hit it hard from the side, back by one of the rear wheels. If you do that, he'll fishtail right off the road. Then we'll have him."

Clayton shook his head and patted the truck's wheel. "What do you say, Roger? I reckon you're even tougher'n that big ole thing . . ."

"You can do it," Jack said with confidence.

"I got my doubts," Clayton admitted. "Ain't no point in lyin' 'bout it. Comin' outta this in one piece is gonna take a miracle, but if we do it, then the two of us gotta be the luckiest fellas alive!"

"That's *exactly* what I'm counting on . . ."

The huge truck raced down Main Street, darkened storefronts whipping past in a blur. For a moment the bark of a dog could be heard. Wind blew hard and unrelentingly through the open window, blowing Maddy's long red hair every which way. She stayed as far away from Jeffers as she dared.

No matter what it took, she knew she needed to escape. Her life depended on it. If Jeffers made good on his attempt to get away, if he somehow managed to evade capture, he was going to have his way with her just as he'd disgustingly promised. There was nothing she could hope to do to stop him then, but now . . .

The truck kept gaining speed steadily. Jeffers drove as fast as he dared; undoubtedly, the only thing that kept him from standing on the gas pedal was a fear of flying off the road at a curve. Within minutes they would be at the edge of Colton, with nothing but woods and little-traveled roads beyond.

I've got to do something!

But even as she struggled to decide what

she should do, Maddy noticed that Jeffers kept glancing at his side mirror, his face twisted in a scowl. Seeing him like that gave her hope. When she saw his attention was focused on the mirror, she quickly craned her neck out of the passenger's side window and immediately saw what had made him so concerned; another vehicle pursued them down the dark and deserted streets, its lights bouncing while it kicked up plenty of dust. It was clear they were quickly gaining ground. Maddy knew it had to be Jack. But before she could do anything to signal him, she was abruptly yanked backward.

"Don't you dare try nothin'," Jeffers warned with a growl.

Even after everything Maddy had been through, though she had every reason to be frightened out of her wits, anger began coursing through her, a fire that burned in her belly. "Jack is going to catch you," she said defiantly. "He's going to hunt you down no matter where you go. You'll pay for everything you've done, for every law you've broken, for everyone you've ever —"

The back of Jeffers's hand struck Maddy's lip, snapping her head violently to the side. Blood filled her mouth. But instead of cowering, flinching, and covering her face so that he couldn't strike her again, Maddy felt even more empowered to stand against him, to show him that, unlike everyone else in Colton, unlike how she'd been that first day he'd entered the store and proposed the speakeasy, she was no longer afraid of him.

"He's going to make you pay for that, too," she said, bracing herself for what she knew must be coming.

But before Jeffers could react to her boldness, the truck was suddenly rammed from behind, the collision an explosion of metal against metal, and both of them were jerked back and then instantly forward, whiplashed by the force of the terrible impact. For a moment the truck fishtailed one way and then the other, but Jeffers managed to hold them on the road.

"Goddamnit!" he roared, looking into the mirror. From close by Maddy heard a vehicle's horn blare and understood what'd just happened; Jack and Clayton had rammed them.

Maddy looked ahead through the windshield and desperately tried to think of what she could do to help. The landscape continued to blur past. Jeffers drove even faster, taking a sharp curve dangerously quick, and then, in the starlight of early morning, the familiar framework of a bridge loomed up, dark against the night sky. It was the bridge Maddy shared with Jack.

An idea formed in Maddy's head as they drew closer. It was daring, it undoubtedly would put her at great risk, but in order to save herself, to put a stop to Jeffers's criminal schemes, to get back to Jack and the love they'd rediscovered, nothing could be ruled out. As the truck's wheels started out onto the wooden planks at the start of the bridge, she knew it was time. When she acted, she did so without thinking; if she stopped to consider how reckless her actions were, if she hesitated, it'd be too late.

Lunging from where she sat, Maddy grabbed hold of the steering wheel and yanked it toward her with all of her might. While Jeffers was unquestionably stronger than she could ever hope to be, the impulsiveness of what she'd done took him by surprise, allowing her to change their course and direct the truck toward the side of the bridge.

"What the hell're you — ?" was all Jeffers had time to shout before they collided with the steel frame, the whole truck shuddering. In a symphony of twisting metal and the explosion of glass the truck leaped over the railing, caught in the steel like a fly in a spider's web, before settling slightly to the side. The front of the truck's cab hung precariously over the river below. Crates of illegal booze were tossed out, landing on the bridge, their contents destroyed.

Maddy felt as if she were moving through a fog as she tried to get her bearings. Tenderly, she touched her forehead, and when she looked at her fingers they were wet with blood. She heard moaning. Jeffers was slumped awkwardly across the steering wheel, his face streaked crimson. He'd taken the worst of the crash; she wasn't sure if it was because he'd slammed his chest into the wheel or if he'd cracked his head against the door frame; either way, he was a bloody mess. The cab itself was at an angle, trapped in the bridge, with Jeffers's side closer to the ground. His door was slightly ajar, the ground a few feet below.

". . . make . . . pay for doin' . . . gonna make . . . ," he muttered.

Furious anger boiled over in Maddy's chest. Though a sharp pain flared in her hip when she raised her leg, she began kicking Jeffers in the side, wanting him as far away from her as possible. Relentlessly, she struck him again and again, putting every last bit of her remaining strength into each blow. Jeffers tried to raise his hands and protect himself, screaming in pain every time she struck, but he'd been too badly hurt.

"I hate you!" she shouted. "I won't be used! I won't!"

Drawing her foot back as far as she could, Maddy drove it straight into Jeffers's shoulder. Desperately, he tried to hold on to the steering wheel but couldn't. He fell out of the truck's cab and landed with a loud thud on his back on the bridge below.

Jack couldn't believe what he'd seen. The truck that Jeffers was trying to escape in, with Maddy as his hostage, had shockingly veered to the side, running headlong into the bridge's railing. Smoke poured out of the wrecked engine, while broken glass and spilled liquor littered the bridge. Jack and Clayton had unsuccessfully tried to knock the vehicle from the road and were just about to try again when something did the job for them.

Or someone . . .

Clayton brought Roger to a skidding stop behind the truck; one of the disabled vehicle's rear wheels had been lifted from the ground by the crash and was still spinning. Jack raced across the bridge, fearful of what might've happened to the woman he loved.

"Maddy!" he shouted. "Maddy, can you hear me?"

There was no answer other than the clanks and hisses of the wrecked truck's engine.

Jack hurried around to the driver's side; with the way the truck was hung up in the bridge's framework, it was easier for him to reach. His feet slipped on the spilled spirits, but he managed to stay upright. Looking up at the cab, the nose suspended a few feet out over the river, he hoped to see what was happening inside, but everything was dark, the driver's side window spiderwebbed with cracks. Faintly, he heard a dull thumping. But just as he was about to leap up and investigate, the driver's side door suddenly fell open and Jeffers plummeted to the bridge, hitting hard.

As the open door swung back and forth, Jack saw Maddy. Her face was bloodied, but he could see that she hadn't been badly hurt. A scowl creased her still-beautiful face, but when she saw him it softened, making his heart thump hard.

". . . not over . . . not yet . . ."

Jack was surprised to find that Jeffers had somehow managed to make it to his feet. He looked exactly like a man who'd just been in a bad automobile wreck; blood caked his shirt a disturbing black, while one eye was swollen almost shut. Still, to under-estimate him now would be to take a terrible risk.

"You'll find that I'm not so easy to deal with when I can see you coming," Jack informed him, ready to fight.

Jeffers took two unsteady but lumbering steps to close the distance between them and swung a heavy left. Jack dodged with plenty of time to spare; the wounded man nearly fell on his face from the effort but somehow stayed upright, coming back for more. Another punch meant another miss, and then another. Patiently, Jack bided his time, waiting for the opening he wanted. With one more miss, there it was. His punch landed squarely on Jeffers's exposed chin, making a crunching sound that was a smaller echo of the truck's crash. Already wobbly, the bigger man fell onto the bridge. With great effort, he tried to raise his head, his eyelids fluttering, and then he was out, unconscious.

It was over.

Maddy had watched with delight as Jack finished off Jeffers. No sooner had the criminal fallen still than Jack was beside the truck, his hands reaching up to her through the battered door. Dropping into his arms, Maddy couldn't believe that it was finally over, that she was safe, or that she and Jack

456

were back in each other's arms. Even as she dissolved into tears, her face nestled into the crook of his neck, she felt as happy as she'd ever been.

"Shhh," Jack soothed. "You're safe now."

"I knew you'd come for me," she sobbed. "I just knew it."

"I'll never let you go again; I swear."

Maddy looked up into Jack's eyes and knew that he meant what he'd said. Standing on their bridge, the brilliant starlight streaming down on them, she no longer had any doubts.

Just as he'd done seven years earlier, on this very spot, the day before he'd left her, Jack said, "I love you, Maddy."

She couldn't help but smile. Back then, she'd been a child, not the woman she had become. Theirs was a love that had been given a second chance to be kindled and now burned brighter than ever before.

Nothing would ever put it out.

"And I love you."

Their kiss was tender, not as passionate as those they'd shared in Jack's bed only hours before but every bit as powerful. Though their lips touched lightly, their hearts pounded like thunder. Maddy was just hoping that their embrace would go on forever when a low whistle interrupted them.

"I don't know 'bout you two," Clayton smirked, looking at the wreckage while a hand scratched at the back of his head, "but if this here ain't occasion to have a drink, I can't 'magine what is."

"No way." Maddy shook her head. "That's what got us into all this trouble in the first place. No drinking!"

"Oh, I don't know." Jack smiled. "Clayton's got a good point."

"That's just what I wanted to hear," the other man answered, scurrying off in search of an unbroken bottle.

Maddy frowned, still held tightly in Jack's arms. "You're an agent of the Bureau of Prohibition."

He shrugged. "I don't have my badge with me."

"It didn't stop you from trying to arrest Jeffers."

Jack ignored her argument. "Relax," he said. "This calls for a celebration."

"Of what?"

"Of tonight, tomorrow, and the day after that," he explained. "I can't say for certain what's going to happen when we sort this whole mess out, but I can say that this time, we'll find out together."

"So we're going to celebrate the future?"

"*Our* future."
Maddy would certainly drink to that.

EPILOGUE

Chicago, Illinois
December 1931

Maddy stood beside her baggage on the train platform in Union Station and shivered before pulling her coat tighter around her shoulders. Even inside, the icy cold managed to chill her to the bone. Looking up at the high windows, the sun peeking through the fast-moving clouds, she could see snow swirling against the glass, like an animal desperate to come indoors.

All around her, people hurried in every direction, travelers coming and going for the upcoming Christmas holiday. Women and children walked hand in hand, pointing up at the large tree that had been erected opposite the station's entrance, its boughs decorated with colorful balls and strung with lengths of beads. Men sat at the shoeshine stands, smoking cigars and reading papers they'd just purchased at the newsstand. Couples left restaurants, laughing as they buttoned up their coats and headed out into the winter afternoon. Voices could be heard in every direction.

". . . just in time, too, because . . ."

"When Aunt Ruth gets here we can go down and see the . . ."

"It'll be the best Christmas ever!"

For Maddy, Chicago was a bit overwhelming. Ever since she'd arrived, it had felt as if she truly was a stranger in a strange land. The crowds, the automobiles, the towering buildings, and especially the *noise* of it all were constant reminders that she wasn't in Montana anymore. She'd been excited to come, sleepless the night before boarding the train back in Colton, but the truth was that it hadn't been quite what she'd expected.

But then, what had happened to her and Jack just a couple of months earlier would never have been expected, either.

Even now, months later, it often felt as if it had been a dream. But there were reminders, too; every morning when Maddy stood in front of the mirror, she saw the small, white scar that marred her forehead just beneath her hairline, an unwelcome memento of the truck's crash. Still, she did what she could to put it all behind her and concentrate on how much her life had been changed by that fateful night.

In the hours after the crash, after Jack had rescued her from Jeffers's clutches and put an end to his criminal schemes, there'd been much to do. Sheriff Utley had finally been rousted from bed and told what had happened; when Jack informed him that he was a fellow officer of the law, as well as telling him his real reason for returning to town, the sheriff had ashamedly admitted his own role in allowing the speakeasy to exist. Jack had waved the man's guilt away; there'd been too many other loose threads to worry about.

Once Sheriff Utley had rounded up enough men, he'd followed Clayton out to the abandoned house where Jeffers had stored the booze. They'd seized everything, but there'd never been a sign of the big-city mobsters who were supposed to come for it; Jack figured that they'd been watching the place and, when the law had shown up, had hightailed it for the hills. Jack would've liked to have bagged them along with the bootleg liquor, but the ring was significantly damaged nonetheless.

Things got even trickier after Jack contacted the Bureau of Prohibition. His superior officer, Lieutenant Pluggett, had shown up a couple of days later to start an inquiry into what had happened. Jeffers, his face a smashed-up mess, his hands and feet cuffed, swore to anyone who would listen that Maddy had been in on it with him, that she'd known every little detail and encouraged him to use the mercantile's cellar storeroom to hide their spoils. He claimed that it was Maddy's idea to open the speakeasy to make even more profit and even went so far as to offer to testify against her in the hopes of receiving a reduced sentence of his own. Maddy figured that regardless of Jack's assurances to the contrary, she was going to go to jail in the same wagon that took Jeffers.

But then something happened she never would've expected.

One after another, the people of Colton came forward and swore that Maddy had been forced into helping the two criminals against her will, that she'd gone along with the illegal tavern in order to protect her father and sister from the threats that Jeffers and Sumner had made against her, and that when it came to breaking the spirit of the law she was completely innocent. Even Anne Rider and Mike Gilson, the couple she'd once been so envious of, had spoken on her behalf. In the end, no charges were leveled against her.

Jeffers Grimm wasn't so lucky; he was currently serving the first of twenty-five years at the State Prison over in Deer Lodge.

Sumner Colt's fate was even harsher. Miraculously, his fall down the lift shaft hadn't killed him, but smashing into the crates and barrels of alcohol had broken his back. There'd been nothing Dr. Quayle could do; Sumner would never walk again. Instead of sending him to prison alongside Jeffers, the criminal Sumner had idolized, the judge had shown leniency and returned him to the custody of his mother. Maddy had met the woman once on the street, her face worn and weary, and imagined that it was she who had really been sent to prison.

But there was one person who'd seemed skeptical of the story concocted to explain away Maddy's role at the speakeasy. Jack's partner, Ross Hooper, recovering slowly but surely from his burst appendix, regarded her with sly glances every time she accompanied Jack to the Belvedere. She doubted very much that Hooper believed them, but he ended up leaving without stirring up any trouble; Maddy always wondered if Jack had made a deal with the man, letting him take more of the credit for the arrests than he deserved in exchange for his silence.

Either way, she was grateful to have avoided arrest.

Afterward, things had slowly returned to normal. Without the speakeasy to provide him with drink, Seth Pettigrew had become a bit more irritable than normal, but whenever Maddy saw him he had a quick smile at the ready. Occasionally, he'd come to the mercantile and regale her with another story about his days as a lawyer; Maddy always put her elbows on the counter and listened intently, a remembrance of their time at the makeshift bar.

At home, her father's condition hadn't changed much. For Silas, some days were better than others, but when the pain of his arthritis took him, he would struggle through it without much complaint, always a fighter. To help with his care, Maddy hired Karla Teller, the simple girl who'd helped clean glasses in the speakeasy. Silas liked to good-naturedly tease the girl, who gave it right back, which made them both laugh, music to his daughter's ears.

Helen continued to pine for something better than the life she had, to go someplace different, although Jack's tales about the rougher underbelly he encountered in the big city seemed to have tempered her desire a bit. Yet a further complication was a young man named Andrew Mungovan who'd just moved to Colton; Maddy was reminded of how she'd met Jack, and wondered if everything her sister held true was about to change forever.

"Maddy!"

Looking up, she saw Jack running toward her, looking smart and handsome in a well-fitted suit. A bundle of flowers was clutched in his hand.

"You're late," she said when he reached her.

"I got caught up in traffic," Jack explained breathlessly. Thrusting out the flowers, especially beautiful given the time of year, he added, "I hoped that these might somehow make it up to you."

"Bribery, is it?" She smiled slyly.

"Guilty as charged, Mrs. Rucker."

The biggest and best thing that had happened to Maddy since that fateful night in June was that she and Jack had been married in October. They'd promised themselves to each other in the church they'd attended as children, with Reverend Fitzpatrick leading them in their vows. Her father had insisted on coming to the ceremony, his old tune about Jack not being good enough for his daughter discarded, and beamed broadly from the front pew.

The questions about their future that had haunted her, whether she and Jack would stay in Colton or she'd follow his career to a big city, had been answered for Maddy the day he'd turned in his badge and gun, resigning from the Bureau of Prohibition. She'd tried to talk him out of it, telling him that she'd be happy as long as he was, wherever that happened to be, but Jack insisted that he'd had enough of seedy dives, bar fights, and spending weeks undercover.

But that didn't mean he'd given up the law.

When Jim Utley had retired as sheriff in Colton, most folks figured he was ashamed of what had happened with the speakeasy. The person immediately hired to take his place was Jack. His first act was to bring on Clayton as deputy, extending an unlikely partnership that'd both upheld the law and undoubtedly saved Maddy's life. Once Jack and Maddy returned from their honeymoon in Chicago, he would take up a different badge and gun.

As for Maddy, she was happy to stay in Colton and would do everything she could to see that Jack never regretted his decision.

She'd return to the mercantile, working with her new husband through the tough times, saving whatever was needed to pay the bills and care for her family. Her hope was that it wouldn't take long before they could have a child of their own, a boy or girl to take with them to the framework bridge, to make it a special place for three instead of just two.

And then four, then five . . .

A train's shrill whistle blew and they both looked back down the tracks to see a locomotive pulling into the station. It was the first they'd board on their journey back to Montana.

"Are you ready?" Jack asked.

In answer, Maddy leaned forward and kissed him, finding his lips warm but his nose cold from his run to the station. Even now, married, after all that'd happened, she still was delighted she was able to feel his touch again.

"What was that for?"

"Love, the future, everything," she answered.

And we'll discover it all together.

SPECIAL THANKS

To Dr. Bob Borgman for his invaluable medical knowledge, as well as the patience to answer all of my many questions.

ABOUT THE AUTHOR

National bestselling and award-winning author of nearly fifty romances that often feature the exciting backdrop of the Old West, **Dorothy Garlock** is one of America's — and the world's — favorite novelists. Her books, all enthusiastically reviewed, now total more than twenty million copies in print in 36 countries with translations in 18 languages. She lives in Clear Lake, Iowa.